Award-winning Moroccan novelist and screenwriter **Youssef Fadel** was born in Casablanca in 1949, where he lives today. During Morocco's 'Years of Lead' he was imprisoned in the notorious Moulay Cherif prison, from 1974 to 1975. *A Shimmering Red Fish Swims with Me* is his tenth novel, and the final part in his modern Morocco series that included *A Rare Blue Bird Flies with Me* and *A Beautiful White Cat Walks with Me*.

Alexander E. Elinson is an associate professor of Arabic at Hunter College of the City University of New York, and the translator of *A Beautiful White Cat Walks with Me* by Youssef Fadel.

T0351619

A Shimmering Red Fish
Swims with Me

Youssef Fadel

Translated by
Alexander E. Elinson

hoopoe
AN IMPRINT OF AUC PRESS

First published in 2019 by
Hoopoe
113 Sharia Kasr el Aini, Cairo, Egypt
200 Park Ave., Suite 1700 New York, NY 10166
www.hoopoefiction.com

Hoopoe is an imprint of the American University in Cairo Press
www.aucpress.com

Dar el Kutub No. 21952/19
ISBN 978 977 416 937 3

Dar el Kutub Cataloging-in-Publication Data

Fadel, Youssef
    A Shimmering Red Fish Swims With Me / Youssef Fadel.— Cairo: The
American University in Cairo Press, 2019.
        p.   cm.
        ISBN 978 977 416 937 3
        1. English fiction
        823

1 2 3 4 5   23 22 21 20 19

Designed by Adam el-Sehemy
Printed in the United States of America

Foreword

His throne was on the water

—The Quran 11:7

INSPIRED BY THIS QURANIC VERSE, Morocco's King Hassan II first announced his plan to build a grand mosque on the edge of Casablanca overlooking the Atlantic Ocean during his 1980 birthday celebrations. Designed by the French architect Michel Pinseau and built by the Bouygues Group of France, work on the mosque began on July 12, 1986. The original plan was for construction to be completed in 1989, to celebrate Hassan II's 60th birthday, but due to construction delays, the formal dedication was held on August 30, 1993—the 11th of the Muslim month Rabi' al-Awwal, AH 1414—which corresponds to the eve of the Prophet Muhammad's birth. From the Quranic inspiration for building the mosque over the Atlantic Ocean to the timing of the project's announcement and proposed completion date, the construction of the Hassan II Mosque was a bold assertion of the king's power and religious authority.

The Hassan II Mosque is truly a dazzling edifice. Over thirty thousand laborers worked on it, including six thousand artisans who cut and set the zellij tiles, carved the marble and granite, shaped the stucco moldings, and meticulously fashioned the cedarwood that made up the decorative woodwork and elaborately crafted ceilings. The mosque has a retractable roof that allows worshippers to pray under the sky's vault. At 690 feet high, the minaret is the tallest religious structure in the world, with a laser beam at its tip which points toward Mecca. The mosque and the patio surrounding it can accommodate up to 105,000 worshippers. It is the largest mosque in Africa and among the ten largest in the world.

Beyond the sheer size and scale of the work, the mosque is an architectural and artistic gem that references much of Morocco's Islamic history, which includes that of al-Andalus (Muslim Spain) as well. As then minister of cultural affairs, Mohammed Allal Sinaceur, wrote in the book published for the mosque's dedication in 1993,

> This synthesis is not the result of chance. It is born from accumulated experience, determined by time and inscribed in the project of a new al-Andalus. The Hassan II Mosque comes at the end of a long line of Islamic buildings, Moroccan in particular. In its general design and beautiful perspective it borrows its nobility from the centuries-old Qarawiyyin Mosque in Fes. It inherits the sober elegance of the Hassan Tower in Rabat, the Koutoubia of Marrakech and the Giralda of Seville, all three having been built by the same Almohad ruler, Yacoub al-Mansour. Like the Merinid madrasa schools, the Hassan II Mosque has a library as well. But the museum that tops it off makes it an authentic cultural complex that enriches the entire building and orients it toward a spirituality for the future.*

And just as the mosque is built as the culmination of a proud legacy of Islamic works, King Hassan II places himself at the

---

* Ploquin, Philippe and Mohammed Allal Sinaceur. *La Mosquée Hassan II*. Photography by Philippe Ploquin and Françoise Peuriot; assisted by Mustapha Kasri, Ali Amahane, and Houceïne Kasri (Drémil-Lafage: Éditions Daniel Briand, 1993), 4. Translated from the French by Alexander E. Elinson.

forefront of great Islamic rulers, those who built the Qayrawan Mosque in Tunisia (the Muslim general Uqba ibn Nafi in 670), the al-Aqsa Mosque in Jerusalem (the caliph Abd al-Malik in 690), the Umayyad Mosque in Damascus (the caliph al-Walid in 706), and the Great Mosque of Cordoba (the emir Abd al-Rahman I in 784), among others.

Despite the grandiosity of the project and its political, historical, and religious significance, the financial and human costs to build the mosque were enormous. While Hassan II's vision and aspirations were grand, Morocco is not a wealthy country by any stretch of the imagination, and carrying the large cost of this project (585 million Euros; well over half a billion US dollars) was beyond the state's means. Therefore, the financial burden fell mainly to Moroccan citizens who were required to help pay for it through a public subscription program. This was controversial at the time as this burden was quite substantial for a great many Moroccans, and the mosque's dominance of the Casablanca skyline ensures that people never forget it. Stories of public shaming, defamation, and even imprisonment of those who didn't, or couldn't, pay are not uncommon; many families had to pay the equivalent of a month's wages or more in order to fulfill their obligations. In addition to the financial costs, many laborers died during construction and many people's homes were razed to the ground. The mosque is located between the Port of Casablanca and the El Hank Lighthouse, a site that used to house an old and densely populated residential neighborhood, along with the Casablanca municipal swimming pool. When one looks at aerial views of the area, it is quite clear that the mosque, its surrounding esplanade, and associated buildings, displaced a great many residents whose houses were cleared to make way for construction.

A Shimmering Red Fish Swims with Me is Youssef Fadel's tenth novel, the final book in his series on modern Morocco, preceded by *A Rare Blue Bird Flies with Me* and *A Beautiful White*

Cat Walks with Me. It deals with many of the themes of the earlier two novels, including government corruption, emigration, crime, unemployment, and love; all of this with a masterful attention to detail and focus on the working classes. In all three novels, Fadel uses a fragmented narrative structure that moves backward and forward in time, and that results in a suspenseful unrolling of plot from one section to the next. This novel's narrative moves between the present and various points in the past as Fadel examines life in Casablanca in the 1980s and early 1990s, a period when Moroccan society was buckling under the economic pressures of a failing economy, an unsustainable and unwinnable war in the Western Sahara, and a regime intent on vain self-preservation at all costs.

The original Arabic title of this novel is simply *Farah*, which means "joy." It is also the name of the eponymous teen-age girl who runs away from her hometown of Azemmour to Casablanca to follow her dreams of becoming a singer. The mosque and its construction dominate the novel which follows Farah and the ill-fated love story between her and the novel's main narrator, Outhman. The building is always there, wherever one turns, and it embodies the beauty and tragedy, the resentment and hope that permeates a world where life is cheap, and dreams and memories are all that exist to keep people moving forward. The lives of the characters are not particularly filled with joy, yet it pays tribute to those who seek to overcome adversity and attempt to find some measure of success and happiness with, or in spite of, the hand that they have been dealt.

Alexander E. Elinson

I

1

THE MAN IS STRETCHED OUT on his bed. He'd rather not know who the woman is whose body is underneath it. It's been a while, a long while, since the man has had any dreams, unsettling or otherwise. He usually wakes to a chirp from the magpie sitting on one of the posts that stretches the barbed wire around the field not far from the railroad tracks. The magpie is black during the day, white at night. Its beak is gray regardless. When it lets out its lone chirp, its tail moves to the same rhythm, as if it is singing with its entire body. It always lets out just one chirp. This bird comes to sing a song just for him, so the man waits for a few moments—savoring or rushing them depending on his mood, and on what the bird expects, so taken it is with this exceptional attention—so that he can respond with his own drawn-out note: *tweeeet.* Just like that. This time, the nightmare wakes him up before the bird sings, so he gets out of bed wondering what time it is. It is close to three in the morning. He hasn't been asleep for more than two hours. He tiptoes across the hall. The light burns in the next room. He stops for a moment and looks in through the crack of the open door. His wife, expecting their first child, isn't sleeping. Her mother is sitting on the edge of the bed holding her hand and wiping the sweat from her fore-head. There's a wicker chair in front of the house. The man collapses into it, weighed down by this recurring nightmare. The field is in front of him. The moon spreads a greenish

3

turquoise glow over it. The field stretching out before him pulses with nocturnal life. The field does not sleep. Because of this, the nightmares don't completely overwhelm him. Once in a while, the flapping of a bird that has just woken pierces the silence. The bird hasn't woken up because of a nightmare or a calm dream, or because of a drop of dew falling gently to the ground; rather, it's woken up because that's what birds do. So, let him forget the nightmare that has so unnerved him. His mind is occupied with what minor worries the new day may bring. Daybreak is coming, and he still doesn't have a story to tell the judge when he arrives. And the baby that's on its way? He also asks himself whether he's happy with the baby's imminent arrival, but he doesn't wait for his own response. He wonders for the sake of wondering, just to pass the time, so that he doesn't have to go back to the corpse. He hopes to go back to the dream *without* the corpse. But there it is, waiting, in the brightest part of his thoughts, underneath the bed. Her name is Farah, meaning "joy," if you didn't already know. Burns obscure the features of her face. Her hair is blue. In the dream, in the moonlight that streams in through the window and envelops them—him, the bed, and the dead girl underneath the bed, dressed in a sheer purple robe—in the dream the man is always frozen in place with his legs stretched out in front of him, a distorted image of what's under the bed ever-present in his mind. He tells himself that the only thing for certain is that he killed her and threw her body underneath the bed so no one would see it. This is a fact. Still in his dream as he lies stretched out there in the same position, nervous and unsettled, with the dead body underneath him. Imagining the hubbub that will rise up outside in a little bit while he wishes for the day not to come, so they won't discover the body. He also wonders whether he has seen this dead body before. He doesn't dare look too closely at the face to determine whether he had had a previous relationship with her. Her name is Farah, if you still had any doubts! What are these burns on her face and arms? Is there a knife or a cleaver lurking next to her, or any other weapon that might tie him to the victim? He doesn't dare look underneath or around him for blood, or the deep wounds the sulfuric acid left behind. Still in the dream, he opens his eyes and realizes he has dragged a part of the nightmare along with him, so right away he closes them again, because he isn't sure whether he has actually woken up. And now, sitting in front of the door, having seized upon this story, he remembers the judge who loves stories. This is a story that deserves to be told. It will amuse him. His friend, the judge, loves to listen to stories on Sundays.

Farah. He used to sit for hours contemplating her small feet with their perfectly arranged toes, elegant, like fishes brimming with life even out of the water. Once he'd asked her to get up on a chair to grab a hammer from the shelf. She laughed because she could see in his eyes how much he wanted to stare at her white toes. This happened twenty-three or more years ago. They met and they parted in a game the meaning of which neither had understood. She appeared when he had least expected, only to disappear after a day, or a few days or weeks. Like the chaos that was filling her head at that time. The man tries to gather the scattered pieces of a life that had not been lived for very long. Farah used to love blue, the color of the dress she appeared in the first time he saw her. And she loved to sing. Once she said that she liked the sound of Naima Samih's voice. Afterward, when they were in the carpentry shop he and his father had built in order to construct one of the ceilings that would furnish the mosque, she said she had come to Casablanca to sing. While waiting to become a singer like Naima Samih, Farah used to love to roam between the mosque's towering columns, walking around the marble fountains, listening to her singing echo all around: "There's no one, no use in calling, there's no one . . ."

Another time, this happened: In Casablanca there is an old lighthouse not far from the mosque, at the farthest corner of the city overlooking the ocean. It's a hundred years old now. Its stairs go way up. Farah was unable to make it all the way to the top. At the halfway point she went back down. When he looked down at her from the top of the lighthouse, she had gone back to the ice vendor's cart where they had just bought some sweet-tasting scoops. He smacked his lips and the berry flavor flowed over his tongue. Lemon, berry, and apricot. All the fruits were drawn on the sides of the cart. He remembers all of this—the ocean, the wind, the lighthouse and its dizzying height, the seagulls flying around it—and he specifically remembers the moment when he heard her scream. A long, painful scream at the side of the road. She raised her head to the sky, not knowing where to put her hands. She stumbled around like a drunk, turning and turning with her hands over her eyes as if she had been blinded. Then she disappeared, swallowed up by the gathering crowd. Before rushing down, he could still hear her screams ringing in his ears, something between wailing and weeping. The passersby gathered quickly. Where had they been before? They hovered around her with every possible explanation, every possible insult, and every possible expression of hopelessness, coming over from every direction. He turned around, trying to cut a path through the growing crowd. He saw the men and their unsettling movements. With difficulty he broke through and finally looked at Farah on the side of the road, stretched out unconscious. Her face was badly burned, as were her neck and arms, cut deeply by the acid. The fiery heat of the sulfuric acid was eating away at her. The ambulance, and the sound of its siren—he hadn't heard it until the vehicle stopped. A woman threw a towel over her face, and Farah disappeared. He can hear it now—the ambulance's siren—as it moved into the distance, rushing off with its dreadful cargo. He doesn't remember if he actually saw all of this—the woman who covered her face; the two paramedics who lifted her into their ambulance. He may have seen it all without realizing it at the time, like someone who finds it hard to ride the bus because he keeps thinking it will never come. He continued to search for her, for Farah. After the ambulance disappeared, he continued to look for her among the other cars and trucks that had stopped there, among the fruit sellers and shaved-ice vendors, in front of the lighthouse, then behind it. The passersby who were still coming took the place of those who had left. Summer lovers (in a summer that had begun unusually early) were coming from behind the lighthouse or up from the beach—relaxed, the sun's gleam still washing over their tan skin—wondering what had happened, as if they were asking about whether the bus had passed by yet. And him? He still believed in miracles, imagining Farah sitting in a small blue car like the ones she loved so much, applying lipstick to her lips, or under the trellis near the lighthouse, singing, "There's no one, no use in calling, there's no one," with the red, berry-flavored ice having melted and dripped over her hand.

The man sits on the house's doorstep in the dark rather than wait in bed for the bird's chirp like he usually does. Now he is sure he has a story worth telling. It is Sunday, dawn. He has a story that isn't new, but he'll tell it to the judge when he's asked to. There is no longer a corpse or a dead person or blood or a cleaver. Farah has taken their place. As long as the sun rises. But why is daybreak so late to come? Farah is like a bird perched on a balcony looking out over the wide, verdant life spread out all around it, ready to jump. Farah remains at the ready, flapping her blue wings, prepared, all set to jump, but she doesn't. She waits for a good wind—ready, trusting, optimistic, prepared to go. The only thing that happens, though, is that the wind never comes. Then the first traces of dawn shoot up. Not in the form of pale lights tracing their way across the horizon; not in the form of a captivating red that mutes the sharpness of a glaringly bright day. Rather, in the form of a chirp that comes from somewhere close by. *Tweet.* The man turns to where he is accustomed to meeting the eyes of the white bird, before it turns into a black bird. It's there, on the same post, moving its tail as if singing with its entire body. A hymn comprised of one note. *Tweet.* As if written in letters known only by him. The man leans over a little and sees the grass glistening at his feet. He says to himself, "In a little while, another hot day will dawn. This is what its heat smells like." He chirps as he always does in response to the bird. This time, for reasons he does not understand, its echo fills him with delight. Perhaps it delights the bird also—*tweet*—because today he has this story. He is looking forward to the judge's visit so he can tell it to him.

2

A Smooth Green Stone

I WATCHED THE FISHERMAN, TELLING myself he had to turn around, and when he turned around he'd have to see it, and when he saw it he'd have to give it a hard kick that would return the animal to its senses. For a while now, practically since I left the house, it had insisted on following me through the streets and alleys, and I had no idea why. But the fisherman, even when he did turn toward it, gave it a look I didn't understand—extremely tolerant, affectionate, and unjustifiably well-mannered—a completely incomprehensible look, as if he knew it! Then he went back to watching his fishing rod. And the animal, what did it do? It sat not too far away, next to the basket, like any friend might do, also watching the fisherman as if there existed an old affection between us. That was what anyone rushing by would have said if they didn't know what had just passed between us as we ran, overtaking one another like competitors in a long-distance race. I too watched the fisherman and his rod sticking out in front of him as he sat on the rock smoking, paying us no mind. As a distraction, I said to him that fish don't eat at this time of day. The young fisherman responded that it depends on the type of fish; there are those that don't stop eating because they never get enough. Then I told him that fish don't eat during the fall because the water's too cold this time of year. For its part, the animal also watched the end of the rod for a bit, and then it peered into the fisherman's basket like someone who understands fishing. Its red eye shone in the middle of an ugly black patch. Maybe it was hungry and searching for food, and the fish in the fisherman's basket smelled delicious to it.

I had gone out early looking for the residence of the guy who had made my sister Khadija's head spin. Just to pass the time, I wondered whether the month would end the same way it began, because of the sun that shone suddenly above my head. I recalled this strange thing—in this cold month, the sun was multiplying in a way that made no sense. There wasn't just one sun like you'd expect; there were multiple suns. Everyone had his own sun following him. It was waiting at every corner, around every turn. I said to myself—and I don't like sunny days at all, in fact I despise them—that the month of October had begun extremely badly. It wasn't a pure, healthy, hot sun like a desert sun, for example. The sun above me now was weak and small, which begged the question what such a weak, small sun was doing above our heads at this time of the year. Not at all hot or useful. But it did have needle-like rays. They penetrated your bones and the very top of your head; a vicious sun aiming its lethal beams at the most sensitive spot on your forehead, piercing it. Always in the same place, as if looking to destroy it with its hidden pickax. Wherever you staggered and meandered, it staggered and meandered with you, turning where you turned. In the end, all you could do was curse it and give in. It fixed itself high up in the sky, at just the right angle so that no matter where you turned, its arrows struck your brain's most sensitive spot, making you think this was its only function, this was the reason for its existence: to ruin your day. If it didn't follow you at night into your house, getting into bed with you, even into your dreams, then it would spend the night waiting for you around the corner of the first alley you came to. It had come for no other reason than to destroy your resolve, ruin your spirits. This damned sun only lasted a few days, but it was enough to ruin an entire lifetime. A truly wicked sun. And anyway, generally speaking, sunny days are only good for lizards and those running away from prison. That was how things looked to me on a morning that had begun so oddly. I crossed the street, sadly enumerating my problems to myself: My sister Khadija's senses had been stolen from her by a man whose face none of us has seen. Also, there was this sun drilling a hole in my skull. Until it disappeared or melted away or disintegrated or set in one or another of the earth's cardinal directions never to return, until it disappeared entirely, I'd take refuge under the tin roof and look at the fancy storefronts, while casting a glance at the newspapers and magazines displayed on the sidewalk. My eyes caught the large headline in green that still dominated the top of the front page of *Le Matin*: "Citizens! Contribute to building the mosque." I wasn't especially interested in this, despite the resentment that occupied a special place in me every time my eyes fell on this headline, as I remembered my uncle Mustafa, who had refused to pay his share of the cost of building the mosque. He had been forced to carry his rifle to defend himself against the gendarmes, and the result? He came to us with a bullet in his right side. Seeing the headline every day at the top of *Le Matin*'s front page always reminded me of my uncle. This caused me to feel a deep sadness. It didn't have the look of a temporary announcement or just any old news item. I looked away from *Le Matin* as one might do when passing a grocer to whom money is owed, but no matter how much I might run from him, the debt would continue to increase and the higher the bill would get. When I thought the sun had weakened, I left my hiding place. I crossed the first street I came to. Not far away, I heard children shouting. I walked to another street, but the shouting didn't stop. This time I heard them behind one of the doors yelling, "That's him! That's him!" I turned, but saw neither the children nor whatever it was they were yelling at. I walked forward a few more paces on the same street and turned again to satisfy the devilish whims hidden with them behind the door, and then resumed walking. This time, I heard the children right behind me barking—*woof, woof, woof!* I told myself they were just the rascally neighborhood kids joking around. Finally, I let them be. I was thinking again about my sister Khadija when I saw it—or did I?—playing with a cow's rib that had a few bits of meat on it. It might have been the kids' idea to give it the bone, because kids love dogs. I don't know why, because I don't like dogs at all, no matter what kind. My interest in it stopped there, with these details. When I turned around again after passing a number of small streets, it seemed to me that it was playing another role. We were in the middle of a rainless season. Despite that, the dog was walking along close to the wall, as if trying not to get its fur wet, or perhaps it was a way of trying to blend in and seem inconspicuous, just like humans sometimes do. Or maybe it was playing with its shadow like I sometimes do when my mind is clear. Nasty sun or not, the time is always right for this sort of clowning around. This ugly, useless sun is what brought us all of these misfortunes, among them this dog. That's the short version of it.

A red dog the color of henna-dyed skin approached until he almost came into contact with my shadow. When I turned, he stopped and pretended to be preoccupied with the scenes of everyday life bursting all around. I almost fell for it, but he walked across the same alleyways I crossed, turning where I turned, and stopping when I did. Despite the cautious measures he was taking, I finally realized he was following me. There was no longer any room for doubt over this point. I stopped, wondering whether I could guess his intentions. What did he want? Short legs and a fat head. They're called pit bulls, some rare breeds of which are for sale. I've seen them in the dog section of the Derb Sultan flea market. It's not a market in the literal sense of the word—more of a wide sidewalk outside the actual market. If it weren't for the dogs tied to the utility poles or the puppies peering out from cardboard boxes, you wouldn't know that the people standing around on the sidewalk were dog buyers and sellers. That's the only market around that sells this kind of ugly dog. A wide mouth with a repulsive tongue hanging out. Thick yellow drool streaming from the sides of his lips. The head was covered by a black patch with a red eye shining in the middle of it, as if seeing with one eye made him look twice as mean. What remained of his fur had taken on the dusty color of dirt. We stopped at a corner. I turned around, and so did he, looking in the same direction I was, as if we were both looking for the same missing person in the passing crowds. In the end, when he had gotten so close to me that I saw his shadow had become one with mine, I said to myself that I wouldn't find a better place than the mosque's plaza to hide. There were fewer workers than there had been in previous years. The carpenters were still there, as were some metalworkers. It was then, as I approached the plaza, that I noticed my walk had become more of a trot. And what did the dog do? It ran along behind me, sometimes getting so close that it almost brushed my legs. I stopped when it became clear that this was becoming ridiculous and futile. With feigned calm, I approached the stone ledge overlooking the ocean and found myself engrossed in an awkward conversation about fish with a fisherman I didn't know—"Do they eat in the fall or the summertime?"—my gaze not straying from the dog for a moment!

I felt around in my pocket, knowing I wasn't going to find a fish to give to the dog. I gave him an apologetic look and felt in my pocket again so he'd see the effort I was making. It was then that I heard him ask whether it was true that our family hadn't paid its share of the cost of building the mosque, as all the other citizens had. It must have been sunstroke from the morning sun that caused me to hear the dog's voice in my ears. Didn't I say it was nasty and that it had only come to ruin my day? First, I avoided looking at him. I continued to watch the end of the fishing rod. To buy time and come up with the proper response, I fixed my gaze far off over the ocean, which had clouded over, and then I heard him say that he had come only to remind me, just as he had done for so many others who had forgotten their obligations. The dog went back to looking into the fisherman's basket. The fisherman fed him a sardine and the dog devoted his attention to licking it, completely forgetting about the matter at hand until I found myself wondering whether I had really heard the animal's question, and whether he was the one who had asked it. Or was it the fisherman? I continued looking off into the distance, scratching the top of my head in order to give the impression that I was giving serious thought to the matter, even though I had made up my mind about the mosque and about having to contribute to the cost of building it, ever since I had seen the bullet lodged in the rotting flesh of my uncle's hip. I don't know where he is now. He might have died on account of the bullet having rotted inside his bone, and this dog may have contributed to his killing, or at least to his arrest. I looked at him angrily as he continued to lick the sardine. This ugly dog wouldn't dare broach the subject of contributing to the cost of building the mosque with my friend Kika, who has strangled other dogs like it with his bare hands. As for me, I won't be able argue with him, saying, for example, that I stood with my uncle. I've always been a coward. Whenever someone stops me in the street to ask about an address, the first thing I do is think about what his reaction would be if I don't know it, so I pretend I *do* know, making a show of thinking it over for a long time, pointing to a street, then a second one, confused all the while and trying to avoid entering into any conversation during which he might learn that I had never actually heard of that address in the first place, especially if the person asking is elderly and able to detect bad intentions in every face because he had grown up in a thicket of bad intentions. Then, as if I finally realized what the dog was driving at, I said that we were exempt from this tax because my father and I had been working on the mosque since the

14

beginning of the year. "We carve and adorn the wood for its ceilings, you see." This time, the young fisherman was the one to respond rather than the dog. Did he *really* respond rather than the dog? The young man, as if to reinforce the pit bull's words, said, "This isn't a tax. It's every citizen's contribution to building God's house. Aren't you citizens? Aren't you Muslims? Are you unbelievers?" It was enough for the dog to nod his head, malicious and domineering from the outset, as if he had found in the fisherman an unexpected ally. Their words were weighed down with all possible violence and hatred, and for what? The ringing in my head didn't allow me to find the appropriate response. Apologetically, I said to them, "Soon we'll finish work on the mosque and we'll receive our full pay, and then . . ." This is how I do it, and it works when dealing with these types—I apologize and show understanding and enthusiasm, while in my head all I'm doing is mocking them and what they say. This thought granted me some courage. Then the fisherman stuffed his hand into his coat and pulled out a gold frame with a piece of paper in the center of it on which was written in golden ink: "*His throne was on the water.*" He continued to brandish and study it from every angle before kissing and placing it on a nearby rock, allowing me sufficient time to study it as well. The damned dog studied it too. His eyes glistened with tears as if he was about to cry. Then, with a sad yet optimistic tone, the fisherman said that ever since this certificate had been hanging in his house, he'd felt a calmness he had never felt before. He added, "You'll see what sort of serenity will settle over your house when your family pays its share and hangs one like it in the house's courtyard, or over the couch. Everyone has one in their house." That's how I found myself apologetically telling the dog and the fisherman that I was going to pay. I cursed myself because I didn't even dare look him in his ugly eye. Would something like this have happened if I had had a pistol in my belt? What could a dog like that do, no matter how vicious? What could it do in that

15

situation except beg for help? I'd calmly draw the pistol out of my pocket and place it above its ugly red eye. "What do you want? My share? Here it is!" Then I'd fire. Two bullets—one into the dog's eye, and the other into the temple of the fisherman who had allied himself with him. Two bullets would be enough. I calmed down a bit when I saw the dog stretch his paws out in front of him, lay his head down, and close his eyes, like one whose mission has been accomplished. The fisherman went back to watching his fishing rod. At that moment I began to think seriously about the possibility of forming a relationship with him, if only temporarily—with the dog, I mean—in order to avoid the evils to come should he reappear. As for the fisherman, whatever the extent of his involvement, my knowledge of people assured me that he had already completely forgotten about it. I also knew that were I to ask him about the dog, he'd deny any connection to him. He might even completely deny his existence and, looking me straight in the eye, say he hadn't seen any dog. Rather than get into a useless debate, I asked him, "And now what about the fish? Have they started to eat?" He didn't respond.

Before the incident with this repulsive dog, I generally respected dogs, or at least I used to respect them and continued to respect them as long as there remained a comfortable distance between us. More than once I had thought about buying one of those friendly dogs, not the mean kind. Today I swore—just as I had three months before when I saw the bullet in my uncle's leg—not to spend a single dirham on this mosque. This time I was completely justified in sticking to my decision, because what concerned me more, what was of the utmost importance to me, was that construction of the mosque be completed so I could get paid, and rather than give it to this or that dog, I'd join my brother Suleiman who, at the beginning of the year, had gone off to work in the Gulf.

3

AFTER GETTING SHOT IN THE hip, fourteen days passed before my uncle came to us. He had been hiding in the forest until the pain overwhelmed him. My sister Khadija brought him a glass of milk and then returned her attention to her hair, which was falling out. She was worried it would all fall out before she got married. Abdullah, my sister Habiba's husband, didn't notice him come in, or that's what he wanted it to look like. He was watching television, pretending he didn't care that my uncle was there. My mother's eyes didn't look up from her sewing machine, but they were watching him, watching his movements. The *tak tak tak* of the sewing machine echoed through the house, but she wasn't sewing anything, preoccupied as she was with my uncle Mustafa, who came yesterday with a rotting hole in his hip. We examined the hole, and didn't see the bullet, but it was festering. I went to the toilet so as not to cry in front of him. I noticed that some fuzz had started to sprout around my penis. In the past year, not a single hair had grown, but now some fuzz was sprouting around it, as if my uncle's arrival had somehow hastened its growth. I wiped my tears and left the toilet. From the moment my uncle arrived with the bullet in his hip, we watched Abdullah. My mother and I were scared that one of the neighbors had seen my uncle come in. Then we transferred our fear to Abdullah. We don't trust him because he's a snitch who would sell anyone out. He might go at any moment to inform the authorities if we were to let down our guard. We take turns watching him, Mother and I—watching for what he might do. My uncle limped in, but it was a slight limp, no need for concern or worry. That's my uncle. He always loved to joke around. When every standing position he tried was too much for him and he settled into a slight lean to his right, a spot of blood appeared, soaking through the fabric of his djellaba. He satisfied himself by turning to my mother and apologizing because he didn't want to trouble anyone. My uncle didn't feel any pain and didn't want to trouble anyone. Ever since he came, he would say that he had never troubled anyone in his life, and he didn't want to trouble anyone now. My uncle always loved to chat. He could have avoided the bullet if he had just moved a bit to the side, or had hidden behind this tree instead of that one, but that night! May God curse that night. Everything is fated, no need for worry . . . The baby screamed from Habiba's room so she offered it one of her large breasts. Abdullah was sitting not far from her listening to the Arabic channel, hoping all the Jews and Christians on the face of the earth would be slaughtered. My uncle limped toward the toilet. The blood spot on his djellaba limped along with him. My mother looked up from the sewing machine. But the limp was slight, no need to worry. The baby's scream got louder rather than softer. Habiba's husband asked her to shut it up. Her nipple was large and black like a raisin. She shoved it into the baby's mouth. The *tak tak tak* of the sewing machine took advantage of my uncle's absence from the room and rose up again. The bundle of clothing was ready to go. Mother had spent all week sewing it. Abdullah said that he'd take it to the bazaar. Mother said no. She wasn't done with her work yet. It sounded like she was compromising, like she was pleading, but her suspicions about what his real intentions were remained in her voice. If Abdullah left he'd stop at the first police station he came to and tell them, because he was a snitch through and through. We worried for the whole day. Afterward, Abdullah said, "Why don't we take him to the doctor before the wound gets infected?" For the first time Abdullah had taken an interest in and spoken of my uncle, like someone wanting to improve his image, to alter our view of him. We don't like him. My uncle stood at the door of the toilet smoothing his djellaba. His djellaba had been white, but it wasn't anymore. It was covered in blood. That's my uncle. He loves to laugh and chat. Short and fat. His head is large, round, and bald—his head was always funny. My uncle sells music cassette tapes in the markets. He doesn't need a bullhorn to call out to his customers because he's got a big mouth, as if his mouth is what chose his profession for him. And if he's limping now, it's because of the bullet lodged in his right hip, but no need to worry! And no need to bring a doctor, he said. When the doctor comes, he'll see the bullet, and all the problems and all the other things that will be dragged in along with it. He's not completely sure the gendarmes escaped his shots because my uncle was also carrying his rifle, his hunting rifle, and a bullet is always a bullet, and thank God it's resting someplace in his hipbone with neither gendarme nor doctor having seen it. No need to disturb it, especially when the doctor comes wanting to know the details of what happened. Details only bring problems. May God curse the details! "And what do we tell the gendarmes if they come asking questions?" Abdullah asked. We'll say, "We don't know any man named Mustafa. There might have been an uncle here who went by that name, but he's in the countryside. My uncle was in the countryside the whole time and we've forgotten all about him. We don't remember him or what he looks like, we've forgotten him completely." We'll wonder, both us and the gendarmes, and we'll say disapprovingly, "And why didn't this man (who we don't know) pay his share of building the mosque like the rest of God's creatures?" Then we'll curse him a bit to give the impression that we were on the gendarmes' side and that we were just like them, in order to make them look the other way. My uncle headed to my room, with the same limping steps as before, the same blood staining his djellaba. Mother sat there scratching her nose, looking where she didn't want to look. I went to the door for a second to see if there was anyone watching our house. The alley was empty now, but that didn't mean anything. The authorities always appear when you're least expecting them. Mother continued to worry that he was going to go to the police to tell them about the bullet. Someone formed from the same clay as Abdullah will always be a snitch.

I love my uncle Mustafa because he used to take us— my brother Suleiman and me—to the movie theater twice a month as if we were his own children (because he had none). Or he'd take us to the municipal pool when it was there, before it was filled in with cement. We loved movies about gangs who would chase the police down wide boulevards because my uncle Mustafa loved them. And we loved movies about the Mafia, because they defended the poor, and killed the police and gendarmes. After two years of marriage, my uncle's wife got into the car of a man who sold household goods and ran off with him to Italy. Mother cried because she hadn't known about the marriage. Before going to the movies or the swimming pool, we would go with my uncle to eat a plate of fried sardines with fried eggplant and fried potatoes, and we'd carry the smell of frying oil with us to the cinema, its taste remaining with us all day, even staying with us when we got into bed at night. He was about to get married again, which is why we were seeing him in this white djellaba spotted with blood. Mother didn't know what a bullet looked like, or what it smelled like. She brought in some bleach along with poultices and boiling water. The hole's edges had turned black. My uncle clenched his teeth and didn't look at the black hole. She also put some crushed herbs on top of the hole. And what would happen to the bullet when the hole closed? My uncle answered wryly that bullets were made to stay in the body. "Would this one behave any differently just because it's in your uncle's body? Your uncle's bullet, my boy, will remain right where it is, like all the world's bullets, like a shell your uncle found on the beach and forgot in his pants pocket." Then mother bought a treatment that didn't work because the bullet couldn't be removed by ointments or pills. Drugs didn't work either. "The only thing that'll work is a doctor," said Abdullah. Neither Mother nor my uncle wanted the doctor, whoever this doctor might be, to ask them where the bullet came from. So, either because of this or for some other reason, my uncle said that he could barely feel any pain. "Who says a bullet pierced my hip?" he'd say while touching his side. "Where's the bullet then? Do any of you see a bullet?" Then he'd laugh, rub his hipbone, press on it, and continue to laugh. And what had been a laugh, all of a sudden, without him realizing it, without his face knowing what it now looked like, turned into a miserable, desperate wince. My uncle had memorized a lot of songs, having so many cassette tapes that he sold in the market. He knew the names of all the singers and their birthdates. This time Mother cried more loudly, but for no reason. My uncle, who thought she was crying because of his second marriage, said, "What marriage? The marriage never happened anyway because of the gendarmes and the mosque." And right then, I didn't understand the mosque's connection to the marriage or the gendarmes or to anything they were talking about that was making my mother cry so hard.

I left the room again to watch the door.

In the late afternoon, Father came in, greeted my uncle, and took a look at the hole. He asked about the bullet. He scolded my uncle because his problems with the authorities were never-ending. He reprimanded him as if he were a child. He drank a glass of tea with us and told us about the mosque's roof he was constructing and the types of wood he had bought. Then Mother suggested that it would be better to find another place for my uncle to hide out. In a way she was asking Father to take him to "the inn," which was what they called our old house. Father went back to scolding my uncle. Why hadn't he paid his share? Doesn't the mosque belong to all of us? Then he proudly said that he wasn't like my uncle since he was exempt from contributing because he was building the mosque's ceiling. It was as if he hadn't heard what Mother had said. She herself didn't expect any more than this. She sat back down at her sewing machine. She put her head down on it and went to sleep, as if regretting the words that had come out of her mouth without having reached Father's ears.

That night my uncle's condition took a turn, from that of a man in hiding to one whose smell betrayed him—a smell that overwhelmed the room, a strong smell, the smell of a corpse that has started to rot, the smell of my uncle with a bullet in his hip. It seemed that now he was in serious pain. His fingers started to tremble lightly. The pain showed more in his hands than on his face. The pain was causing his senses to come undone, like someone starting to think with his eyes, or dream with his tongue, or sniff light rather than see it. My uncle no longer knew his own body. His eyes were open now, unblinking, fixed on the ceiling. They were looking at what was beyond the ceiling, open onto a world seen by his fingers like a man pursuing the echo of a dream that remains on the other side of sleep. The same look that said he didn't want to annoy anyone, when he had been able to say that with nothing more than a finger's movement. What if his leg had been amputated—would he have been able to forget about the bullet, because the pain would have been even greater? My uncle possessed but one form of pain, and for this reason he focused all of his attention on it, which wasn't good for anyone. It would have been better for him to be able to choose between a number of different kinds of pain. The skin on his face began to dry and darken, and its surface started to look like dirty toenail clippings. Two red tears, like drops of blood, hardened and stuck in the corners of his dull eyes. His violent trembling prompted me to put my hand on his shoulder without even thinking about it, in order to calm him down and comfort him, but the trembling did not subside. His whole body was shaking now. I left the room so as not to cry.

A strange tension came over the house the next morning, as if our body temperatures had risen. Mother, who was aware that something was happening, was no longer able to control her movements. It was as if we needed nothing more than a cloudy morning like this one for her to be sure that Abdullah could inform the authorities without even getting up from where he was sitting. A sort of agitation afflicted her eyes and hands. Things fell from them, slipping out without any explanation, as if everything had lost its desire to be touched by her hands or seen by her eyes. Things would fall as soon as her shaking hands got close to them, as if they had suddenly malfunctioned, or an unseen shadow had wrapped itself around them. Her gaze would shift slightly, her head leaning to one side, as if she was no longer seeing the same things we were. Her eyes would be fixed on the lamp while she talked about the door, for example; or she would turn toward my uncle in the bedroom while watching Abdullah's movements; or she would talk to Abdullah while shaking loose threads from her dress, as though people and objects no longer went by the same names. Even when she pricked herself with a needle on this cloudy morning, she didn't notice, as if things were operating outside of her volition. Different sized and colored pieces of cloth were scattered all around her. She sucked on her pinkie and spit into a rag she wasn't looking at, and still Abdullah hadn't left the house. But she felt as if he *had* left and come back.

Then, as she unsheathed the razor, I heard Mother say, "Your uncle Mustafa wants to shave his beard." My uncle's condition must have improved if he was thinking now about shaving his beard. The way he thought about himself also improved. She had a red plastic basin in her hand, as well as a clean shirt and pants. I took the basin and filled it with water. I placed the towel, pants, and shirt over my shoulder. The towel wasn't red. The shirt had big squares on it, which would make my uncle laugh. I asked him if he wanted to shave his beard, the razor blade at the ready between us. He opened his eyes and leaned his head toward me. This had become his way of speaking. The basin and towel didn't concern him; it seemed that he didn't see them. His gaze was fixed on the razor, which was nothing more than a blade with a metal handle, cold like any other razor blade. Maybe it reminded him of the bullet. He remained looking at it for a few moments, mesmerized by its shine, by its lethal edge. He reached out and touched it. He went back to how he looked before, the same empty look of surrender, but without any optimism now. Then he raised his eyes to the ceiling, saying that never in his life had he heard of a man stopped at his own door on the eve of his wedding day by gendarmes demanding money, even if it was money for the mosque. My uncle doesn't like gendarmes. He doesn't know anyone who likes gendarmes, or if they do, they like them the same way they like thieves, in that they hope to be like them. That's my uncle, and that's what he says with regret stuck in his mouth and bitterness in his eyes. We—the razor, the basin, the soap, and I—walk toward him. I hold my father's pants and shirt up in front of his eyes and wait for him to laugh. I hear a long, resounding sigh. Her name was Sabah. Twenty-two years old. He heard her voice before he saw her. "Do you have any Abdel-Halim Hafez?" It was as if her voice had blown in unexpectedly from somewhere. His wife deserting him had left an emptiness inside that Sabah filled. He handed her two cassette tapes that had a bunch of songs on them. Day after day, as was his habit, my uncle filled his car with cassette tapes and made the rounds of markets near and far. Then the markets were no more, remaining only on Tuesdays, so the Tuesday market came to mean something to the two of them. I set the basin aside, telling myself he was no longer in pain. The memory of Sabah had absorbed all of his pain. He lay on the bed in what seemed like a suddenly calm state, floating in an apprehensive silence that enveloped the room like a cloud of light. My uncle told us that he had started to wear cologne, groom himself, and wear the nicest clothes he had. He stood behind the counter pretending to sell, but in reality he wasn't selling a thing. He would praise this or that singer in front of the customers, uninterested in any of them. That was because he was only waiting for Sabah to show up, preceded by her perfumed smile and Abdel-Halim's song, which came to ring out in the shop before her arrival, and would play over and over in his head for the entire day. The car that he used to drive from market to market—the Thursday market or Friday market—didn't run on gasoline, but rather on the music of Abdel-Halim. In the streets where he walked, he wore Abdel-Halim songs rather than clothes. At home, the singing didn't stop until late at night. As if it was playing for her. And on the eve of his wedding, instead of opening the door for her, he opened it for three gendarmes. My uncle had started to stand in front of the mirror many times a day. He was thirty years old. Sabah had come at just the right time, neither too soon nor too late. Sometimes they would stand in front of the mirror together, comparing their faces, saying to one another that they had met at the right time. If only it hadn't been for the gendarmes. If only they hadn't knocked on his door at just the wrong time. My uncle took the shirt I handed to him and sniffed it. Was he smelling it or concealing his pain? Bullets hold a pain like nothing else. I was deeply affected by my uncle's condition. I resented the gendarmes and the mosque. I had never seen anyone with a bullet lodged in their hip for fourteen days, with or without pain. I went to the window and saw that there was no one there. I watched my uncle from above, imagining that he was sleeping peacefully. I held the razor in front of his eyes above his beard, which had grown thick, so he could see it and know what it was about to do. "What do you want, Uncle? Do you want to shave your beard or your head, Uncle?" He didn't hear me. He was still floating up above in his cloud. Once, they had gone down to the beach. She said to him, "Come on, let's go swimming." The sand took on a green color around him. Instead of swimming, he took out a small tape player and placed it on a rock, whereupon they let Abdel-Halim finish what they had started. I put my hand on his head. His bristly hair stuck up like barbed wire. I placed the towel on his chest. I rubbed his beard with shaving cream and his misery disappeared. He became a person ready to have his beard shaved. He dreamed of a wedding that never happened. The corpse smell that rose to my nostrils filled my eyes with tears. It was not so much a smell as something intangible, resembling thin spikes that pierced the corners of my eyes. I removed the covering, and other things that hadn't been clearly visible enough to me before made me turn away. As if, one way or another, I had known and expected what was waiting for me, even before thinking about removing the covering. The hole had gotten bigger and maggots were moving around inside it. In the middle of the sticky hole there were small maggots, white and yellow, a world of maggots moving around amid green and brown fibers, as if playing in a small pool. Millions of maggots, full of energy and life. My uncle showed no sign of pain on his face. He had transcended it. His eyes were watching a world we weren't a part of, attentive in a particular way, in a piercing way that allowed for no interpretation, paying special attention, alert with a bitterness that would not have been possible were it not for the gendarmes. I could not continue because the tears were choking me and pressing down on my head. My resentment grew and I said to him, "No worries, Uncle. Even we didn't pay our share for the mosque . . ." The words emerged out of my resentment. I ran out of the room before I could see his tears.

I went out into the foyer with the basin still in my hand, along with the towel, soap, and shaving foam. She was standing there at the open door. The car had finally shown up, as if Mother had been seeing it since yesterday on Abdullah's face, in his eyes, and in every movement of his face, especially when she woke and found the door open. "Once a snitch, always a snitch," Mother said. Then she went back to sit down at her sewing machine—*tak tak tak*—as if there were no car in front of the door and there weren't two men in gray coats standing there calmly; as if the two men were waiting for Mother to invite them to lunch. As the men opened one door after another, Abdullah grabbed his sheepskin and began to pray in his usual corner. The two men came back out of the bedroom with my uncle. One of the men lit a cigarette while the other leaned up against my uncle to keep him from falling over. Neither Mother nor I had a chance to say that we didn't know a man named Mustafa, and that perhaps there was someone in the family who went by that name, but he was in the countryside, and other things like that. The calmness that accompanied the two men as they entered was now gone. They grabbed my uncle, one on each arm, and dragged him toward the car as they cursed, perhaps because of the smell. And instead of looking toward the door this time, Mother was looking at the hole in her sock. She didn't appear to be angry. "Where did that come from?" she said. I wasn't sure whether she meant Abdullah or the hole in her sock. I told myself that my uncle was a parrot, and that he had flown away.

4

A CHILD RAN ALONG THE beach. The employee standing on the raised path craned his neck in that direction. Kika was hiding behind the rocks singing. And I was there with the small stone in my hand that I had picked up without even realizing it. It was the beginning of a cloudy afternoon on the beach, close to the stone jetty that supported the mosque's foundations. Between the rocks and the sand, the horizon line was invisible because the water and sky were the same color. I realized that there was a small stone in my hands and that my fingers were playing with it. My hands were thinking about the dog in their own way. A smooth green stone. Should I throw it at the dog if he showed up again? My fingers closed around the stone and it disappeared. I stood there for a bit in order to examine the situation from different angles, telling myself that it was time for me to grow up. It was time to overcome my fears. I wouldn't find a better way than contributing to the cost of building of the mosque.

On the shore, behind the black rocks, Kika continued to throw pieces of glass and sing his dirty songs. Kika only sings when he's drunk. And the employee? Here he was coming back for a third time, the National Department of Electricity employee, the one overseeing work on the mosque. He was on the other side, on the raised path, wrapped in his khaki wool coat, walking back and pretending he was examining the minaret, passing the same spot he went by just a little while ago.

He was wearing a wool cap. Ever since a construction worker fell last week, he's been watching the places where other workers might lose their lives while he tries to make it look like he's completely uninterested in what's going on around him; that he's passing by quite by accident, even though this is the third time. Anyway, workers don't die under anyone's watch. Nonetheless, he doesn't stop watching, looking all around. The employee made one last round then disappeared. Kika was still throwing his empty bottles at an indistinguishable black lump splayed out on the sand at the edge of the water. I watched Kika from behind the rocks after he had stopped singing. I forgot about the employee and Kika. I grabbed another stone and threw it into the water. The stone skipped twice then sank. When I opened my hand, the first stone was still there, looking like it was smiling. Light, cold, wet, and green. A rare stone, its transparent greenness and lightness tending toward something ephemeral with no real presence. It didn't deserve to be thrown at a wretched dog. Everything about it evoked a sense of calm and awe. I watched the secret vibration that passed between the stone and the skin of my fingers. It was as if my fingers were holding onto a small dream, clinging to it so it didn't shatter or get lost. They say those who think too much die before they're twenty. If that's true, I'll die this year because I'm always thinking about something. I think about all lives, even the tiniest of them—the small stone, cats, ants, and all the other insects. As for dogs, I never gave them a thought until the pit bull burst into my life the way he did, which was, to say the least, quite unreal.

Kika stopped playing with the empty bottles. Now that the employee was gone, he got up and walked toward the mosque with hurried steps. Kika didn't expect anything from the sea—neither fish, nor treasures, nor consolation. All he was waiting for was the visa so he could cross it. His mother, Kenza, paid a certain amount of her share of the mosque so her relationship with the officials in the Makhzen would remain good, because her job is sleeping with men. Outside of the house, of course. She wouldn't dare do that work at home. Now she's running around between her contacts in order to get the visa for Kika. In her room she has the same gilded piece of cardboard paper I saw with the fisherman. Kenza is a lucky woman. I put the green stone in my pants pocket and forgot about it immediately, only to find it later, unexpectedly, like pay for work I hadn't yet done. I approached the dirty black lump and saw that it was a crow that couldn't fly. What was a crow doing on the beach? The bird was still alive even after all the glass Kika had thrown at it. I passed my hand over the smooth feathers. Maybe it was a black seagull. Its blackness had a captivating sheen that made it seem almost blue. The crow opened one eye, like someone doubtful that the danger had passed. What came to mind was how miserable he looked. The black bird was dying alone, surrounded by water, sand, and the broken glass Kika had tossed all around it. Its black feathers weren't wet. Rather, they had thin streaks of blood on them. The crow, in a desperate final attempt, stood up and weakly flapped its wings twice. The urge to fly that had once made it swagger was gradually leaving it. The intoxication of flying high had let go of it and was fading away before our eyes—me and the unlucky bird. I don't feel any sympathy for it. A blind hatred toward it and its total incapacity to fly ate away at me. A blind hatred for all forms of incapacity ate away at me, whether it involved a person, place, or thing. I'm not the sensitive type, the type that easily feels sympathy. The bird stayed where it was rather than fly away. That was what made us equals. It didn't fly into the sky and it didn't dive into the water. Like us people, it was satisfied with crawling along the ground. I started to watch it with increased curiosity, reading its thoughts and trying to guess at its intentions. And it watched too, first with one eye, then the other. Thinking. It and its repulsive fat black beak. It waited for what was coming next. Perhaps the bird was wondering whether I'd stomp on it with my shoe or pelt it with the empty bottles Kika had left on the sand or grab it and hit its head on a tree (lucky for it the tree it might have been imagining wasn't there). Then I began to feel surprise at the reason for my hatred toward it—two large wings not strong enough to carry it. That was the reason. What good are the wings? It was the first time I'd looked at a crow so close up, and at one so appallingly weak. For the first time I realized that crows, in spite of all of their smugness and impudence, don't just need wings to fly, but legs too. Here, the bird at my feet was no longer of any use—neither its feathers nor its huge beak nor its legs. The same was true for its large wings and annoying call. This wasn't what crows normally do anyway. I yelled threateningly at it, my face close—*caw caw caw*—like it used to do when it was a real bird flying above us with real wings and too much arrogance. At that moment, its chest quivered lightly. It moved again and opened its wide beak toward the ocean's water that was just a step away from it, as if looking to take a gulp, as if this gulp would be enough to return it to its previous arrogance. But it seemed more pathetic than it had before. Right then I walked away from it, satisfying myself with a mocking sideways glance. I put it out of my mind before walking past it. The bird cocked its head slowly to the side, so slowly you could barely see it, plunged its beak into the sand, closed its eyes, and fell asleep. It had lost its passing blackness and returned to being a seagull, as it had been before.

I walked up the sand dune behind Kika toward the mosque. There used to be a big swimming pool here, and my uncle Mustafa used to bring us on Saturday mornings when he was driving back from the market. The municipal pool was gone. The mosque rose up in its place. After years of work, it was almost done. The minaret rose up high. All it was missing were the zellij tiles. Its yellow stone floated in the early-afternoon fog that hadn't yet faded. One morning, a thick cloud of dust spread over the old city, excavators coming in from every direction. The metal buckets of bulldozers rose like gigantic masts of ships moving around haphazardly. Trucks, steamrollers, cranes, cables, and all sorts of dump trucks that looked like destructive animals. Tools screeching, metal rumbling, the loud nonstop howling of tractors. After the hole that was once our swimming pool was filled in and the ground was leveled, workers' barracks, piles of wood and tin, grocery and vegetable shops, and places for fresh and fried fish popped up all over the place. And up above, flags of every color were raised, flapping in the wind like the temporary banners of conquerors. All of that because they were building a huge mosque on top of the municipal pool that we used to do somersaults into when we were young. The municipal pool that we used to play in when we were kids, that we used to dive headfirst into from high diving boards, was no more. They built a mosque on top of it, on top of our playing and our laughter, and our dead. The workers who spent five years digging there didn't know a thing about our friends who had drowned in the municipal pool—when the municipal pool was there.

I climbed the hill to look for Kika, but didn't see him. Then I looked toward the road to see if the employee had shown up again to watch us. When I walked farther into the mosque's courtyard, I heard him moving. Then I saw Kika climbing up the back wall like a monkey, on the side where the National Department of Electricity employee couldn't see us at this late hour of the day, hanging precariously from the gas canisters as if he were doing exercises. Another two or three moves and he'd fall on his ass. But there he was. Rather than falling as I thought he would, he sat cross-legged, high up on top of the gas canisters, holding onto the copper pipes that went up the walls in every direction. I heard his enthusiastic laughter and turned around, overwhelmed by a feeling of pleasure that felt a little bit like fear. The employee was gone. Something I didn't understand drew me to what Kika was doing. It was as if he were undertaking a regular task in one of the workshops scattered around the mosque. He wouldn't fall then. I alternated between watching him and watching out for the employee who might now be examining the road or returning to the beach close to where the dying seagull was; the seagull that might in fact have already died. Or an eagle might have grabbed it in its large beak and swallowed it, because eagles have always been stronger than seagulls. That's just how it is and no one can do anything to change it. The sun peeked out from behind the mosque and shone its harsh light over the courtyard. Because of the sunlight, Kika emerged from the shadows and his tall body appeared more clearly in front of me. I heard the sound of his hands as they cut the copper pipes, rolled them up, and threw them down to the ground on top of a pile of other pipes. Then I saw him jump down and rush to grab the pipes and hide them under his broad coat. I wasn't sure why these canisters were here with the pipes on top of them, or where they were going to end up. Maybe they were here for us to sell in the market, to contribute in our own way to destroying the building before it was completed. At that moment a strange enthusiasm took hold of me—like the rush a runner feels when he's close to the finish line—as well as something resembling the desire to cry. I didn't know whether to move forward or backward. I was thinking that the time had come for me to grow up. Like Kika, who was twenty-one. And I was thinking at the same time about leaving the mosque's courtyard before getting caught. I thought about talking to Kika about the green stone resting in my pocket that eased my nerves. The time had come to grow up. A seagull took off over by the ocean, letting out its sharp cry. Was it the same bird? But it wasn't black and no blood could be seen on its feathers. It didn't look like it had just emerged from the jaws of death. I followed its path for a moment. Maybe it would land on the top of the minaret. No—the bird gently crossed the gray expanse above my head, giving itself up to the wind, and finally settled on top of the mosque's roof. The view of the ocean and the sun and the bird distracted me, and for a moment I forgot about Kika. Then, at that same moment, I remembered him again because he was walking toward me. He stumbled as he walked because of the pipes underneath his coat, trying not to look like someone holding on to stolen copper pipes. Kika's hands are strong, and when we were young, he had used them to strangle a rabid dog. All the dog had done was sink its fangs into Kika's wrist. The dog died but Kika didn't. His hand was swollen for a few weeks, and then he got better. When I thought to myself, "Kika will be struck down by the same thing the dog was," Kika was saved because, like me, he doesn't like dogs. Now he's immune to rabies from all types of dogs. I wouldn't be able to strangle a rabid dog with my bare hands, and I wouldn't be able to give it my hand in order to inoculate myself against rabies. I'm not Kika, even though I wish I were like him.

Now I saw him moving forward through the thicket of high, interlocking metal scaffolds that cast all sorts of shadows down below. Kika limped a little because of the awkward load he was carrying. The polished marble on the ground reflected the sunlight onto his face, making it glow. At a certain moment, it looked to me like a pipe was about to fall to the ground. After a few steps, I heard the sound of copper crashing onto the zellij tiles, and it just kept on ringing. I was delighted, even though it was a normal thing that didn't deserve any special attention. Kika's face was shining at the edge of the sheet of water. I forgot about the rain. The night had been rainy. His upside-down reflection in the water mirrored his limp as he approached. Kika reached the courtyard where I was now standing, not knowing whether the time had come to leave. Another chorus of seagulls flew by, soaring above the mosque's roof in noisy circles. Perhaps the seagull had died, and this was its funeral dance. The seagulls are happy because they love one another. They stick together, whether on the beach or at the dump. This is well known.

Then, finally, Kika stopped in front of me with his awkward load, looking strangely swollen because of the copper pipes. I stared for a long time at Kika's wrist, looking for the deep scar left by the rabid dog, but I couldn't see it. Finally, he raised his hand, placed it on my shoulder (like a brother putting his hand on his younger brother's shoulder), and said, "Tomorrow we'll go sell this copper at the market so you can pay for the mosque." I remained frozen, standing there without comprehending what was happening to me, a small lump moving around in my chest. Right then I thought about throwing myself into his arms, embracing him, and kissing his cheeks. My eyes were suddenly flooded with tears. What was causing me to feel so strange? Not the idea of a financial contribution, that's for sure. The hand Kika had placed on my shoulder and the words he had said—they were the reason. The notion that we were friends came back to flutter above my head. Was this joy? And did it come in the form of a lump rising and falling inside until one's eyes filled with tears? I told myself that joy also brings tears. All of this on account of the hand and the sudden warmth it had brought. Friendship is also a beautiful thing. Yes indeed, the time had come to grow up. Without surprise, I saw now that I loved Kika, despite the worrisome scar on his wrist. Kika had been going out with girls since he was fourteen. I had always thought about being like him, even though I lied to him when I said that I thought I never wanted to get married. Given the choice, I'd rather be like Kika than anything else. His mother buys him fancy clothes from the shops on Mohammed V Street. There's no doubt that she loves him a lot, so much that she goes out with men every day in order to buy his clothes and shoes from the Indian shops on Mohammed V Street. I skipped behind him, thinking about the small stone there in the bottom of my pocket. The time had come for me to show it to him. I was now thinking about the stone completely differently than I had been before. I put my hand in my pocket and touched it. Now that I'd grown up,

I could show it to him. But then I reconsidered, as if I were celebrating a special occasion, telling myself, "Later, later!" I was having a ball. I skipped behind him. I imitated his limp. I said to myself, and only to myself, that now that I was with Kika, I wouldn't be needing a stone to throw at a dog. Also, with the same joy that had been swirling around inside my chest since that moment, I thought that only pleasant things would happen to me from now on. I continued to skip along behind Kika. The beautiful green stone was no longer bouncing around in my pocket because I had tossed it away.

5

WE BROUGHT THE WOOD FOR the ceiling from the workshop to the mosque's courtyard, all the wood that we had cut, polished, and smoothed. Moving it all took the better part of the morning because the workshop is outside the mosque grounds, pretty far away. The whole encampment of woodshops, metalworking shops, and storage sheds for the building and excavating tools is located some distance from the mosque, so we crossed the empty expanse between the two locations, having to go around the mosque's walls from east to west numerous times. Many of the storage sheds were locked, and the giant excavating machines were still. Their work had been done for some time. Now they crouched on the ground like animals with nothing to do. I held the compass and leaned over the piece of wood. My father approached. I heard him above my head saying, "Hold the compass firmly." I held onto the compass firmly. I drew a messy circle. He took the compass out of my hands and squinted in contempt. I felt a strong desire to go to sleep, so I yawned. Right then, Father came back carrying a piece of carefully sanded wood with freshly painted colors on it. I examined my splattered fingers. Father followed my fingers' movements uneasily. He didn't like the way I worked. Kika had worked for a week at another carpenter's shop. The guy he worked for was a homosexual who spent his days singing melhouns and checking out the asses of kids who passed by the workshop. Kika feared for his ass, so he stopped going to work. Father walked away toward the niche that was going to be the mihrab and sat cross-legged on a box, like someone who had lost all hope. I began to gather up a piece of the ceiling that was going to be the principal dome. I added some new drawings that weren't in Father's sketches—two horseshoes, and above them some floral designs. Improvised drawings. Why had I put them there? To make Father angry? Perhaps. Or maybe it was because I was distracted. I was thinking about my brother, Suleiman, who had run away to avoid having to work with Father. He was mending sails in the Gulf and wouldn't be back anytime soon—that is, if he was even thinking about coming back at all. When he disappeared at the beginning of the year, Father said he no longer had a son named Suleiman. He had gathered up all of his scorn and placed it into that single sentence. There was no longer a son named Suleiman in his family. Before that, when Mother had decided to move to the house she rented in the old city, she said to us, "I'll buy you a color television set and a refrigerator so you can drink ice-cold water." She said that so we'd follow her there. And follow her we did, the whole tribe—Suleiman, my two sisters, Khadija and Habiba, and I, along with her numerous suitcases and boxes. And she really did buy us a television set, but not a color one. Our humiliated father said that in order for him to join us, we'd have to return to the home we had left and apologize to him. For five years we didn't know whether he would live with us or whether he would tenaciously hold on to his dilapidated house that threatened to collapse on his head someday (while Mother asked God to make that happen on a daily basis). She knew he stayed there because of the women, and for no other reason. As it was, he came and went as he pleased, as if our move to the old city had granted him another life, one that didn't include us.

When I meet up with Kika, I'll tell him about Father, mainly about his hands. My father's hands have always been large, with crooked fingers and rough skin like a crocodile.

The blood that used to flow through them dried up long ago, and on the top of them there are veins knotted like an old palm tree. The hands of a man who has lived with wood for a long time, who's married to it. Kika has no father. He says his father is in Spain and that he'll join him when he gets his visa. But I know that he was born without a father, in the desert waste like a snail (and this is the best part of his story). God gave my father two skilled hands. With care and patience, they create something out of nothing, bringing form to something that had no form before. They steal secrets from colors. Sometimes he applies it to the wood like an adversary, as if pushing it to give up its mysteries. Other times he uses fine, delicate strokes. Either way, what was nonexistent is now there, embodied in a delicate form that possesses beauty and splendor. All of this happens outside of his own will. My father doesn't think about the drawings he does. They come to him all on their own. They race with one another to appear first on the wood. All of a sudden, what you think is the wing of a butterfly appears. And then, just as a rose has opened before your eyes, its full meaning manifests itself: attractive, brilliantly colored, complete. Everything that comes from his hands is beautiful. He spends hours drawing a field of colored butterflies. Little by little he detaches himself from the world around us, as if he has left us for gardens we cannot see, where there are creatures we could never imagine existed except in the disorder he takes control of. As the minutes and hours pass, as the sun moves across the sky, Father's feverish excitement appears ever more clearly in his fingers, as if intoxicated by the nectar of the plants they tame. He takes the brush and fixes the drawings I had thought were butterflies, then thought were a field of roses. He uses his brush to dab at them with some final, violent strokes, and lo and behold, in front of me there's a beehive brimming with activity.

I put the paint can down when I heard him ask me to bring him the adze. It was then that I remembered the dog. It might have been sitting in the courtyard waiting. I wasn't worried about it when I was with Kika, but I remembered it now that he wasn't here. Maybe he had gone to the embassy with his mother. I left for the courtyard thinking about how much I had come to love Kika and hoped that he would stay with me forever. The sky was just as depressing as it was yesterday. The mosque's courtyard was a wide-open stone expanse covered in water. A large workshop opened onto the ocean—columns and countless arches scattered about; large, bare rooms and stables with what remained of the metalworkers' workshops erected inside them, their work adorning the balconies and stairways; what remained of the carpenters' workshops where doors, windows, and mashrabiya that would separate the women's prayer space from the rest of the mosque's pavilions were to be built; workshops for the gypsum and marble that would adorn the floors, hammams, and fountains; and leftover stone, alabaster, wood, metal, sand, and dirt, as well as the wind blowing over it all. The minaret rose in front of me on the north face of the mosque. It was still wrapped in steel and had holes in it where, as soon as the opportunity presented itself, some seagulls had built their nests. High cranes were moving all around it, its tip almost disappearing in the fog. My eyes followed a worker who was climbing the scaffolding fastened to the minaret, and I was sure he was going to fall. Would he be the latest one? I stopped, waiting for his end to come. The worker stopped too. He looked down as if measuring the distance or listening for the thwack of himself hitting the ground. For reasons I don't understand, people are drawn to death as moths to a flame. I've been thinking a lot about death these days. The difference is that moths don't actually think about death and what goes along with it, as if they'll rise from the ashes after the fire has consumed them and they've disappeared completely. Moths aren't concerned with such things. All they care about is the distance that ties them to the flame. The worker continued to look down into the abyss, as if to test the wisdom of the thoughts swirling around in my head. I ignored him for a moment, then followed him out of the corner of my eye as he climbed. Now he was going to fall. No, he wouldn't. Or, and this would be more likely, he'd fall as soon as I forgot about him. That was how suicides went. They loved to remain hidden. A feeling of shyness overtook them when they felt like they were being watched. I followed him as he climbed, in order to give him the chance to reexamine the course of his miserable life. I followed the unspooling tape in my mind, then I stopped again, intent on surprising him, determined this time to follow the path of his about-to-be-extinguished life to its very end. Other workers had fallen before, from the same place, the same height—or even from lower down—and they died immediately. Why should he be an exception? Not to mention the fact that we were building the mosque over the old municipal pool where the custom of death was deeply rooted; rooted in the very idea of the pool. It was in this pool, when it was there, that our relatives, friends, and neighbors' children drowned. And now we were erecting a mosque on top of their bodies. So why should this worker be the only exception? There's no height from which people don't fall. There's no place where people don't die, especially when it's a mosque built over the bodies of our friends. Work on the mosque was in its final stages. All that was missing were two more dead bodies, three at the most. So rather than being empty, the courtyard had been invaded by architects, carpenters, metalworkers, gypsum and zellij craftsmen, electricians, sewer cleaners, and builders, as well as those who hadn't mastered any craft at all. Everyone who had worked before on the mosque and was no longer needed still insisted that the work was not finished. They still insisted that there was plenty of work awaiting them. And why so insistent? For death to continue its work, nothing more. Even those who hadn't worked a single day sat, their arms outstretched on the rock overlooking the ocean, or along the road. They played cards, waiting for the need for their death to arrive so that construction could continue and the mosque could finally rise up high in all its glory. When I turned around this time, the worker had disappeared. Had he fallen, or had he climbed up to the sky?

A man parked his old car in the middle of the courtyard. He said he wanted to see Father. It was the National Department of Electricity employee who had taken off his cap and khaki coat so I wouldn't recognize him. His bare face now resembled that of a frog. His short body was stuffed into a green suit, and underneath it was a red-and-white plaid shirt. His head was bald, with a deep groove running down the middle of it, as if he had two heads—he'd pushed one to the front, and the other to the back. Perhaps he had come in disguise, with two heads and wearing the clothes of someone who works in a circus. Because of the stolen pipes, he was wearing clothes unbefitting of a respectable employee of the National Department of Electricity. Thus, when I saw him, I told myself that this face was one I didn't know, one I hadn't seen before, to allow him to continue his ruse of disguising himself. I think his disappointment became even greater when he saw that I had met him before, and that the ruse he had cooked up to surprise me didn't bear any results. That's what disappointed him. We left the car behind and crossed the mosque's courtyard, moving between the intertwined columns that provided little shade because the sun had risen so high in the sky. The employee shuffled his dusty shoes through the thicket of steel, with me in front dragging my feet lazily as I ignored him and looked at today's life all around me with greater optimism. The smell of cedar wood rising up around my father didn't surprise me the same way it surprised the employee. The accumulated smell of long years surrounded by wood, by entire forests of cedar. Perhaps it was surprising to the employee who didn't know that wood has a life, and that it has good times and bad. I looked at the frog's face, waiting for the effect of the smell to show on it as I walked between the columns underneath the prayer room's ceiling until we arrived at the mosque's interior. I chuckled to myself: "Who is this man walking behind me?" Father was standing on a high bench and satisfied himself with turning his paint-spattered beard in our direction. His nose was also dabbed with paint, as was his forehead. However, it wasn't as funny as I wanted it to be. I told him that this was an employee from the National Department of Electricity, then I plunged my brush again into the can of red paint. Father stepped down from his bench without giving the impression that he had noticed the employee was there. He stood over me watching, while I waited for his torrent of dissatisfaction and nagging, along with his steady flow of disappointed observations. I saw him roll up his sleeves, take the brush from my hand, and plunge it into the paint. Then he walked away for a few moments, deep in thought. He wasn't concerned with us standing there in front of him. Father recalled his glory days. He retook the lead. He took the bull by the horns as if this unexpected observer was all that was needed to spark his enthusiasm. His legs were slim and graceful. He walked away from the pieces of wood, then walked back toward them. He took some measurements and recorded them, and then he started drawing. But his two steady hands had been replaced by two shaking hands; the confidence they once possessed was gone. They weren't as delicate as they once were. I could see the top of his head as he leaned over the wood. A red circle shone in the middle of a little bit of white hair that fell over its sides. In his hand he had his brush that had been plunged into the red paint. He held it upright at an odd angle, as if he were holding a red line, trying unsuccessfully to find a place for it between the lines he had already drawn. I repeated, "This is an employee from the National Department of Electricity." The frog's face came closer. He placed his hand on Father's shoulder and tapped it gently, nodding and saying that building the mosque where the municipal pool had been was a nice idea, providing Father with this job after such a long period without work. He continued to rub his shoulder with the same calm, reminding him that he would always be a great carpenter, adding that the ceilings he had done in the past were at one time exemplary models their owners would show off, and that still, to this day, adorn the rooms of great palaces in Fez and the ancient mosques of Marrakech. In the good old days . . . Father began to nod, saying, "Great days, ha!"— dazzled by the moment, adding, "Yeah, yeah. When the work deserved it." Father put his brush into an empty pail next to him. Perhaps he felt that this would be an opportune moment to tell of his past glories. The employee took advantage of this unexpected moment of relaxation to tell Father that his lines were no longer as straight as they once were, that his hands shook, and that permanence belongs only to God, as if his hands had forgotten the craft they had once mastered. Yes, that was what I thought too. That in itself was embarrassing. I no longer worried about him. I was only going to be worried if it had to do with the stolen pipes, and I would have been more worried if it had something to do with the employee playing his private investigation game with Kika and me. As it was, the employee was talking about lines that weren't straight, shaking hands, and slow work. Father wiped his brow with his sleeve several times. I looked again at his gnarled hands. I saw that the red-splattered fingers were trembling, and that his clothes were splashed with other colors. A look of severe disappointment came over his face, which also had paint on it. A sound like a whistle rose from his chest, and then I saw him walk around the ceiling examining the work we had done over the past months. He grabbed a piece of ceiling we had spent a week arranging, ripped it from its place, and broke it apart. He raised his finger. He extracted a splinter from it and blood shone on its tip. He looked at the splinter, dazed. It was as if he considered it to be the embodiment of all the blood wasted on this work. Calmly, the employee returned to pick up the brush and put it back in the pail, leaning over the piece of wood.

He stood there for a while following Father's lines and curves, the unpleasant surprises that his colors had imprinted on the wood. As he continued to examine the work, he said, "They say that your hands are no longer as skilled as they once were, that the craftsmanship is gone from them. *There is no power nor strength save for in God.*"

For a long time after the National Department of Electricity employee had left the mosque's courtyard, Father didn't get up from where he had been sitting. His paint-smudged nose looked as if it were mocking a situation he hadn't been expecting. His nostrils were moving to the rhythm of the wheezing coming from his chest. With exaggerated calm he grabbed the saw and began to cut the wood we had spent six months smoothing, drilling, and cutting. Six months of hard work, and many more months drawing, calculating, assessing, examining, appraising, and reappraising; all of it coming apart bit by bit before my eyes with calm, patience, and a strange pleasure. The smell of sawdust grew strong around him. The forest smell still emanated from his body. His hands, even as they were destroying what they had built, no longer obeyed him as they once had. I went as far as the door to the mosque's courtyard. I watched the seagulls fly across the square of sky there. Were they black or white? When the birds landed on the roof of the mosque I couldn't see them anymore. I pictured their feet scratching the roof, their annoying sound getting on my nerves even though I couldn't hear them. Everything about these birds gets on my nerves! What were these birds that live in marinas and on deserted beaches doing on the mosque's roof?

6

WHEN I TOLD KIKA THAT it would be better to go someplace else, and he responded, "We're good here," it was too late, because the girl had already lodged herself in our minds a while ago, like a spotlight that shone brightly tonight. Kika repeated, "We're good here," as he turned toward her. Her dress was blue. I saw it before I saw her. Then I saw her looking into the room, scrutinizing the faces there. A thin girl you wouldn't say was older than fifteen, although her eyes shone with the spark of a mature woman. She stood between the door and the counter, blinded by the blazing light coming in from the hallway. Even before Kika put his hand on my shoulder, he asked, "Why is she looking at us?" I pretended not to hear or see, even when he leaned toward me and whispered tensely while squeezing my shoulder excitedly, gleefully even, "She's been looking over here for a while." Tense. Excited. Squeezing my shoulder. Yet relaxed at the same time. As if the cords that kept him balanced had slackened slightly.

I said to him, "Since when, Kika? She just showed up."

"Then why would she look at us this way? Not like how women normally look at men?"

"And how do women normally look at men?"

Instead of answering, his eyes continued to mull it over while I looked at his pants pocket to see if it was bulging as much as a pocket with a wad of cash should be. Perhaps she was looking at us through the color of her blue dress. He took two steps toward the door, then walked back. I told myself that Kika wasn't limping because he wasn't still carrying the pipes he had been yesterday. Still, he was limping a little, and it was then that I saw and confirmed that he had the money in his pocket, the money we had gotten from the pipe deal. I think I had come to trust Kika ever since he first put his hand on my shoulder and I had lost all fear. Like someone absolutely comfortable with his future. She was closer to the door than to the counter. She moved hesitantly as her eyes flitted about, like a ewe that has lost its way from its pen. Sometimes the shadow of a girl passing by blocked her, or the head of a man leaning toward his friend. Other times it was the body of the bouncer who stood between her and the room, not letting her move forward. A young brown-skinned man, tall, with an excessively ample belly, an eagle tattoo on each bare arm, and around his wrist a wide red-leather wristband. The eagle occupied the uppermost part of each arm, its large wings outstretched and facing downward on the sweaty skin, creeping toward a woman and a forest. There were symbols and numbers surrounding them, and delicate drawings resembling flowers. The young woman behind him continued to look at us. I wasn't close enough to say for sure that she was looking at us. There were lots of men getting drunk, with an equal number of girls laughing, and there was music and the sound of clinking glasses. A singer in the middle of the room beneath a colored spotlight sang out into the darkened room. The singer's presence under the colored light made the surrounding darkness seem a little less dreary. The people in the light were like shadows being moved by a drunken wind, as if the singer and his voice were trying to light up a darkness in the customers' souls, but couldn't. I fixed my gaze on Kika's legs and saw that they wouldn't stop moving. One leg went up as the other went down, out of his control. In their own way, they were thinking about the girl. "There she is again," Kika said, running a hand over the back of his neck, wiping the sweat from his forehead with the other, wondering if he'd go and bring her over. He looked at me, and at her, with what appeared to be a confrontational glare. I was content with looking at Kika's back pockets to try and guess the amount of money they were hiding, because the amount we got from the pipes was in one of them. Sometimes the bulge was visible in one pocket, sometimes the other. Kika is usually unaffected by young women in bars. They're not his type. It's schoolgirls and factory workers that get his attention. For them, he'll wear the fancy clothes his mother, Kenza, buys for him. He's tall. He says it's the Adam's apple that sticks out of his throat that attracts the girls. The girl behind the guard's tall frame looked inside, craning her neck this way and that, ceaselessly talking and gesturing. When Kika wondered, in simultaneous protest and anger, "Why doesn't he let her be?" squeezing my shoulder with his trembling hand, I noticed that she was looking all around, and that I was looking at her as if she were disoriented, lost, a stranger to us and the place where we were—me, Kika, the men, the young women, and the singer. As the moments passed, his body leaned over more and his legs sped up. Now I lit a cigarette because his agitation was contagious. I drew on it nervously and exhaled a cloud of smoke from my nostrils in order to forget about Kika and the cash (I still didn't know which pocket Kika had put it in). I saw him put his hand into his pocket. I waited for the bills to appear, knowing that they wouldn't right then. Maybe they'd never appear, because I no longer trusted him as I had just a short while ago. I was amazed at the amount of smoke coming out of my nostrils. In the meantime, the girl had disappeared. She left through the cabaret's entrance with the guard, but what seemed like a shadow of her presence lingered. I told Kika that it would be better if we went somewhere else. He replied, echoing what he had said before, "How come? We're good here." I bit down on my cigarette and turned toward the counter. Finally, Kika took out the cash that the copper pipe deal had netted us and began to count it. Then he raised his glass, laughing, pointing to the bills scattered on the counter in order to give the impression that he had forgotten all about the girl. The girl, her dress, and the memory of her dress were all behind us now. The clock hanging among a row of different sized and colored bottles in front of us pointed to quarter to nine. The two hands were stuck to one another, and there was no way of knowing if they were going to stay that way. I focused on them. Instead of looking, I listened closely, but I didn't hear them ticking. Then I heard them, *tick tick tick tick*. As I kept looking, I realized the clock had only one hand, and it had stopped. I think I saw her even before turning around. Even before Kika yelled, "There she is again!" with the same determination, the same eagerness, without surprise, with the same agitated joy, without the least bit of shock. As if I had been expecting her to show up at any moment. She appeared without the guard, neither in front of her or behind her. I turned toward Kika, imploring, "Better we go somewhere else."

Unlike before, the girl with the blue dress didn't stop between the door and the counter. The music stopped. She moved toward the middle of the room, approaching the spotlight, as if this time she knew which way to go. We were interested in her now— she was someone who had just entered an unfamiliar place, with lots of movement and noise, under the circle of light that, just a little while ago, had enveloped the singer. Kika was no longer interested in anything other than the girl. Kika seems like a thirty-year-old man with his deep voice and Adam's apple that juts out from under his jaw like a real apple. Suddenly, the girl was alarmingly close to us. The blue of her dress bloomed near us in an elegant blaze. The color of her dress reminded me of the blue in Father's ceiling. The dress brought me back again to the mosque, which I had forgotten all about. I almost placed my hand on the dress. Maybe, after all, she came back on our account. We didn't know her and hadn't seen her before, but nonetheless, maybe she came because of us, or because of an idea she had

in her head about us. Why else would she wear a blue dress—
the same blue that floated across the sky of the ceiling? Why
would she be wearing a blue dress if she weren't thinking the
same thing you and I were? Why else would she be looking at
us that way as soon as she came in? I noticed that I had started
to think like Kika, and I too wondered why she had disappeared and then come back. Why was she walking so slowly
toward us that we could see her dress, and see that it was blue?
And why was she looking at us as she approached to make
sure that we saw her? "This girl isn't looking for anyone. It
would be best if we went somewhere else," I said to Kika. Just
then she was grabbed by a young man close to her, who was
wearing strange leather clothes. He had a line of hair sticking straight up like a rooster's comb. The girl trembled like a
frightened goose and backed away until she almost bumped
into the counter. When she made it clear that she intended to
retreat, he grabbed her forcefully by the arm. This time she
didn't retreat. She remained looking at him, determined not
to be scared of him or his threats. He leaned over close to her
face and whispered a few words that were enough to make
her blush. Her eyes filled with fear. Then he began to pull her
toward the door. She looked around with pleading and terrified eyes that said this was the first time she had entered the
bar in her life. As this was happening, Kika was gripping the
counter with his fingertips, wondering why the man wouldn't
just leave her alone. I knew what was going to happen when
I saw his fingernails dig into the countertop. Then I saw Kika
moving forward in a deliberate manner between the other
customers. A sudden uneasiness came over everything; the
shadows stopped dancing around the anxious patrons. He
walked out. I was no longer as concerned with his pockets as
I had been before. I turned toward the stopped clock and, in
my head, proceeded to count the money Kika had taken out
of his pocket and then put back in, telling myself that Kika
was my friend no matter what. I saw him come back with the

girl, his hand in hers. Then I heard him say proudly, "I present to you Farah. She's come looking for her friend Naima." Farah gave a light, bashful laugh. She had spent the entire day looking for her friend, but hadn't found her anywhere. She didn't know anyone in this city. Casablanca is like a huge island. And in the end, they pointed her to this place! Kika happily handed me my share of the proceeds from the pipe deal as if he were making up for the fact that his other hand was holding on to the girl's. Then he began to count out his share like someone well practiced in counting money.

I began to count my money just as Kika did. I looked at Farah, moistening my finger and moving my lips so she'd see that I was counting real money, just like Kika, but better. I may not have actually been counting it, though, because I was nervous, really nervous. When I'm overly nervous I can't do anything, especially something that requires focus such as counting money. Kika is better at this than I am because his fingers are long, and long fingers are good for counting money, no question about it. When he finished counting his money, he put it in his back pocket with his usual overconfidence. Farah was content to smile a bit wider and attach herself to me, putting some distance between herself and Kika and the way he was looking at her. Every time he tried to get closer to her, she became uneasy and backed up. I thought to myself that this girl was just like me. She didn't know anyone in this bar, and Casablanca must have seemed like a huge island to such a lonely girl. She wasn't used to places like this. She didn't go into bars—she didn't generally even go into coffee shops—and now she didn't know what she was supposed to do. I asked her if she wanted to see the mosque. At that hour I didn't think it was the right time for that. I took a piece of paper from my pocket, put it on the counter, and began to draw circles and squares on it, explaining the work Father and I were doing. Kika stood behind us. I could feel the heat of his breath on the back of my neck as he looked at the piece of paper. I wondered what he was thinking. He carefully studied the circles I was drawing. Then he grabbed the pen angrily from my hand and violently drew a line across it, tearing the paper in two. With his other hand, he scrunched the paper into a little ball and threw it into the air, hitting it with his head while letting out a strange laugh. He walked toward Farah. She walked around me to stand further away from Kika. I told myself that maybe the time had come. The time had come to leave, because Kika had changed. Kika was definitely giddier than he should have been. This time she didn't let him hold her hand as we crossed the room to go outside. The angry flash I saw in his pupils changed my mood, and I was no longer feeling as cheerful as I had been before. The place got louder—clinking glasses, chairs, and tables scraping the floor, girls laughing. In place of the other singer there were now women singing whom I hadn't seen get up on stage. A group of cheikhat were singing songs while they danced, clapped, smoked, drank, and shook their fat bellies like bears, all to the drunks' delight.

7

SUDDENLY, IN FRONT OF THE cabaret's entrance, I remembered her name—Farah. It was as if I were hearing it for the first time. As if I hadn't heard Kika utter it just moments ago. Farah! Standing on the sidewalk across the street, Farah fixed her gaze on the door as if she had already forgotten us. She was waiting. Her friend Naima might show up. I thought about the cash Kika had given me, and the uncomfortable situation we now found ourselves in. The bills sat in my pocket in place of the green stone that was no longer of any use. I touched my pocket and thought, "There, now it's bulging like Kika's pocket." I put my left hand in and touched the bills, knowing each denomination by how soft it was. A calmness passed through my fingers, but it didn't make the anxiety swirling around inside my head go away. Despite that, everything was fine. Outside the bar, it was lit up bright as day. Taxi drivers waited in a long line for customers who were pissing on the bar's wall, calculating how broke they were. A lot of girls came out of the bar wrapped in heavy coats with high collars that hid the fatigue that comes from staying out so late. None of them was named Naima. They fanned out into cars lurking next to the sidewalk and disappeared into them, laughing drunkenly—the laughter of a night at its end. One was being followed by a drunk whose last cent she had swallowed before taking off. Another sang because the echo of the cabaret's singing still pursued her and surged inside her head. Yet another wavered between two rivals who were staggering and reeling, and ended up seeking refuge in a third car. None of them was named Naima. If there had been someone named Naima, or someone who looked like her, we would have known it right away. That's what Kika said. He tried to hang on to Farah, talking to her about his house, which wasn't too far away, pointing toward the old city where we lived. He looked at his watch in order to give an impression of balance and calm. At this time of night, his mother was somewhere else, whoring herself to other men. Under the lamplight I carefully examined his face, which betrayed his thinning patience. Kika has little patience. He gets angry for no reason. I keep pace with him so he doesn't run out of what little patience he does have. I wasn't sure why Farah ran from him, seeking my protection. I had grown up. Her face was small and round. The redness of her lips was clean, tempting, like the red of a winter fig. Had we seen her before as Kika claimed? There are those cheerful faces that seem so familiar as soon as you see them, making you think, quite naturally, that you've seen them many times before. Was it possible that I had seen her on the beach last summer, or at the International Fair, or in some other place I couldn't remember? It doesn't matter whether I remembered or not. Farah held on to me as if seeking my protection, which made me genuinely confused. The square in front of the bar became completely empty and dark. After the last car took off, its noise having faded away in the distance and the silence of night having settled in, she walked off with us beside her, one on either side as if to protect her from some danger that might jump out at her at any moment. Then she came around me from behind and clung to me. She sought my protection once again. She held on to my arms. I thought to myself that she didn't like Kika. He wouldn't be taking her to his room like he did with the schoolgirls. This gave me a hidden pleasure. I stole a glance at him and saw that he no longer commanded the same sense of authority and power, satisfying himself by kicking a stone with his new shoe. He no longer walked as arrogantly or with as much self-importance. Middle-school girls and factory workers are easy to seal the deal with. They're already won over. But Kika's luck betrayed him this time when he saw her holding on to me. Perhaps his luck had been betraying him ever since Farah first set her eyes on the cabaret. Kika makes a habit of sleeping with young girls, whether or not his mother is around. He has a room all to himself, and he tries to provide us with every minute detail of the color of its walls, the type of lamp hanging above the bed, the starfish that adorn the ceiling. Fury steered his ship now, along with pride and gruffness, all because Farah hadn't held on to him. A light breeze played about my head and I could see that Kika finally understood that even if she didn't hate him, she was repulsed by the notion of getting anywhere close to him or his bedroom, despite the Adam's apple upon which he hung so many great hopes. His hands were in his pockets, his shoulders rocked back and forth, and his nose was high in the air. All of this meant a great deal. I remember the color of her dress, joking to Kika, "Maybe she walked by us last summer and we didn't recognize her because the dress she was wearing hadn't been blue . . ." but Kika wasn't in a joking mood. He circled around to get next to her as she moved away to avoid him and held tightly to my arm. Derisively, he said that the way I was holding on to her was shameful. It was the first time I'd found myself in such a situation, in the company of a strange girl whose origins I didn't know. With Kika behaving as if he had won her in a contest. Then we started to walk in front of him, leaving him standing on the side of the street. Her fingers squeezed my arm. She wasn't comfortable with what was going through Kika's head. She looked around, a little bit lost, a little bit frightened, not at all comfortable. I wondered whether I should grab her hand to comfort her, but I didn't. Twice, and then a third time I wondered whether I should grab her hand, but I didn't. Then Kika swooped in and grabbed her by the wrist, dragging her as he said threateningly, "What's wrong? Scared?"

"Let go of me . . ."

"Scared of me? Am I scaring you?"

"Let go of me or I'll scream . . ."

Kika's hand was strong. He gripped her wrist as if holding onto a poor little kitten. It wasn't the same hand that had patted me on the shoulder two days before in the mosque's courtyard, or just a little while ago under the dim lights of the cabaret. Rather, it was the hand that had strangled the rabid dog, the hand with the deep scar, the one immune to rabies. And then, as if the poison in the hand gripping her wrist had seeped into her veins, Farah jumped in fright and let out a sudden scream—a single long, piercing scream that you wouldn't have expected such a skinny body to be able to keep inside it. A disturbing scream. One capable of tearing the night in two. The kind that makes the hair on your head stand up on end. It was as if some other person had inhabited her body. Kika let go of her hand and backed off, shocked. He looked at her in disbelief, and only when there was a reasonable distance between them did she stop screaming. I put my hand in my pocket and counted the cash while Farah grabbed my arm once again without hiding her discomfort. Kika passed his hand over his hair very slowly, as if granting us a rare opportunity to see just how much he hated and despised us. His upper lip was quivering in a bitter sneer. I wondered how he saw me right then, with her hand holding my arm. What would my friend, Kika, say? I stared at him, overcoming my fear, with a measure of self-composure that, for the first time, didn't betray me. This in itself was an overwhelming victory. As he rocked back and forth from one foot to the other, he said that I'd regret it, that there would come a day when I'd regret what I'd done. She began to scream again before he retreated, reiterating his threat as he walked off into the jet-black night.

For a few moments after Kika left, I wondered why he hadn't told us about his mother who was turning tricks at this time of night. Deep down inside I had a feeling of delight I hadn't known before, and a hatred as well. Kika running off into the darkness. Ha! I'll bet he pissed his pants he was so scared. Hee hee! And I'll bet he's never slept with a girl in his life—student or factory worker—even though he's claimed to have slept with lots of girls! These are just claims, like the one that his father is in Spain and that he was going to join him there. Kika loves to boast!

I noticed that, rather than screaming, she was laughing. The contempt she had for Kika made her laughter down-right ecstatic. Soft, flowing laughter accompanied the calm that had suddenly set in, pushing aside the night's disarray that the scream had caused. I slowed down a little to savor the moment, and to see if Kika was following us. No trace of him. He had disappeared. Vanished. The darkness had swallowed him up. Unsurprisingly, I found myself behind her, deliberately walking in step with her. Cheerful. My hands were moving along with hers. We walked according to a hidden rhythm that Kika would never know. I heard her say, "If we go . . ." but I didn't hear the rest of what she said because it drifted off with the wind. Right then I told myself that I was going to place my hand in hers. My hand was sweaty. This wasn't encouraging. Then I heard her again: "If we go now, we'll find Naima at home." She walked next to me and far from me at the same time, lightly, as if a breeze were pushing her along, as she repeated that she had come from Azemmour to see her friend Naima. We walked through narrow alleyways with few lights and lots of cats whose shadows were running silently behind one another. I watched all of this with keen interest, because a bit of her lightness had moved to me. I walked along like someone who, all of a sudden, felt reassured, like a person who was now heading in a specific direction. Farah skipped along next to me, repeating that she had come from Azemmour only because of Naima. And that her neighbor, the brown-skinned woman, had told her that Naima was most likely staying late at the lawyer's place. If Naima didn't stay out late at one of the places where she was singing, she would spend a good part of the night at the lawyer's. "Do you know where the lawyer lives?" Farah asked. "I don't know where the lawyer lives." "Do you know who this lawyer is?" "I don't know who this lawyer is." Because there are lots of lawyers in Casablanca, and it had gotten so late, it was difficult to think. Then she said, "If we go now, we'll find Naima in bed because the brown-skinned woman said that she didn't make it a habit to sleep away from home, even if she does stay late at the lawyer's." That's what she said. Nothing more, nothing less.

A light rain started to fall on our faces and the asphalt glistened under our feet in a way that made me feel sad. After walking around the old city, the mosque appeared in front of us, the gray water stretching out behind it. She passed her hand over her wet face and laughed gaily. She continued to walk a few steps in front of me, not far from the low wall that surrounded the mosque's courtyard, differently than she had been walking just a short while ago, as if finding her friend no longer mattered to her. This sparked an additional bit of enthusiasm in me as I told myself that now I would take her hand, but I didn't. She kept on going in the rain, in her blue gypsy dress, talking like someone singing. A feeling of delight returned to me as I looked at her. I saw the minaret's shadow rising up between us. The wind howled around us, carrying our words every which way so that the girl only heard half of what I said, and I only heard half of what she said. I made do with sign language. The wind became more ferocious in the exposed area where we were standing. I strained to think of something entertaining to say to her—a funny story or an amusing piece of news, something about actors or singers. I discovered that we both loved Fairouz and hated Farid al-Atrash, not because of his singing, but because of the name Wahid (meaning "lonely") that he would use and that would always appear in the movie credits. That really made us laugh. As if the night had invigorated me and I was an actor who had finally found his role, I began to skip on top of the short wall that ran alongside us, forgetting about Kika and what might happen with him. My emotions told me that I should thank her for that rare opportunity that allowed me to see Kika defeated, destroyed, humiliated. I turned to see her walking alongside the wall. I asked her how old she was and she jumped up delicately, ending up in front of me on the wall. Now both of us were skipping along the wall. Farah was in front of me, spreading her arms to the wind, unfurling her wings like a dove pursuing its dream of flying away. As if she had become reassured, and this was really the strange thing! I skipped past her. She stopped and saw that I was now ahead of her. I also stopped and let her come closer. Should I grab her hand before she passed me? Or should I describe the different types of wood to her and explain the different ways they look until she laughed some more? I didn't do either of those things. I mean, what would a girl do with such knowledge about different kinds of wood in the wee hours of the morning? Farah was seventeen years old.

We were approaching the workshop when I heard her say, "If we go now, we'll find Naima in bed." This time I didn't think about whether to hold her hand to help her inside. Farah wasn't the type who could be easily held. That was what I was thinking. Farah hesitated before crossing over into the workshop, as if she were apologizing for the problems she had caused. I lit a candle and we sat looking awkwardly at one another, and at the shadows dancing around us. Farah told me that her friend had left Azemmour two years before to sing. The brown-skinned woman told her that she now sang in lots of places, in fancy cabarets and rich people's houses. Naima had always loved to sing. She'd sing at home and in the street. In class too. Naima knew nothing other than singing. At that moment, I wasn't interested in Naima or anyone else. All I was interested in was Farah. In the candlelight, I'd swear she didn't look seventeen years old like she said she was. We remained silent for a long time. As if we were wondering, both she and I, what to do with this young girl who had come to stay in the workshop. The clock indicated that it was past three in the morning. She sat under the window. I lay down far away from her. I hid myself among the pieces of wood inside the workshop in order to go to sleep, and at the same time to make her realize that Kika and I were different. When I opened my eyes, I saw that dawn had broken—a gray-blue dawn, as light as it was dark. Everything was strewn around the room. And the money I had made from the pipe deal was gone! I looked out through the open window and remembered that I had locked it before going to sleep. And Farah? She had disappeared as well, without a trace. All that remained was the memory of that strange night, which followed me around for days. Still, it had been a beautiful night that left a scent somewhere between lavender and wild thyme in my memory. Her scent! I spent days thinking about the strange perfume that had entered my room and my head that night, like a breeze passing through into a dream. Other thoughts filled my mind too. Something of that night did remain, something I didn't say. It might not have occurred to me to mention it at the time—the light that fell on her round breast as she walked toward the counter had colored it a warm purple.

8

Farah

THE TUNE THAT PLAYED OVER and over in my head was blue. It made me feel less sad. The bus that brought me to Casablanca passed through villages and towns I had never heard of. "Life goes on even outside of Azemmour," my friend Naima had said. This thought renewed my sense of relief since leaving home and continued to do so for practically the whole trip. The bus was slow and it stopped in every town it passed through. "Casablanca isn't far." I had to reassure my sister Raja with these words and others as well, such as, "It's only an hour. It'll be as if you've gone to the market and back, Raja! An hour or less." "Casablanca's just another city on Azemmour's doorstep, just outside *our* door." My words fell like water on sand and didn't really comfort her at all. The tears welled up in the corners of her eyes. I told her to bring me a glass of water so I wouldn't have to see the tears in her eyes. She's young. This twelve-year-old child thinks it's just a matter of time before everyone's desires will evaporate into thin air. My sister Fatima offers each of her two nursing babies a breast. Two fat breasts that look like white inflated waterskins. The nursing twins weren't even a year old, each one grabbing onto its prize, sucking greedily. Their eyes overflowed with joyful mischief as they watched me sitting on the same mattress smoothing the kerchief over my hair. I wasn't waiting my turn to nurse. I was waiting for my father to go down to the river so I could leave. He wasn't going to go now because he was waiting for his cigarettes, and the man who brings them hadn't come yet. Our father retired last year and now he sits on the doorstep of the house preparing his fishing rod and waiting for his cigarettes in the rising morning light as he stretches his lone leg out in front of him. Our father doesn't sleep, as if he's afraid he'll lose his other limbs during the night if he does. He was wearing his heavy djellaba that he never takes off. He didn't have the slightest inkling of my impending departure. Comfortable in that regard, thinking about his first cigarette. He didn't have a clue about the cash that was hidden underneath my dress. Comfortable in that regard as well. He was thinking about the cheap army tobacco his friend who hadn't yet retired supplies him with. He'd come by in a little bit to sell him the pack for double the price and they'd smoke together. Before they headed down to the river, they'd argue about a fish that had disappeared decades ago. Father was waiting for the fish to appear on his hook, whereas the soldier said that the fish no longer existed. The tobacco-selling soldier hadn't shown up yet. The fish was called the North African shad. I'd never seen it. This fish only existed in Father's imagination.

Our father is unhappy because of us. He didn't expect our mother to bear him girls—three daughters one after the other. However, he never seemed to grumble or complain. On the contrary, he spent his days fighting to make sure people respected us. That was what he thought about, its shadow settling over his days like a perpetual cloud. He thought he'd stumbled upon a solution when he asked whether there was any better way to gain people's respect than by working in the army. We didn't know if he was asking us or himself. "Is there anything that gets more respect than the military uniform? You could be nurses, or aides, or any profession as long as you're dressed in military garb." This is what he said to us, Fatima and me, because Raja was still young. He hadn't started to worry about her yet. The uniform was what would protect us from people's insults and vile talk. Vile talk informs vile deeds. That's how things have always been. Raja laughs when she hears our father say that she, too, will someday become a soldier, after he's finished with us, once he's forced us into any old job that comes with a respectable, khaki uniform. People here don't respect anyone. Raja will get used to the uniform and learn how to clean and iron it. She'll learn how to tie the necktie and lace up her shoes later on. Our father says, "Soldiers are respected wherever they go, whether they're a man or a woman. People respect the uniform. They'd respect it even if it were draped over a piece of wood. People don't respect anything other than this scrap of cloth we drape over ourselves. Take, for example, the man who has thoughts and ideas. Do people respect him for this? Everyone's heads are filled with thoughts, but nobody sees them. Only the lucky ones get to put on a uniform, though. Thoughts receive no more respect than a mosquito because thoughts stay inside your head, and as long as they stay inside your head they don't intimidate anyone. Not so with the military uniform. The military uniform has its history, luster, mystique, glory, prestige. Prestige! That's the word. We soldiers have our prestige. As long as we were in uniform, people would always respect us. Have you ever heard of a soldier who's been raped or assaulted?" Maybe Father didn't choose a path that corresponded to what we wanted to do, but it made perfect sense for someone like him who had spent his life moving from base to base. Fatima didn't get the military job he had been hoping for, but she did marry a soldier, and that's the important thing. A regular soldier without rank or anything. This was the most Father was able to arrange, but it didn't matter. Even with this modest achievement, Father could boast about his daughter's new status. Soldier or married to a soldier—same thing, isn't it? A soldier the same age as her. Twenty-seven years old. Low-ranking, but that has never been important to the success of a marriage. And what happened? Fatima came back home after a year of marriage with two children, one in each arm, dark blue bruises around each eye, divorce papers in hand, and a miserable view of her ruined life. But this was never important, because Father continued to boast about his daughter and her short life in the military. Even after she returned to her parents' house, he still felt that she was fully respectable. Respect isn't like a shirt you toss aside after wearing it for a week. Respect doesn't wear out. Once you acquire it, it stays with you forever. Proof of this was that she still went out without anyone getting in her way! I left Mother in the kitchen kneeling and rolling out bread for the day. I left as if I weren't hiding stolen cash in my belt.

My friend Naima went to Casablanca two years ago to sing, and there's no doubt that her voice is now ringing out in all the fancy spots—salons, cafés, party halls, and stadiums. "After two or three years," Fatima said, "you'll forget all about singing and Naima and everything else. Your head will be filled with other concerns. Three years isn't such a long time. They pass like a flash of lightning. After that, you'll forget all about Casablanca when you give birth to a beautiful son who looks just like you, and together we'll sing him to sleep. Together we'll watch him become a child and we'll take him to school, each of us holding a hand. He'll learn how to be a good person and he'll get a good education. A good boy who only wants the best for people, or a girl who'll work in the carpet workshops or the milk cooperative earning an honest living." "Well, I'd rather go to Casablanca than have Father shove me into one of his military barracks." This is what I continued to explain to her over the course of many long nights. "When you're in Casablanca, you're out in the world, living life, ready for every chance encounter, every interaction. Casablanca has lots of opportunities. The world begins there." Naima would say to me, "Casablanca's a big city. No one sees anyone there. No one asks about anyone there." She told me about the yacht where she had spent an unforgettable night on the open sea, her voice dancing over the water as if in imitation of the big city's lights that twinkled before her. As if the city and its lights and its buildings and the thousands of lives it was overflowing with were all living to the rhythm of her singing. In Casablanca you can do whatever you want with your life. I left early so that I'd arrive early, but the bus didn't come until almost noon.

I left Azemmour and here I was on the bus. I even said to myself that this was a morning brimming with optimism; despite everything, it had finally arrived. Then came some short rain showers that had been holding back before falling steadily, albeit weakly. They weren't enough to wash the ground. They didn't get rid of the dust or the anxiety that had built up in the air. Nonetheless, they left behind enough light to give the impression that we were on the verge of a new day. They left behind a soft calm that provided me with a feeling of optimism like the restfulness one feels after being tired. A veil wrapped around fields of green corn that stretched into the distance, there, anxiously awaiting the same rain I was waiting for. I saw it from the bus window and heard it tapping weakly on the glass, *tock tock tock*. I left Azemmour early in the morning carrying this slight optimism with me, despite everything, because the sky had spent the entire night holding its breath. Then, after we left the station, the heat returned like it had been before—heavy and stifling. I liked picturing myself running away, with the woman next to me not knowing anything about it. I looked at the woman sitting next to me on the bus and thought to myself that I'd grown up all at once. From now on I'll need to think about older, rational women. Women traveling unaccompanied to the city, on the verge of something completely new. I realized that more clearly now that I was alone.

Above us there was a gray sky that was practically white. The woman next to me was appealing to God to pour His mercy down on us. She might have thought that it was still summer. I was thinking about noon, obsessed with it. When noon arrived, I'd find Naima in bed. At school, Naima was always cheerful. She loved to laugh and play. She left Azemmour two years ago in order to sing. Naima left school because the only thing she was good at was singing. She would sing at home, in the street, at school. Maybe she'd wake up this morning with a new song in her head and jump up, humming. She'd leave the house happy because she'd think she'd found the tune that suited her voice. And at that very moment, I'd be knocking on her door. What if I didn't find her there after all of this? Usually I'm a pretty optimistic person, so I didn't know why these thoughts assailed me now. I'm not a complainer or more stubborn than necessary. I'm always hoping for the best, for myself and for others. I see people in the best-possible light. I closed my eyes. Most of the time when I close my eyes, I see lots of faces. Faces I know and faces I don't know, always cheerful and accompanied by music. This relaxes me. Its effect on me lasts for a while. This was how I thought of her, my friend Naima. Would I be luckier than her? I didn't know. I removed the headscarf from my hair. I opened the window and put my hand out while holding the scarf, and the wind made it flutter as it considered its unclear fate. Then I opened my fingers and the scarf flew away with the wind. I opened my eyes and followed it until it disappeared.

There's a road that goes up for a while. Then, when you get up to the top, the buildings appear, all one story tall. Any other time they would have looked normal, just houses painted with yellow plaster. To me, though, it was as if I were looking out over a richly colored garden that I had been dreaming of, whose time had finally come to present itself to me. So, I'd arrived. As soon as I stood up, I touched the money. Bills still there in the same place, wrapped in cloth and halfah grass, waiting. The money was there now, tucked into my belt like an apple that had been on display for years, and that I had grabbed because no one else had. It would have gone bad if it had remained where it was, hanging on the tree or hidden in the halfah-grass stuffing of the bed. That was how I thought of it. It had been hidden in a small hole in the mattress that Mother and Father slept on. Even when we were in the other room, Fatima and I could smell the cash. We wondered what those bills were doing among the halfah reeds. They'd rot if someone didn't come along and grab them. Getting to them was always tempting. It was just a loan I'd repay when I returned from Casablanca. This thought relaxed me.

Just as I feared, I didn't find Naima at home. After I knocked on her door several times, I realized that it wasn't a bit of luck I needed to prop me up anymore. What I needed at that moment was a bit of shade, a wall or a tree under which I could take cover. I sat on the doorstep. To my right and left there was a line of doors that all looked the same, reminding me of the doors in military neighborhoods. Their walls were painted with flaking yellow plaster. There was an empty space stretching out in front of the houses, above which was a dark sky that tired my eyes. There was absolutely no wind. Plastic bags clung to the branches of thornbushes like crows caught in unseen traps. Rigid. Mummified. What was I doing here? I was waiting for Naima. Rocks, people, everything stood still for a moment, suspended. As if the earth had stopped turning and the sky was about to rain down lead. There wasn't the slightest breeze. The heat became increasingly brutal, grabbing the skin and seeping into the pores to suck up what remained of its sap. I thought about the Oum Errabia River and about Father waiting for the shad to show up again. There's a river down the hill from our house. My two sisters and I can see it from the window. When I lay my head down on the pillow, I can hear it running lightly over his fingertips. Was the water still running, or had it been hit by the same drought? This day was endless. My sweaty body was struck by a weakness that practically numbed me. I thought about Azemmour as if I had left it a year ago. I thought about the small room, occupied now by Raja and Fatima and her twins. From this morning on, Raja would sleep in my bed. I thought about the refreshing breeze that would always blow through the room no matter what time it was. I thought about all of these things the way someone trapped in the snow thinks during his final moments before his body freezes for good, thinking of the sweet drowsiness that makes his eyelids heavy, in the moments when a delicious numbness comes over each part of the body, one after the other, and the mind begins to work feverishly, racing, seeing at that moment all the good things that had happened to him over the course of his life. That was how I felt. I think I lost consciousness and during that time I saw a dove flying, then a long set of stairs. I climbed them reluctantly. I stopped on every step to turn toward the brown-skinned woman climbing up behind me. Every time I stopped, I heard her urge me to keep going up, a friendly smile on her lips. Then she asked me if I'd like some water. The brown-skinned woman wasn't a dream. It wasn't the oppressive temperature or a trick of the darkness. Rather, she was standing over me as I lay in the bed, not looking for water or for Naima, but wondering how I came to be in her bed, as if my discouragement at not finding Naima had turned into utter exhaustion. I wondered whether the night would end as the day had, without even the smallest surprise. Instead of water, the brown-skinned woman held a damp cloth in her hand, which she placed on my forehead. Behind her, musical instruments hung on the wall. The man sitting in the chair was looking at me as he polished his violin. His hair was jet-black, his face extremely white, and he had a thin moustache. He wore dark sunglasses. Was he blind? Had I returned to the nightmare? Or had I gone to another nightmare? Through the small, square window, lightning flashed. I sat up and heard a distant thunderclap that sounded as if it was coming from the deepest depths of night. Other instruments hung all over the four walls of the room, along with djellabas and kaftans. Another peal of thunder. Would it rain tonight? The brown-skinned woman said, "Naima doesn't usually keep set hours. She doesn't have a usual time when she comes home, especially on Saturday nights." Was today Saturday? "If she's spent the evening at the lawyer's place, she'll usually be out late, but she won't be out all night." I don't know Casablanca, and I don't know any lawyers. The Naima I know is a shy girl; just passing in front of a man would be enough to make her blush. At school she was always cheerful. She loved to play, laugh, and sing.

II

9

THE MAN WHO HAD BEEN sitting in the chair for hours finally lifted his head. As he had been expecting, the bird's note echoed across the wide-open space—*tiii*—as the sun's first rays appeared. He turned. He could see it without having to turn around. It was there on the same post, on the edge of the dirt road. The man responded to it with a long *tiiiiii* of his own. And as it did every morning, the bird repeated its note. It left the note ringing behind it as it flew away, echoing above the head of the man sitting in the chair. This was the moment when the day came to life. His wife's mother opened the windows to air out the house. The smell of coffee wafted out in front of him and he breathed it in deeply. When he went back inside, his wife was pacing to ease her pain. Then she stopped and looked in the mirror. Without the mirror, she can't see her belly. There were secrets inside her belly just as there are secrets at the bottom of the ocean. She thought about the new life growing inside her as if she could only measure how far along she was by looking in the mirror. Her damp, jet-black hair stuck to her forehead and fell over her shoulders, and her cheeks were red—not the red of blood, but the red of a woman who was just about to become a mother. Her breasts were swollen and warm. For the past few weeks she had been amazed that no milk was coming out of her breasts, swollen as they were. What prevented it from flowing? Her mother told her, "The milk doesn't come before the child." But the woman didn't understand how it could be that the milk didn't come before the child. The milk should come first. No one likes to go somewhere and not find food waiting for them. How can a child come into the world and not find its nourishment on the table waiting for it? Her mother moistened her chest with milk at night. Its rotten smell filled the room. Her chest was damp now and had large, nearly dry splotches on it. The woman thought the milk flow had burst forth during the night while she was sleeping, in preparation for feeding the newcomer. A captivating calm enveloped the woman as she studied her body part by part, acquainting herself with it, looking at the changes in her face, examining the splotches of milk that her mother had put on her chest during the night, saying, "It's coming, it's coming!" She held up her hand and weighed the amount of milk she believed she had collected, drop by drop, the result of all her thoughts, all her senses, her movements, and appeals day and night. Not to mention those of her mother over the course of many nights. Satisfied, she touched the generous, translucent white liquid on her dress, and said to her mother, "The milk always comes before the child, Mama." And it would continue to flow to feed her newborn for a year or two until it got big and strong. Was she happy now that she was on the verge of something new, something she was now more clearly conscious of? Not something so abstract as a happy dream, or a multicolored rainbow dancing around inside her head, or a radiant star floating up in the sky illuminating her nights to come. Rather, a body with a real head and real hands swimming around in her belly; a body that would grow up enough to upset the calm of what remained of her days. She had enough time in front of her to experience all of this.

For about two months now she had been complaining of chronic constipation. She was incredulous. "Two months?" The man replied, "Constipation is what women get, just like diarrhea is what men get." She pointed to her belly. The man came closer and leaned in a little without touching the belly. She asked, "Do you hear it?" He continued to wonder what he was supposed to be hearing. She insisted, "Do you hear it?" Up until then, the man had no desire to hear anything, but she insisted. A small life was pulsing underneath, moving, growing little by little. How could he not hear it? Was this its leg? As if the fetus were a cat trapped inside a box. Separated from them by this patch of skin as thin as a piece of bread, so thin that the woman imagined the fetus's leg might become visible to them at any moment. Then he passed his palm across her belly. The skin's softness didn't awaken any feeling in him. The belly was warm, and that was all. Maybe he was expecting more than this—more than the heat of the skin and that of the fetus hiding beneath it. He passed his hand over the small lump as if testing his sense of touch again. What was the fetus doing right now? It was playing. But how could fetuses play? No, it wasn't playing. It was growing. It never stopped growing. The thought of not growing never occurred to it for even a moment. If only the man had just an hour without it being there so he could think. But that was no longer possible. The fetus wasn't too concerned with what the man was thinking about. Then her mother appeared with a cup of coffee in her hand. Having her put it down seemed stupid to him, so he got up. The woman lay back down on the bed. The little mass growing inside her was what she possessed. It was palpable, definitive. There was no going back. No one could share this with her. This was what she had tried to show him when she recoiled from the sting of his cold hand and went back to bed. As soon as he left the room with the cup in his hand, he didn't care anymore about the small fetus that was making his wife so happy. And the woman? A terrifying feeling that she could give birth at any moment had settled in. She didn't want the man to see the child when it came out, the first treasure of hers that she would present to this world. He left her with her mother's advice and sat back down in the chair as he placed the cup of coffee on the box. Her mother had been advising her to eat turtle meat so the baby would be born male. This too was of no concern to him, as if he weren't awaiting an event that would likely change his life. About two months ago she had brought home a cage with a hoopoe in it because swallowing the raw heart of the hoopoe is supposed to make male babies more intelligent and she wanted her grandchild to be an intelligent male, not like the neighbors' children who didn't possess an iota of sense. This too didn't concern him.

The only miracle he was waiting for was for Farah to appear. The only miracle he was still waiting for—even after the ambulance disappeared, even after the square emptied out, and even after that as he sat in the doorway of the workshop—was that she would appear from behind the mosque or coming up from the beach. Nothing of the sort happened. Farah was languishing in some hospital; a stranger in a hospital the location of which he didn't know, nor how to get there. He spent a long time searching for her in broad streets and narrow streets, in twisting alleyways and obscure administrative offices, unable to hold onto a thought or recognize a road, preferring to continue the search before the trail went cold, before regaining his composure and seeing that there was no use in rushing. Then he saw that the time for searching had passed and realized that finding her was becoming less and less likely. He ran after traces of her as they moved from one clinic to a larger clinic, from one hospital to another, before the thought faded away. Finally, he came across an ambulance driver in the neighborhood prefecture office who alerted him to her presence in such and such large public hospital located behind the church (not in any other hospital), in such and such wing that takes in burn victims (not in any other wing). The driver couldn't keep from asking, "Where do you know her from? Is she your sister? Your niece?"

The faces were covered in bandages, nothing showing except for the eyes and mouth. Seeing them didn't help him at all. Three small, round holes were all that connected these faces to life. Other faces were completely covered. Then there were the bodies hidden behind curtains. How could he possibly find a young woman named Farah among these ghosts? The place had no faces. No bodies. The smells weren't human smells. The only visitors were sitting in silence, as if at a funeral. With no smell, they gave the impression that the place was filled with temporary, transient beings laid out in these rooms to rest for a little while before continuing on their journey. Silent pain was the worst. Closer to death than pain that announced itself. It was always there. The visitors sat in silence. As if the time for painful crying and wailing had passed. They were all preparing for the funeral, getting used to the idea of it. The overall impression was that of death. What oozed from the faces and walls and floated in the air in the rooms and danced through the hallways was death, or some notion of death, more present there than anything else. Resigned. Resigned because they were helpless. How could he find a young woman among them who went by a name no one knew?

"Her name?"

"Farah."

"We don't have anyone here with that name."

"She came in this morning."

"Lots of people came in this morning. Where do you know her from?" Then a measured silence.

At the front door and the reception desk, the same question: "Where do you know her from?" Followed by the same silence. In the rooms and hallways. In all the places that hinted at some form of life. Inside him there was a heavier silence he didn't know how to express. A nurse took him by the hand and led him to one of the rooms, but even in this room, though his intellect told him that it was the right room, he didn't recognize

Farah. He stood at the door staring at her face, scrutinizing her. There was no trace of the happy times he had spent with her. He tried to recognize her underneath the bandages, with the swelling on her neck, and bruises and bloody wounds on her arms. She looked like the many drowning victims he had seen in the hallway, or in other rooms throughout the burn-victim unit. He had looked at all of them, one after the other, pursued by the moans of victims caught in buildings that collapsed all the time, until he finally found her in the last room at the end of the hall, just when he thought he'd never find her. She was lying without a cover on a bed splattered with spots of dried blood. Her thin body wasn't covered by anything. She was wearing clothes he had never seen on her before. He didn't recognize her. He didn't recognize her hair. It was as if it had grown longer. Her jet-black hair fanned out over the pillow. Her face was different from the face that had shone with vitality in the workshop just a few days before. The calm happiness that it had radiated was gone. Her face was covered in bandages. Her lips were split, bruised, spotted with dried blood. There was a black swelling around her eyes and a blueness on what he could see of her cheeks. Blood stuck to her black hair and forehead, which had still-fresh burns on it. Above her forehead a strange-looking indentation had formed, and there was another blue one above her arms. Was this enough for him to recognize her? Her small body was shaking like a dying bird. Her shoulder blades were more prominent than they had been. Her hands were the same white color and they shook lightly. The burns hadn't disfigured them too much. Was she going to get up in a little bit? He didn't recognize her long fingers. The fingers were clasped peacefully on her belly. He especially didn't recognize her toes, or was it that they would never again have the same effect on him? The small, perfectly arranged toes that had been so filled with life, with Farah's joy. On the bed across from hers was another girl the same age. She looked like her. She was also sleeping. She had the same spots on her face, the same fever that made her lips tremble, even while she was sleeping. The two of them were sleeping. Two orphaned children forgotten by a tribe that had gotten through the ordeal and moved on. All the patients looked like one another. The room was bare. No comfort. No visitors. No flowers on the bedside table. The walls were green, the color of death. The patients' rooms also looked like one another. He remained standing in the doorway for a while, and when he walked toward the bed—he might not have needed to right then—he did so to reassure himself that this wasn't Farah.

Salih, the cistern guard, carried a hunting rifle on his shoulder. He walked between the train tracks. He crossed the tracks and walked down the hill, and his shadow and that of his rifle, which for a few moments had broken the calm line of the horizon, disappeared. He crossed the dirt path that ran alongside the railroad tracks. He had come to ask about his daughter and her mother. The man came outside with another cup of coffee and stood across from the door, giving the impression that he wasn't ready to talk yet today. The cistern guard sat down on the box. He didn't talk about his daughter. He was preoccupied with the rabbit that had crossed the river. It wasn't normal for this land to shelter rabbits. The guard had been preoccupied with the rabbit since dawn, but the man who had been sitting there since before dawn hadn't seen any rabbits cross the river. When the man was ready to think about rabbits, the guard had changed the subject to thieves who had shown up again, and when the man was ready to think about thieves, the guard had gotten up and walked into the field that had been invaded by weeds. He walked with heavy steps. After each step he would stop to closely examine the ground. He leaned over the dirt, picked up a handful, and sniffed it. He crumbled it and let it flow through his fingers like water. The man sitting in the chair watched all of this and didn't think it had anything to do with a rabbit. The guard took a few more steps, performing the same meticulous task over and over. The cistern guard owned sheep and cows. When thieves began swarming around his flock and those of the neighbors, he bought a rifle and began to sleep among his animals, and when he laid his head down on it, the new rifle smell brought dreams that he was firing at the thieves. For the first time, today at dawn, he had seen a rabbit dashing across the empty land. Perhaps it was the rifle propping up his head that had seen the rabbit. Why would a rabbit leave its hole unless it was running away from thieves? Thieves don't steal rabbits. They steal entire herds of cattle. Rabbits are rabbits, and the only thing we understand for sure is that rabbits run when they smell humans. The guard came back and opened his hand in front of the man—sure of himself, of the truth of what was in his palm, completely convinced—saying they were rabbit droppings, as if these small, round balls were the smoking gun that proved thieves had been there. He sat down again on the box. He grabbed the rifle between his legs and leaned on it like a cane, looking toward the horizon, which was blazing. Whatever the case might be with the rabbits, the thieves had shown up again. He heard that two days before they had stolen a full herd of cattle. He was the cistern guard and not a farmer. He needed a full night's sleep. These thieves didn't understand such things. This whole time, the man thought about how he didn't have anything to steal, neither cows nor rams. He had a ewe once that had died during the last drought, and that was it.

Two pigeons flew low past them, practically right above their heads. They were in a hurry, unconcerned with what was going on inside the guard's head, unconcerned with whether he was standing or sitting, unconcerned with the man and the son he was waiting for. The only thing that concerned them was discussing the day's sustenance. No one passed by on the road. In fact, there was no road at all other than the train tracks. And the only train wouldn't pass by until two in the afternoon, empty as it headed toward the southern mines.

There was no shepherd driving his flock to the fields whose grass has dried up because of the rain that didn't fall. Would it rain now that it was May? It was enough for Salih to say, "The sky's blue." The fields had dried up. No harvesting machines would come here this year. Work wouldn't go on as it had before. Instead of spreading fertilizer, planting seeds, and preparing the soil for the coming season, all he'd be able to do was gather up the dried crops and store them for the cold days to come. As for the other train, the one loaded with fertilizer, it had passed by at two in the morning. At two in the morning the man was asleep.

10

The Mailbox

I WAS IN THE TAXI, crammed in the back with three other travelers who were laughing nonstop as they discussed football, Morocco's preparations for the Africa Cup, and the opportunity other nations would have to make fun of us and our preparations. With a burst of laughter they recalled the parachutist who, during a previous game, rather than landing in Honor Stadium, found himself hanging from a lamppost near Ain Diab beach. Their laughter grew even more hysterical as they beat their chests and pulled at their hair, so much so that they paid no attention to me and how annoying their moving and writhing bodies were. Maybe they couldn't see me, even though I was glaring at them with visible contempt. And I didn't understand what was so funny and interesting about being made fun of by other people. I attributed it to the fact that they were old, past forty, maybe even fifty. This added to their bizarre way of hating one another. Never in my life will I befriend men their age. Were they heading to the same city I was? If so, I'd rather head somewhere else than remain with them in the same car. I had never set foot in Azemmour. Hatred for them had infected the driver at the same moment and he began to hit the steering wheel with his two large hands, shaking like a bear. The older a person gets, the more feebleminded he becomes. What he says becomes increasingly trivial. That's what I think. That's why I don't place any importance on what they're thinking. I'm not thinking about the parachutist hanging from a pole on the beach, or his friend who landed on the roof of City Hall. I'm not thinking about Africa or its Cup or the other nations getting ready to laugh at us, just as I'm not interested in the hysterical laughter of my fellow travelers, so preoccupied am I with the girl who burst into the cabaret that night. What was her name? I tried to forget her name, but then I called it back to mind so as not to have to think about the noise rising up around me.

I spent the last few days thinking about her. For many long weeks I couldn't think of anything but her and the way she had appeared and stood there between the door and the counter in her blue dress, and the way she had disappeared. I wasn't thinking about how much money she had taken with her; the money we had made from the copper deal wasn't enough to cover even one week's expenses. Besides, contributing to the cost of building the mosque was no longer on the table after I'd seen the maggot-filled hole in the lower part of my uncle's belly. Still, there was an alarm going off in my head, telling me that she hadn't shown up only to disappear. She hadn't spent a whole night with me for nothing. Quite simply, she had come to stay. The cash she had taken with her was proof that her disappearance was temporary. That's how I had come to think over the past few days. If her intention had been to disappear for good, she wouldn't have needed to leave behind any sign. Like other women, she would need to meet multiple times before becoming intimate, to get used to me, and to stay. That was how I thought about it, and it seemed reasonable. She may have taken the money to get back at Kika and the bizarre way he had behaved toward her. I thought about all the possible paths she might have taken. The morning she disappeared I shaved, put on cologne, donned a clean shirt, and stood at the window waiting for Farah. All day I saw signs in her disappearance that indicated she would come back. I told myself that when she did come back, I'd repaint the workshop and buy a new suit. And what happened? Nothing happened for two full days, for a whole week. As if the workshop and the thought of painting it, and the suit would be enough to bring her back. How funny was that? It was the first time in my life something so strange had happened to me. A girl I didn't know before and barely knew save for a couple of hours we spent together in a dark room and in even darker roads and alleyways. Despite that, I couldn't stop thinking about her. She might not even go by that name that smells so sweetly optimistic—Farah. I'm not sure how I started this morning thinking she was close by, living in the neighborhood with or without her friend, Naima. Maybe she was waiting for me, seeing my search for her as some sort of amusing game, following my footsteps as I followed hers, watching me from behind a crack in the door so I wouldn't see her, expecting me to find her the whole time, or something like that. But I didn't find her. It was enough for me just to think about her. This was how I'd get to her. Because she'd notice. A sign would come to her and she'd appear, or she'd be satisfied with some other sign. I remained standing at the door of the workshop waiting for plenty, but not expecting anything in particular. I'd spend whole days in the mosque's courtyard, forgetting about work, forgetting about Kika and his odd behavior, forgetting about Father and his ceiling that was scattered all over the courtyard. Sometimes I'd climb the sand dunes and find myself on the coastal road pretending to watch the truck drivers while they followed the progress of the mosque as it took its final form before they headed toward the marina. For a few moments they'd bare their muscular forearms, which looked like ships' masts, before heading off. I'd remain standing in the middle of the road, directionless, without a signal, without a sign that she was anywhere around. And so, little by little, without thinking about it, without any forewarning, I found myself preoccupied with the letter that was going to come from her. I continued to wait for the letter, and for the mail carrier who would bring it, dressed in his dark uniform and carrying his heavy satchel, coming up from the ocean like someone emerging from the clouds. I anticipated what my response would be: Would I write some lines of poetry like the ones I wrote in elementary school? Sometimes I'd picture the mail carrier before he appeared, with the letter sitting at the bottom of his satchel bouncing around to the rhythm of his steps. Because he would have so many letters, I would always imagine him walking slowly. When I didn't see him at the usual time, I'd leave the workshop and wander around the neighborhoods behind it for an hour or two to give him the chance to show up, for his sack to reveal what was inside it. Then I'd go back. I'd turn to see if the mail carrier had left any footprints in the sand on the beach as he passed by. I'd walk toward the mailbox with dread in my heart. A small box made of colored wood that I had constructed the morning she disappeared. Gentle, friendly. Its mouth yawning wide. Dark and laughing innocently. I looked inside, trying to make out in the deep darkness of the box whether anything might indicate that there was a piece of paper there, something resembling paper, a bit of an envelope, yellow or white, lurking in its depths. Anything that might possibly indicate that a sign had arrived.

This time the entire car shook. In fact, the laughter had become a veritable earthquake. Since I was an outsider to their world, I didn't know the reason for all of this violent shaking and the frightening sounds that went along with it. The driver almost went through the car's roof, as the contagion had stricken the passenger seated right next to him as well. Rather than bursting into hysterics like the others, he chose to get out of the taxi, covering his mouth with both hands. Then, for a long while, they didn't even have to say anything. It was enough for one of them to raise his brow or twitch his nose. Even without these signs, a mere glance from one to the other was enough to cause them all to burst into irritating fits of laughter. I asked the guy sitting next to me to let me out. He turned toward me, but couldn't see me because of the tears in his eyes, and my words didn't reach his ears. The demons of laughter had completely overtaken his senses and he went back to it, turning his face toward the window. The other two passengers had pulled the hoods of their djellabas over their heads, unable to regain their composure. They laughed, guffawed, and shook the car, shaking my skinny body along with it. They laughed because an hour of rainfall had inundated an entire city due to faulty sewage lines. Then they laughed because of a man who tripped over his djellaba and fell down. In the end, they laughed for no reason whatsoever. Could there be anything worse than this? There was no way I'd go with them. For his part, the driver leaned on the door of his car chewing on his moustache, having remembered that it was up to him to call over the passenger who would save him from waiting, from the laughter coming at no charge, from his own bad luck. He didn't know anymore whether he needed two or three more passengers.

Before the letter, I stood like a night watchman for two nights in front of the Saâda Cabaret until the last drunk stumbled out and the last taxi drove off, until the last light was turned off. No trace of Farah. Two bitterly cold nights waiting, wrapped only in the hope that she would appear with her short hair, blue dress, and that little bit of fear and shyness on her face. That's Farah. Before that, the night before, I stood where she had been standing, between the door and the counter, scrutinizing the singer with the light shining down on him and the drunks swaying all around. All I was missing were the short hair, the blue dress, and the terrified face. All I was missing were the two narrow eyes. I stood there struck by this thought. Her eyes looked Asian. Two small, cheerful almond-shaped eyes that prompted delight and lust at the same time. I thought that perhaps what had attracted me to her so intensely were her foreign-looking eyes. They didn't look like any other girl's eyes in that, despite the fear etched on her face, these eyes held an eternal tenderness. That gave me enough of a reason to think about her the whole time. Other customers, another singer, other music. But the same girls and the cheerful atmosphere that lifted the day's burdens helped me feel a sense of release, of freedom, of rapture. I did almost exactly what she had done. I asked the guard about Naima, the same guard she had asked and who had tried to keep her from entering. I told him that it was my first time in this city. I had come from the city of Azemmour asking about a friend named Naima, a fun game that allowed me to move around the counter and all over the place asking about Naima. I was talking to the customers just as she had spoken with me— about the lawyer, about Azemmour, about the Oum Errabia River, about the father who had lost his leg in the war in the Western Sahara and who spent his time sitting on the river-bank waiting for an extinct fish to return. At a certain point, I became her. I wished I could have been wearing her blue dress so I could have seen myself the way I had seen her. I put on a feminine face, an embroidered dress, a bouncy walk, narrow eyes, and a little bit of fear, because we girls are born with our fear. It grows with us just like our hair or our finger-nails. We trim them as we please, but they always grow back, even continuing to grow after death. Did I seem handsome and friendly to her that night, unafraid of a reckless hand or a vicious tongue? I'm only two years older than her. It's easy for me to pretend to be a girl. It wasn't the first time such ideas had entered my mind—that I saw myself as a girl. Could this be attributed to the fear that overwhelms me for no reason so much of the time? Sometimes I call it fear, sometimes shyness, and sometimes it's a tactic. Whether I'm walking or sitting down, my heart always beats quickly, as if it's on the verge of jumping out of its cage, and I don't see any reason for it other than the fear of something that hasn't yet happened. If not for this feeling, I wouldn't have hung out with Kika, I wouldn't have been afraid of the dog, I wouldn't have feared Father or any old person who might take his place.

Why didn't she show up now? Going back to Azemmour or coming from there? Just like that, all of a sudden, in her blue dress, or not in her blue dress? What surprised me was seeing Kika with his mother, Kenza, slinking around a group of travelers whose numbers had dwindled, just when I had been waiting for a pleasant surprise. They were still chasing after the visa. For her son's sake she was going to knock on the doors of other people she knew after having exhausted all of those in Casablanca. Kika was wearing a brown coat and wiped his sweat with the sleeve. He bought it last summer, a coat like Columbo's that he'll take with him to that country. From that very moment he's been picturing himself waiting in front of the Metro for the blond girl he's been dreaming about ever since we were in grade school. Blond and slender, with green eyes like those of an angel. The passport, the working papers, the residency permit, and everything. But he's not going anywhere because he's always had bad luck. He looks ridiculous strutting about in his long coat. It would have been better if the carpenter boss had fucked him and knocked him down a few notches. I made myself small and buried my head between my shoulders, happy to wait there for as long as it would take to avoid running into them, so as not to have to say hi to them. I remained in that uncomfortable position for a while. It became clear to me that night that I should not expect anything from Kika anymore. The time had come for me to put a definitive end to that friendship. In fact, he had never been a friend in the first place, even though I'd tried to show him otherwise. Maybe the time had truly come for Kika to go to Sweden, or Hungary, or Hell. Why was I even worrying about him? Was he my brother? Or my cousin? I have one brother named Suleiman and he's in Abu Dhabi making lots of money. He wouldn't worry about Kika if he were around. Anyway, like I said before, he doesn't look like he's going anywhere. He'll stay here scratching at the walls and wasting away until he vanishes completely. I felt safe because it had suddenly become silent inside and outside the car. This allowed me to sit back up. When I straightened up, Kika and his mother were gone, along with the loud commotion of the passengers who had been in the car with me, because they had gotten out of the taxi. The driver and I remained, waiting for them and for five passengers now, rather than one. The taxi stand was pulsing with travelers, none of them going to Azemmour. This was completely understandable, because none of them had met Farah. Most of them were wrapped in more than one coat or djellaba because of the cold weather.

Suddenly, I found that I was all right. Not because Farah had appeared or because Kika was gone, but rather because a small sun had emerged from behind the clouds, cheerful and sending out calm, cool rays on this morning that had begun so depressingly. This small, cool sun filled my eyes completely and I thought that surely my eyes were smiling too. Neither the noisy passengers nor the driver whose annoyed voice was still chasing after other elusive passengers would see it. Then, for no apparent reason, the blood rushed to my heart with a force I hadn't known before, as if rising and falling in my throat rather than pulsing playfully in my heart. I got out of the car, trying hard not to think about Farah anymore, just as I had done before with Kika, and the dog. This was also significant, extremely significant for someone like me who didn't know anyone.

11

ON THE ONE HAND, I started to see lots of dogs at night, their howling getting to me even with my head under the pillow. On the other hand, during the day I acted like someone who needed to take every precaution, like going out the window instead of the door, for example, and constantly following the headlines on the front page of the *Le Matin* to see if anything had changed there, not to mention closely watching the work being done on the mosque. With each step that the work moved toward completion, it became more certain that the dog would disappear from my life. Because after the work on the mosque was completed, the shaykhs, the officials, the police, and the gendarmes wouldn't be able to justify taking people's money anymore. That's what I was thinking. The headline on the front page of the *Le Matin* continued to be the proof by which I would measure the path toward this end. Does it still occupy the uppermost part of the page? Are its letters still prominent and green?

With these thoughts, I get up this morning in a foul mood. Wavering between searching for the man who made my sister Khadija's head spin and going to the mosque to finish the work Father had abandoned. His hands had betrayed him. My brother Suleiman, whom we relied on a lot, was of no help to us at all. Why he had abandoned us, I didn't know. Right when Father had landed the contract to construct one of the most prominent ceilings in the mosque (maybe two or even three, depending on how quickly and expertly he could work), just when he had begun to see the future a bit more brightly after years of being fully unemployed, just when he had declared that our days of destitution were behind us and that he was truly ready to abandon his days of wanton depravity and come home. It was then that Suleiman chose to set off, or as Father put it, to run away to the Gulf. So I said to myself that the least I could do was gather up the scattered bits and mend them as best I could. I walk toward the bedroom door and open it gently, expecting to see Mother leaning over the sewing machine. Scattered all around her are the little things she sells in the back alley: washcloths, veils, undergarments. There's also a cardboard box that contains things she bought in the markets up north or in Derb Sultan, along with goods smuggled in from Ceuta and countries as far away as India, China, and even Korea. Abdullah, my sister Habiba's husband, prays behind a wall of cardboard boxes that Mother has erected between the two of them. To each their own world. Mother sews the smuggled goods, Abdullah prays, and his daughter, Karima, walks back and forth between them. Mother asks me about Suleiman. She doesn't wait for a response. "Suleiman will come back with all the beautiful things we've been dreaming of. When Suleiman comes back we'll have enough money to pay off our debts and contribute to the mosque just like our neighbors . . ." She doesn't wait for any commentary on what she says, continuing to weave her small dreams. "If we don't pay our share, they'll prevent us from praying there. What will I say to our Lord on the Day of Resurrection?" I nod, agreeing and not agreeing at the same time. Then she remembers the landlord. "The landlord is a good man. He'll give us an extension until the end of the rainy season." She had promised to pay him all that was due when Suleiman came back. "Suleiman will come back when he sees that the time has come. That's what migrants always do. They come back when they're needed."

Habiba is my older sister. She's lying down on the straw mat in the bedroom next to her nursing son. She's always hungry. So are her husband and daughter, Karima. My sister Khadija's skin is pale and yellow like pomegranate skin. She's four years older than me, and she's always been kind. She never leaves the house except on the day she goes to the hammam. Khadija is like my second mother. I call her my second mother because she used to take me to school. When I came out she'd be waiting for me and would buy me a piece of honey cake, and then we'd go back home together. Another reason I call her my second mother is because she is all grown up even though she's only twenty-three years old. She has grown up and gone gray, and she looks like Mother. Now she's walking back and forth across the foyer, humming a tune, preoccupied. She's been preoccupied for two months or more by a man we don't know. We've never seen him. She—Mother, I mean—casts a glance at the goods scattered around her, pretending to be unconcerned with what is happening to her daughter. Suddenly, just like that, as of two months ago, she was no longer herself. Her sadness had disappeared. She had calmed down. Her face had become noticeably less pallid. Her nonstop menstrual bleeding became lighter—sometimes it would go on for two full months before allowing her a few minutes of limited rest, to the point where I wondered how much blood she could possibly have that it flowed so freely (women must store up unimaginable amounts of blood). Her breasts no longer hurt her like they had before. And the sharp pain that had lodged itself in her lower abdomen for so long had disappeared too. She no longer paced while holding her belly in her hands, grimacing in pain. This used to go on for a long time until she would collapse and completely lose consciousness. No more. She calmed down as she waited for the man who had changed the course of her life, as she put it. Now she sings. But perhaps the pain hadn't completely disappeared. Every once in a while she lets out a sigh or a scream or a moan, depending on the sharpness of what remained of the old pain. It might have been another form of singing for her.

I walk to the door. I peer through a small crack at the alley and see the dog lift his ears. It's ready to start its day, there, in front of the door. The very same dog with the same black spot that covers half its face, even though I can't recall right then which side of the head it covers. It doesn't move, happy to follow me with its ugly eyes. But it's there, and that alone is enough to shake me in a way I didn't need. A fury overwhelms me and I shout epithets and names at it: Blackbird! Swine! Tyrant! Dog! I slam the door violently but it does nothing to soothe my anger. I walk away from the breakfast table propped up next to the goods, with the image of the dog distracting me for a while. I grab a cup of tea. Without bread. I don't like tea, with bread or without. I don't even like its smell, which conjures up bad memories for me. I force myself to take a sip so Mother will think that I'm eating breakfast to get ready to go to work. She asks me about the mosque. I remember the minaret and tell her that it's leaning slightly. That's how it sometimes looks to me, but I don't know why. "Come on, you must be kidding," Mother responds. In order to look as if she's preoccupied with the household expenses, she takes out a small purse and counts what remains of the change, wondering out loud whether it will be enough for the day. I leave Khadija propped up by her hazy dreams and go back to my room. I walk to the window. I look out onto the street behind our house. There's no sign of the dog. I wonder if today I'll find the man who has caused Khadija to burst out singing. I close the window shutting out the sounds of the world. I go back to the middle of the room, resolved not to leave until more of the day passes. Meanwhile, I think about the dog, about a radical way of getting rid of it. There are gangs that steal dogs; in one year, twenty-six vicious police German shepherds were stolen. They feed them drugged food, then stuff them into sacks to sell them in the market the same way slaves are sold. This thought puts my mind at ease and I begin to wait for the right moment to acquaint myself with such a gang, while at the same time searching for more radical ways to get rid of it.

I go back to open the window and, taking all the necessary precautions, I jump out. I walk so close to the wall that I'm touching it. I raise the collar of my coat and light a cigarette like a secret agent in the movies. The higher I raise my coat collar, the more confident I feel. I cross the street as I look behind me, walking among the vendors who have spread their wares out early this morning. I don't see the rascal. Tables and boxes and notebooks all piled up next to one another with no trace of it among them or behind them. I'll pass this day peacefully and won't run into any dog, nor will I bump into anyone named Kika. And anyway, Kika isn't my friend anymore, because he abandoned me just like Father did. I'm not going to give him a second thought, whether he stays here or goes to Spain or the Comoros. This strengthens my conviction that I don't like him at all, which is how it will be until Judgment Day. I walk most of the small street, passing through the group of ever-present checkers players. They're here summer and winter, shouting things I don't understand. They've always been here. To make me forget my own grumbling, I look at the electrical wires tangled above my head, listening from time to time to the water sellers' bells, the vendors and porters shouting, the ambulances, the children. Usually I only hear the ambulance sirens at night, but here they are encroaching on my day as well. November's cold stiffens the joints and doesn't allow you to get anything meaningful done. The only type of job I've mastered is working with wood, and Father has brought that to a humiliating end. I remember the man who made my sister's head spin. I don't know where to begin looking for him. Everything at home has come to depend on finding him. I cross two streets and stop at one of the doors, not knowing if this is the appropriate place to begin such a search. My sister

Khadija said that he doesn't live too far from us, behind our house, three streets away. There's no trace of the man three streets away, Khadija. Then she said that his name was Omar, or Hassan, or Hussein. She tossed out all the names at once as if her only goal were to get rid of them and stick us with having to choose. For the past two weeks, Mother wondered how the girl had met him without leaving the house. "No one knows how she met him, Mama." All she says is that no other man is capable of filling her empty heart. As for when she first saw him, when she met him, and how they came to their mutual understanding, no one knows. No one knows when or how this phantom entered her blocked-off heart. "He doesn't live far," Khadija said. "Three or four streets away." Does he work at the mosque? If he works at the mosque, I may have met him and said hello to him; I may have drunk black coffee with him. Lots of young people from the old city work at the mosque. "He doesn't have a job." And what's his name? "Omar, or Hassan, or Hussein . . ." What are we to do with all these alleys and all these names? Meanwhile, she doesn't know who he is or whether he has a family. In fact, she doesn't even know how he made his way into her dry heart. So what could I do, before what was left of the lifeblood that was still flowing through her body dried up completely, except look for him and his family—if he even had a family—like a spy or a private investigator, or someone who didn't have a job? For a moment it seemed to me that I was searching for the dog rather than avoiding it, and that this is what I'd rather be doing than looking for the man. I walked up and down the street a number of times, stopping and asking about him at every open door. Of course, I was speaking a language that no one understood, because when you're asking about a man whose name you don't know—nor his address or his work or his father's or grandfather's names—all the listener can do is not answer. Until I find this son of a bitch, Khadija won't stop singing. She'll sing day and night. Khadija had completely changed. She's thin, but she had become even thinner. She had never been pretty, but she'd gotten even uglier. She became even feebler, all because of this person with no fixed address. Maybe he didn't even exist. She's losing her mind. This man only exists in my sister's sick imagination. She walks among us now, sashaying lightly across the patio like a fashion model. Actually, she doesn't walk. Rather, she floats between the two rooms or up to the roof to hang the laundry. Flying and singing the song of her first, and only, love, "I've given you the key to my heart which has grown wings," and on it she soars above us, her song rising high over the stuff of our regular lives. She won't come down. In order for her to calm down, to come back to us, to come down from her dizzying heights, I walk through the neighborhood streets without purpose, or rather, with the one goal of finding Omar, or Hassan, or Hussein. But this person whose name is Omar, or Hassan, or Hussein is nowhere to be found, either three streets away, or four, or anywhere else, not even in the mosque or around it or close to it. There's just this cardboard plaque that the fisherman waves in my face with the gold writing running across the top: *His throne was on the water*. They hang in storefronts and on house walls in their gilded frames. Our house doesn't have a piece of cardboard like this. Without realizing it, I look around me as if I've committed a crime. Anyone could stop me and ask if I've paid my share, like the dog and his accomplice the fisherman did. Or he could ask, "Do you have the certificate?" And not knowing whether I am feeling frightened or nervous, and without realizing that I am speaking out loud, I'm able to get a grip on myself, enough to realize that, fortunately, the street I am crossing right then is empty. No one sees me as I look over the Quranic verse. It really does hang in storefronts. And in new gilded frames. I see them in houses through open windows hanging in the middle of their walls, too. *His throne was on the water*. The strange thing about it is that I actually feel pride in being the only one who has not paid up until now, and who hasn't paid any attention to their threats. These scenarios and the thoughts accompanying them grant me a measure of intoxicating boldness. My uncle Mustafa and I aren't afraid of anyone. I quicken my steps and leave the street like someone running off with some sort of spoils.

Finally, standing in front of the minaret, I remember the pieces of wood strewn about the mosque. The minaret is unfinished. Someone passing by might think it's a tower or an ancient ruin. The zellij tiles barely reach halfway up and there's no place for the muezzin to call the prayer. There are twenty-five thousand pieces of wood inside the mosque that once comprised part of the ceiling. They're waiting for someone to put them back together the way they were before Father's broken-down hands delivered the coup de grâce that destroyed it. Twenty-five thousand pieces—half of them stripped red pine, which was going to form the underside of the ceiling, and the other half smoothed, blue-painted cedar, which was going to form the flat sides. I leave them all spread out on the green marble like a scattered sea whose water had lost whatever it was that it needed to keep it together. Twenty-five thousand wood pieces of every shape and size that had been smoothed with care. Seven months of grueling, constant, backbreaking work, strewn all over the prayer room floor, stirring up all sorts of reactions in me.

I walk toward the mosque, trying to assemble the drawings in my mind. I try to pick up the pieces that Father had scattered all over. I can smell the wood. Pine, which woodworms don't bore their way into as they do with other types of wood. I recall the patterns that Father had laid out before destroying them. Red, white, blue, and black. Colors that have been chaotically and completely mixed up. I line them up, then go back and line them up again without succeeding in finding the right arrangement. The round and square miniature pieces are precise and intertwining. In addition to the images, there are little pieces, each made up of sixteen stars that need to be arranged next to one another. They are what will form the concave shape of the ceiling, to give it the proper depth. So I walk toward the door thinking about how the new ceiling will look. I look out over the mosque's courtyard. It's empty. There isn't a trace of a single piece of wood, not even half a piece. It's as if a stream has passed through and washed it all away. My work on the mosque is done. It ended first when they got rid of Father, and then again after the pieces of wood disappeared.

Nothing to do. I sit behind the mosque watching the giant freighters anchored offshore, thinking about what sailors do at this time of day. They smoke, get drunk, play cards, and roar with laughter. When they get tired they dangle their hooks in the water and fish for rare types of red or blue fish, depending on the dream flickering in their minds at that particular moment. Happy with their precarious state, their untethered, temporary existences. Most of them grow their blond beards as they like because they no longer have any need for a mirror. And maybe they don't even need money because no mosque will ever be built on the ship's deck. They exist outside of any place. They're not like us. They don't follow our same orbit. They go around with the sun, the earth, the moon, and the stars. Moving along for nights at a time if they wish, and then more again during the day, with ports and their quays replete with smells, laughter, and music. They aren't worried about yesterday or tomorrow because they don't actually live anywhere. They only stay in the same place long enough for a dance or a kiss. They don't occupy the same time as we do. And I think about my brother, Suleiman, who knew just as much when he went off to the Gulf to toil in the palaces of the wealthy where he would work, save money, and come back—or travel to Thailand instead of coming back, like I would do if I were in his place. I'd travel to Thailand, live in fancy hotels, and sleep with young girls. I remain sitting for a while, trying to understand the big empty space where the ceiling is supposed to be. The ocean's waves crash into the rocks below, their refreshing spray hitting me. The sea is rough this time of year, its waves breaking violently on the rocks, causing the ground to shake as if from cannon blasts, rocking the mosque's foundations, shaking my unsteady thoughts. The smell of fresh seaweed rises from the ocean as if it has been ripening all night over a low fire. I throw my cigarette into the water and a wave swallows it immediately, not giving it the slightest chance to breathe even for a moment on the water's surface. Then . . . then, when I turn around, I see him, ten paces away or less, lying down on his side. He opens an eye and then closes it again as if all he had wanted to do was to see me, like any good dog reassuring himself that his owner was comfortable with him sitting there. Lying there stretched out, the dog doesn't give any real indication as to its type, breed, or intentions. If it wasn't for what had happened before, I would have said that it was the nicest dog in the world. Nonetheless, I pretend not to show any more interest in him than I might have in any other dog. I give him a passing glance as if I don't know him (despite being a bit puzzled), as if I had never seen him before. Then, as I turn to him again, he forms himself into a ball and rolls around in the dirt, letting out a growl that sounds like a sigh. Then he sits on his rump while he continues to growl. I stand up. My plan, which seems reasonable, is to run away. This is what my feet are planning as well. They tremble violently, as if they intend to run away without me. I hear his voice, as if he were talking to himself, or something like that. My feet stop shaking. He doesn't look the same as he did before. He isn't ugly at all. His eyes are gentle, like those of a small child, smiling with wide-eyed affection. And I, so as not to raise any suspicions, greet him as if I have just realized at that moment that he is there. Then, in order to win him over, I speak as if finishing what I had been saying before. ". . . I've been working on the mosque you see behind you for months now, and as far as I know, whoever works on the mosque is excused from paying." He nods, as if encouraging me to continue, so I add, "The amount they're asking for is really quite high. If it were just a matter of a few hundred dirhams . . ." He continues to nod for a while until I think I will break out into hysterical laughter. He shakes the dust off his body as if to give himself a moment to think, then says that he completely understands, that he has known from the start that I worked at the mosque, and that he has known all about my father ever since he began working as a carpenter in the old marketplace.

12

I ROLL AROUND IN BED with some difficulty and can't figure out what's keeping me from being able to move my feet. I don't open my eyes right away, so that what I first thought was a dream can continue. I try pulling the cover up but it proves difficult. Then I remember the dog lying at my feet. I open my eyes and see him curled up, lying on top of the cover. His belly rises and falls lazily. He moves his ears slightly as if conscious that I'm watching him. I scratch the back of his neck. His fur is soft, velvety to the touch. He opens one eye. I can't tell if he's returning my smile because his mouth is hidden between his legs. I cast a glance at the cage hanging in the window. Only two birds are left. I jump up. It's right in front of me. I open the cage door. The two birds are hesitant to leave. Two goldfinches that a few days ago were flying around in far-off skies, casting their shadows over forests and fields, flitting about between spikes of grain and tree branches. Now they're facing an altogether different fate, deliberating with one another as to which one was going to sacrifice himself to allow his brother an additional hour or two of life. One of the birds takes the plunge and launches himself out of the cage. With eyes half closed, the dog follows its flight across the room, without showing the slightest sign of curiosity, as if watching a butterfly fluttering above his head. The bird bumps into the wall in front of him, circles the room twice as it lets out a bewildered tweet, then lands on the armoire. It surveys what's going on down below for a bit. It considers the life it has lived. They say that those who are sentenced to death do that the moment the noose is placed around their necks. My bird is on the brink of death, at the end of its heroic struggle. A snake in the bush didn't swallow it, nor did a game hunter's bullet kill it. A fox didn't catch it in the many fields of corn it landed in. Rather, it is in a modest room in one of the houses of the old city, looking down from the edge of the armoire like someone reviewing the course of his life, which is ending—or on the verge of ending—starting from the moment it jumped for the first time from its nest, spreading its wings to the wind. It also recalls the nests it built in the company of lovers at different moments of a life full of successful marriages. Thank God all of its progeny lived. It always preferred leafy trees so the kites couldn't ambush its chicks. Thank God it found mates and left behind good, solid offspring that bring joy to people all over the world. And the females it lived with—it always liked the slim ones. It lets out a short chirp then takes off from the armoire again, displaying the three yellow lines on each wing, hitting the window's glass before landing on top of the cage, as if regret were eating away at it at the last moment. All the while the dog sits, following the bird's acrobatics. His shrewd eyes are almost closed. The other bird inside the cage eats rye-grass seeds indifferently, dropping the shells out of the cage. The door is locked, and what's going on outside the cage is of no concern to him. Then, as if his comrade who is still in the cage has reminded him that it is time for breakfast, the bird swoops down to peck at some imperceptible pieces of bread on the floor. The bird doesn't forget a thing, neither his fate nor the fate of those who came before him. This is the moment when the condemned finally realizes that his life has been one big mistake, and that the hour of deliverance has finally come. The bird feigns caution. He pokes furtively at the floor, raising his head with the same speed to look all around him, and between the third and fourth peck, the dog pounces down on him. No surprise. Always exciting. I hear the bird's bones snap between the dog's jaws as they are slowly and deliberately crushed. His eyes remain closed, and I'm not sure which of us is enjoying the sound of cracking bones more. I picture the beautiful bird now singing inside the dog's stomach, remembering its children and their warbling that soars across the sky. I open the window and Rihane jumps through in one leap. A yellow feather remains quivering on the floor tiles.

His name is Rihane. Rihane and I pass by the workshop. I cast a glance at the empty mailbox, and then we cross the mosque's courtyard, heading toward the beach like two old friends. Fishermen stand on the distant rocks thinking about the migratory fish. Have all of them caught their share so that they can now sit and relax with peace of mind? A few steps away fish is being prepared in the adjacent shops. This is what it smells like. Shops selling fried fish, eggplant, and potatoes are scattered about here and there, and inundate the place with their smells. Deep inside their gloomy interiors, certificates shine in their gilded frames—*His throne was on the water*. We pass by some shacks. The children who play in front of them stop playing and step back—stunned, frightened, nervous—until Rihane and I pass. The same strength that feeds the pit bull's muscles flows through my body. I prefer Rihane's companionship a thousand times more than Kika's.

I don't brush his fur from my clothes, which are covered with his reddish-brown hair that's been accumulating these past two weeks. It's as if I've grown the same fur. My gait resembles his and my head sways to the rhythm of his steps so much that I don't recognize myself as I walk next to him. I feel like claws have appeared in place of my fingernails and toenails, and my muscles have started to bulge and become hard as wood. Cautious, on guard, sprightly. I've grown a small tail, which I wag cheerfully. Can the poor losers passing by see it? Instead of my own blood, Rihane's blood flows through my veins. It flows like a full, rushing pack of vicious dogs.

For close to two weeks I've forgotten all about the mosque and everything to do with it. In truth, the feeling that no one loved me and ambivalence toward my very existence became as sharp as the magical effect Rihane's presence imposed on me. I am now truly changed. After all the time I have spent with him these past two weeks, I have learned many things—that sleeping outside is no more frightening than sleeping in a comfortable bed, for example, or that human flesh is sweet, especially the fingers, and other equally important bits of information. I tell him stories that make him laugh for a long time—about the copper pipes that Kika and I stole; about Farah, who ran away with my share of the money from the pipes; about Father and his ceiling that disappeared before he could finish it. I spend my days walking up and down the alleyways. Rihane walks next to me, licking the sides of his mouth. We're happy together. Cocky together, as we scare the little kids, rifling through their wallets and taking their money if they have any.

We go places I hadn't known about before, each one stranger than the last. One time, he takes me to an odd place—a tall, black, three-story building hidden among some high eucalyptus trees. He tells me, "There are hundreds of secret prisoners crammed inside these walls." I look up at the windows. Small open windows covered with steel bars that are hung with drying underwear. There isn't a window that doesn't have a woman's blouse or pants, or children's clothes. What strikes me about it is that entire families, including children, have been thrown behind these bars. Then he says, "These are the apartments for the guards' families. The cells are in the basement. The guards' families live above them. They can't get away from them, like birds that are unable to live far from the swamp. The prisoners are thrown into subterranean vaults. Dark halls that are dank from humidity and crawling with rats. They remain lying down day and night. Hands bound, blindfolded, forbidden to stand, sit, or speak."

I wonder if they were imprisoned because they hadn't contributed their share to the building of the mosque. Rihane says, "Pretty much," and adds that he had guarded the gate in front of us for six months, before they transferred him following this depressing and disturbing visit. We go to the section where Rihane now works. There's always a fat man in front of the door. Sometimes the fat man is happy enough to shoo us away. Sometimes the office is locked for no reason—it isn't Friday or Sunday—but then it might happen that the office is open. In those cases, we look in and find it empty. We stand there for a while looking at the gray office and the papers strewn about on top of the only desk and all over the cement floor. Just to prove to me that working at the information desk no longer matters to him, he grabs a piece of paper and swallows it without chewing. I have nothing to prove. I try to recall events that were just as strange, but I have nothing to tell or show him. Sometimes I say to him, "Come on, let's look at the fig tree that's losing what's left of its leaves." We play in the dried leaves until we get tired, like two nature lovers. That's all I can do. I pick up a piece of paper from the desk and toss it into my mouth.

Then we arrive at the Sunday market. We can hear the dogs barking before the market comes into view, before I buy the birds that Rihane will swallow for the rest of the day and in the days to come. We check out the vendors. The dog sellers come first because they've been inundating the sidewalk since dawn and now they're completely blocking the entrance to the market with their dogs, bikes, carts, and smells. I really like this place where people and animals exist naturally side by side. We walk along together on the same sidewalk, toward the same goal, side by side, accomplices, moving up and down the rows as if walking around a bazaar or in a public park. Barking comes at us from every direction, through the air and from under the ground, from places I can't even see, as if the spirits of all the dogs that had passed through here were still flying above us, filling the place with their cacophonous presence. All sorts of dogs mill about, tied to the market fence or standing without a leash, on the lookout for anyone who might buy them, looking deceivingly friendly. Some sit next to their owners, eating bread or soup with them as if in a popular café. Others wag their tails as soon as we stop in front of them, thinking we're new buyers. Puppies in cardboard boxes, stepping all over one another, their eyes closed, not having yet seen the light. Then come the pigeon and bird sellers. Goldfinches are the most plentiful. There are hundreds of them, stuffed into narrow boxes like mice. They still flap their wings, futilely searching for a way out, knocking into the sides of the cages, thinking they can fly away. Caught in a trap last night or the night before, and they still think there's a possibility of returning to where they came from. Kika and I used to catch dozens of them because they travel together. They drink water together and they fall into traps together. Rihane strolls next to me with a dignified manner, like someone who still has all the time in the world to choose which restaurant to go to. Indifferent. A judicious walk. No sign of impatience. He doesn't even turn to look at the birds that jump around on top of one another and call out from underneath the nets covering them. I buy six birds and stuff them into a cardboard box, poking holes in it so they can breathe for what remains of their lives. Before they come to rest between Rihane's jaws.

13

I CAN'T THINK OF THE house Father settled into without remembering the smell of wood everywhere. It was originally an inn with lots of interconnected rooms. It was built about a century ago on the edge of the old city, flush against the walls surrounding it on the western side. I pass through the doorway at Bab Marrakech and plunge deeply into the alleys of the old city. A plucked chicken—wounded, without feathers, with broken wings and paralyzed legs, blue spots on its yellowed skin, bare, miserable—looks out from between the bars of a battered cage. It doesn't seem to be in the slightest bit of pain. Despite its injuries, it seems calm and clearheaded, waiting for whoever will end up eating it as if waiting for a savior. I don't like how it looks at all, nor how those yelling at it so wretchedly look, either. I forget about it. I try to forget its repulsive smell, that disgusting smell that hits you as soon as you enter the alley. Bab Marrakech begins right here. At this smell. I speed up in order to move past it. Luckily, after a little bit, the smell of fish will allow me to forget all about the chicken and its miserable life. To forget about it, I think about Maymouna too. I call her Aunt Maymouna so as not to think about her in any other way. Sometimes I consider her Father's new wife. She lives with him without any documentation, like all the women who came before her. Ever since the woodworking tools went silent and we left this house five years ago, women have come and gone with no set schedule. They live with him for six or seven months, without ululations or rituals or marriage papers or anything of the sort, and then they go back home the same way they came—without papers, pockets empty, their heads filled with the stupid stories he tells them, always the same stories. He tells them about the years he had lived the easy life and about the influential people whose palaces he has worked in. I'm not sure what appeals to them about a man older than sixty. His hands shake. His teeth fell out a quarter century ago. No money or status. The only thing he knows how to do is tell stories about his past glories, along with tales of things that had never occurred, adding details that never happened. He has an old set of dentures in his mouth, left over from more prosperous days, which he places in a cup of water before going to sleep. The women enjoy these made-up stories. They're enthralled by the lies. They picture themselves sitting at his make-believe gatherings with princes and ministers and other men of high standing, warming themselves like he does in front of the fire of their false greatness. I think they picture him sitting atop a great fortune that someday, they'll inherit some or all of it. That's the impression he gives, which is why they stay with him for so long. There can be no other reason. Also, I call her his wife so as not to call her by another name that would only make Father mad. Instead of the invigorating smell of fish, I find myself surrounded by the smell of mint. This is the biggest disappointment I have felt all morning.

The paint has worn off and many of the ceilings have caved in. The house's interior resembles a small, ravaged village with its deteriorating walls, pockmarked pillars, and exposed steel that look like the ribs of a corpse. Window frames have fallen out. Chickens have left droppings everywhere. When we were small, the woodworking tools ran day and night before they finally fell silent. Suleiman and I stopped hiding behind the thicket of wood that filled all the floors of the house. The smell of cut wood remained nonetheless, but without the refreshing moistness it used to have. Now, mixed with the droppings of chickens and birds that came in from everywhere, the smell has turned humid, rotten. The strong smell sticks in the throat like a tiny germ, and that's what I feel rising from it now as I look at the house. Between me and the house there's an open area covered with dirt, cactuses, and wild thorns, along with an old barbed-wire fence. Our echoing footsteps used to fill the yard with happiness, but now it is empty and silent, floating in a depressing calm under a light mist.

Father isn't there. In the middle of his room there's a desk and two chairs. I picture him sitting there. A large, imposing desk constructed of good, thick wood. Heaped on top of his desk are pens, torn-up papers, inkwells, and folders, along with a cup of stale coffee and some crumbs. There are pieces of dried cookie all over the desk and scattered on the floor. A long line of ants takes advantage of the emptiness to carry their booty back to their storehouses. Maymouna sits on one of the chairs painting her nails, with her foot on the edge of the other chair. She's the one who said that Father isn't there. Her arms are bare, just as I'd imagined they would be when I was in the market a little while ago. What are her pinched lips doing? Are they tracing the brush's movement as she applies the red polish to her nails? Should I keep looking at her nails with the smell of alcohol wafting up from them? Then Maymouna gets up. She casts a not-so-innocent look in my direction. She says that two days ago, my father had picked up his tools and left. Her words suggest the opposite of what she is saying, as do the way she walks and looks at me. Her clothes are practically see-through, her panties visible. This Maymouna is still young and alluring, and she is lying. She likes to play like a kitten, and she looks like a cat as she jumps up from the chair and leaves the room with me hopping along behind her like another cat that wants to play with her. I'm not at all surprised to see that the hallways have been invaded by black-skinned renters: by their women and children; by their brightly colored clothes; by the strong odors of their cooking; by the smell of onions and bluefish. I figure Father has disappeared into some corner or another of the house. I tiptoe carefully. I turn the doorknob to one of the rooms and it opens up. From inside, large eyes peer out. Doors are open. Many doors, and just as many shining white eyes. I ask her how much rent Father is charging for the rooms. She doesn't respond. I walk ahead of her so I can look for him on another landing. The rustling of her clothes catches up to me. Then I hear her say, "The old man. No one knows where he went." She says she doesn't even know if he's coming back because he took his clothes with him too. Her tender years make her lies acceptable, likable even. Her clothes, behind me, then in front of me, don't stop swishing. I'm not thinking about my father or his disappearance. Like her, I'm no longer searching for anything. For the time being, I'm not concerned with Father. I move through these twisty hallways and decrepit stairways that are brimming with bare-chested black people. An entire African tribe has taken up residence in this abandoned inn, but nothing matters to me anymore other than her body undulating behind me, in front of me, all around me, in my head. This morning I left the ocean behind, and here I am returning to it with a practically naked woman, swaying in the shadows of ancient hallways that are ready to collapse. Her waves shake me, throwing me onto the sand, and then they come back to drag me down into the depths of the crashing sea. The rooms are filled to capacity, there isn't a single room free of them and their eyes that shine from deep in the darkness, or their boisterous naked children. And me? What do I want from her in the end? I ask her if she likes children. She rushes off. Her body in front of me urges me to ask again. She moves ahead, swaggering like one of the queens of ancient Ethiopia. I catch up to her like a king from the same timeworn Ethiopia. A bunch of clucking chickens runs between our legs. When she stops at the door of the room she has just come out of she raises her skirt above her knees and says, "Come look at my toenails." But instead of looking at her nails, I look at her knees that shine in the darkness, my blood boiling as I count *one, two, three*. I'm about to pounce on her but I don't, because the children burst in. She laughs loudly. We go into a second, empty room. Father isn't anywhere in the room or in my thoughts. It doesn't seem like she's looking for him either. She just wants to lose herself. I hear her say, "Over here, over here," but I can't see her. I hear her clucking, and see her lying down on a box motioning for me to come closer. That's when I realize that the chicken under the box is what's making the clucking sound. She puts her hand out and in it there's an egg that the chicken sitting underneath the box has just laid. She giggles and runs away. I search for the egg in another room until I forget about it. I hear her cursing Father, calling him the devil. I don't know why she calls him that. I go into a dark room. It's so dark I can't see her. I can hear her moving behind me, or in front of me, or in my mind. Enthusiastically, I do as she does. I count *one, two, three*. I'm about to pounce, but I don't. I feel her hand on my shoulder. This time I'm the one who moves back toward the door. I hear her say, "Come." I don't move. I hear what sounds like a cat's groan when it twists and stretches, or it could be a snake. She stops under a beam of light and pulls her skirt up high. She moans and flicks her tongue in her mouth like a young viper. In the other room she sat crying next to the window where I could see her and the black kohl from her eyes running over her cheeks in long, crooked lines. Was her nail polish also running? I walk over to her. I touch her. "Everything all right?" "Don't take pity on me." She says she's miserable in this dump and that she's going to leave Father today. I hear her say that Father is working in the back garage, and she wipes her face and lets out a loud laugh. I think about jumping her—I count *one, two, three*—but I don't because she's left the room. This third room is dark too, or is it the fourth? Then I hear the tools, so I stop playing around. I pause for a moment with my eyes closed in order to listen more closely so I don't lose the music of the tools as it penetrates the walls and flows through the halls.

I rush down the stairs with the flock of chickens and their chicks running in front of me. Loudly they cross the courtyard that's grown over with boxthorn. They remain in front of me as if to guide me along the path to the wooden garage that stands behind the house. Their tail feathers dance to a rhythm I don't hear. The noise of the tools grows louder the closer I get to the slanting garage door. The chickens and their chicks disappear behind the boards leaning against the wall. I stand by the window rather than the door. I see him sitting in his old chair, covered in sawdust; a chair that looked like a throne, which he had spent long weeks carving before tossing it behind the piles of wood when his skills had become obsolete. The back is high, and there are curved lines on it, between which are the words "Allahu akbar"—God is great. Underneath them on either side there's a long floral design with the same words, then another floral design, running all the way down to the bottom. The chair's two arms are shaped like snakes with their mouths open, going down the sides as if in search of an elusive prey on the ground. All of this is in front of me. The noise of the tools, the sawdust, the chirping of birds that flutter above our heads flying in and out of the pane-less windows, the chickens and their chicks searching around him for food somewhere among the twenty-five thousand pieces of wood that had disappeared from the workshop. All of it had made its way here. Father studies a large drawing that's hanging on the wall. This also faces me. The ornamentation that Father had carved in wood is drawn on pieces of paper hanging on the wall, a second version of the ceiling topped with celestial drawings; others are in red and white like the hallways. Some shapes are square; others are like stars. Then arches shaped like eyebrows underneath which are bulls' eyes, scorpions, and beehives colored Roman red, which Father calls Casablanca red. I stand next to the door. Instead of looking at me, he moves around the forest of wood that's standing up and strewn about all over the floor amid a chaos of birds and the din of machines. He holds a steel ruler that he waves around in every direction, as if threatening someone he can't see. He's in his old djellaba, not caring that I'm standing there watching him. When he turns around, it will be too late for me to turn back. He goes back to the pieces of wood and begins to count them rather than look toward where I've been standing for three minutes. I distract myself by thinking again about the shapes he draws, so as not to have to see my own confusion. On the wide table there's a pile of muqarnases shaped like beehives and filigree. He walks around the table, hair disheveled, sawdust covering him like snowflakes. Then he stops to examine them from another angle. He takes a red pen from behind his ear and draws an arch on the wood, then examines it while chewing on the pen. I stand at the door, unsure whether he knows I'm standing there. He walks away, recoiling from the chicken as if allowing me the chance to leave, or to come closer. I can't move, thinking only that I am behind him now, able to see the back of his neck and the arch of his back. I take satisfaction in the fact that he has aged and that the ceiling won't turn out as he had been picturing it. Nothing good will come out of this head from now on.

14

FATHER CAME FROM THE OUTSKIRTS of Marrakech, from a small village called El Kelaa, during the carnival of famines that struck the country in the forties, when families would leave their children on the sides of the road because they couldn't find enough food to fill their bellies. He settled for about a year in Marrakech before marrying and moving to Casablanca to have six children, two of whom died. They didn't die during the famine, but afterward, during the most fertile season, when Father said the wheat grew as tall as a man. I lived, as did my two sisters, Khadija and Habiba, and Suleiman, who went to the Gulf. The moment my father came to the big city, he saw that a great future awaited him. He became a carpenter as soon as he arrived in Casablanca because, in my mother's eyes, it was a serious profession. A special kind of carpenter—a wood-carver. He did the ornamentation on mosque pillars and mausoleum ceilings. Was this the future that had been predicted for him when he left Marrakech? I think he sensed this in his hands after years of carpentry work. They were hands that had decorated many palaces and museums, and over the course of three years, by the time my grandfather on my mother's side died, he had accumulated a great deal of money. A mere three years were enough. He was touched by days of rare luxury that lasted for the ten years that followed and I have no idea where the money went. I figured he had many women and that he bought them houses and cookware and wristwatches. I also think he didn't know the value of money and that, despite the fortune he had amassed, despite our being with him, despite the presence of the other women, he lived in a world where there existed nothing other than the wood he carved and the forms that only took shape in his hands. Even after losing all that he once had, the money that flowed through his fingers and that was cut off so suddenly didn't interest him as much as the flood of shapes that teemed inside his head. No one asked about them or expressed amazement at how fastidiously they were crafted. He continued to carve wood that no customer asked for, and to invent shapes that were of no value to anyone. The future he had been anticipating for himself had passed. He's still waiting. That's what I think.

Later, his dementia increased so much that he began to wander the cold, wide, deserted streets around the villas that he had once passed through, calling on non-existent passersby to bear witness to the ceilings inside and the decorations his hands had carved. "These two hands that worms will eat . . ." His eyes brimming with tears. Then came a time when he began to board trains, going to Marrakech to contemplate the water-wheel ceilings he had carved in some of the passageways there during his days of greatness and glory. For hours on end he would demand that people walking by bear witness to his genius, which was lost on the ignorant. "This beautiful zellij work that's so snugly assembled on the columns, it isn't me who put it there. I'm no zelliji. I'll leave zellij tiles to those who know how to do it. I'm a carver of wood—that wood up there. That's work. That's craftsmanship. It needs no words. It needs no praise. To this I say to you all: 'Lift up your eyes. Forget the zellij and look closely at the wood. Pure-smelling cedar wood. Then look what happened after the profession went to pot with cheap, manu-factured ceilings—worthless and tasteless—that look like plastic . . .'" At that moment his eyes would glisten with a strange joy. He'd place his rough hand on the shoulder of the first person to pass by in front of the waterwheel with the carefully carved ceiling. "Look at this masterpiece. Do you know who made it? It'll remain there long after you and your children are gone because it was made with heart as well as hands. It will remain there until Judgment Day. Do you know whose expert hands stood here crafting it from A to Z? For the sake of your eyes before your mouths? But your country doesn't recognize art. It doesn't see genius where it exists. It looks for geniuses under the turbans of ordinary people, common folk, idiots. How can they walk by this masterpiece every day without stopping and bowing down to pay tribute to this pure genius?" He'd raise his hands high toward his masterpiece. His thick, powerful hands, gnarled like an old walnut tree. By this point, those few who had gathered around him would have heard enough. But rather than quiet down, he would become more agitated, as if all he had been waiting for was for them to leave so that the flame that fired his buried rancor could glow brighter.

Father doesn't like anyone, not even his children. He thinks he came into this world at the wrong time. No one values his genius. "I'm not a carpenter like the ones in the souiqa marketplace." Life hasn't given him his due. That's why he hates everything—he hates night and day; he hates the sun and the moon; he hates summer and winter; he hates the country and the way it's governed; he hates monarchism and republicanism; he hates the neighbors, their children, and their children's children. But his hatred for Mother, unlike anyone else, has remained constant. His hatred for her has not diminished for even a day. A perpetual, continuous hate that's always the same. Neither more nor less. As if it were part of what kept him stable. He hates her with all his strength. A blind hatred, violent and black. All he has in him is expressed through this all-consuming hatred. They argue for hours on end, far apart and without either one turning toward the other, as if they were fighting with the neighbors. All the insults, all the epithets passed over our young, lurking, frightened ears. Then their voices lowered, only to rise up even louder than before, each one hoping the other would die or disappear from the face of the earth. This battle only strengthened the equilibrium they felt together. And this continued even after we moved to the new house in the old city. No longer in the same daily way, but not a week would go by without him coming over for his share of insults and counter-insults. Because he remained busy, even at his most broke, with the carvings that floated around in his head and that he continued to complete at the same pace, with the same passion he had before, believing, absolutely sure that lovers of decorative art would show up once again.

Then, when he turned toward where I was standing, I hid behind the window shutter. I stayed there for a little while listening to his strange ramblings. The way Father was acting reinforced what I had always thought, that he was not my father. This notion always sat well with me, even transforming the way I walked, like someone who depended only on himself, without expecting help from anyone. That's how I walked across the empty space that separated the road from Father's house as I thought about him and everything happening around him. Then, as I got closer to the mosque, I stopped because of a strange overwhelming feeling. At that moment I didn't know what to attribute it to. Was it because of the sky-blue mailbox standing in front of the workshop, or because of the workshop's open window? Was it the door that wasn't securely closed? Or was it because at that moment I felt a violent shaking inside of me? I quickened my steps. I pushed gently on the workshop door as if afraid to disturb the unclear thought that had taken root in my head. I stopped, holding onto the doorknob, fearful and in disbelief. There she was, standing, looking at me as if she had been expecting me. I had forgotten all about her. Prior to this moment, I hadn't given her a thought. It hadn't occurred to me even to imagine her. But all of a sudden there she was with this serious look, completely unexpected, in a green dress adorned with butterflies of every color, like a banner blown in by a passing wind.

15

Naima

FARAH DISAPPEARED YESTERDAY MORNING—TUESDAY—at just the right time, before I would have had to throw her out anyway. This might be the best thing she's done in her life. The lawyer said, "If we leave now we might find her leaning against the wall of the house, waiting, because she doesn't know anyone in this city." So we went out looking for her, but didn't find her, neither sitting against the wall nor anywhere else. We searched everywhere for her today, and at the end of the afternoon we returned without any sign of her. We looked for her in the market, at the beach, in the cemetery, in police stations, at the mosque, but we didn't find her. The first thought that occurred to the fee-bleminded lawyer when he woke up yesterday morning was to look for her at our neighbor's place. He went upstairs in his pajamas, knocked on the door, and came back as disappointed as he had left. At ten o'clock he went back up the stairs, but this time I went up right behind him. She had gone to the market—our neighbor Rabia, that is. The door was open, just as she had left it, and her house was there for everyone to see, with its two rooms and kitchen, but no Farah. Musical instruments hung uselessly on the wall, just as they had before. Dust had settled on them years ago. Her blind husband woke up. He sat in his usual chair moving his head left and right, polishing his violin. He hadn't seen Farah either, because he's blind.

The lawyer forgot all about his court files. He forgot about eating and drinking. He just sat waiting for her to come back. He didn't understand why she had disappeared after having spent such an enjoyable evening next to him. She had been happy. There had been nothing eating at her. He didn't understand what had happened to her! He spent Tuesday sitting and thinking about it, and when night fell he was still sitting in the same place obsessively hoping for her to come back. He spent the night listening to the footsteps of people passing by in the street. No sooner would we doze off for a moment than he'd bound toward the door shouting, "She's come back!" He hadn't really been sleeping in the first place. He spent the night listening at the door for a knock that never came. Then, when it got late, he wrapped himself in a blanket and stretched out with his shoes on, fully clothed, his eyes on the door, listening for any sound outside. This girl named Farah had destroyed his whole sense of reason. "This is a good start," I thought. I hoped the day would continue as it had begun—without Farah. Neither in my house, nor at our neighbor Rabia's place, nor anywhere else. That's what I wanted from this day, and from God. Was that too much to ask? Why couldn't luck be on my side this time? Just this once. I hadn't had any luck since leaving Azemmour three years ago. For the first six months I worked at Saudi Arabian Airlines, a job that held no importance except for the possibility of finding a pilot who'd marry me and buy me two apartments, one in Casablanca where I'd live with my family, and a second one in Riyadh where I'd go once or twice a year to bear the children necessary for maintaining my permanent residency status. This is the plan my friends at Saudi Arabian Airlines (and other airlines) put into action, and they were successful, but I had no such luck. When I worked at the Najma Cabaret, after my dreams of marrying a pilot had evaporated, a lawyer seemed more within my reach. Most of the cabaret's customers were lawyers, collecting their clients' money during the day and throwing it away at night. Then, barely surprised, I began to notice that I was in love with the lawyer who made me forget the pilot I never found. Then he promised me—and continued to promise me for the two years I spent with him—that he'd buy me an apartment that would be the envy of friends and enemies alike. Spacious. Three bedrooms . . . three bedrooms and a bathroom. And in the bathroom there'd be a roomy tub that I'd fill with hot water and stretch out in anytime I wanted to. I promised him, swore to him on the Quran with the apartment as a guarantee that I would never sleep in another lawyer's bed. Then, on Monday night, I got worried when I saw her hand in his. Not three weeks had passed since she had come to stay in my home, and here she was giving him her hand to read her future, this girl who called herself my friend and who had come to Casablanca to become a singer. As if singing were out there in the streets just waiting for her talent to arrive! If singing actually provided a living for the singer, she would have preferred to sing on television and at public soirees. She didn't know that singing while surrounded by drunks and repressed men brought nothing but trouble, and that after just a few months, the most she could hope for would be to become a prostitute like so many others, and she wouldn't find anyone to help her with that. Do you think she didn't know that? She knew and then some, but she pretended to be blind to it. Her hidden agenda was to get into the lawyer's head, and she would have succeeded had I not gotten involved in the nick of time. He was playing with her fingers and telling her about the singers he had helped, uninterested in the green bag she had taken out from her dress as she said that she was prepared to do any-thing for the sake of singing. He told her that Naima Samih had become a singer thanks to him, and that he was the one who had gotten involved so she could buy a Mercedes when she became a famous singer—a new black car like the ones ministers had. He was a well-known lawyer, he whispered, and there was no door that didn't open for him, especially since he had become a member of the local football club's office, and would soon become a member of the Royal Federation for Football. I was consumed with what was happening in front of me, completely consumed. I saw his hand in hers, his lies taking root in her head. And I could only see one explanation for all of this: Soon they'd fly away together. They'd disappear. I wondered what the connection was between singing and her being in my house. What was it that had made her knock on my door in the first place? Perhaps she was running away from Azemmour, leaving behind some resounding scandal!

After I met the lawyer, I no longer sang at the Najma Cabaret because he made it a condition that I stop singing. That's how lawyers are. They always have conditions. And in the end, what women are looking for is a man to protect them, as my mother always said. After I met the lawyer, I was no longer looking for any other man—airline pilot or otherwise. For five months I saw him from up on stage. He came in every evening and sat there—drinking, clapping, drinking—until closing time. Sometimes I intentionally gave him the impression that I was singing just for him. I don't know whether that's how he himself felt, because his applause was always louder than everyone else's. And then? Here I was, seeing him as my second chance, but not knowing when it would come, because he didn't seem to have any more interest during the soirees. As if he were measuring the distance separating him from the abyss that was going to swallow him up. As for me, I prayed to God at the end of every night that He'd pay attention to me and help me through this ordeal of waiting. For months I visited tombs and saints and bought amulets and talismans, putting them under the chair he would usually sit in, in the doorways through which he would pass, and everywhere he could be smelled. And when the lawyer finally came into my house after the many traps I had laid, he told me that he was sticking with his wife and children. The things men say in these sorts of situations are always ridiculous. Mere words that all men say to show that their conscience is clear. But men are men. Essentially, they have no conscience. He played his trump card, the child card, as if announcing a defeat ahead of time. After one month living with me, he began to make fun of his family. He would take out a picture of his wife and explode with laughter. What was a lawyer like him, famous like him, known by workers and ministers alike, occupying a high position in the Marrakech Superior Court, what was he doing with this pale, ugly, long-nosed woman in the photo? She might actually look worse in real life. How had she been able to trick him for twenty years? And now here he was having woken up this morning from his slumber only to see the hideousness that he had been wallowing around in for decades without having noticed. And his resentment now was greater, and his thirst for revenge more fearsome after having discovered that he had children she had forced him to bear. How had she managed to take control of him, a woman this ugly? He swore he was going to go home and put poison in the glass of water she drinks before going to bed. Was this the luck I had been waiting for? Why not take a little bit of this luck while I still had my beauty and youth? I had everything a lawyer who wants a woman worthy of him needs. A woman to show off to his colleagues at weddings and funerals. I had everything except the luck I needed. And the proof? This girl came bursting into my garden without a care in the world to pluck any fruit she wanted. She claimed that she loved to sing. She doesn't know how much effort her ripe youthfulness has cost me. Women don't seek the men they dream about. That man remains solely in her dreams. I was happy to see her the day she showed up, just as any woman is happy to see a friend she hasn't seen in a while. Farah isn't much younger than me. She's seventeen, I think. We used to go to school together because we're from the same neighborhood. But was this enough of a reason to let him play with her hand and read their future together in her palm? I should have thrown her out that first day. I should have realized right then what her intentions were. Instead, I didn't see in her affected naivete the danger she posed to what I had built, stone by stone.

Monday evening, the lawyer rushed in as usual, coming straight from the courthouse. He and his heavy briefcase both groaning under the weight of a day burdened with work. He said he wasn't going to stay for more than half an hour. There was an important case waiting for him at the courthouse for which he was going to request a temporary release because his client hadn't confessed to killing his mother with an iron. Would a son kill his mother with a hot iron? Did that make sense? But when he saw Farah in her short dress that scandalously revealed more than it covered up, he was no longer in such a hurry. Rather, he would postpone the case in order to party with his new friend, even though three weeks had gone by since she had first arrived. He took a bottle of whiskey out of his briefcase with a silence befitting the celebration he had begun to prepare without anyone asking him to and poured himself a glass. He poured me a glass, which I drank in one shot (although the pain that raged in my blood and the dark thoughts that dominated my mind didn't go away), and a third glass for Farah, but Farah doesn't drink. She was content just to sit next to the lawyer who had thrown the keys to his new car on the table, enumerating its merits. Then he took hold of her hand, kissed it twice, and predicted a bright future for her in the world of singing. She laughed. She might as well have been sitting there naked, as if we had been in a whorehouse. That's Farah. And that's the man I picked, who was becoming a stranger to me. I'm nothing more than a simple girl who isn't seeking fame; who only wants to build a nest for herself that won't cost too much, to prepare his food, wash his filthy underwear, and happily go to bed with him; to happily open her legs while avoiding as much as possible allowing him to place his heavy body on her chest and smelling his bad breath, putting off my real orgasm (setting it aside on the cabinet next to us) while moaning and trembling to make him think that my orgasm has come on top of his blessed penis. I tell him that he has a large penis, that he has vanquished me, in order to make him happy. I add a final shudder to make him orgasm quickly so I can get away from the smell of his sweat and the whiskey on his breath, to relax, to put an end to the battle. As for my orgasm, it comes as I like it, and I reach it without needing him, without the need of any man. It's enough for me to pass my hand over my pubic hair while thinking about all the beautiful things I haven't achieved on this earth. Little by little the water rises up to my mouth as if emerging from a secret spring, then it goes down, down until it settles in my belly and becomes music that plays and plays, then, bit by bit, I feel it going down further, down until a pleasant shudder comes over my entire body, flowing from every pore in my skin, its springs welling up between my thighs, until finally it bursts. Then I go to the washroom and clean up, laughing after being kept up so late Monday night. It seemed like forever. I stood at her bedside and said threateningly to her—to Farah, "I don't want any problems with the police because of some scandal that may have forced you to leave your home in Azemmour . . ." I didn't find her Tuesday morning when I woke up.

We left our neighbor Rabia's house and headed in a direction only he knew. I saw him walking in front of me, turning every which way. He'd stop for a moment, and then go the other way. Suddenly, he headed toward the beach and climbed up onto the rocks. This made me laugh. Was he looking for her under the water? Or between the rocks? Was she a sea crab he was looking for between the cracks in the rocks? I wish she really were a sea crab. Then I saw him turn and go around the lighthouse, telling the guard that he was looking for a girl named Farah. "She has a round face and narrow eyes, and she's wearing green and yellow. She left home this morning."

The guard asked him what a young girl would be doing alone at the top of the lighthouse. Then he walked alongside the old houses that had previously been used as barracks by the French army. It was almost eleven o'clock and the sun was practically right above our heads. We weren't going to find her. This was what I had hoped, even before we left the house. The lawyer walked in front of me in his wrinkled clothes looking defeated, like someone who has lost his mother, hunched over, shoelaces untied, which caused him to trip with every step. He walked along fully expecting to find her, whereas I, in the depths of my soul, hoped we wouldn't find her. Women sat here and there on the bare ground, warming their bones which had been chilled by the dampness of a rainy night. The lawyer walked up to a woman and told her that we were looking for a girl named Farah. "She has a round face and narrow eyes, and she's wearing green and yellow. She left home this morning." She's not a child at all. She's seventeen or older, but that didn't mean a thing. I stood next to him, listening but not adding anything, as if she had come from Azemmour for the sole purpose of taking control of him, of tirelessly plucking the fruit from my tree. No doubt the man's smell was what drew her to my house—the smell of an easy prey, within reach, fresh. To think of all the amulets I had prepared and the dried lizards I cooked. The lawyer didn't turn toward me because he didn't hear what I was saying.

All of a sudden, the sky became clear. Blue as if it were the height of summer. We searched in the forest that stretches along the coastal road and asked the guard if he'd seen her. "What would a girl with any brains be doing in the forest?" the guard replied. We walked through the cemetery before reaching the mosque and asking about her there, because one night he'd heard her say that she had visited the new mosque. We left the forest and the coastal road and headed back toward the old city, and there too, even before the walls of the old city loomed before us, I heard people say, "What would a girl with any brains be doing on these unsafe streets?" He peered into kiosks we passed, thinking we'd see a picture of her on the front page of the newspapers. He wouldn't go any farther than the municipal park. That was all he had left in him. Or perhaps he'd venture as far as the Jewish cemetery. But what would she be doing in the Jewish cemetery? I watched him. He had lost his mind. He was raving mad. I was sure that whatever he was doing no longer had anything to do with me. I also felt relaxed because I had been able to get rid of her. My heart couldn't take another catastrophe. I hadn't swallowed a single bite since yesterday morning. How could a single blessed morsel of food enter my mouth with such rage stuck in my throat?

16

THE MAN SITTING IN THE wicker chair, brushing the ground impatiently with his feet, had settled on this land years ago. A land where he has no roots. A land with no name, or rather, with a name that is difficult to remember. He'd planted his walking stick here, as any weary traveler might do. One day he just left the city, without family or baggage. Without illusions. Was he a fugitive from justice? An adventurer thoroughly exhausted by life on the road? A refugee who lived as a stranger among the crowds and clamor of the city? Or was he just a man whose hair had gone gray, not yet forty-three years old? And what was he doing on this desolate land, alone, with no friends or neighbors? Without children. The closest human soul in this vast emptiness—the closest neighbor from whose chimney smoke rose up—lived four kilometers away. There, where three eerie, lonely eucalyptus trees loomed, lived his in-law, the public cistern guard. And, while waiting for the judge who visits his village on Saturday evenings and who would pass through on Sunday on his way back, what does this man do with his time? He plows when it's time to plow. He plants seeds when it's time to sow. He fertilizes when it's time to fertilize. He watches the sun as it moves across the sky. He watches the seasons come one after the other. The cistern guard's daughter came one afternoon, the summer before last, carrying a loaf of bread fresh from the oven in her basket, a round loaf made with fresh wheat wrapped in an embroidered white piece of cloth, sent by her father, Salih.

She showed up at the house again on a fragrant summer evening a few days later. He was preparing dinner when she knocked gently on the door. She entered like a dove that had found its nest, bringing with her all the summer fragrances from outside. Figs and wild wormwood, along with a strong smell of straw. All those arousing smells. In a white dress and barefoot, as if she had just come from the next room. Her arms were bare. The lantern behind her made the light silky down on her arm appear golden, and it shone with a breathtaking femininity. The light from the lantern revealed the contours of her tender body. Her neck, her buttocks, her thighs. She remained standing there, waiting. The crickets were chirping in the distant fields. He had to say he was preparing dinner, what with the knife in his hand. His hands were wet. Anything to take the edge off the tension and excitement. He no longer remembers what was going through his head right then. He might not have been thinking about anything in particular. He might not have moved for a few long moments, as if the white of her dress had blinded him and prevented him from moving at all, or as if he feared that the fragile image that had burst in on his solitude would vanish if he did move. A puff of wind would have been enough to cause this precious, fragile form to fade away. He ran back into the kitchen with the knife as if to give her a moment to turn back. But when he returned, she was still standing there with no discernible expression on her face, the green of her eyes now shining more brightly. Then, with a light movement, she removed the belt with the butterfly drawn on it, and the dress fell off with little more than a light rustle. Here was Hayat in front him, completely naked, her breasts standing firm, jutting out, full, making his mouth water. Suddenly he felt hot. The juices of desire between his legs began to boil. Rather than think about her in this rare moment he had been given, he found himself thinking about his penis. She headed toward the bed and lay down on it. The man followed her to the edge of the bed and stood there gazing at her naked body. Her hair fell haphazardly onto the pillow. He stripped off all his clothes and lay down next to her, catching his breath, afraid to touch her. Her fragility was still there, and the closer he got to her the more it pushed him away. He waited for the fever in his head and between his thighs to subside. He told himself that Hayat had surprised him. She should have come to him slowly, gradually—not like this, all at once, sweeping in like a storm. Did what he was thinking even make sense? Lying down next to her, his penis touched her cold body. He waited for a few more moments, hoping she would make some sort of movement, hoping she would moan or shiver. He was also scared that she would become frightened if he put his hand on the small mounds on her chest and the two pomegranate seeds adorning them. Then she moved gently, turning as he did. Her back was warm and her bottom was cold. The pleasant smell of her hair covering her face surrounded him. Its smell went right to his head, filling up the dreadful void in him. He placed his hand underneath her throat and touched one breast, then the other, then the first one again, then the other. He twisted her nipples and played with them, gently rubbing them up and down. Little by little he felt a movement between his thighs like a swarm of ravenous ants. "It's coming, here it is, it's coming," he said. Hayat turned to him and grabbed him, smiling. Now it was her turn to play with him. Between her fingers he grew, becoming firmer, becoming human, warm, hard. He smiled, then let out a loud laugh like a child when his mother takes him and throws him up in the air. Life washed over them. The man closed his eyes and said, "This is happiness." She filled his head and the rest of his body as well, and after a little while he would explode with pleasure.

Just a year ago she came leaping in with all of her fifteen years, and here she is now in his house, belly swollen, having reached the end of her pregnancy. And he? He's sitting in his chair not thinking about her; not thinking about her labor,

139

about whether it would be easy or difficult, about whether the baby will be a boy or a girl. He watches the slightly raised railroad track. It passes by over there in the distance. In place of trees, steel poles run alongside the track. A straight gray track devoid of all movement, as if its only function were to separate the ground from the sky. He watches it for no reason, without curiosity, with neither joy nor sadness. Do you think he's waiting for someone? No, this man isn't expecting a visitor. He doesn't count the judge because he belongs to other circles. The judge greets him as if he were greeting a tree. He isn't waiting for a relative to come to congratulate him on the newborn baby, and he's not waiting for rain. The pickax he used to dig up the earth in previous seasons is dry now, leaning up against the wall, spots of rust starting to show on its blade. Next to it is a box in which is a frayed sack full of unplanted wheat. He'll plant it if it rains, but it hasn't rained yet. It's too far past the month that's best for planting for there to be rain. Maybe he's waiting for the two o'clock train, the fertilizer train heading to the southern mines that won't stop at any point along the way. Maybe he's waiting for it so he can count its cars, so he can see that a good part of the day has passed. Nonetheless, the man is satisfied enough, like everyone is. He hates those who finish their prayers while he is still praying. He hates those who pray when he isn't praying. Like everyone, he hates those who are lower than him, and praises those who are higher. He hates love stories, especially when he thinks about the woman with her legs wide open in his room, happily awaiting her firstborn child to arrive. When he thinks about Farah, he hates those who have never felt love in their lives, just like everyone else does. He gives to the caid when requesting a permit to dig a well, he gives to the muqaddam when he begins digging, and he gives to the water official so that pipes will come to his land. The official takes, but no pipes come that might bring water, drinkable or not. He gives to the official from the National Department of Electricity so that utility

140

poles will come to his land, but the official takes and no poles arrive. He befriends the gendarmes, though he has no need for them, betting that he will someday. Who knows? Satisfied nonetheless, drawing water from the well and getting light from gas lanterns. Completely satisfied. He has a little piece of land—two hectares—that his father had forgotten to sell and give to the last woman to visit his bed. He has three puppies that eat scraps and moistened dried bread like the other poor dogs. He has a wife who has no desires or thoughts. Nothing like Farah, the girl who loved to dream, who loved Fairouz, and who loved the way her voice echoed in the mosque when she sang her songs.

The man's eyes follow a black plastic bag rising up from behind the train tracks. Its brazen indifference breaks the blueness of the sky. The plastic bag doesn't draw anyone's attention other than that of the man sitting in the chair. It doesn't matter to it if it rains. The lives of thousands of bugs crawling along the ground and chirping harshly don't concern it, nor do the lives of those that crawl underground in silence. The plastic bag is filled with its exceptional life, as if a special hidden life force makes it move. It seems happy with this arrangement of mutual disregard. It turns in the air to its own secret rhythms. Happy with its youthfulness. It emerged from the factory just thirty years ago, and it has five hundred more to live. Overflowing with the same calm haughtiness with which it began its life. Free. Relaxed. Without people. Without relatives. Its whole life in front of it. The plastic bag has no family. It floats down to the ground when it wants, and stops when it wants. It puffs up with a deep, bold laugh, then contracts, then laughs and laughs as it falls quickly to the ground, until the man sitting in the chair in front of his house is sure that it will be blown onto the thorns, snaring and tearing it as it rips apart and dies, so his eyes widen and his ears perk up as he waits. No, the plastic bag knows neither life nor death. In the moment of truth when the man thinks it is living out its final moments, it trembles and rises up with the same lightness. The plastic bag flies over the thorny plants and rises once more, then lands again in an exciting dance. It settles down between the two railroad tracks, warily steering clear of the thorns and stones on the road, avoiding all snares. Then, after a short rest, it continues with its game, this time showing off its strange dance as it glides riotously along the train tracks, reflecting the sun's rays as if it were itself a small black sun that's pleased with itself, its own sense of humor, its agility, and its freedom. The plastic bag won't board the train. It's playing with the morning sun. The train won't pass by, or perhaps it already has. The track is occupied right now. Don't you see that the track is occupied right now? It hasn't rained in months, and the year's crop slowly burns in front of the man's eyes. The man looks at the hair that's disappearing on his fingers, the gold ring on his second finger surprising him. No sound comes from inside. His wife is in a hurry. She's been waiting two days for the baby to come out into the world. She's been waiting since the day she was born. As for the man, he's in no hurry. He's not waiting for anyone. Why isn't the ring on his middle finger rather than the index finger? He counts his fingers.

He didn't find her in the hospital, and he wouldn't have recognized her even if she were to be found in one of its rooms. She remained anonymous among all the other nobodies every single time he came looking for her. An unknown surrounded by faceless beings. After eleven days, he found her at the door to the workshop. That's right—that's how things go when you want them to get better. He remembers her after she came back from the hospital, how she stood in the workshop doorway, a white veil covering her head and face. He stood watching her from a distance. He remembers that he hadn't stopped thinking about her for those eleven days he had spent looking for her in the hospital wards, as if she had occupied his entire body. He walked toward her and saw that she hadn't completely healed yet and wondered why she had left the hospital without having fully healed. She had come this far, and that was what was important. They were the worst two weeks of his life. The man believes that now. The man believes that the two weeks that followed her return were the worst. He watched Farah sitting, hopelessly playing with her fingers or lying down, every once in a while letting out a soft moan like a deep sigh, as if trying to console herself. He watched his hands as they covered up the burns on her face with ointments she brought with her from the hospital. Or maybe they were the best of days! He brought her hot food from the café or from his mother's house, hoping she wouldn't get up so he could stay up all night taking care of her, attending to her every moan, fulfilling her every request, along with those things she hadn't asked for. Tears came to his eyes whenever he saw her fingers searching out his hand, and when they found it, they clung to it like a drowning person holding on for dear life. Her pain gave him new life and lit an additional spark of love in his soul. Truly the best two weeks. And all the while he hoped she wouldn't get up so he could continue to lean over her, and examine her face through the transparent veil as she smiled at him with a hidden half-acknowledgment of something beautiful he hadn't done. Every moan, no matter how faint, brought her closer to him and him closer to her. Pain was the bridge that led to her. Her beautiful, silent pain. He also recalls her prominent collarbone and how he would become erect when he looked at the thin white bones under the rays of light coming in through the window, and at the spatters of sulfuric acid that had splashed black and brown spots all over her fine skin. Her arms, folded over her lightly shaking belly, were just as white, with the same spots on them. Was she going to get up? He hoped she wouldn't so his gaze could roam freely over her and his eyes could cheerfully take in their fill of her body's hidden maps—perhaps what he was seeing on her body were the delicate drawings he had etched in the mosque's wooden roof. Her pain was the mountain he scaled so he could see the vastness of his love for that garden of calm in which Farah lay. Its flowers blew to and fro in a gentle breeze that rose from an unseen stream. They were hidden together under a shady, luxuriant elm, far from anyone else. This dove that glided up above built its nest in his garden. But she did get up. One morning she got up. He was the one hoping she wouldn't get up so that she wouldn't disappear again. But this time she had come to stay. He helped her stand up, and when she expressed a desire to sit in the sun in the workshop doorway, he led her there and helped her sit down. And as she sat there sunning herself, he sat down next to her. She had her hands on her knees. He didn't know what to do with his hands. His mind raced. She asked him if he had been waiting for her. He replied that he had searched for her in all the hospitals but hadn't found her. But had he been waiting for her? Yes, he had been waiting for her. She placed her hand on his and squeezed it with her thin fingers, holding on and squeezing hard. The mosque was in front of them with its green roof tiles. Its minaret up there in all its splendor. Complete. Its zellij tiles reflected the sun's glistening rays. Did Farah still love to sing? Would the sound of Fairouz's voice be sweeter coming from underneath the white veil? Perhaps she had guessed what he was thinking about, and perhaps right then she remembered the song she had sung in the mosque. She removed her veil, and her voice emerged meekly, completely inaudible.

They remained standing and talking next to their gray car for quite some time. Pistols at their sides and malice in their eyes. Their eyes weren't black. They were like wildcat eyes—somewhere between yellow and brown. Their voices scratched like wildcat claws; claws just the right size for hunting mice. The car was parked ten meters away. Two gendarmes in full uniform were searching the area with all of their senses—smell, touch, hearing, and sight—with the audacity and confidence that their pistols gave them and the official appearance their bearing granted them. The man had been watching the car ever since it had appeared on the horizon. He might have been following its movement even before it appeared, just from the sound, then watched as it crossed the roadway that ran alongside the train tracks until it came to a stop. He invited them to sit down. One of them sat on the box, but the one with the epaulettes on his shoulders remained standing. The man offered him the wicker chair he was sitting in. The mother brought two cups of tea and freshly baked bread with butter, along with a towel for them to wipe their hands with when they were finished eating. They were here on a mission and wouldn't stay longer than necessary. They wiped their hands on the towel and got up from where they were sitting. Their work didn't allow them to sit. Since dawn, they'd been tracking thieves. Thieves become more numerous in the days leading up to the holidays. The man knew they weren't tracking cattle thieves. However, there was nothing to keep them from talking about thieves if talking about thieves made them happy. The man knew that the cistern guard wasn't tracking a rabbit, but there was nothing to keep him from talking about rabbits if that was what made him happy.

The man said he hadn't seen any thieves.

They appeared unconvinced by what the man said. That was part of their job. They knew he had woken up at three and sat down in this chair at quarter after three, right?

Had he heard gunshots during the night?

He replied that he hadn't heard gunshots.

At dawn?

Nor at dawn.

Had he seen a herd walking along the tracks?

He hadn't seen a herd walking along the tracks.

A herd of cows.

He hadn't seen a herd of cows walking along the tracks.

They remained standing there. They still had some time. The two gendarmes drank another cup of tea, ate some more bread and butter, wiped their hands on the towel, and said that thieves become more numerous in the days leading up to the holidays.

The man repeated that thieves become more numerous in the days leading up to the holidays.

"Keep your eyes open."

The man said he'd keep his eyes open.

"If a cow shows up walking along the track . . ."

He said that if that happened, he'd inform the gendarmes, as he always does, because he loves the gendarmes, and always wishes them success in what they do.

"Salam alaykum. May peace be upon you."

"To you as well."

17

A New Year's Present

SITTING ON THE ROCKS WATCHING the ships at sea in front of me, I hadn't imagined that I'd meet her again. But Farah was standing right there in front of me, inside the workshop. All the day's worries disappeared. I wasn't sure right then what was different about her face. That was because I hadn't looked closely at her, cautious as I was, scared, first and foremost, that it wasn't her, and then scared that if it was her, she'd become frightened and turn to run away. As I walked slowly toward her, my blood pumped faster as if my heart had been turned up a notch. I could practically hear its thunderous thumps beating violently in my ears. Her shoes were green. Her white legs were bare and she moved her small suitcase from one hand to the other. On her chest was a swallow made of black glass that moved to the rhythm of her chest's light trembling so that it looked as if it were flying around this small green garden with vibrantly colored butterflies fluttering about. There was a look of worry on her face, or it might have been distress, or the beginning of a question, or a certain pallor. Farah looked more faded than she had before. She shivered because of the cold. I don't like it when the cold comes unannounced. I didn't think about whether she was hungry or not. That question didn't even enter my mind. I extended a hand toward her in an attempt to show her that *it* was neither nervous nor surprised. It didn't show the same excitement and agitation that was on my face. I inquired about her health and made a joke about some nonsense that made her laugh and blush. Then I swore that I had thought of her just that morning when I woke up. I swear to God! I had to add that I had seen her in a dream wearing the same green dress, and why not? Perhaps I had seen her and forgotten. I no longer had anything else to think about other than making her laugh and spending the day searching for words that would touch her in some way, that would allow me to forget I had been missing her for at least two months. Now, when I heard her say she was hungry and would love to eat some little sardine balls with olives and lemon, I didn't say a thing. Would I be able to find conditions favorable to fulfilling such a small desire? What use was speaking? I also wondered whether I should grab her hand, knowing that I wouldn't, as if I were seeing her for the first time. That's why I couldn't find the right thing to say. Should I ask her about her friend Naima? Should I talk to her about the different types of wood I know about? What's a girl to do with a knowledge of different types of wood? I didn't have any other way to bring her close to me. I drew some squares on a piece of paper and began to explain what they meant, explaining the meanings of other squares I didn't draw as well. The square is neither a beginning nor an ending. The dot is the beginning. A hailstone. A drop of water. A bird's call. A knock on the door. All of them are dots that humans did not come up with. They existed before humans, and they'll exist after humans are gone. She looked at the piece of paper. She may have been trying to understand. It was a good start. I lit a cigarette and blew the smoke out. I was feeling better. There was still plenty of time. I saw her lean toward the drawing as if she were following the corridors I had drawn in my imagination. Should I grab her hand now? On the roof above our heads, seagulls walked around. The female usually walks with heavy steps. The male's walk is always rushed. Their walk turned into a noisy scamper. The male was chasing the female above our heads. A loud clamor. Like a full tribe of mice. Yet they were nothing more than two seagulls who couldn't wait. Two seagulls making all of this racket! I told her I knew a shop where they sold this kind of food. I didn't grab her hand.

18

MY SISTER KHADIJA CONTINUED TO worry about her hair falling out up until the day she left home, saying with neither joy nor disappointment, "Look, look. My hair isn't falling out any-more!" The man named Omar, or Hassan, or Hussein came late one afternoon and asked for her hand, all on his own, without any family or friends or conditions. How could he have conditions when he didn't even possess enough for his own dinner, having nothing for her or for himself? All he pos-sessed were his three useless names. A man currently out of work (and who had never worked a day in his life), living in a dark, cramped, empty room with a ceiling and walls that were crumbling because of the dampness. There was a patched blanket and a table wobbling on three legs. This is what Mother and I said to her: "Khadija, this man isn't suitable for you. You'll die from the cold before the end of winter." She remained silent, and in the end said that she wasn't thinking of herself. We didn't understand what she was getting at. Who was she thinking about, then? In any case, she talked so little in the last few days before she left that we had to remain opti-mistic. She fattened up a little—her chest filled out and her buttocks plumped up—as if she were being nourished by her illusions, as if it were her special way of getting ready for mar-riage. She didn't show any signs of joy or sadness. On either side of her eyes and above her upper lip an intricate web of fine wrinkles appeared that gave her face a sort of sternness.

Khadija had grown old and gray after so much waiting. Like a fruit that had over-ripened before being picked, but she was neither delighted nor pained. Rather, she had simply ripened quickly, so quickly she had almost rotted. She could be forgiven for that. Perhaps she was right.

I didn't find her in the room she rented after leaving us. I finally found her in the early afternoon on one of the roofs. Mother had been wondering what had happened to her daughter ever since she left in mid-November. She thought of her as she sat in front of the sewing machine. She thought of her as she sat at the dining table. She thought of her all the time. Anxiously, she wondered about the hand her daughter had been dealt. I didn't find her in the second room either. The entrance to the house had no door, like the alley. The hallway was dark. I tripped as soon as I stepped in. Still, I stepped in and was immediately surrounded by a rotting smell, rancid enough to make your eyes water. I went up some narrow stairs that led to a long hallway where some nearly naked children less than a year old were playing, wrapped in rags that revealed more than they covered up. An obese woman was hunched over a tin washbasin squeezing her laundry, moving her lips without making a sound, as if speaking to her unhuman inflated chest. The woman was completely soaked; behind her there were clothes dripping on the line. The naked children jumped and pranced all around her. I asked her about the room where Khadija lived. She didn't respond. She contented herself with a meaningless look, as if she were looking at the wall. She went back to her washing. I tried again, practically screaming, "Khadija! Khadija! I'm asking about my sister Khadija!" The obese woman didn't lift her head this time either. Instead, a man with angry eyes appeared in the downstairs hallway, in the entryway I had just passed through without seeing him. He hit the wall with his cane and yelled that the woman was mute. I looked down at him from the top of the stairs. I could only see the white turban covering the top of his head and his cane raised up toward me. "The woman is mute. Mute!" His cane was the only thing that remained clear in my mind. What he told me about Khadija and her husband when I went down caused the blood to go to my head. Blood, anger, and tears. I told myself that I was the cause of what had happened to my sister. If her husband beat her, it was because no one had been asking about her. No one had asked about her since she went off with him. And where were they now? Who knows where they went. To another alley. To another hell. Her husband never paid the rent he promised to pay. How could he pay a single day's rent when he didn't work? Then he'd come home drunk every night and beat her, after which he'd throw her out to spend the rest of the night in the hall or on the stairs. The man was wearing two heavy wool djellabas. Standing in front of the house and boiling with the same anger I was, he hit the stone-hard ground of the alley with his cane as if he were smashing the head of the criminal, my sister's husband. "If he's going to end up killing her, let him do it someplace else . . ." I didn't hear the last part of what he said because I was unconsciously repeating that I was going to kill him—knowing that I wouldn't—or that we would kill him, Kika and I. We wouldn't hesitate to slit his throat from ear to ear, Kika and I. Together we could slaughter an elephant. Especially Kika, because he happily slaughters the holiday sheep. But Kika isn't my friend anymore. I don't know what he's been up to ever since Farah and I left him behind in the street.

The third room where I found my sister Khadija resembled a neglected wooden box on one of the rooftops. A seven- or eight-year-old girl led me to the building's entrance, pointed to the roof, and disappeared. No smoke. No food smells. No running water. No clothesline indicating that there was any life on this roof. Just a narrow open door at the end of the stairs that I didn't doubt for a moment led to the wooden cube Khadija called her room. As soon as I moved toward the door, the body of her husband Omar, or Hassan, or Hussein got in my way, rushing toward me as if a supernatural force had thrown him out of the room. Naked as the day his mother had given birth to him, enraged and yelling that Khadija had sucked him dry. Squeezed him. Sucked his blood. Sucked his last drop of water. I was bumped back to the top of the stairs. "This woman is never satisfied. Her hole always wants it. She loves it all the time—day and night, morning and evening, all the time. She loves it in every position—standing or sitting, kneeling or lying down, on her back or on her belly, in every position." Then he headed toward me, forgetting that he was naked, as if I were someone with whom the secrets of the wooden room could be shared, the secrets of the room where her legs are always pointed up toward the sky. "And even afterward she stays there in bed rolling around like a cat." I still wondered whether he had seen me. Had he seen me and recognized me? Right then, Khadija appeared in the doorway, also naked. Her breasts hung down like two dried eggplants. Wrung out. Black. Some birds flew off over our heads. Khadija went back into the room and threw on something so skimpy it didn't cover a thing. Had she changed? She was the same Khadija, except for some faded bruises on her forehead. Perhaps she had gotten a bit fatter. And her skin had darkened a little. As for her husband Omar, or Hassan, or Hussein, the way he was standing was ridiculous. His penis looked funny too, hanging like a small intestine with green, dimple-like spots all over it. They might actually have been dimples. His testicles hung like two dried figs. How could my sister feel any passion for this sickly, pale body? And what could he possibly want with her breasts that hung like two droopy eggplants? What was it that attracted them to one another? They didn't make me angry anymore. They looked funny. The scene was completely ridiculous. I went into the box she called her room to get Omar, or Hassan, or Hussein something to cover himself with. However, because of the awful, stomach-turning stench, I came back out before I had a chance to finish examining the few things that were in there. A room with no windows. Empty, with practically no furniture. It smelled of sleep, cheap liquor, sweat, semen, and whatever other foul odors come out of a body. I asked Khadija if she wanted to come back home with me. Omar, or Hassan, or Hussein seemed happy with this suggestion. He yelled gleefully, "Take her, take her!" as his body shook with delight. "Take her, take her! Free me from her!"

"I want my things."

Mother had bought her a double bed and a refrigerator when she went to live with Omar, or Hassan, or Hussein. "But the room is empty. Empty, sister." Except for the bed. No cabinets, no refrigerator, no dishes. Khadija said, "He sold everything."

"The refrigerator?"

"He sold it."

Omar, or Hassan, or Hussein said that the dishes weren't good for anything since they didn't cook at all.

"And the bed?"

"What about the bed?"

"I want my bed."

I told him that Khadija wanted her bed. He replied that the bed wouldn't fit through the door because it was too narrow. But hadn't it gone in through the same door? Did it come in through the roof? The man who looked like he had an intestine between his legs stood there solemnly, looking at the door as if he were seriously thinking it over. Then he said, "Go ahead and try." Surely he was being sarcastic. The sarcasm of someone who knew that the bed was bigger than the door. That was how I found myself measuring the bed's dimensions against those of the door opening. First by eyeballing it, then with my arms. This time I didn't ask him how the bed had fit into this room because it would only make The Intestine mock me more. I didn't want to give him the chance to mock us. If only Kika were here. But Khadija wasn't going to leave without her bed. "Her bed won't fit through the door," The Intestine said, laughing as he straightened the covering wrapped around his waist. Happy now that he was done with his nightmare. He headed toward the room, walking like a triumphant pimp. Khadija remained standing in the doorway, determined to take her bed before Omar, or Hassan, or Hussein sold it to some other man to sleep on with some other woman in some strange house she'd know nothing about. I stood there waiting. I no longer thought about how that bed had gotten through this door. I no longer wondered how the bed had grown larger than the door. All I was thinking about was why such a wide bed was so important. What use did she have for a double bed that only she would sleep on? Then I thought about the wisdom behind the invention of these sorts of beds; a bed wide enough for two people who don't know one another. I thought about why a man and a woman needed to be in the same at all. What was the wisdom in remaining attached to one another for thirty or forty years? Who says that they have to live a full lifetime in the same bed? It's not as if this custom can be found in any book. Khadija says that she won't leave without the bed, because it's her bed.

19

SHE WAS SLEEPING INSIDE THE workshop. The rain had stopped early. At dawn. It didn't stop completely. At ten it turned into a light drizzle. My thoughts were calm and peace of mind washed over me. I stood in front of the mirror and flexed my left hand to see how solid it was. It was as muscular as could be. I was fine. When I heard something rattling outside I stopped moving and listened. I wondered if there was someone at the door. Then a light knock made me more than wonder. I was really terrified that the knocking or the person knocking had something to do with her. I took a look at her as if to assure myself she was still there. Then I walked toward the door and placed my ear against the wood, but I didn't hear any sound or movement. I peered out the window but didn't see anything in particular. The courtyard in front of the workshop was empty. The ocean below had turned back to gray. The sky seemed to have descended and turned gray too. We were at the start of a dark day that would bring little light. Gray clouds had rolled in over the workshop, the courtyard, the ocean, and the mosque. I put out the lamp that was still lit and opened the door, only to see the dog Rihane, or rather his corpse, laid out straight, his tongue limp and hanging out of his mouth. It caused me to take a step back. His lifeless legs were outstretched on the dirt. His eyes were half closed, flat and lusterless like two pieces of cheap glass. I stepped out of the workshop. Perhaps someone had thrown him onto the doorstep and run away. No one was there. I went back to Rihane and turned around to see if Farah had woken up. Then I satisfied myself with sitting on the rocks, thinking about his unfortunate and unexpected end. There were no wounds on his body. Maybe he died by poisoning. What use were the precautions he had always taken? And why would he come to my door to die? Perhaps his presence on my doorstep was some sort of threat, a way of telling me that there was no way out of paying my share of the construction, which was just about finished. Or maybe his death had something to do with how he felt about the job he was no longer doing as he was supposed to. Or he might have died a natural death and preferred that his end be at the workshop's door so I could bury him instead of leaving him to rot out in the open like all the other dogs. All of these black thoughts were finding fertile ground now. Then there was a less-black thought: with Rihane's death, I was truly and irreversibly alone. There was a grapevine we had sat under one day. A bare grapevine. The strange thing about it was that its purple color couldn't be seen all year, but only revealed itself at the very end of the year. I buried Rihane in the shadow of its branches without shedding a single tear. I tried to, but couldn't. Look how harsh and hard-hearted I'd become, like Kika, and even more so. Look how I'd changed.

Farah hadn't woken up yet. She'd slept a lot since she arrived, and spoke very little. Perhaps this was for the best. The things people say always make me laugh because, at the end of the day, they don't say anything important. What they say usually means nothing. So why do they speak, then? Maybe they find themselves somewhere in all that chatter. They don't know themselves except when they're making noise. Over the course of eleven days we only exchanged words that were absolutely necessary. I let her tell me what she viewed as essential: the small room she rented after Naima kicked her out, the work her father used to do, the Oum Errabia River, her sister

Raja. I asked her about where the room was, but she wouldn't say. It was a small room on the first floor, which she might get rid of the first chance she got when she straightened things out. And the address? When she didn't respond, I asked her about her health and what she wanted to eat that day. We didn't need anything else. Yesterday, after she had eaten some delicious little sardine balls that Mother had prepared with olives and red peppers, she went to sleep. During the days she stayed in my workshop, I noticed that she didn't seem as happy as she had been before when she had first set foot in Casablanca. She didn't walk along the seawall, arms outstretched, trying to fly. She was preoccupied. Long periods of absentmindedness, or complete absence. Not once did she laugh like she had before, not even a little bit. Farah wasn't with me. She was far away. I just didn't know what was worrying her. My joy was incomplete. It remained that way the whole time she stayed with me.

Then I became preoccupied with the notion that perhaps she was tired after what it had taken for her to convince herself to come back. In reality, this meant nothing. No one would be convinced by it. It was an attempt to console myself. I didn't go to sleep until late. I spent hours mulling over all the possible reasons why she'd come back in the end. I couldn't keep myself from thinking about it, always ending up at the same result: Perhaps she had done something bad. Maybe she had been living in the street, got hungry, stole, and in the end came to hide out. She didn't say anything to that effect. It was up to me to figure it out on my own. Just as she didn't say a thing about the money she had stolen from my pocket. And I didn't ask her about it. After I buried Rihane, I stared at her through the window. Weak sunbeams streamed in and settled on her face. Her collarbone stuck out dramatically. Before, she hadn't given me a chance to worry about her, but this time it was up to me to show my concern for her, wanting her to regain her confidence and joy. For a time, the image of the white skin between her throat and shoulders never left my mind. Her delicate fingers. Her thin, white, translucent toes. For a moment I felt a spark of desire inside me, but I snuffed it. A hidden heat caused my body to tremble shamefully; why don't we wait until the beginning of spring like other creatures do? From the ocean, despite the bitter cold, or maybe because it, the smell of seaweed wafted up from the beach. Some fishermen were out there catching octopuses out of season. I wondered whether she remembered the spotlight that had shone down on her round breast, giving it a warm purple color the night of the cabaret. She seemed to be in the right place, surrounded by stacked pieces of wood that were strewn everywhere, each piece painted with care as if in any forest in bloom. That was what I tried to convince myself of. She slept calmly. What would Father say if he saw her stretched out in his workshop, surrounded by his wood, tools, drawings, ideas. Then I went back to where I had been sitting to look out over the mosque's courtyard, allowing myself another moment to clarify things in my mind. I was filled with misgivings. The chaos of her life wouldn't get any better as long as she felt that I was distant from her, as long as she didn't feel that I was with her, as long as she didn't realize that my heart and my thoughts and every hair on my body were with her. As long as that was how it was, she would remain like this. As long as I remained unconcerned with her, she'd remain oblivious, distant, cold like this, like any rock.

The seagulls reappeared. Because of the clouds, they weren't fully visible. In the middle of the courtyard there was a podium that hadn't been there before. In the far corner of the courtyard that looked out over the ocean, metalworkers' and carpenters' workshops had been erected. And there, this podium rose in the middle of the courtyard as if it had sprouted up from nothing. Standing on the podium was the National Department of Electricity employee motioning with his hands, as if delivering a speech to the workers who were covered in gray, the color of the bags of cement they carried day and night, rain or shine. Down in front of the podium were enormous yellow spools of cable that would bring electricity to the mosque. I walked forward a bit, only to realize that the employee was scolding the workers, threatening them because work on the mosque hadn't progressed far enough after five years. It was as if work had just started. The mosque and its courtyard were an enormous open-air workshop on the ocean. Covered in dirt, all dug up. Columns strewn about and arches too numerous to count. Ceilings still being held up by wood and steel scaffolding. A ceiling that wasn't there—our ceiling. Huge piles of rocks, sand, dirt. The wind blowing. Metal blackened by the rust that had accumulated over time. In the middle of this ruin, in the middle of this enormous marketplace, the employee stood on his podium pointing to the four corners of the square in disapproval. "All of them are cheaters. All of them are thieves. They steal the mosque's copper and the latches from its doors. They even steal the toilet fixtures. But when it comes to work, they waste time. The good Muslim worker is a pure person who doesn't steal." The National Department of Electricity employee couldn't understand how thieves could enter into God's house. "What will all these sinful hands say on the day when they stand before God? And on top of this you want new houses? On top of this you spread rumors? Who said that the new houses aren't there? And that your old houses were going to be destroyed to make room for a wide boulevard? The mosque doesn't need a boulevard so it can be seen by believers." As soon as they heard about the new houses, the other workers who had been pretending to be busy with their tools now hovered around the employee. For a little while, they forgot all about their hammers and ladders and sweat. Look at how they waited now that the employee, after his usual threats, was going to explain to them the benefits of the electricity that had barely made its way to their closed eyes. Soon. The employee stood up straight on his high podium. Around him were electrical cables and boxes of different sizes. The workers, as well as some women from the old city who were sitting on the low wall that formed an extension to the mosque's courtyard and some elderly retirees who were pretending that they were looking at the ocean view—this whole crowd was now surging forward around the podium. And the National Department of Electricity employee, like a professional actor in his long khaki coat and black cap, explained with elaborate gestures how every wire and every plug worked. He clarified for them the many benefits that electricity would bring to their new homes. "After the work is done, not before. Do you hear me?" It seemed that he finished off his speech with one of his jokes, because laughter rose up from a number of spots in the crowd. It might not have been a joke though, because people sometimes laugh at things that aren't funny. The employee now leaned over the box and took out a black panel with a number of lights on it, which he showed to the onlookers wondering what it was. In front of the baffled crowd he pressed a button, after which lights began to flash without any intervention from anyone. Praise God! Then he turned them on again and explained how life was going to change in their new houses with electricity instead of candles. "When electricity enters your dark hearts, you thieves, these are some of the benefits that will come from working on the mosque. As long as work progresses, you'll see the affordable housing project move forward as well, right? Because in the end, God's light is what will illuminate your houses and your minds, you ignorant illiterates!" In the same sharp scolding tone he asked them, "Has your work progressed one inch in the past four months?" He responded to his own question: "No, of course not. Because instead of working you're protesting in front of the prefecture or assaulting the security forces." Then he leaned over the box again and replaced the lights with different, colored, ones—yellow, blue, red, and green. Then he pointed to a man standing at the foot of the podium. "Ahmed! Write down how many rooms each family will need, and how many electrical outlets in each room." The man pulled a small notebook out from the pocket of his djellaba and began to write: "Three rooms, six plugs, five lights, inshallah, God willing." And here's one who needs four rooms and ten lights, or thirty. It depends on how many people are in the family. Inshallah. Not to mention the cables and electrical wires and plastic tubing, inshallah. "The proper place for the breaker box is by the house's front door. That's for the inspector who will pass by your houses once a month when it's time for you to pay your bills, because electricity isn't given away by the state for free. Do you think the state is a charitable organization? You'll even be able to put a bell at the door, and its chime will be heard in every room. Yes, a bell, like in the big houses. Each with a different tone, depending on your taste. From the particular ring of the bell you'll be able to know who's there and you'll open the door for him if you so desire, or you can keep him from coming in if you feel that he doesn't deserve to see your new house. Ahmed! Write this down: 'A bell at every front door.'"

Maybe Farah had woken up. Should I go back to the window to watch her wake up? This would also be enough. I wouldn't find her sitting drinking the milk I bought for her yesterday, because she doesn't like milk. I headed for the workshop, then stopped halfway and retraced my steps, giving her the chance to wake up on her own. I liked this game. I forgot all about Rihane's death. Perhaps a car hit him while he was on his way to my workshop. All dogs die under car wheels. Why would Rihane be an exception? I put aside all of those negative thoughts, happy to replace them with all of these pleasant ones. Then I seemed funny to myself. This was also something that felt soothing, now that I thought about the world around me so joyfully. The voice of the National Department of Electricity employee waxed almost poetic. "Electricity changes life. With electricity comes the refrigerator, then the radio, then television. Once you get used to electricity, your mentalities might change too, and your children's sensitive eyes won't strain in the candlelight as they study their nationally mandated lessons. The light will illuminate their young minds because electricity, as I explained before, changes lives . . ." Then he switched off his lights. He looked at them now, and they nodded as if they'd finally understood. The employee watched each and every one of their movements. Every change on their faces further convinced him that they hadn't understood. He watched their nodding heads and their fake enthusiasm. Had his words changed their way of thinking at all? The employee seemed calm, and then he seemed unconvinced; disappointed almost. Without hope. Despite the explanations he had just presented, as he had the day before and all the days prior to that one, he saw that work was progressing slowly. He jumped down from the podium with surprising lightness and stood in front of the man with the notebook. He repeated his orders to write down what everyone needed—how many rooms each family would need, the number of lights each house would require, the number of outlets and how many meters of electrical wire. "Don't forget a single house or the price of the electricity that will be within every household's reach." Then, when the throngs surrounded and obscured him from view, his words could no longer be heard amid the din. But I still got their meaning. "There's nothing more effective than electricity for fighting the sinful thoughts that have taken root in your heads . . ." Then his voice disappeared completely.

All of a sudden, sheets of water poured down from the sky, as if buckets were being emptied over everyone's heads.

20

THEN SHE DISAPPEARED. NOT LIKE the first time. It was a cold night that chilled the bones, but I didn't care. There were no stars in the sky that might guide me. In any case, this didn't matter now. The ocean's fury was hidden, which allowed for a false sense of calm. A December night. I was sitting on the sand of the beach, unable to feel how damp it was because my clothes were wetter than it was. My hair was wet and dripping, too. The cold water penetrated my bones, flowing, seeping deeply into the folds of my soul like poison, drop by drop. On top of all that, I was distracted and tired after the painstaking effort I had exerted looking for her. The ocean, like the sky, was concealed behind the jet-black night. I looked at the glints of light on the waves flashing in the darkness in front of me, and I thought about Farah. No hope. I thought about the eleven days she had spent at my side, with the slight hope that she might return. I blamed myself. I beat myself up over it and told myself that I was the reason for what happened. Farah disappeared eleven days after she arrived. How painful is that for someone like me who had been expecting her to disappear the whole time? They were days filled with nothing but anxiety. I swung back and forth between this shore and that one. She'll stay—she'll disappear—she'll stay—she'll disappear. I could smell her departure with every passing hour, with every look at her absent face, and in every move she made. During the eleven days she spent in my workshop, I couldn't think about anything else so long as my thoughts remained stuck on this point: When would she disappear again? As if expecting something like that to happen. I put it off after each passing day, expecting it, waiting for it and for nothing else. It was as if I was counting on her disappearing just so she'd reappear and stay for more than eleven days the next time around. Each disappearance would make her stay longer than the time before. Maybe that's how she was thinking about it. Who knows? What I wasn't expecting or imagining at all was that she would disappear the way she did. Farah came at the worst possible time, the least optimal. She didn't seem hesitant or cautious. Even though, really, she had come back to the place that had been waiting for her. Beautiful and radiant. For the first two days, she didn't show any aversion to the workshop I had crammed her into. She acted as if she were living in a palace. That was what reassured me, despite the warning bells going off in my head. Isn't that strange? Like a feral cat you've lured into your house. She didn't say whether she was going to stay for an hour or spend the night. She didn't say that she was going to stay forever. She didn't say a thing. As for me, my whole being was turned upside down. After she showed up, everything inside me and around me was transformed. I no longer had to turn to see her, as if I could see her using another sense entirely. I could recognize her without seeing her. Not by the blue dress she had come in the first time, nor by the green coat upon which the colored butterflies flew; not by the uneasy way she stood at the cabaret entrance looking for her friend; not by the cash that was in my pocket and had disappeared, nor by the harsh thoughts that formed in my head afterward; not even by the fragility she displayed inside the workshop, behind her a thicket of painted pieces of wood that almost swallowed her up. Rather, I recognized her by the muddled image she planted in my head. Present and absent at the same time. Despite all that, I was overflowing with a happiness I couldn't deny because she was there. Eleven full days, short and long at the same time. Eleven days with the feeling that something had changed inside me and around me. This in itself was extremely important. There was also this: Farah showed no signs of joy or sadness. This didn't concern me any more than was necessary, not as much as did the matter of her staying put, as I said before. I had been worried about her impending absence from the start, as soon as she first stepped into the workshop!

I walked toward her with some of the food that I brought from my mother's house. She was standing at the open window waiting, leaning her arm on the windowsill, blinking as if her eyes hurt from the rays of a sun that wasn't there. I was happy, thinking she was waiting for me to come back. She is the mosque's baraka, its blessing. She let her two short braids tumble down over her full chest. She looked like the lady of the house. For the first time, this Farah had matured, after only eleven days. I placed the bundle on the table. She walked forward and opened it up. She looked down at its contents. She sat eating hungrily, while I worried about my deteriorating financial situation. While it's true that most people are born poor, no one wants to remain poor. That's how it's always been and that's how it will always be. The idea of going to the Gulf became more immediate, more so than getting a new shirt or a pair of pants. It was just as tempting as it had been before, but now the question of whether or not to join my brother Suleiman was no longer as pressing or important. Remaining at Farah's side was the most important thing in life from now on. I contemplated this confined space—a workshop constructed of wood and sheets of tin, smelling of sawdust and glue and paint and sweat. I was absorbed by the misery Farah and I were floating around in together. No shiny mirrors or soft cushions or generously set table. Shelves in place of a cupboard, a furrowed mattress (like a plowed field), an old rug with some pillows thrown on top of it, an ancient radio held together with pieces of string, a forest of wood rising up around us with its heavy smell, a crummy table with a rusty candlestick on top and a threadbare cloth with leftover potatoes and eggplant on it. Was this all we deserved? Was this living? But Farah didn't seem to have any misgivings about the place. And why should she feel such misgivings? She now possessed a bed and a mirror. She now possessed what a girl without a girl's experience needed. She now possessed what a woman without a woman's experience needed. Still, it was true that in the last two days before disappearing, Farah had changed. She spent hours silently passing her hand over the wood, and because people don't like to feel total isolation, or at least they'd rather not be isolated for no reason, she would sometimes make an effort, saying for example, "Cedar wood is a noble wood that loves to be taken care of." Words that held no meaning, but that let me know she was there. Maybe they held a meaning I didn't get, but they were words regardless. Or she would lift her skirt up above her knees when she saw me looking in her direction and flash a shameless smile. Or she would say with feigned anger that she had lost half of her weight and that her hair, once black as coal, had lost its luster. In those last two days before disappearing, she changed. Those two days weren't like the ones that had come before.

On the last day, she took a turn for the better, as if she had awoken from a long slumber or had decided all of a sudden to brighten up. This started first thing in the morning. I suggested that there was no better day to go to the movies, to see *The Sins* starring Abdel-Halim Hafez and eat lunch in a popular restaurant with the few dirhams we had. Like any woman accustomed to doing housework, she opened the window to air out the room, standing for a little bit to look out at the ocean then turning toward me with a smile because, from here, she could see the ocean and hear the crashing of the waves. Farah was beautiful with her cheerful eyes. I watched as she cleaned the workshop. She swept all around the room, making it her little kingdom. I watched her small red fingers as she wrung out the rag and plunged it into the black bucket. Then I watched her swaying as she walked, picking flowers along the side of the road, yellow wildflowers awakened from their slumber by the recent rain—their spring having arrived—shooting up along the entire length of the sidewalk. Then, having remembered the housework, she returned home. I walked toward her but she ran away with the cloth she was carrying as I followed her into the workshop. She let out a flirtatious scream because I grabbed her. I placed my hands on the curves of her hips. I stood there looking at her for a long time, submerged in her hazel eyes. Then I heard her say, "Do you still like me or is the magic gone?" From a prolonged silence to nonstop chatter. She talked about how short she was, about her fingers that turned red when she scrubbed the floor, about her hands that weren't good at anything—plates shattered in her distracted fingers. She asked if I liked singing, because singing was all there was in life, and whoever doesn't like singing doesn't love life. In the end she said that she came back to see what sort of creature I had become. She came closer and told me to open my mouth. She spit into my mouth, then gave me her open mouth for me to spit into. For a few moments we tasted the flavor of each other's fresh saliva. For the first time I realized that saliva had a sweet taste, sweeter than rainwater. Then she pulled my head toward her with a delightful violence, leaned over, and planted a furtive kiss on my lips, or rather on my lower lip, a single kiss that was closer to a bite. I wondered whether this was a new type of punishment. After that she picked up the bucket and went back to her work, as if she had forgotten what had just passed between us. I wouldn't say that the pain I felt was sweet. Does being pricked with a needle made of gold make the pain feel any different? I wouldn't say that this was what I had been expecting from her. I don't know what I was expecting. I was expecting something the essence of which I didn't clearly understand, as if I had been waiting for a delayed promise. Finally, she sat down next to me and began to talk about her father and her two sisters. For the first time she felt like chatting—the father who had come back from the Western Sahara missing a leg; his friend who would bring him cheap tobacco from the base; the veil she had put on her head because of the wind, but that her family and neighbors and friends understood differently. This last story made her laugh a lot.

That night, our final night, she didn't give the impression that it would be our last. A calm night, normal, but still cold, like any December night. I was leaning against the side of the workshop looking at the minaret. It looked like it was about to take flight, cloaked in the pale light from the lamps that the workers had left on before leaving. Then I began to count the many stars in the sky. I could hear her inside humming along to the music coming from Father's radio. I felt intoxicated for no reason. All of this—the night, the stars, the ocean—deeply affected me. So much so that this night seemed clearer than it should have been, its stars so close, fixing themselves in the heart rather the sky. I entered the workshop. I found her looking at her face in the mirror. Perhaps she was scrutinizing her new situation by its light, saying to herself, "How did I get here? I've made pretty decent progress since I left Azemmour." She said that strange things she hadn't experienced before had happened to her ever since she first settled in this city, and that these changes were what made her behave so strangely. Then she apologized and asked me to forgive her for everything she did that I didn't like. I wasn't able to hold back my tears this time. I too began to look into the mirror at Farah. As if I wouldn't be able to see her true face without the mirror. As if only through the mirror could I measure how sincere she was being. I went back to where I had been sitting and wiped away my tears. After a moment, Farah came over. She took my hand and we went down to the beach. We walked for a little while, hand in hand. My hand was sweaty and sticky, and this caused me some alarm. I pulled my hand from hers and sat on the sand, lifting my eyes up to the sky. Farah walked away, looking delicate in the moonlight. She came back and sat down next to me without making a sound, as if afraid of disturbing the clearness of the night. I gathered some wood and lit a small fire. I stretched my body out like a lizard in the sun. A moment of profound, pregnant silence passed between us. She placed her head gently on my shoulder and I felt my heart beating in my ribcage. I wished that this moment would last forever. I had changed. I had become sensitive, light-spirited, weak. This had never happened to me before. And it wasn't what I would have expected from myself. I gave her a sidelong glance. She looked green. Instead of looking red in the firelight, she had taken on the color of tarnished copper. I thought about throwing my coat over her. She stood up and threw her sandals down, walking toward the little waves that were gently breaking on the sand. She began to laugh and play in the water. I looked at her and thought that I felt just as she did in every possible way. I stretched out on the sand, content to listen to her silvery laughter. The night carried the echo of this intoxicated laughter back to me. I could see the color of her laughter, and I could see her in all the images that had accumulated during this whole irreplaceable period of time. I could hear her moving in the water. Maybe she was swimming, although this wasn't the season for swimming. I turned toward the water but I didn't see her. She had gone underwater. What was she doing underwater at this time of night? I heard a light stroke like the movement of a fish when it jumps in the water, but I couldn't see a thing, waiting for her to appear with the lightness and grace of a sea lion—first her hair, then her laugh—but neither appeared. She hadn't laughed for a while now. She hadn't yelled or screamed for help either. I imagined her movements receding and growing fainter as they moved away. I looked toward the water where she had been, or where she went under, or where she disappeared. There was nothing in front of me except a black curtain upon which long, white bands appeared and disappeared. I walked toward the water, staring at it again. No sound. No real cry for help or even a pretend cry. I looked toward the waves where she had been playing. I walked toward the water, then I walked in, but all I could see was the night in every direction. Wherever I fixed my gaze, all I saw was night. Farah had disappeared. She had drowned. The water had swallowed her up while she laughed. I dove in, looking for her. The salt burned my eyes. No trace of Farah and no sound except for the crashing waves. My eyes attempted to penetrate the intensely dark confusion but were prevented from doing so by the salty spray. The cold of the night chilled me to the bone. I got out of the water and continued to look for her, shivering. I waited futilely for the stars shining above to guide me. A wave knocked me onto my back. I clung to the notion that she was still fooling around. Then, after more than two hours of walking around barefoot, searching for her between the sharp rocks, on sand dunes and in the dark folds of the night, looking in the seaweed spit out by the ocean or sliding on the slippery rocks, I went back home without having found her. I stopped every once in a while, looking around in every direction, but no shadow disturbed the blackness of the night, nor was there any movement or rustle that might have provided some hope in the darkness. I listened closely but no sound came to me except for the crashing of waves as they rolled onto the sand or smashed on the rocks, accompanied by my heavy breathing, because I had begun to pant without realizing it. I climbed a tall rock, but could see only my own shadow reflecting in the mirror of the water below. Finally, I went back and sat on the sand, my clothes dripping wet. The water burned my eyes. The night around me floated over everything. I looked at the flashing waves and told myself that she might appear now, but nothing appeared except for endless darkness. Without hope. Sitting like a rescued stray cat, trembling, unable to get up, unable to make even the slightest movement, I peered into the emptiness Farah had left behind her. I lay down on the sand and cried like I had never cried before.

That's how I was for days afterward; content to sit on the rocks in front of the door to the workshop like someone sunning himself and waiting, wondering why she came and then left like this. In a bad state, like someone sunbathing without a sun, waiting for other disasters to come. It was as if an enormous void had inhabited me. Things around me had no life—the workshop, the rocks, the mosque, the minaret, the ocean—all were suddenly emptied of meaning. My eyes couldn't see a thing. They had turned into empty holes. As if a kind of death had taken root inside me and risen up rebelliously against the shell that contained it, consuming everything around it, the way lava does. There was no longer anything but me, empty, contemplating the emptiness all around. I thought of her. All of my thoughts revolved around Farah. Farah used to love fish. I'll wait for her to show up to buy her lots of fish. She didn't last long in this life because I didn't manage to care for her as I should have. I remained sitting on my rock like someone who wouldn't be able to utter words like these next time. I'll have to show her how much I care for her and how much I want her so she'll be able to regain her optimism for this life. The image of the white skin between her collarbone and her shoulder. The delicate fingers. The small white fingers that used to animate her special life were all gone far away. Where was she now? Floating in the water with little fishes swimming in and out of her empty eye sockets, swimming around ecstatically inside her empty skull after having eaten what life it had contained? Was she at the bottom of the ocean where the seaweed tied her up, keeping her from being able to return to the surface, jellyfish having stopped up her mouth so she couldn't scream? Or was she in the belly of an enormous whale? Were the fish all done with their feast or were they still savoring the taste of her succulent bones? I went down to the beach and walked up and down it for days, morning and night. I was barefoot, my clothes soaked. I rolled around facedown in the sand. I found the same worries I had before. Inside me an old hatred for myself boiled like a volcano, hissed like a snake. Oh, how I needed someone to tie me up and take me to an asylum—I generally like asylums. How I needed someone to give a full-throated yell, to insult community and religion, the mosque, the flag, the nation, just to allow others the opportunity to watch. So they could get an eyeful. To smell what the earth smelled like from the time of its creation. I left my skin for a little bit and hopped around like an acrobat. I turned. I twisted. I leaped and danced, giving others a chance to laugh at me, mock me, or just insult me. In desperation I stopped in front of the ocean, mulling it all over, like someone who no longer had work at the mosque, here or anywhere. I'll join my brother Suleiman in the Gulf, or maybe I'll go with Mother, who has dreamed for years of performing the hajj pilgrimage. Or perhaps I'll travel to Milan and join the Mafia that we used to see in the movies with my uncle Mustafa, before the gendarmes opened fire on him. I was feverish. I had to find Farah so I could save her from drowning. I sat down and closed my eyes so I could see with greater clarity. I went to the same bar, the Saâda Cabaret that bore witness to our first meeting, and asked about her inside and outside. I stood in front of the bar waiting for her in the same place we had stood before, but I didn't find her because she had preferred to drown. That's when I started to see her everywhere. She was always there— when I was awake, and when I slept. I saw her tonight too. A gentle morning brought us together, lulled by a clear sun as we lay on the white beach so bright that it was difficult to look at the water, or our naked bodies, what with the sunbeams dancing all about.

21

I WAS MOVING THROUGH A bad dream when I heard it. The voice came to me from far away at first, so far. Then, when it started to get clearer, I rolled around in my bed, and shivered when I heard it. I had forgotten all about it. I hadn't heard it since last year. When I was fully awake and knew what it was, I wondered if the reason I hadn't immediately recognized it was because it had never sounded so mournful as it did at dawn, at this hour when the earth is born anew. The voice came clearly from the depths of the night: *To God we belong, and to Him we shall return.* It went on this way three times. Ten times. More clearly than it should have been. *To God we belong, and to Him we shall return. To God we belong, and to Him we shall return.* Soft and tender, like a sad song we had all forgotten. The voice might have been coming from the top of the minaret. And the child? Our first dead one this year. I didn't wonder which house it came from. I didn't think about which room it lay in, this first dead child of the year. All I remembered was that it was winter, and that children die in the wintertime. Death finished up its work in my sister Habiba's room, just as it had been doing for years, ever since work began on the mosque. Was there any wisdom behind this as Abdullah claimed? Death began here, and always at the outset of winter. Abdullah knows this better than any of us. He used to spend the day in front of the tax administration building filling out all sorts of applications and forms that were needed in that office. He didn't actually work inside the department, but rather in front of the door like a beggar. He spent his day filling out the sorts of forms that public administrative offices overflow with. His wife, Habiba, split her time during the day between sleeping, helping Mother with the sewing when there was something to be sewn, and sitting in front of the mirror putting on makeup while she ate. When construction began on the mosque, Abdullah stopped doing this work because death's scheme began to cut his children down at around same time. At the beginning of the second winter, he lost his first son, who was eight years old at the time. He considered it a clear sign that marked the division between one period and another, and that God had turned specifically to him in order to test him, so he stopped working and began to pray. After losing his second and third sons during the following two winters, he became certain that it was God who was demanding this heavy annual sacrifice. God had chosen him from among all His other servants to offer up his children as a sacrifice and an offering on everyone's behalf. The neighbors said that it was a tabiae, the kind of djinn that follows a family until it completely annihilates it. Abdullah doesn't approve of such nonsense. He was the one who was offering up his flesh and blood to atone for everyone else's sins so that construction could continue, people could have jobs, and he and his neighbors from near and far could receive recompense in this world and the next. Wasn't that a lot for one man to bear? All of this made him even more smug, more vain, more unreasonable.

Mother was uncomfortable with this man from the get-go, ever since he worked as an officeless public scribe, filling out forms in front of the tax administration building. She avoided him as much as possible after Habiba forced him on us. Now Abdullah had become another man with a mission greater than spending his day begging for customers outside the tax administration building. He considered it his duty to feed himself and his progeny. And he no longer permitted Habiba to work. "I'm no pimp. I'm not a pimp who would let his wife leave the house to go to work." Even though she doesn't go anywhere, happy to help Mother sew the clothes they sell to merchants in the bazaar. No, Abdullah, her husband, isn't like the pimps like us who work. Who is he talking about? Everyone. Me, Mother, Father, my sister Khadija, my brother Suleiman, the neighbors. Everyone who works. What citizen would force his family to work after the harsh trial he has faced, is currently facing? Which he has taken upon himself to accept as an unusual form of contribution in order to provide the sustenance we receive? This time, when his wife heard him talking about sacrificing his children, she came out of the room swearing he had smothered his child with a pillow. I don't believe she was lying. I think he was killing his children in order to get a job at the mosque. And rather than listen to what his wife was saying, he went on and on: If it weren't for his sacrifices, our business wouldn't last a single day. If he didn't sacrifice his children, the mosque would have collapsed on top of the workers inside it on day one. No man could possibly give what he had given. None of us citizens could do more than he has in terms of giving over his children for God's sake! "Not one, not two, but *three* children!" The oldest would be more than twelve years old now had he lived. And the youngest? The last of the bunch? He still had his milk teeth. What Muslim could stand before him, look him in the eye, and accuse him of not performing his full duty? "What are *you* and your neighbors doing? Your pushcarts half filled with mortal sins and crimes, mixing sand with sand rather than with cement, you cheaters! You sell watered-down milk and rotten vegetables! How do your deeds compare to what I have given, and continue to give?" He goes up to the mosque and staggers back again along the main streets, telling everyone about his children who have died one after the other, voluntarily, one after the other, without pain, with a smile on their lips, knowing why they were dying, understanding the meaning of martyrdom.

Ever since our trials with him began, a beard spread over his face, covering his lips and almost swallowing up his eyes, the hair on his cheeks growing whiter and thicker—white hair standing up straight, resembling tangled thorns. His skin darkened, and he began to pray. He partitioned off a spot in the foyer behind a wall of cardboard boxes that Mother dragged in every week from the wholesale market. That's where he erected his mosque because he had taken it upon himself to make up for the prayers he had neglected for the previous forty years he had spent in a duped and deluded state. Years straying from the path and wandering aimlessly. Yes, he used to lie, steal, and bear false witness, but then he repented. For this purpose, he got a number of old diaries, colored pens, and a small calculator to add up the prayers he performed, and the ones he still had to do. And there were a lot. More than a million prostrations. He said it with an air of superiority over us pimps. Abdullah the martyr. He'll die praying. Prayer will suck the last drop of his blood before he falls down as a martyr. And when he wasn't praying or recording his prayers on the wall, he was eating. And when he wasn't eating he put a stick between his teeth and sucked on it all day, making disgusting sounds as he repeated, "Praise be to God," then spitting wherever he wanted to. He counted off his children who had died. The white wall behind him was filled with black lines (vertical and horizontal, corresponding to morning and evening), red squares to keep track of the weeks, crescent moons and half-moons (I'm not sure what they represented), suns and circles, and other, more complicated, drawings. And now Abdullah has lost his fourth child. This morning at dawn. A dead one every year! Isn't that a miracle? Only the chosen are so afflicted. Only the daughter remains living. Her name is Karima. She didn't die in her first or second year. Karima has reached six years of age without any problems. Girls don't count when it comes to martyrdom. That's what was happening as I looked down onto the foyer. The most recently deceased of Abdullah's offspring was lying on an old sheepskin wrapped in an old cloth, his face blue—the face of a nursing child who died by being smothered under a pillow, as Habiba said. She was the one who'd shaved his head to ward off the djinns that held onto his hair. Clumps of wet hair mixed with pitch were scattered around him next to a bucket of dirty water and a cloth and soap. The floor was wet. Was he dead? No, he hadn't died completely. A yellow foam was coming out of his mouth as if he had been eating soap. Our neighbor who was holding the cup of pitch said, "This wicked djinn, Oum al-Subyan, has come back." She looked at the white eyeballs turned up in his head. Maybe he hadn't died yet. She rubbed his head with a bit more pitch while reciting some incantations to ward off the King of the Djinns and his entourage, which includes this wicked one that devours young boys. Then Abdullah came in, composed, standing gravely, moving his lips, looking like someone used to receiving disasters with open arms. Should I comfort him with words that aren't heartfelt? I'd say the words to him and then run off to my bedroom to avoid becoming absorbed in his stories about this world and the next. That's what I would have done had Kika not arrived. The first of the men to arrive, Kika asked Abdullah, who was standing on the doorstep, whether he had called for the doctor. Abdullah's face became more sullen as he indicated that Kika should close the door, as if the doctor were hiding right behind him, waiting for just the right moment to steal his child and destroy his life's work. The women looked in and asked if there was anything they could do to save the child. They went into the room and sat next to Habiba, who had become accustomed to crying years ago. Abdullah went back to his corner to pray, subtracting the prayers he had completed and recording them on the wall. The yellow foam had dried on the child's face and mixed with the hair scattered around him. As the sun came up, some men gathered in front of the house. The unusual smell of the dead body and the melodious sound coming from the top of the minaret had attracted them. Now the women were searching for a clean piece of cloth to wrap the dead body in. That was what was awaiting Abdullah when he came back to stand in the middle of the foyer. We were in the midst of a harsh winter that wasn't going to wait for anyone. The dead body wasn't going anywhere without a suitable shroud. The house was full of many types of cloth that Mother had bought at the wholesale market, all with patterns and designs on them. Cloth made in China that had traveled thousands of miles, and there wasn't a single white one among them. They were all decorated. The Chinese don't produce white cloth because they don't want us to take it as a bad omen. So that we'd continue to buy cheap Chinese cloth. But none was white. And so? There wasn't a single piece of white cloth in the house that was suitable for serving as a shroud for Abdullah's last son, martyred so that the mosque would remain forever. As always, Abdullah was composed. Patient. Something as trivial as not being able to find a piece of cloth wasn't going to get the best of him. He had experienced much worse. I indicated to Kika that it would be best to avoid him and wait by the door until the corpse left so we could walk behind it. Maybe we could console him after the burial. I wasn't surprised that Kika had come under these conditions, as if I had been expecting him to visit. I considered it a form of apology for what he had done. I think he had been waiting for an opportunity like this. Deep down inside I welcomed his return and was flooded with warmth when my shoulder touched his. We stood at the door. And the singing voice? I had forgotten all about it. It was still coming from the top of the neighborhood minaret. *To God we belong, and to Him we shall return*. As long as the voice continued, heads peered out from the windows. There were a few men waiting for the small dead body to emerge, but it wasn't coming out because it didn't have a shroud. One of them said it was a small corpse with no need for a shroud because he was just a child and didn't even know what a shroud was. "That's right. Just bury him as is." Someone else said, "He came into the world naked and will have gone back to where he came from naked, as if he had never come." The first one said, "Dead like these don't want anything from this world, even this half meter of cloth you want for him." But Abdullah saw things differently. He wasn't like the other dead, and his father wasn't like the other fathers who let their children go meet the Lord of Majesty without a shroud. He was no pimp, you damned pimps! Abdullah wasn't like them. Death strengthened rather than weakened him. Abdullah stuck to his guns, and finally one of the neighbors brought a piece of cloth that she had been using to wrap bread in. It had no shape whatsoever, but it was white and good enough. It was then that he allowed them to get close to the deceased, wipe the foam that had dried on his face, and collect the hair to save with bunches of his other children's hair that rested inside the pillow where he laid his head, the one Habiba said he used to smother the last branch of his male offspring.

We walked away from the door when we saw them bring the deceased out and place him on a cart. A small, skinny lump no more than half a meter long, wrapped in the sheepskin Abdullah had laid down in the foyer. Because of its small size, the corpse on top of the wide cart looked like any old cheap piece of merchandise, which almost made you wonder what exactly these men were walking behind. The few men who were walking silently behind the cart were led by Abdullah. His lips were dry and he had dark circles around his eyes, which were shining with arrogance and self-importance. He slowed down as the procession passed in front of the mosque, expecting the workers—all of them—to join the procession, or for them to stop working until the funeral procession passed, or at least to quiet their hammers. The workers were busy. They pushed heavy carts filled with stones, they climbed up stairs, they pounded metal, they assembled the zellij tiles—they were doing everything except paying attention to the wretched procession of no more than seven men, followed by a stray dog whose ribs practically poked through skin that had completely lost its color.

The gravedigger grabbed his pickax and dug the hole. Abdullah, the father of the deceased, sat off in the distance, his hand supporting his head as if it were weighed down by his worries. Was he crying? When they finished preparing the hole, he got up, lifted the light, skinny corpse, and handed it to the digger standing in the hole, yelling at him to pay attention to the way the head was facing. "The head faces Mecca, gravedigger!" The gravedigger felt around the shroud. He couldn't find the head. Because it was so small, it was the same size as a hand or a foot. He felt around the skinny corpse for a while, finally yelling from the bottom of the hole, "Here's the nose!" But Abdullah had his doubts, preferring to make sure of it himself, so he asked that the corpse be brought back up. While he was feeling around the white shroud trying to find the head that couldn't be found among the other parts of the body, his neighbor asked him if he had died clean. Abdullah said that, at dawn, in his final moments, he had washed him and his mother had shaved his head, just as they had done with the previous children, so he wouldn't go to the next world with all of his filth and dirt. All of his children met their Lord in a state of cleanliness. Then he grabbed a small mass the size of a lemon and ran his hands all over it, as did the others, until everyone was sure they had finally placed their hands on the head. "Are you sure?" There was still some doubt. They went back to feeling around the shroud, one after another. When they were filling in the hole, the gravedigger took a stone and threw it at the dog, who ran away with a yelp. Then he brought over a large rock and placed it on top of the grave, explaining to Abdullah that the rock was necessary to keep the hungry dogs from digging up the corpse. The emaciated dog sat away from us, as if waiting for us to finish our task so he could begin his. I wondered what the dog was thinking about now as he looked at the heavy rock that had been placed on top of the grave by the gravedigger. Then Abdullah remembered that with all of the hubbub, they had forgotten to pray for the deceased. The dog came closer when it saw the corpse appear for a second time, as if he thought they no longer needed it. After praying and returning the corpse to its resting place, then pelting the dog (who walked away limping, or pretending to limp) with curses and rocks, they stood around on the muddy ground in silence.

We returned from the cemetery. I sat on the short wall that encircled the mosque's courtyard, waiting for night to fall while thinking about the deceased. He'd turn into dirt after a few days. And that dirt would become fertilizer for plants and vegetables that we'd eat and fortify ourselves with. For this, the dead are useful, if they're useful for anything. I felt depressed. Then I saw Kika sitting next to me, and I heard him let out a deep sigh. I asked him if he was thinking about the deceased. Sort of. He was thinking about his father. Maybe he had died. Moroccan prisoners die in Spain more than the Spanish ones do because no one visits them. The first thing he was going to do when he got to Spain was visit him in prison. But he wouldn't be able to. Kenza had stolen his visa. Right then I noticed that he was making me nervous. But couldn't he think happier thoughts? He calls his mother "Kenza" as if she were the neighbors' daughter. This Kenza had betrayed him. She had led him on for more than a year, and in the end she had taken his place. He said he would kill her before she could pack her bags for the trip. Because she loved a man who wasn't her husband. She had continued to sleep with him illegally without papers, before he was thrown into prison. We laughed, remembering that Kenza only slept with convicts. Everyone she slept with did prison time at some point in their lives, or at least were fit to do so. We laughed more at this last thought— that these poor fellows had been free men, but as soon as they met her they found themselves in prison. He said that she had always been a whore, sleeping with whomever. I didn't know if I liked Kika or not. Despite the friendly atmosphere that surrounded us, I was still hesitant. I wasn't expecting at all to see him like this. Completely destroyed. Head in hands. Kika is truly luckless. Our neighbor Kenza sold her jewelry and entered into relationships with agents and embassy door-men in order to get him a visa, and what happened in the end? The visa found its way into *her* passport instead of his. I felt his pain, even though I knew he had no father in Spain, or anywhere else for that matter. It seemed that Kika had cleared his head when he put his hand on my shoulder and rubbed it warmly. I wasn't hating him at that moment. Two warm tears welled up in my eyes. I didn't want to turn toward him. There might have been two similar tears forming in his eyes as well. The sea breeze was refreshing and the wind was strong—the smell of seaweed, oysters, and those who had drowned. Per-haps I like him just a little bit, hoping at the same time that the black thoughts that had been messing with my mind over the past few days would disappear.

22

Our Neighbor Kenza

NEW YEAR'S DAY IS AN exceptional day as far as I'm concerned. You always think the earth will stop turning, that the day will be longer, and that it will be unusually sunny. The night before is always rainy and you think it will be like this until the following day, but then you wake up to a clear blue sky. Always. For as long as I can remember. Praise God! I spread out all the fruits and vegetables I bought yesterday and remained at a loss, not knowing where to start. After buying all the fruits and vegetables and everything, and returning from the market, after paying the taxi fare, I only had a few dirhams left, with which I bought four Marquise cigarettes. I gathered up the vegetables and put them in the basket. Mounir's been in prison for three years. He'll get out in a month. He's waiting for the basket I'm to bring him this afternoon. He doesn't know that he'll never see it. This time, I'm not bringing him a basket. I'm not happy, despite the visa I finally got. After more than a year of back and forth, begging and waiting. During my last visit, Mounir said that I had written him off. He's always known that I go out with other men. But I stopped, pretty much, as soon as he asked me to quit working. I haven't gone out with many men after promising him. And now he says I've written him off while I've taken it upon myself to bring him his weekly basket for three full years. All so he wouldn't lack for anything in prison. When I visited him last week, he said that I had humiliated him. I think he's searching for some justification to break up because of his imminent release. Nothing else would cause him to change like this. So as long as I've humiliated him, as he puts it, let him look for another woman to bring him his basket. I think the visa came at just the right time. He'll have nothing but air in front of him when he asks, "Where's Kenza?" She left. She went to Spain to earn some honest money. He wouldn't be able to find me even if he were to turn the earth and sky upside down. I don't need men anymore. I won't expect a thing from them from now on. They don't add anything to my life except for problems. May they all rot in hell! From the beginning, I've always looked after myself. I won't come back from Europe with less than thirty million. I'll buy an apartment like I've always hoped to, with a bathroom and a balcony looking out onto the minaret so I can hear the call to prayer all the time. I swear to God I won't come back without that thirty million. Before that, though, I'll buy a table and refrigerator for Kika so he won't lack for anything while I'm gone. He didn't say a thing about the visa I got. What's he going to say? That's how things are, so what can you do? Instead of giving him the visa, they put it in my passport. They handed his back as it was, its pages blank, with no visa. I explained the situation to him as best as I could. I put the basket to the side. I light the gas burner and put some water on to boil. I promised my neighbor that I'd make a batch of vermicelli with cinnamon and sugar. Mama Fatima loves vermicelli the way I make it, with cinnamon, sugar, and almonds. Instead of almonds, I'll put in a few peanuts. Almonds are expensive these days! I light a cigarette and blow the smoke out down between my legs. It's a funny habit, and I'm not sure where it came from. Am I happy now? I've never been happy in my life. Why should I be happy? I don't have anyone next to me telling me what to do and what not to do. People just love taking advantage of others. There isn't a person in the world who, given the chance, wouldn't take advantage of someone else. I was ten when my father brought me from Taounate to work. When you work for rich families, you're always working for idiots. I'm not sure how God decides that they should be so stupid. They never stop asking mean questions, and when you ask for a raise, the lady of the house asks you, "Are you building an antenna that makes you think you should be paid four thousand riyals, you ass?" Father would come once a month to take the hundred dirhams. I didn't make much money. There were days when I went hungry and days when I had enough to eat. Then there was the fact that I didn't like living locked up in other people's houses. I didn't work in any house after that experience. These people don't deserve you wasting your good health on them. There's good and bad waiting for everyone. That's how it goes. It's enough for us to be in the right place at the right time. I'm no longer hoping to meet a man who'll buy me a watch or a car. They say that the work is hard in the strawberry fields in Spain. I was born for hard labor, but not when exploitation or contempt come along with it. And if I have to be exploited, at the very least there are other places I could choose instead. Exploitation along with poverty exists only here with us. I'll come back and buy an apartment in a clean neighborhood. I'll quit smoking. All so that Kika can see that it's possible to aspire to something better. I don't like the name they've given my son, Abdel-Haqq, but I've gotten used to it, and I too have started to call him Kika. His father used to work in construction. He was far away when Kika came into the world. Off building somewhere. Where? One time in Agadir. Another time in Tetouan. Every time the same question: "Where?" I'd spend the day at the post office attached to the telephone, because he wouldn't stop asking, "Where are you?" "In the post office," I'd reply, handing the receiver to the woman standing next to me so she could verify that I was in the post office, and that we were waiting for him, the little one and I, while he was going from apartment to apartment, building to building, city to city, saying that he was building us—the child and me—a house. I was sixteen when I gave birth to him. He said we'd get married as soon as the house was done. He said that he was jealous. That the jealousy was consuming him. But he disappeared. The last time I spoke with him he said he was going to Las Palmas, and then he disappeared. We never saw the man or the house. We didn't hear anything more about him, neither good nor bad. He had disappeared from the world without a trace, as if the earth swallowed him up. At least I had some relief from the pressure of the phone receiver on my ear. The first thing a man talks about when you meet him is marriage, but it's the furthest thing from his mind. Because we're fools, we open our legs for them knowing full well that they're lying, because we love to get a taste of their fruit before we wilt. When he asks about him, I tell Kika that he's in Spain, in prison, so he won't mention his name again. So I lied, may God forgive me. Mounir is the latest man I've met, and in the last few weeks he's been saying that I've written him off. I've never written anyone off in my life.

I switch on the tape player and let the faqih recite some verses. I always relax when I hear a Quran reciter, especially if it's Abdel-Basit, or a voice that sounds like his. I put out the cigarette, put the vermicelli in the couscoussier, and leave it to simmer. Mama Fatima says I should learn how to sew and work in one of the embroidery ateliers. I missed the boat for learning anything, Mama Fatima. Moreover, those ateliers are far away, on the other side of the world, and the women who work there leave their houses when it's dark and get back home when it's dark. They never see the light of day, and I love the daytime, Mama Fatima. I won't sacrifice my days for six thousand riyals a week. Locked up in an embroidery work-shop or in some idiot's house, same thing. The ones who own the embroidery shops are like the rich people whose houses I worked in. They're all sons of whores. My visa is in my pocket. The work is better in the fields of Andalusia, out in the fresh air rather than in suffocating embroidery shops. Or maybe I'll go to Sweden. Why not? My friend Atiqa says that she's comfortable in Sweden. Sweden was always better, my God! Atiqa, who used to drink and smoke cigarettes, weed, and hashish, met a movie producer who married her and took her with him to Sweden. After all of the sins she had swallowed in Ain Diab, she finally found her happy ending in Sweden. She goes with him to film festivals in France, the US, and Canada. The important thing is that this is an opportunity not to be missed for someone like me, who's thirty-six years old. God brings about every blessing. I'll forget all about Mounir and everything connected to him, and I'll start from scratch. I'm no longer willing to go on any more adventures with men I don't know and who expect who knows what from me. Especially when it comes to Kika. All the toil that awaits me is for Kika's sake. I don't want him to be looking for his mother in courtrooms and in the backs of police vans when he gets older. Poor Kika, he's always been high-strung. That's why he could never hold down a job. I used to say that abroad was the most appropriate place for a boy like Kika. But he has no luck. He came into the world a bundle of nerves, because he was born without a father. That's what I say.

I can hear the sewing machine downstairs. Mama Fatima is working on a day like this! Her machine never stops. She's always consumed with work because she feeds so many mouths. I let the vermicelli simmer and take out the flour to make some cookies. I pour boiling water over the flour. Mama Fatima also likes cookies with lemon.

The basket next to the wall is overflowing with fruits and vegetables. I walk over to it and check to see if anything is missing. Women are fools because they'll believe anything. I light another cigarette and go back to preparing the basket. This time I put a cover over it so I don't have to go back to it. I get up. Evening is still far off. I remove the couscoussier from the flame. I won't make anything right now. Maybe later. What did he say? That I'd written him off. Now I've become someone who writes people off. That's all I am? I always helped him after he was arrested for hashish, even though he denied it. And I followed him from prison to prison so he'd have everything he needed. I spent a lot of money. And what did I get in return? After the trial, I spent more than two years going between home and the municipal prison. I borrowed money for the weekly basket, and he didn't lack for anything. If people were eating an orange at home I'd buy him a kilo of oranges so he could show off in front of the other prisoners. If people were eating a piece of meat I'd cook him a whole chicken. I fulfilled his every request, small and large. All the food he craved. I didn't keep anything for myself. Baskets filled with fruits and vegetables and everything. And add to this the fact that I was stuck at home, not going out with other men unless absolutely necessary, so as not to give people the wrong idea. He kept on saying we'd get married as soon as he got out of prison. He said he was ready for that day, and that he had prepared the paperwork and everything. I was also ready for that day, as every woman is. Birth certificate, certificate of residency. Divorce papers weren't among them, though. Marriage is a relationship between a man and a woman, not between papers. Marriage is a mutual understanding. Instead of that piece of paper I paid ten dirhams at the district office for a certificate of celibacy. And after all that, he says that I've written him off. How will I make do with the money I spend on him if I don't go out and meet people? Not to mention that he's pretty well off even though he's in prison. He sells hashish to the other prisoners, but he keeps it a secret so I won't ask him for anything. His take from one night would be enough to last me a whole month. Why am I running myself ragged with this shit? I'm not the one who's coming out ahead here. I've gone through more difficult periods.

I take a look around the room I'd been living in for fifteen years and tell myself it's time for a change. I won't find a better time than now. The room is small, but it's enough for two people. It has everything I need. A gas heater. A blue plastic strainer. A television on a stand made of chipped, peeling wood. Various types of cookware. An ashtray that has yesterday's cigarette butts in it. A table that has everything on it I need for cooking—oil, sugar, green tea, flour, and all sorts of spices (with cockroaches walking all around—I consider these insects members of the family; they've lived with us since day one), buckets for the bathroom, toothpaste, mint, tomatoes, and potatoes. The time has come for a change. I stand in front of the mirror. I don't like how my face looks in the mirror with these rotten teeth. I no longer have the hair I had before that used to knock men off their feet, nor the dark eyes. Under the mirror are a few pictures, including a picture of Kika and me when he was four years old. We're laughing. Then there's a picture of him alone after he was all grown up. And a picture of Mounir with his siblings and mother. In the snow. In the picture they are laughing, just as they did in real life. They have everything they need because Mounir spends money on them. There are people who are always lucky. Even while he's in prison there's this idiot woman who provides for him, borrowing money and drowning in debt so he'll lack for nothing. And one month before getting out of prison he has the nerve to say that I'd written him off. Great. I swear this New Year's Eve I'll sleep with ten men in one night. Just so he knows what sort of pen women use when they're intent on writing someone off once and for all!

Then I take out the purse I had hidden in the cupboard. While waiting for the vermicelli to boil and the cookie dough to rise, I go to my neighbor Mama Fatima's apartment. The door is always open. She is in front of the sewing machine like she always is. Her daughter, Habiba, is rolling out dough, with Karima beside her forming a small loaf. I stand there hiding the purse behind my back while she tries to guess what I'm hiding. "A loaf of bread?" "No." "Cookies?" "No." She doesn't know what I am hiding. But she remembers that it is New Year's and draws in her breath. She smiles. Then she says, "Perfume?" "No." Karima shouts, "A purse, a purse!" while I stand there with the purse in my hand for her to see.

I hand her the purse and tell her that this year would be better than the one we had just said goodbye to.

"How much did you buy it for?"

"Four hundred," adding, "May God bring health and wealth with it. A nice purse. Practically new. All that's missing is the strap. It just needs a good polish and it'll be as good as new." She picks it up and turns it over. Then she looks inside, laughing. Maybe she'll find a thousand or two thousand dirhams.

Mama Fatima gets up and comes back out of the room with a small wooden box. She sits in front of the sewing machine, takes out a simple mirror, and begins to apply black kohl to her eyes. I sit cross-legged in front of her, no longer feeling like I had just a short while ago. I feel much better watching Mama Fatima lining her eyes with kohl.

"Who're you putting kohl on for, Mama Fatima?"

"For the new year," she replies.

Then I add, "May this year bring health and wealth to you and your children." We hug, cry, and say, "Amen."

Life is like this dough Habiba is kneading. Without a hand to combine all the ingredients together, everything will stay separate.

IV

23

THE MAN SITTING IN THE wicker chair brushing the ground impatiently with his feet listens to the familiar roar, the roar of the judge's car engine. He's passing by in his Oldsmobile on his way back to his house, his office, and his family. It's Sunday then. He's returning to his other life, which he had left behind when he moved to the city. The judge lives in the city. He comes to his farm on Saturday nights when he wants to get drunk with one of his many mistresses. Barbed-wire fences separate the man's field from the judge's vast land holdings. He could walk in them for three days without covering all of it. He passes by in his old American car so no one will recognize him, just like he did yesterday when he was coming from the city. On his farm he drinks alone and in silence so that no one sees him getting drunk. But he doesn't walk the courthouse hallways silently, and he doesn't skirt the walls to avoid attracting attention. The judge is everything in the courthouse. The courthouse is his kingdom. He sends whoever he wants to prison and he pardons whoever he wants. On his way back from his farm he sits with the man and they spend some time exchanging news about everything under the sun. He's a mysterious man. Secretive. The man doesn't know why the judge likes sitting with him on Sunday afternoons before he returns to his family, his house, and his office. Every Sunday afternoon he waits for him to tell him why he sits there. The judge says he likes talking with people. He likes the bread the man's mother-in-law bakes, and the breeze that blows in the late afternoon. Instead of bringing bread, the mother-in-law brings boiled eggs with oil, olives, white cheese, and two forlorn cups. And the bread? The mother-in-law forgot the bread. The two cups remained forlorn until the judge poured their share of whiskey into them. It was an exceptional day. Maybe he came to ask about the newborn. This was also possible. But he didn't say a thing about the woman in labor or the baby. Nor did he say anything about the land. Was he planning on taking ownership of his land? If that idea occurred to the man, it certainly occurred to the judge too. Or not. The judge didn't say what he was thinking. The man knows he doesn't count for anything next to whatever it is the judge is thinking about; next to all of the ideas that emerge from the judge's brain, or from that of the gendarmes—any gendarme, with or without epaulettes on his shoulders. His life is empty. It doesn't amount to anything. It hasn't known anything worth mentioning. There's only one story in his head and it is named Farah. There might have been other stories. He could have gone to the Gulf to join his brother Suleiman. He could have become a skilled carpenter or a famous thief (but all he had stolen in his life were some silly copper pipes not even worth thinking about). He could have been anything. But now he's nothing. Nothing to his wife, who's ready to swap his life for a pup that will come out into the open soon. He's nothing to the judge, to the thought that hasn't yet emerged from the judge's head. He's nothing to the plastic bag. The judge is fifty, but from so much use in courtrooms, his voice has come to resemble that of a seventy-year-old. The judge said, "This is Najat." He forgot that he introduces her every time. "This is Najat," and she got out of the car with some difficulty because she's fat. The judge doesn't like beef. At his farm, in order to stay thin, he only eats lamb that has had the fat removed in order to avoid the cholesterol. However, his passion for fat women remains. She got out laughing loudly, her djellaba pulled up above her knees so it didn't rip. Her lips were bright red, as were her fingernails and hair. Her pocketbook was tucked under her arm and her mouth was filled with laughter. Sounding like an old lady, the judge asked, "Do you know the story of the man who was stung on his penis by a bee?" The woman laughed, showing all of her teeth, and the judge threw an arm over her shoulder. The man wondered what wind blew him in on Sunday afternoons. Why did the judge love to sit with him every Sunday afternoon? The country was his country. The borders were his. Rusted wire that had long ago lost its ability to intimidate anyone separated their lands. The thought that the judge was planning on taking over his land made the man grow larger in his own eyes. The thought that the judge was interested in him and his land made him feel his own presence. He was happy to be with the judge whether he spoke or not. He felt protected. No harm could come to him while he was with the judge. Harm had been left behind, praise God. Harm is the judge himself, praise God. Harm, when it comes from the judge, is a blessed form of harm. But the judge didn't say a thing about why he had come. The judge turned to Najat and asked her to retell the bee story without omitting any of the details. She couldn't speak because her mouth was full of olives. Afterward. Maybe he came for another story. Then the mother-in-law brought some bread. The judge said that he had seen the gendarmes' car by the dam. The man told him that they were searching for cattle thieves. The judge replied that they were chasing after a young man and his lover who had been caught in the act. No one had seen cattle thieves in these parts for at least two years. The woman with the red hair knew all the stories about thieves that were in the judge's head, and on the judge's desk.

The judge grabbed the bottle, but rather than open it, he asked the man what time the afternoon prayer was. The man looked up at the sky as if he understood things such as prayer times. He didn't add a thing, as if this gesture was enough. Without moving from where he was, the judge said, "Prayer comes at its appointed time." The judge was well versed in religion. The man held him dear for this reason too. He enjoyed matters of religion simply because they came from the judge's mouth. Because the judge—in addition to his jokes, his saucy stories, his drunkenness, and the lovers that he exchanged every four months—was always happy to dive into matters of religion with rare enthusiasm, with all of his friends, lawyers and defendants alike. These are the things the world should revolve around. The noblest form of knowledge is knowledge of God. Attaining it should be the goal of all people, animals, inanimate objects, and every creature on the face of the earth. Always with new additions. The judge is a religious scholar and the man holds him dear because of his knowledge too. "A time will come when everything will disappear, with nothing remaining except for His exalted face. And this time has started to manifest itself. Don't you see that God is stronger than everything? Inside and outside. Stronger than walls, cars, and storefronts. Hands, foreheads, and mouths. Perfumes and clothing. Humankind has disappeared because time belongs to Him, the Exalted One." The man listened, nodding, so the judge would see that he realized the importance of what he was hearing. No longer was he that child who would walk naked into the hammam, not caring what people said, or the one who, along with Kika, used to steal the babouche slippers that those praying had left on the mosque's doorstep, running away with them and laughing. No, the man had become serious. He listened to the judge. He listened to the gendarme. He said, "Amen." He was tolerant. They could enter his house anytime they wanted, and leave anytime they wanted. They used his kitchen. They used his cookware. They used his bed for their afternoon naps, and when they left, their smell remained behind in the house. Deep down, he realized that there was no other way. Deep down, he knew that he was prematurely older than his forty-three years. Praise God, his life had passed with hardly any problems. He was comfortable.

Following the afternoon prayer, and after tossing back half a glass, which allowed sufficient time for his veins to swell up and his face to become flushed, and after a long fit of coughing to cover up his sudden lapse, he took out a small camera and asked Najat to take a picture of him like she always did on the Sunday afternoons they spent together—one time with a thick beard, another time with a short beard, once with a moustache and once without one, wearing sunglasses and with no glasses at all, with his judge's robe on and without it. The judge hadn't yet found the right look. After the photo session, Najat leaned over the judge's neck to search among the hairs on the back of his head for the black spot. She knows just where it is, when it first appeared, and the stages of its development. She couldn't find the black spot because of the grease, the sweat, and the strong smell. She told him that his hair smelled like a goat, and this comparison made him laugh for a while. Then the judge fell silent, his head comfortably resting on Najat's thigh in anticipation of the pleasure he'd been longing for, saying, "I'm your goat," and scrunching himself up like a cat does when you pet its head. His face had disappeared between her thighs and, with eyes closed, he waited for the erotic purring that would start at the knees and move ever so slowly upward through his tendons and veins until it reached his nostrils, putting him at the edge of bliss. He'd ask her to slow down a little bit so as to savor the pleasure drop by drop before it faded away. Najat knew all of this. And she knew where the other black spots were on the judge's body. Here was one on his shoulder, and on his buttock was a bigger one. And two above his rump. When she got to this point, she'd tell him that the flesh was fatty, which made it difficult to grab onto the two black spots, as he waited for her hand to move down to that place that was closest to his heart.

What pleasure does illness derive from awakening our pain at night? When a person is sleeping, he is less resistant, less prepared. No more than a night had passed since Farah had come back from the hospital. As he sat beneath the window watching her fitful sleep, she let out a scream that made him jump and hit his forehead on the window sill, causing it to bleed. There's nothing worse than illness ambushing you at night. Death and sickness swoop down at night for reasons that, to this day, are unexplainable. It wasn't really a scream. Less powerful, yet more severe than a scream. It was more like a thick rattle in her throat, as if Farah had exerted a great effort to remove a rock that had been blocking her windpipe. He lit a candle. Blood covered the pillow. No, not blood. Rather, it was small black bits of flesh floating in a sticky mixture of blood and nasty chunks. Everything she had swallowed since this morning was now all over the pillow. She continued to sleep. The small piece of cloth that had been covering her face had slipped off, but she continued to sleep. It was as if the burns caused by the acid had cut through not just her skin, but her internal fibers as well. The burns, after having caused so much external damage, were now attacking her insides. His testicles contracted with a sharp, quick sting that made him jump. Was she asleep? He might have been able to forget all of this. He might have been able to forget the shock he felt in his testicles. He might have been able to forget the thunderous rattling that came with the nerve-wracking images. He might have been able to forget the face sleeping in a pool of dirty blood. However, the crow and its chicks that were perched over the gap in the window—what was he supposed to do with them? He went over to the door to fetch a bucket of water, and even before lifting the bucket up, he wondered where the sound of rustling wings was coming from, and he also wondered who had opened the window after he'd closed it. They were craning their necks from the window opening, the black bird and its three chicks, surrounded by a halo of translucent light. It was only then that he realized dawn had taken him by surprise. The light gave their feathers a purple sheen, which made them look a little less gloomy. Even now, after the passing of all of these years, he didn't remember whether it was really a crow or that bad-luck seagull that had lost all of its color the day he had gone with Kika to steal the pipes. The bird hopped onto the pillow and proceeded to peck at the bits of flesh, bringing them back to its three chicks as they hopped around it chirping ravenously, their wings flapping boisterously, their beaks opened cavernously wide as if they were smiling, gladdened by the rare feast. They flitted around their mother's open beak with childish impetuousness. Then the sound of birds chirping rose up all around. Birds of every color thrown into the first feast of the day by the rising dawn. All of a sudden the workshop was filled with their noise. Did they want their share of the feast? Or did they just want to provide their own musical accompaniment? They flew around the workshop without landing on anything, flying over the crow and its chicks. Over the pillow that was, little by little, going back to how it had looked before. Over a sleeping Farah. Was she really sleeping, and was what he was seeing actually her dream? The reflection of the dawn's first rays of light on the flapping feathers gave the workshop and everything in it additional color. When he went back to stand beside her, everything was over. There were traces on the pillow, the pale remains of blood, some spots that were no cause for concern. She was looking at him with quizzical eyes—or what remained of them—leaning on her forearm, which had put a small indentation in the pillow. "When did you wake up?" He no longer needed the bucket that was still dangling in his hand. Even before he put the bucket down, even before he thought of putting it down, everything had ended. Except for the silvery smile that continued to shine between the two of them.

At that moment, the man got up. He walked toward the slanted door, but for the first time, he noticed that the door wasn't slanted. It was because the man was walking with his head cocked to one side because of the strange footsteps that were attracting his attention. As if his ear were moving ahead of him. They weren't footsteps that he recognized. Something more lively, with more vitality, brutality, and stubbornness, like the buzzing of a forest full of bees moving forward slowly, with an unbearable calm. Even so, they were still secretive. He stopped, waiting at the door. The blueness of the sky had become even more overbearing. The spikes of grain had turned completely yellow as if they had shrunken and faded. All the fertilizer that had been spread out had either been absorbed by the thirsty soil or evaporated. But now there was a cold wind blowing in the air. It might rain tonight. Little by little, the footsteps turned into what sounded like horses trotting in the distance, approaching insistently. The sound reverberated under his feet. Then he saw what it was. A human throng was coming toward him like a gray cloud creeping over the earth—with all of the contracting and expanding that distinguishes a cloud, and with all of the running, dashing forward, people racing with one another, pushing and pulling that distinguishes a human throng. He could see all of this, but not completely clearly. Then what had been a buzzing sound changed into a complex noise that was difficult to decipher, and what had been a cloud turned into thick swirling dust as it moved forward. The gendarmes' car passed by first. Yes, before the human throng appeared, the car passed by, coming back from someplace or heading someplace. That was how gendarmes' vehicles moved. You didn't know which direction they were heading. The two gendarmes asked the man about the two rabbits. Had they shown up? They let out a piercing laugh, but the car didn't stop. In their haste to rush out of there, their laughter didn't have time to clearly express what it meant. The car disappeared, but the roar of its engine didn't. That was because it was barely there in the first place. The whole area was filled with the other roar. The continuous roar. The human roar.

But they weren't approaching as quickly as the man thought. Crowds always move slowly. The dust dances above them as if swirling in place. Then a part of it began to move, the part closest to the hill. With its dust, its commotion, its jostling. His in-law Salih, the cistern guard, who had come back with the crowd, stood beside him, his rifle on his shoulder, clearing the way for the torrent so it could continue to flow and flood onto the dirt road. Then they all stopped at the same moment before crossing the railroad tracks, a blind sense driving them as precisely as a clock, definitive, even more intense in their silence. The cistern guard said that the children hadn't slept since the previous night. They wanted to catch them. Jokingly, or responding to a joke he had heard before, the man said, "Maybe it has something to do with the two rabbits." The guard responded, "None of them have slept, nor have their children, or their cattle, or their grudges." Children's grudges are blind. That was what betrayed them, at dawn, hiding in the thicket. Maybe they weren't hiding there. In the same joking tone, the man said, "Or maybe it's connected to the two thieves. No thief can remain hiding in the same place until dawn, especially not a cow thief!" The cistern guard said, "This has nothing to do with thieves or cows. A man and a woman. The woman is married and has children. And she does such a thing with a man younger than her children! And where? Out in the open like cats. *There is no power nor strength save for in God*." They all turned around together like a single person and went back the way they had come, with the same enthusiasm, the same persistence.

He saw them now, gathering in a circular motion at the top of the hill. A mixture of colors, signals, riotous sounds, and what looked like hats flying in the air, as if the hats were doing the yelling. Then, at the bottom of the hill, the crowd appeared to be parting. Like two hills being pushed apart by opposing currents. There was only one prey. The first group disappeared behind the hill, but the second continued to move along the path it had been following. Then the two met in a more coherent current, one moving with greater conviction. The current flowed in front of him now like a river whose tributaries had finally come together. It flowed silently toward the same goal, toward the thicket where the children said they had found them at dawn—the young man and his lover, who was old enough to be his mother. Disheveled hair and dusty beards. Eyes white because of the suspense and excitement. Really, they were looking for the woman. Because Salih, the cistern guard, told him before joining the crowd himself that the poor young man was no older than eighteen and that the woman had seduced him. Women are devils, and she's the cause. It was as if they had regressed decades in time. Mouths were opened by an explosion that hadn't yet left their throats. Anticipating the moment they had been waiting for, the moment when the prey would bolt out of its hiding place. All feet were loudly crunching the dirt and stones on the ground with rare resolve. A single cohesive crowd with the image of the anticipated, coveted prey in its sights. The crowd was attracted by the smell even before it spotted and recognized it. The two lovers were out there someplace trying to elude their fate, eyes shining with fear, their faces betraying the same agitation, the same anticipation, in the thicket of trees or in the middle of the forest's dense growth, or by the dam. They hadn't yet determined their whereabouts. The children passed by them at dawn and taunted them with their sticks and stones. They might have thought that they were two young foxes waiting for their mother to come back. And the man? He stood by the gate picturing it all. The fate of the two lovers. Their corpses that would be ripped apart, and their skulls that would be crushed. The crowd disappeared momentarily, and along with it the threat it posed. The man went back to his chair, the judge still lying facedown, pressing his nose between the woman's thighs.

24

The King's Drums

I CLOSE MY EYES AND open them again. I close my eyes and tell myself that it will be there, but when I open them all I see is fog. It also happens that, in a dream, I see that the minaret has disappeared. I'm not sure why that terrifies me and I jump out of bed to see if it is actually gone. The thick ocean fog really has swallowed up quite a bit of it, or else the ocean has washed over it. Some time passes between it disappearing and then reappearing. A lot of time. It might have been an entire morning. After Farah drowned, I went regularly to the mosque and slept in the workshop. Sometimes I slept in the mosque, in the main prayer hall. I noticed that my relationship to it was improving little by little. I spent the morning hours watching the changing colors of the minaret. From here, I don't see it, even when I close my eyes and open them three times in a row; nor can I see the mosque. Usually the minaret is there to welcome me at this time in the morning, though there are mornings when it refuses to do so. Like this morning. This isn't at all connected to the weather. It might disappear even when the weather is clear, as if it had just picked up its stonework and gone to the other side of the ocean, but this rarely happens. Right now, it's obscured by fog and nothing else. I let it take its time. Maybe it has plunged into the ocean's depths to bathe itself, to shake off the steel that's still wrapped around it. It will need a lot of time to wash away its worries and reappear looking clean. When this happens it's always accompanied by the squawking of seagulls. The squawking seagulls drown out all other sounds, including the crashing waves. As long as it remains hidden, the squawking doesn't stop. From time to time, instead of closing my eyes, I crane my neck to extend my gaze, but I don't see it. It has completely disappeared. After an hour of looking for it, not a trace of the minaret can be seen. Maybe it's getting ready to surprise me. And what is Father doing right now? It's been a while since he visited the mosque. What scheme is he cooking up? The cemetery dog showed up three times in the past few days, but then it disappeared. It didn't show up after that. Maybe it was another dog. These kinds of dogs all look the same. And they're there on every street. I'm not that worried. There are many ways to get rid of it should it continue to pose a threat, the most preferable of which is to contact the gang that specializes in snatching dogs, as I said before. Except for the time in the cemetery, and the three times it appeared after that, it has stayed away. Like all the dogs that fill the streets. It keeps its distance as it follows me, far enough to dispel any suspicions, like a spy practicing his craft. Is it the same dog I saw in the cemetery? I slow my pace in order to get as close as possible, trying to get a better look, but it's no use. I have forgotten what the dog looked like. I no longer have the slightest memory of him. All I remember is how he limped as he ran away from the rocks the mourners threw at him. Perhaps there is no connection between the mosque and the monetary contribution, because in the end, with or without the dog, the goal is to crush your spirit bit by bit, as Rihane had told me. To ultimately push you to commit suicide, or toward despair, which is just another form of suicide. That's the plan. To push you little by little to hate life, family, your neighbors, and all of humanity. And even if you don't reach that level of despair, you'll still feel that fear has occupied a distinct place in your heart. I'm not talking about regular fear, human fear. I'm talking about another type of fear known only by the defeated and the oppressed, who can't put a specific name to it. You become a big skeptic, your full-time job being to doubt everything and everyone around you. As you walk down the street or through the market, or when you stop at the tobacconist or the fishmonger, you ask yourself whether any of these people walking alongside you or standing in the same line as you know about you and the mosque. All the while you think they're looking at you differently, suspiciously, hatefully, in a way that's missing something because the matter will have grown larger along the way, and rather than just being about the money you haven't paid, you have become a cursed atheist who mocks the Quran or insults the mysterious sanctities of the state. Their first and last hope is that terror will settle deep inside your very being, that the dog will occupy the deepest recesses of your mind to destroy anything you might set out to do during the day and haunt you in bed at night until you go to their office of your own accord and place a handful of bills on their desk as you apologize for being late, apologizing for everything that you might be responsible for, begging their forgiveness and wishing them and their bosses perpetual good health and long lives. In order to forget about the cemetery dog, I think about Father. And in order to forget about Father and his unfinished ceiling, I think about Kika. And just when I find that I'm feeling fine, I go back to hoping that he has gotten his visa. In the thick silence that wraps itself around me, I picture him in his long coat—the Columbo coat he bought at the flea market last year for just this occasion—hitting the pavement of distant capitals, collar raised and cigarette butt hanging out of the side of his mouth like Columbo. A thin line of smoke twisting upward like a steam viper. And to forget him as well, I begin to count off the capital cities he would visit: Paris, Frankfurt, Stockholm. I watch the minaret appear in New York, Moscow, and Amsterdam. He won't get any farther than Rabat. And to forget the capital cities he'll never visit, I begin to mockingly name the cities he does know: Boujad, Khouribga, Tan-tan, and I burst into laughter. Then I jump! Instead of the minaret I hear the loudspeaker. I had forgotten about the minaret and its loudspeaker. Its siren had never shrieked that way before. Maybe a ship has gotten lost at sea because of the fog. I stand, craning my neck toward where the minaret usually is. Through the fog, I see a specter approaching. It could be the dog. No, from the way it's walking, I think it might be Kika. But instead of Kika, the National Department of Electricity employee appears. He has come to ask for Father's address and request that I go with him to his house. I remain silent. The only thing missing besides some final touches here and there is Father's ceiling. The ceiling—where is it? It seems to me that an opportunity to take revenge on the employee has presented itself to me. That, in and of itself, is too much for me to imagine. I tell him that my father is traveling, as May-mouna had told me.

"And when is he coming back?"

"I don't know. Maybe he won't come back, because he isn't a carpenter anymore."

I see that my words have a negative effect on him, and if I were to continue to sing this tune, maybe he would pull his beard out, or perhaps (seeing as he has no beard) he would rend his clothes. I tell him that he has opened an office for motor-vehicle customs clearance in Agadir, that he is now working in the import-export business. My father is no longer a carpenter. "You didn't know? He only deals with foreign countries now."

The employee takes a piece of paper out of his pocket and, with a shaking hand, begins to record all the ridiculous things that come out of my mouth. "He exports animal feed to Turkey and Japan. He has contracted with the Turks to make ceilings of glass for them, but he'd prefer to be Japanese, so he went to apply for Japanese citizenship." Then I see him tear up the piece of paper and walk away until he is swallowed up by the fog that brought him.

25

Two days ago, we were about to take my sister Khadija to the mental hospital. By the time afternoon rolled around, she was still the same as she had been. The rain hissed lightly on the windows, like a soothing piece of music being played far away. A rain that couldn't be seen from this side of the glass, with no clear sign that it was falling. You could only imagine it. If not for its rhythmic hiss and slight tapping on the glass from time to time, you wouldn't know it was raining at all. We were waiting for the car to come. The damp flagstones of the street were also awaiting its arrival. Abdullah didn't go get the car because he was no longer meddling in our affairs, and we weren't asking anything of him anymore, either. We left him in his corner to make up for all the prayers he'd missed. Habiba was no longer menstruating because she was pregnant. Happy in her second month. The baby was going to be a boy to compensate for his brothers who died. That's why Habiba was chewing on clove leaves. From now until the birth, a large cooking pot with no bottom would sit next to her for the newborn baby to pass through as soon as it was born, before they wash it, so it can be freed from the clutches of the djinn Oum al-Subyan. Mother was the one who went out to call for the car because my sister, Khadija, was sick. Very sick. She had colored pens she used to draw her desires all over her skin, as if on a piece of leather she found on the road. She drew maps of desires which she had left behind in the house of her husband Omar, or Hassan, or Hussein. "Are we going to take Auntie to the hospital?" Karima asked as she gathered up pieces of cloth scattered around Mother and her sewing machine, throwing them in front of me so I could make a small doll that looked like her. It wouldn't look like her with all these different-colored scraps of cloth. She insisted that the doll have blond hair even though Karima wasn't blond. After she said this, I began to picture the car that would take Khadija away. It would look like the ones used for transporting dead bodies, with the same white color and green lettering.

Ever since she came back home, she'd been asking from her bedroom about her bed and whether it had arrived yet. No, not yet. She complained about the pain in her head. Would it hurt less if she got her bed back? Whenever she put her head down on her pillow, she remembered the missing bed. Her weakened body relaxed to the rhythm of this absence. Then the pain moved to her stomach, and from her stomach to her knees. Sometimes she couldn't stand. A mental shock had transformed Khadija. "Is Auntie going to die?" asked Karima as she listened to her singing in the next room. We no longer recognized her either. For days after she came back, she sat behind the sewing machine. Mother wasn't expecting any help from her because she had returned with her old depression. The machine turned all day long without any cloth in it, as if she were stitching the emptiness going around inside her head. Sitting in front of the sewing machine but not paying attention, as if she had lost all connection to what once connected her to it. She didn't utter a word, and when she did open her mouth, it was to ask whether her bed had arrived. She didn't respond to anyone. She only spoke at night, when the lights had been put out and we were asleep. Then the sewing machine went silent, and Mother said that maybe her condition had improved. Yes, my sister forgot all about the machine, but instead she had become obsessed with her body. She spent an inordinate amount of time washing and brushing her hair. Then, to dry her body off, she spent even more time walking around the house wrapped in a single towel that barely covered her. Her hair would still be wet. Droplets of water would fall onto her bare shoulders. The white towel came to her knees. A thin line of water still flowed over her thighs. Mother, who only had her worries to lean on, wiped away tears we couldn't see. She had aged since her white hair appeared this morning. Habiba sprinkled salt around her belly to ward off the evil eye. Abdullah hung Quranic verses over the windows and doors to keep the Angel of Death from getting too close to the house. He told her that the embryo is formed according to how the man wants it to. If he gives his wife something soft to eat, she'll bear him a daughter, and if he gives her something hard, she'll bear a son. All of this so he didn't have to turn toward where Khadija, damp and practically naked, walked by. (I wondered how Abdullah avoided stealing a glance at Khadija's body while passing so close to it!) Then she began to scent her body with every perfume she could lay her hands on. She'd mix her perfumes with water when the bottles were nearly done. Or fill them with orange blossom water when they were empty, or saffron, or lavender if she could find it. Then, in the end, with plain water. No rose or orange blossom or lavender. The house was filled with all sorts of strange smells that surrounded and moved with her like a cloud. Mother said that we would take her to the venerable saint Sidi Wafi. I didn't know where this saint's tomb was, but according to Mother, he treats these sorts of illnesses because he isn't human. There is a group of djinns under his command that specialize in treating all sorts of diseases. Then Khadija's condition got worse, and she started saying that her body was coming apart. Her limbs were coming off, leaving her. She would stick her legs out in front of her for hours. Or, with her colored pens, she would draw lines on her body between the limbs that had gone and those waiting their turn to go. And when she got up, she moved around the house .

211

carefully so as to keep her body parts from falling off onto the tiles in front of us. She walked haltingly like an old lady. Then we got too embarrassed to look at her for very long, and that was when Mother said that we'd take her to the mental hospital. I didn't agree with this suggestion because patients in hospitals—when they weren't tied up with heavy chains, their faces hidden under hair resembling halfah grass, filthy, their clothes torn and their fingernails looking like eagles' talons—wandered the hospital corridors begging for alms. Women were strewn like corpses under beds in dark, gloomy rooms. I knew all of this to be true, even though I'd never visited a mental hospital before.

Until today, when she tore up her shirt, she had only asked about one thing—her bed. I didn't have a clear picture of what was going to happen to my sister when Mother left the house this morning, nor when she came back and sat behind her machine as if she hadn't gone anywhere, as if she weren't waiting for anyone to come; sitting in front of the silent sewing machine with her forearms leaning on it, her head resting on her forearms. The rain tapped monotonously. The afternoon sauntered along even more monotonously, calmly marching toward its conclusion, moving forward with the same stifling monotony as if it were not moving at all. After Mother came back she was grave, absent. Was she thinking about her family that was breaking apart? When the car finally stopped in front of the door, I thought that maybe she was feeling some regret because she was about to send her daughter off to the mental hospital, and that she was rethinking her decision. I saw the black cloth that covered her head, and the white hair that spilled out from beneath the cloth. I hadn't noticed before that Mother had grown old. She lifted her head slowly, as if she had heard what I was thinking. She was wearing glasses. I hadn't noticed before that she had started wearing glasses. I saw Mother's head turn, and at the same time saw my sister Khadija. She came out of her room no longer wrapped in her white towel. She was wearing a pale shirt and had her colored pens in her hand. With the same hesitant gait, she walked by without seeing us, and disappeared behind the bathroom door. Karima handed me a piece of red cloth and told me that this was the hair she wanted for her doll.

The street's cobblestones weren't wet anymore because the car from the mental hospital had arrived and now covered them completely. Its whiteness covered them up. White, but without the green lettering I'd been expecting. The two men at the open door wavered between waiting and entering. They were both extremely tall and thin. One of them was wearing a white lab coat and the other a black suit. They were both wearing knee-high boots, ridiculously high. Karima left the cloth in my hand and rushed toward the two men, laughing at them before asking about the car. "Did it come to take Auntie to the hospital?" They didn't respond. They came in now and stood scowling in the entryway. Their faces were old. They didn't betray a specific age, as if they had been born with these wrinkled expressions. The one in the black suit leaned a little to one side as he walked, but his limp was otherwise unnoticeable. His eyes were blackened with kohl. The walls of our house were bare. They passed their eyes over the walls as if expecting my sister to burst out from one of them. No, Khadija was hiding behind this door right here. They came into the middle of the foyer. Into our midst. We all looked at one another, and then at the closed door. I pictured my sister behind it. I pictured her decorating her body with her colored pens. Then I pictured her gathering up her scattered body parts. I didn't know what the two men were picturing. Maybe they weren't picturing anything at all. They were waiting for Khadija to come out of the bathroom so they could take her to the mental hospital, as Mother said. Now she was holding back real tears. Karima walked up to Mother. "I wanna go with Auntie. I wanna go with Auntie." Habiba scolded her and she quieted down. There was no movement from behind the door, nor was there any sound to disturb the rain's hissing. Outside, some windows closed and others opened as if to set the oppressive, monotonous rhythm. Some women stood in the doorway looking in at us. Habiba shooed them away with her hand as if they were chickens. The women disappeared from the doorway, but their feet were still visible from behind the car. Karima now clung to the pants of the man with the black suit. "I wanna ride in the car! I wanna ride in the car!" She ran up to the car door and opened it.

Then we heard the creaking of the bathroom door. The creaking went on for a little bit and stopped. We stood there peering into the dark emptiness that the creaking had left behind. She came out naked as the day she was born, her torn-up shirt dragging behind her, her body inscribed with every color—circles and lines in red, green, and blue—as if she had stolen one of Father's secrets. Her breasts shone dirty white in the middle of all of this, like two lamps she had forgotten about and left lit. Her black hair flowed down onto her adorned shoulders. We stood there dumbfounded. She asked the two men standing in the foyer whether they had brought her bed. Abdullah pulled her by the arm before she could take another step, pushed her into his room, and locked the door behind them. All eyes continued to stare, fixed on the cloud of smells, colors, and questions that Khadija had left behind.

We all stood there like strangers. After a few minutes, Khadija's voice rose up from Abdullah's room, first a soft moan, then a yell that sounded like laughter, neither soft nor loud. The men were no longer in a hurry. We heard the sound of the wooden bed creaking. The men were no longer in any hurry at all. It was absolutely silent. There was no movement in the foyer, a suspended stillness—like a rope that had temporarily broken, that only needed another laugh for its two ends to join back together. But this laugh that sounds more like a scream never came. We could only hear it in our heads. Other, incomplete, images float around our house. The moaning inside the room started up again, rising and falling, yet remaining constant, interrupted periodically by broken whispers. Following this, there was a single laugh, loud, like a cry for help. What was happening to my sister in Abdullah's room? Mother got up, hands on her knees for support, as she muttered, "Good lord!" The bedroom door opened and Khadija appeared wrapped in a black selham. Nothing of her could be seen. The black selham passed before us, went into its room, and locked the door behind it. Mother clapped her hands as if to say to us that today's party was over. The cloth that Karima had given me was still in my hand, and the blond doll Karima was waiting for had been born disfigured—two sticks forming a cross and wrapped around them were the gathered pieces of cloth. We had no time to worry about that now. The one wearing the black suit took out a small notebook and went over it one last time with his kohl-painted eyes, as if he were concluding one of the chapters in our family's story. He passed the notebook to his companion, who gave it a passing glance, then walked toward Mother. I rushed over and signed on some lines that no one read. Everyone was in a hurry. Waiting to get our house back. The rain tapping on the windows continued with the same indifference. And us? Embarrassed. Demoralized. Destroyed. Happy in the end, or with what seemed to be the end.

26

WE HEARD THE SOUND OF machines even before we crossed over the wires, stopping in the middle of the courtyard that was covered with prickly grass. We didn't go as far as the storage shed door. That was because Father appeared—looking like he had before, all covered in sawdust, happier than he'd ever been, in the bloom of youth, beaming because of a victory we hadn't yet seen, hands on his hips in a deliberate challenge, surrounded by four black guys standing in the same challenging way—preventing us from going any farther. The National Department of Electricity employee seemed small in front of him, worthless and lacking any authority. All of a sudden, he no longer seemed as intimidating as he had before. To be honest, he seemed insignificant to me, inspiring not the slightest bit of fear after his initial defeat. Then, when he came back after a few days, asking whether Father had returned from his travels, he didn't wait around for me to come up with a lie on par with those about the export office, Japanese citizenship, and Turkish animal feed. He just handed me a hundred-dirham bill as soon as he stopped in front of me, a bill I was in most urgent need of. From that moment on, he became the most insignificant person as far as I was concerned, like someone you could easily pass by anywhere without giving a second glance or paying any attention to at all. I could have closed up the workshop and headed down to the beach, leaving him standing at the door like a beggar. I

really could have told him that he had come back from Agadir and flown to Tokyo (this last thought almost caused me
to break out into hysterical laughter). And I could have quite
simply asked for another bill or two. But I remembered the
ceiling the employee had talked about before. The four black
guys looked like they were charged with guarding someone
important. Their faces had the same stern look Father's had,
like a well-trained gang, organized and ready. What could the
employee do? I had never seen him look so fragile. So much
so that I wondered where the fear he used to inspire had gone.
Right then, it would have been better for him to go get his
pail and fishing rod, and head down to the shore rather than
ask about the ceiling or make a fuss about why it was delayed.
Unfortunately, he didn't have this gear with him, and anyway,
it only would have made him appear even more insignificant.
The image of him carrying what looked to be a pail and fishing rod, with the smell of sardines rising from him, cheered
me up in a way I hadn't expected it to.

It was as if we were in an arena, with me watching two
wrestlers and knowing in advance which way the match was
going to go. They stood there facing one another for a while,
each evaluating the strength of his opponent as if trying to
intimidate the other one first. Each concealed the weapons he
had sharpened beforehand, or at least tried to make it look that
way. I walked away a bit so as to retain the drama of the scene.
I stood not too far away, between the two of them, like the
referee; a referee who knew from the start that he was going to
side with one of the two opponents, no matter which way the
battle went. Like someone watching two contestants he knew
very well in open battle, but who pretended that he didn't know
either of them so as not to make the match appear to be rigged.
But he leaned in favor of one of them. Not because of kinship
or blood, but because of a defiant, solemn stance, or because
of each combatant's past history. Out of sympathy for him,
because of the hands on his hips, he favored the man covered

in sawdust. Father shifted his weight from one leg to the other now, like someone who knew how the fight would turn out, and said, "Everything comes in due time," as he looked at the black guys rather than the employee. In a voice containing a little modesty, and quite a bit of mockery, the employee responded, "What time, Si Omar? The time has passed."

"Everything comes in due time."

The only thing missing from the mosque was Father's ceiling.

Working, working. His words were filled with contempt. They contained hatred for his adversary even before they'd climbed into the ring. "Everything comes in due time . . ." His ideas only emerged from his head when he pleased. Thoughts had their moods.

"Do you know anything about wood, my good employee? Do I know anything about electricity? Why don't you worry about your job? What *is* your job? Stringing electrical cables? Well then, string your cables and leave us alone."

"And the ceiling?"

"Why doesn't everyone just stick to where they belong? Do you understand anything about wood, ornamentation, and coloring? Do you know what Casablanca red is? Do you know, first of all, who invented it?"

"But where's the ceiling?"

"It's around."

"Can we see it?"

"No."

The four black guys with their broad arms crossed over their chests moved closer to Father, as if assuring the employee that there was more abuse to come. What flowed from Father's tongue came to resemble a song. That's because Father was a poet. Does the employee even know anything about a thing called poetry? What is paronomasia? What are homonyms? Does the National Department of Electricity employee know what juxtaposition is? It is shade and light together, one next to the other. Now I was hearing Father's old, true voice. I recognized it, and I could tell from its tone that he was intoxicated. Now he recounted his glories. Then he moved to his favorite story—the sixty-sided sittiniya dome that he constructed in the Dar Pasha house. "Do you even know what a sittiniya is? Three full years to make one dome." And his story with the pasha? Does the employee know it? To this day, all Marrakechis recall and recount it. Once, while he was explaining to the pasha what he was doing as the pasha watched him walking in circles around the courtyard for three full days, touching neither wood nor chisel, nor mixing a color, Father told him, "I'm a poet, not a carpenter forced to work out of necessity. I've never begged in exchange for my art." He picked up his tools and carried them back to his house. After a week, he went back to work in the pasha's palace and the pasha didn't ask about anything anymore. He didn't say a word to him about how late the work was or why he stood there with his nose in the air watching the stars at noon. He gave him all the money, food, and clothing he needed and left him alone with his creativity. After three years, the dome was revealed. It was the sittiniya dome, none other.

"And the ceiling, where is it?"

"Someone like me," my father said, "needs more time in order to finish work that's on par with the sittiniya—that might even be better than it—because I'm a poet, not just any old carpenter slapping together cheap, crummy wood or making cupboards to sell in the market. Just finding the right wood is a difficult task. Cedar wood, but not just any cedar. Rather, cedar that when you smell it you say, 'That's it . . . that's it.' You fall in love with it at first sight, and you feel in your heart that it shares the same feeling for you. Then you need to allow sufficient time for each piece to find its special rhythm. The two tempos that will be like Neruda's 'Canto General.'"

The employee's voice was lost in the poetic din. "And the ceiling, where is it?"

"Do *I* understand medicine, or engineering, or radar? Every profession has its experts. This is how the world has always been." He laughed, happy, intoxicated, pleased with this last sentence. The tone of his voice changed, as if he were giving lessons to uninterested students. "When it has to do with carving wood, when it has to do with choosing wood, first of all, and then with preparing it, you won't find a better hand than this one. Then there's the other hand that ornaments it in a way you won't find in any book—gardens, forests, butterflies, or seashells . . . or all of this together . . . or nothing of the sort. Your emotions are what put these visions before you. In the end, they're nothing more than squares, circles, and triangles. Meticulously well-fitted shapes."

The employee had already left.

27

THE MINARET WASN'T GREEN. A half hour passed as we hung on halfway up the minaret, yelling, cursing everyone on the face of the earth as long as no one could hear us from so high up. We yelled ourselves hoarse. From here we could see that we were against everyone, against everything. As if the shackles that fastened us to the ground had been broken. Kika and I were happy sitting on the metal bars, legs dangling in the air. Nothing more than a weak sound emerged from our mouths at this point as we shouted and laughed. We had used up the last of our voices, yelling out our protest. But we were happy nonetheless. Especially Kika, who continued to yell louder than I was so he could forget all about the visa. His mother had gone to Spain after New Year's. Kika continued to believe that some sort of mistake had been made at the consulate. Then he thought that the people in the consulate had taken revenge on him because of the chaos he had caused at its door, and rather than stamp the visa into his passport, they skipped over it and stamped his mother's. But he'd practically forgotten all about that now. Hundreds of seagulls gathered above us—white, gray, distant—floating in the morning clouds like a swarm of flies sliding across an overturned piece of ice. I scoffed at Kika when he said the minaret was green. I didn't contradict him, even though he was wrong. Now the seagulls were gathering in large numbers above us, as if preparing for their winter journey, even though they're birds that don't migrate. As they clumped together it made them look darker. Seagulls aren't always white. In this way they're like the minaret, which only looks green at certain times of the day. Contrary to what Kika says, the minaret spends the rest of its time changing colors— from bright white to deep black. The minaret changes color according to people's moods. Kika's hand felt warm on my shoulder. My shoulder was glad to be so close to this warmth. I remained silent as long as the hand stayed on my shoulder. The feeling remained, along with all the confidence it provided me. I didn't move. I didn't utter a single word lest the hand on my shoulder should move away. We were still suspended half-way up the minaret when this happened. We heard a distant boom that sounded like a large rolling boulder. Then we realized it was the beating of drums, like the ones you would hear in wars long ago. We scurried down as fast as our arms and legs could take us as the roar of the drums drew closer, until the awesome structure appeared, obscured amid a group of bois-terous, clamorous people. We couldn't say who these drums were beating for. We didn't understand yet what was going on.

The appearance of the ceiling surprised us both as we stood at the base of the minaret. We didn't know that it was Father's ceiling until it was right in front of us. I should have recognized it from the smell. An enormous structure made of wood, as high as a small mountain, arched like a lid. The inside of it wasn't visible just yet. Upside down like a bell. Tied down with thick ropes, lying flat on a platform with four wooden wheels being led forward by dozens of young black men. Their clothing was highly ornamented and they were wearing red and yellow caps on their heads, with braids of the same vivid colors dangling from them. Their faces were painted with yellow and red lines. Light sandals were fastened with straps that went up their legs. Behind them were other black men beating the drums. These ones were barefoot and their legs were muddy. Their faces were painted white, which made their thick lips appear redder than they actually were, and their eyes appeared shinier. Large earrings that hung from their pierced ears were jangling. Their chests were bare and adorned with clusters of white shells or yellow frankincense. Pulled up around their midsections they had plaited belts made of straw and hemp, green as grape leaves, going down to their knees and inlaid with colored shells. The cart passed by and the strange procession stopped in front of the minaret, right in front of us. On top of the high ceiling, Father sat cross-legged. Over his shoulders he wore his black selham, which was embroidered with gold thread that sparkled delicately, as if he had come bearing gifts for a king of long ago. His beard was carefully trimmed. In his hand was a cane that looked like a scepter. On his face there was a calm dignity, or I should say, his face had no expression whatsoever, as if it was appropriately frozen, in its final state. The entire scene was completely ridiculous. Drums beating. Bare-chested black men dancing. Behind them there was a rainbow. One of them stepped out of line and pointed to Father, yelling in his ancient language that resembled tumbling pebbles. A thunderous, collective yell followed in the same ancient language, making the same clamorous noise. With the same enthusiasm. With these black men dancing, having donned the costumes of their distant tribes for Father, with these drums beating for Father, with the rainbow that had risen up behind them painting the cloudy sky with its captivating colors, and with the minaret that stood out now in all its majesty, as if we were standing on the steps of a virtuous saint's tomb, and it was the time of year to visit him. The only thing missing was the sacrificial animal. The black men danced to the beat of the drums, kicking the muddy ground. The mud reverberating with their stomping. Bodies dissolved into the African rhythm. The bus that brought the tourists stopped on the main road and the tourists hurried out with their cameras so as not to miss the extraordinary scene. They stood along the sidewalk as if at a public performance, their cameras flashing blindingly.

The black men's muscles danced to the beat of the drums. Sturdy, well-formed muscles. Dramatic. Sweaty. I put my hand on Kika's. I was relaxed, completely relaxed. The sun's rays were silver, faint. They pierced the cloud cover. Its rays fell onto the sweaty black skin in lightning-quick flashes, bestowing a captivating color on this spontaneous carnival. Father raised his cane and the procession started up again as we walked behind it toward the mosque.

Did his resounding fall show on his face as he sat there so broken? When I walked up to him, touched his shoulder, and he didn't turn toward me? Laid out on his back without his embroidered selham or scepter, without the pomp that had lasted for just a few minutes. In the middle of the mosque's empty courtyard. Above him, his cracked ceiling. The tourists had left, as had the black men. Perhaps his fall had appeared on his face even before that moment, while he was making his way toward the minaret surrounded by his strange entourage, as happens in real life. Like that man who walks obliviously along the sidewalk, hands clasped behind his back, when all of a sudden, for no logical reason, without the slightest justification, without turning right or left, without raising his head to see what the building he's passing by looks like, head bowed, he just walks by, but he might be thinking about something. That is to say that somehow, he sees what will eventually happen to him. The stone that will crush his head isn't there at all. Or perhaps it is there, but it can't be seen. He still pretends that it's in the hand of the worker who's fixing holes in the roof. Or maybe he can convince the worker that it's a stone that won't fall. Rather, its task is to plug up all the holes in anticipation of the coming rain. A distance separates them, and there's enough time for the passerby to walk safely by. The man walking by pauses for a moment, a second, just a fraction of a second, which is all that's needed for the stone to lodge itself in his skull. That's because the man passing by can see the stone before it falls, he sees it in his imagination, falling with a single blow. Baaf! The whole time that exists between him and the accident, all his mind does as he pauses, looking for something in his pocket or tying his shoe, is prepare for this blow that won't come as any surprise. Perhaps that was what Father saw as he sat cross-legged on his throne, calm, grave-faced, distracted. In any event, his face had shown nothing except for what was about to happen to him. It might have been there even before he arrived sitting cross-legged on his ceiling like a king from bygone days, surrounded by his new entourage of black men, calm, with no distinguishable expression on his face. Maybe he had brought his fall with him from his house, and it had been with him the whole time he worked on constructing his ceiling. It had been with him night and day. It had slept with him in bed and traveled with him. That is to say that the fall was there, built into the ceiling as well.

For the tourists, in the mosque's open patio, when we finally went in, Father became an eloquent guide, his tongue overflowing with everything he hadn't said during his long years of silence. Ladders and scaffolds rose up, ropes were pulled tight, tractors were hitched, and the ceiling slowly lifted. Workers held on to the ceiling from every side, leaning as it leaned, with the young black men helping them. The young black men had changed back into their everyday clothes, their everyday look. And what was Father doing right then? He was like a ship's captain steering his boat toward its final harbor. He walked around his rising ceiling, examining it as closely as he pleased. A broad smile split his face as he followed the ceiling up with his eyes. Then he stopped and remained there for a moment, frowning, thinking, at the height of excitement. I tried to read Father's face to figure out where his thinking was headed in this rare moment. I saw fishermen storm the mosque's patio with their yellow raincoats, baskets, and rods. I saw the employee approaching. His black cap bobbed right and left, and I could practically hear him exhaling. I asked myself whether he felt the same amount of pride that Father did. Had the anger he felt toward him last time subsided? Had he forgotten about the insults? Then the ceiling appeared above us, dazzling. Gasps of wonder rose up. The most beautiful ceiling my eyes had ever seen. Carvings descended like colored snowflakes from melting snow. So smooth. Ornamentation in red, green, and gold. Channels of blue that gave off just the right amount of tranquility between the descending colors. A forest motif surrounded by little arch-shaped pieces embracing one another on a red background. Father didn't stop talking. "This ceiling that you're looking at contains eighty stars." He began to count them, pointing to each one, explaining, "This is how every part is formed; each has its own fixed shape and size. Nothing can be added or taken away without destroying the complete homogeneity of it." Then Father lifted his cane toward the center of the ceiling and, as if justifying his enthusiasm more than anything else, said, "That in the center is an egg-shaped medallion decorated with fine, interlocking palm fronds on a blue background that brings to mind the overall theme." Father passed his hand over his white hair. I watched the employee rather than him, but I listened only to Father's voice. "There can be no humans or animals or anything else without the connections that tie them together. There exists nothing but connections, neither in the world of human beings nor in the world of objects." He pointed to the other side of the ceiling as if, after an entire lifetime, he had finally found the ideal audience for his creativity. "The totality of this vegetal ornamentation is decorated with gradually fading colors—rose, gray, and green—mixed in with contrasting shadows. Here is a repeating pattern, here is its opposite. Here we have symmetry and contrast, and over here we have a pattern of another type. Contrast and juxtaposition for a shape made up of four elements. Patterns repeating without interruption. They'll remain in your heads even after you've left."

He explained things primarily for the tourists. He didn't consider us. He didn't consider the sweating workers. He didn't consider the black men who were celebrating his achievement. Without actually saying it to us, it was as if he wanted to make us feel that what he was saying was more than we could understand. He explained it to the tourists and their cameras, which hadn't stopped flashing: "I didn't study in a university, but I know things by way of a special sense. There is nothing more beautiful than nature. The shapes of plants and the way they grow according to a known numerical equation that existed yesterday and will remain the same tomorrow. I don't add a thing. I merely take forms from nature and vary them so the eye doesn't grow weary or become bored, know what I mean? The form will deteriorate if the connections between its constituent parts are unclear and undefined. If that happens, a feeling of dissatisfaction will be the result. Same thing if one of the parts is too big compared to another. A feeling of satisfaction comes over me when there's balance and restraint between different parts." Father sat on an improvised chair. He took a break. He wiped away some sweat that we couldn't see. That was because a change had come over Father's face. He looked disturbed. Something was bothering him. I walked up to him and touched his shoulder. Rather than turn around, he craned his neck, looking hard and long at the ceiling. What did he see? Then he got up, his face changing color— an unnerving pall came over it. It went on this way for what seemed like a long time. In the meantime, the tourists withdrew. The show was over. The black men withdrew as well. The mosque's patio emptied. Everyone walked away while Kika and I stood where we were. Father stood in the middle looking up. We lifted our heads and looked in the same direction. Right then, something caused him to stiffen. He took a step backward. I might have realized what he had realized. Only those who know about the decorative arts could see what Father and I saw. He pulled the ladder over and climbed up.

His hand touched the wood. He came back down and saw that the crack wasn't visible from below. He climbed up again. He tried to move the ceiling. It didn't budge. He pushed hard on it. The ladder tilted, and I saw Father falling. We took two steps backward so he wouldn't fall on top of us. I walked over, leaned over him, and touched his shoulder. Then I moved him, to see if there was any blood under his head.

28

Night. A night we're not a part of. We're busy with other things. Sitting on our neighbor, the baker's doorstep watching the entranceway to our house. Kika smokes while I count the people going in who have come to offer words of consolation. In addition to some lit windows, there's a dim lamp that casts a small spot of light, and we're in it. Other than this, the street is sunk in the blackness of night. Kika leaves the spotlight. His cigarette flickers intensely in the darkness. He hasn't forgotten about the visa. There's nothing funny about it, but I secretly laugh because our neighbor Kenza is the one honoring the Spanish streets of Malaga, Madrid, and Barcelona with her presence. There are many cities in Spain, and even more streets. From now on she hopes not to find any Moroccans who will fuck her, or Spanish men who are like the Moroccan ones. The most she hopes for (the most any woman can hope for) is to find men to fuck who don't beat her after emptying their massive loads. His mother, our neighbor Kenza, is the one who got the visa rather than her son. After so many long months of going back and forth, sometimes sleeping propped up against the embassy wall. Isn't that funny? But I don't laugh because I don't want him to become even more enraged (though there's a tremendous laugh stuck in my throat just waiting for the chance to burst out). I know what he's feeling; I know he sees now that he's not going anywhere. A visa good for a year! And his mother is the one who got it. She can come and go whenever she pleases. With this stamp in her passport, Kenza can cross many borders. She can cross the whole Spanish Kingdom if she wants—Seville, Granada, Zaragoza. Kika is the one who bought the brown overcoat to show off to the blondes of Amsterdam after traveling across so many kingdoms and republics. Then he was to marry a Dutch woman, or a Belgian. But her poor son Kika has no luck. He punches the wall, having come back to the spotlight. He chews on his lit cigarette. I stand and avoid looking at Kika in order to keep from bursting out laughing.

The few people walking by brush along the wall like shadows or ghosts. We don't hear the sound of their shoes. Some of them go into our house to offer condolences to Mother. "Did he die?" "We don't know, sister, whether he's died or whether he's hanging on somewhere between life and death." With people like this, we're not sure how to act anymore. We're all waiting for the doctor who will settle the matter. We've been waiting since noon, but the doctor hasn't arrived yet. He took his children to the circus to watch the lion tamer put his head into the lion's mouth, and as long as the tamer's head remained inside the lion's mouth, all we could do was wait. Women go into our house, but most of the men don't. Some of them don't even know what's going on inside. They continue on their way for a few moments before the darkness swallows them up. I'm not sure why I decide to speak to Kika about a letter that doesn't even exist. Everything I hadn't said while we were hanging off of the minaret's steel scaffolding comes back to me now. I tell him it arrived this morning from my brother Suleiman, and I pretend to remove a piece of paper from my pocket then put it back in. "This is his most recent letter, Kika." Even if I had waved it in front of him, Kika wouldn't have cared because it was too dark for him to see it, much less read it. He sits back down next to me. "His fourth letter, Kika. Do you know what letters are good for? They're not good for anything, really. Suleiman says that the papers are ready, and that even the agent who will take care of me is ready and waiting. Housing, salary, car, the plane ticket that will take me, and all the other wonderful things I'll see when I'm there. And when I come back it'll be with two gold watches, one on each wrist, and gold chains around my neck. All I need is a few administrative rubber stamps. This is how administrative offices do things." I don't know if talking about the letter is starting to make Kika angry or not, because he remains stone-faced. "Administrative offices love to take their time. This is well known. But in the end you start to think the same way they do. After a while, though, I won't even have to think about this anymore. In two months. Once I'm there. Comfortable. Suleiman and I. Our pockets full, drinking beer on the sixty-fifth floor, on the balcony of a ten-star hotel. Doesn't that sound good, Kika? As for the letter itself, whether or not we can see it in the dark, whether or not we can read it, how about the news it contains, eh? What do you think? The plane will take me over land and sea. It'll fly me over all sorts of countries—Algeria, Tunisia, Libya, Egypt, Senegal, and if it takes a sharp turn, we'll see Somalia too, even Ethiopia. I won't get another chance to see all these countries in one trip, Kika." Then I ask him, "How many hours is it to Abu Dhabi?"

Kika gets up and disappears into the darkness. I laugh. The laugh doesn't come out as I'd hoped it would, but I laugh anyway.

Women from who knows where are going into our house to offer consolations. Their mournful keening comes into the circle of light even before they appear, but it doesn't disappear when they do. Inside our house the mourners cry. Up until now, they have been gently weeping. It has a painful echo on this dark night. If Father has died, why don't I smell cooking? The deceased's family isn't supposed to light the cooking fire. The neighbors are the ones who cook. They cook, set the tables, and eat. And why do people love to eat so much at times like these? Why do they want to eat so badly in the house where someone has died? To fortify themselves. To know that they are still alive, and to reassure themselves that this time they too have been saved. Death missed their house and knocked on their neighbor's door. And passersby, so as to banish death from their own houses, go into their neighbor's house and gobble down his food in order to confirm that he has died. They eat in proportion to how far they think they are from death. But they can't eat forever. One day they'll be all full. One day they will have had enough. One day death will catch them. One day death will grab them by their throats. One day they'll stop eating. And one day they'll die, like those who stopped eating before them. As I mull this over, I start to feel hungry. I long to see the deceased laid out on my bed in my dimly lit room. From inside, in place of the smell of food, the mourners' wailing emerges more forcefully. I get up so as not to think more about food than the topic deserves, and go into the house.

The foyer is filled with women. It smells of lavender, cloves, henna. The smell of women. That's what gives the impression that death is present. The women's eyes are red from so much crying. Most of them lower their eyes when I walk in. Women sway left and right, moaning softly as if their wailing tanks are empty and all they have left is this low-level moaning. It's their way of sharing in the family's sadness, even though there's no reason for them to keen so embarrassingly. None of them have a reason to be sad. He's neither their father nor their uncle. He's not related to them in any way. I don't know where they keep all the sadness that leaks out of their faces at times like these. Women are always sad, but they love these occasions. They hope that opportunities for offering condolences will never stop coming. My sister Khadija sits among them, but she doesn't cry. She's the total opposite of my sister Habiba, who slaps her cheeks nonstop as she looks all around her, no one paying any attention to her. Khadija is brushing her knee-length hair. It tumbles down and covers her face and chest. Her fingers dig into her hair and pick at each strand with extreme care. Then she puts some oil in the palm of her hand and rubs it over her jet-black hair underneath the hijab, massaging and massaging from the nape of her neck all the way to the tips of her hair resting on her knee. Other women are done with their share of crying and are taking a break now. The few men who are there are in Abdullah's room. I know they're deep in conversation about the hereafter and the punishment of the grave as they wait for the doctor and his family to leave the circus. They couldn't have come up with a better topic to discuss even if they wanted to. I hear roaring laughter, so I turn around. It's Mother who is laughing as she comes out of her room. She's rocking back and forth on high heels I have never seen her wear before, and she has on a green, gold-embroidered kaftan that shines in the light coming down from the ceiling. She says she doesn't see any reason for sadness or tears. She stands with us all around her—looking livelier, more youthful, with kohl-blackened eyes and reddened cheeks—as if she has just come from the hair salon. Standing up straight in her high heels, she's happy because God has saved her. Her gray hair disappears underneath a scarf adorned with orange and blue roses. God has liberated her from the sadness she has lived with her husband. He has saved her from the pain and suffering she had tasted because of him. Now she has to thank her Lord and thank Him again. She releases a relaxed laugh, playfully hitting the shoulder of the woman beside her. God has shown her His love and sent her this gift. There couldn't be a more valuable gift. And she has no place in her house for mourners. "If there's anyone who wants to cry, she can go to *her* house. The one gift that God can give to a woman in life is to hasten the time of her husband's death." She turns on the television. The women stop crying, talking, and everything else. The singing coming from the box distracts them. It soothes them. It dispels their discomfort. Brahim El Alami the singer, the one with the red hair and the long coat, gets them singing while Mother dances to the song's tune. "Leave me far away. I'm afraid of falling for you." She moves to the rhythm of El Alami's music. And what do the other women do? The celebration surprises them and they are unprepared. They have cried enough. Luckily, Mother reminds them of that. Could there be a better time to celebrate the death of a tyrant? Then Mother pulls one of the neighbors in to dance with her. Khadija gets into the middle of the circle to dance as well. This is a singular occasion, not to be missed. Dancing instead of fretting about a dead man who doesn't deserve a single tear to be shed over his corpse. Relief doesn't come every day. A woman asks Mother to turn the volume down because the dead can hear us, can distinguish our voices, and can even recognize whose feet are doing the dancing. The woman pushes the button and the singer's voice disappears. The dead can still hear for a while. The dead can hear what's going on in their house. They can hear the water boiling. They recognize the hand that places the embalming herbs into the water. They know the hands that stitch the shroud. They know the mouth that wishes them well *and* the mouth that comes up with bad things to say about them. Most of the time the dead take this moment to seek refuge by fleeing. Without stopping her dancing, Mother says, "If God takes him to Him, there's no possible way he'll come back."

I take a few steps across the men's room and look down at him. At Father. He's lying on his back in the weak lamplight. Completely dead. In his final repose. His hair is blazing white. I get closer to him and see that he looks like he's sleeping. From here, death doesn't appear to be too painful. I hear the music and turn. I see Mother leaning against the television and pushing the volume button. The singer's voice fills the foyer once again. I turn back to the deceased and see him lying on his back as he was before, except that his eyes are open. There's no sign of death in them. Completely open and looking toward the crack in the door. What does he see? Father lies on his side watching Brahim El Alami sing. Without taking his eyes off of the screen, he asks for some water, without saying anything, with a gesture of his hand. He's more alive than he was before, as if he had woken all of a sudden from a short nap. Father always loved Brahim El Alami.

29

Father

IN A WAY THAT DIDN'T surprise me, I saw that I had fallen into a forest, and I knew right away that I was on time. The first thing that struck me was that I wasn't alone, and that I might have missed the appointment. Suleiman and Outhman were with me. The three of us were looking for the mosque in this extremely shady, sprawling, intensely quiet forest. We couldn't even hear our footsteps as we walked over the dried leaves. The fog didn't help us to recognize anything either. Because of how sweaty and tired we were, and how we were panting, it seemed that we had walked for a long time, and that we had begun the search days before. Maybe we had lost our way. We couldn't be sure of this either, since the trees all looked the same. Outhman was walking ahead of us holding a basket with some paint cans in it. Suleiman was carrying a camera, and every time he pressed the button, the flash went off. Why was he taking so many pictures of a forest where everything looked the same? Outhman said, "Don't you see that we're in the mosque?" I couldn't see anything around me except for the thick tree branches, and I couldn't see anything under my feet except for dried leaves, even though I couldn't hear them at all. Outhman insisted that they were the mosque's columns and not trees, and that we were walking over mosaics in the mosque's courtyard. They were walking in front of me now, pelting each another with paint, colors dripping down off of them. They're good boys. I don't understand why they'd disappear whenever I tried to hold onto them or tell them not to do something. The moon's rays reflected off the ground and turned the courtyard's mosaic floor into a sea of moving colors. A clock struck in the distance and Suleiman yelled that it was two in the morning. We still had a bit of time. Why did they walk in front of me as if I needed them to guide me, especially now that it was clear which way to go? I walked past them and rushed into the courtyard, where I could no longer see them. I could see the mosque, and that was all that mattered to me. I looked closely at it with a wary eye, wondering whether I'd find someone in the mosque if I looked in. The thought made my hair stand on end and my knees shake. I focused my thinking on the mosque so as not to waste time on things that didn't matter. On this intensely dark night, its frame seemed threatening, frightening even. Who would this someone be who would venture into it on this dark night even if he was on time? I walked toward it. I stood facing the mosque, which was missing its minaret. The minaret had been swallowed up by the forest. It was right at this moment of excited thinking that I saw a shadow move inside the mosque, a light breeze playing with its djellaba. The djellaba was wide, like a banner rustling musically. The first thing I said to myself was, "Am I that specter that's walking around inside the mosque?" The mosque was completely dark, but it was an unusual sort of darkness. Cascades of soft light flowed in from nowhere in particular, as if coming from more than one direction, from above and from the sides of the mosque, like in a theater. I watched it from the courtyard, a few steps from the main door. I didn't know whether to walk forward or back. I wondered what a man other than me would be doing in the mosque so late if he weren't the man with whom I had the appointment. Suleiman and Outhman ran around the pillars yelling at one another. It didn't surprise me to see them having turned into children. Two kids laughing gleefully. They'd always been like that. Unburdened with what went on around them. I've never depended on them or on anyone else. I've never relied on anyone in my life. I don't have any children I can rely on. I forget about them and focus my thoughts on the person moving not far from me, on what's about to occur. At two in the morning. Right on time. Not a minute before or after. I told myself that it would be unreasonable for something not to happen tonight. It's not normal for nights like this to pass without leaving some sort of a sign that it has passed, however small it may be. He seemed to agree with my way of thinking. He continued to stare at me. He approached me and I didn't act at all stunned. I didn't tremble in front of him. He too was wondering what a man was doing in the mosque's courtyard so late at night. What were we all doing here? No, he didn't ask. Nor did I. Because at that moment I knew that he was the king who had come to inspect the work. I almost fainted when I realized it. I lost my balance and my limbs trembled in happiness and dread. Where were my children so that they could see with their own eyes? I looked around but couldn't find them anywhere. That's my son Suleiman, and that's Outhman. They've been careless since they were little. Where were they so they could see for themselves? The devils had disappeared. I heard about Your Majesty's upcoming visit to the mosque, and I expected signs, banners, drums, and songs. I wasn't expecting it to be like this, at two in the morning, with no entourage or white limousines or motorcycles or carpets or trilling or fireworks or music. Where were the signs, the banners, the drums, the songs? He looked around as if he too were looking for his entourage, while some shadows that might have been his moved around him. When I heard the rustling of his djellaba as well as that of his shadows' djellabas, I remarked that people always have shadows accompanying them. The king was wearing a djellaba decorated with black and white squares, like someone on vacation. "I present to you my children: This is Outhman, my youngest, 'the last of the line,' as they say. Suleiman, the oldest son, is in the Gulf. He ran off to the Gulf so I wouldn't demand anything of him. I've never demanded anything from anyone in my life. Suleiman's a skilled carpenter. Where is he? Where'd that devil disappear to? He always does this—disappears just when we need him. I taught him carpentry when he was young. Then he ran off. He went to the Gulf to help strangers rather than help his father. He's waiting for me to die so he can sell the ruins that shelter me." The king stood and looked over the mosque's ornamentation, encircled by something resembling a delicate halo of light. I waited for him to lift his eyes to look at the ceiling. The king handed me a pair of slippers with turned-up toes as a gift for the work I had done. I wasn't surprised to see that they resembled *his* slippers—the same yellow, with the toes pointed up. I kissed the slippers three times and put them on, with some difficulty because my feet had swollen from fear. With a delicate gesture, imperceptible to anyone, he indicated that I should take a seat underneath the halo of light emanating from him. He asked, "What do you think about building a mosque on the water?" to which I replied, "Everyone will build their houses on the water to emulate your idea." The response pleased him. Then we discussed all sorts of things— England, the United Nations, the issue of the Western Sahara. All of a sudden, he said, "Did you know that you're the most intelligent man I have in the kingdom?" My eyes overflowed with tears of modesty. I was amazed he didn't see them on my face. I was at a loss as to whether I should talk with him about the ceiling because the ceiling . . . in case the crack appeared . . . Better to talk to him about the boys . . . Where are they? They'd run off. Thank God I wasn't lacking for anything and didn't need kids. Then we sat and talked for a long while about the English capital. He told me that he had spent years there; that he had studied medicine, engineering, and law; and that he had memorized the Quran at one of its universities. Then he laughed because he could no longer remember the name of that university. I laughed too. Ha! On the topic of England,

I said that I too had been there, and we laughed together because he knew I was lying in the hopes of prolonging our time sitting there together. And then, in order to prolong the time even more, I told him that, like him, I liked to laugh too. Yes, nothing delights me more than laughing and making fun of things. I had always loved to laugh. Still do, even at the age of sixty-five. "Between you and me, I don't know how to be serious, nor do I like it. Especially at work. When I used to work, that is. I used to carve magnificent palaces that still bear my name, but it was more like a diversion for me. Work is an art. Not a craft for earning money. Whoever wants to earn money should open up a shop in the bazaar. That's right, Moulay, my lord. I spent three years ornamenting a single dome in the Glaoui Pasha's house, may God have mercy on him. I'd come and go as I pleased. I'd work at night or during the day, before evening or after daybreak. My provisions of food and drink and my share of kif would come to me daily. I'd smoke as I worked. According to my mood and my desires. No one would say 'work' or 'don't work.' Even if the work had taken years longer, no one would have complained, because work, as I see it, is like that. It ends when it ends. No one would trade it for anything. Unfortunately, the profession is starting to disappear. *I'm* not the sort who would bargain, who would ask 'How much?' Because of these silly words, crafts-manship is being driven to extinction. What do master craftsmen do these days? They go from one rich person's villa to the next with nothing in their hands but the words 'how much?' Because of these words, they replace one piece of wood with another of lesser quality, instead of the cedar that I use. They use paints with lifeless colors." Then crystal chan-deliers of different colors were lit and shone above us like a thousand stars, creating a soft, brilliant ringing that sounded like music. "The time for the visit has come," he said as he got up. He began to inspect the ceilings above us, one after the other, asking about the type of wood and paint, the master

243

builder who did the work, and how long it had taken to complete, recording it all in a small notebook—where it came from I didn't know—with a golden pen. He came to a spot underneath the ceiling, and as if the king could guess what I was thinking, he turned to me, placed his hand on my shoulder, and said, "You're right. We won't find a better ceiling than the one you've made here anywhere in the kingdom." He proceeded to examine it at his leisure, writing everything I said in his notebook. That's when I saw Outhman looking in through the crack, and the devil laughed. He was hoping to destroy me. To amuse the king and distract him from the crack, I continued to explain: "For more than three years I calculated. I planned. I recalculated. Chiseling here and there. Calculating again. Planning first on paper, then on wood . . ." I related all of this to him without looking at the ceiling, but he looked up at the ceiling. He took his time looking meticulously at my drawings. The pen between his fingers flowed with golden ink. I told myself that I had to distract him so he wouldn't look up. But I didn't understand how I'd come to be wearing a djellaba just like the one the king was wearing. Right then I remembered what was important. I said to him, "Can you believe it, my lord? While I was sleeping, Buraq the mythic steed came to me and carried me on his wings to my grandfather Bouya Rahhal's tomb. That's right, my grandfather was the saint Sidi Rahhal, who transformed desert sands into wheat seeds and who soared over Marrakech for forty years on a green prayer rug. I've never told this to anyone. You're the first man to know about this secret—the first king to gaze upon this dazzling truth—and I'm telling it to you now because we're practically from the same family. Each has his own grandfather, but we're all the same, as the foreigners say. Ha! Our grandfather traces his lineage to our virtuous lady, Fatima al-Zahra, may God be pleased with her. Do you know what that means? This is a coup d'état, a revolution. Ha! Do you at least know who Fatima al-Zahra is? Do you know how much our lives would change were you to be so kind as to acknowledge us and take us under your wing? We wouldn't need any other form of protection, at least for the moment." I took out the book. "Everything is recorded in this book, my lord. Everything is made clear in *The Methodology of Journeying toward the Knowledge of Shaykh Sidi Rahhal* by the jurist, the most noble and erudite Sidi Mohammed Larbi ibn al-Bahloul bin Umar al-Rahhali al-Mijnawi al-Mishwari, may God grant forgiveness to him, his parents, his teachers, and his loved ones, amen. When someone ignores his lineage, every bad deed can be expected of him, amen. This lineage can be traced back to the son of Adam, who doesn't equal a thing outside of his family tree. Look, my lord, at the long list of names. One hundred and fifty-one pages of names and titles. And where do they end? At the name of my father and paternal uncles. Si Taher. Si Rahhal. Si Larbi. Si Omar, this last one being my father, who gave me his name so I wouldn't forget him, may God have mercy on him." Then I saw him scowl, his face turning red hot with anger. It changed instantaneously. He yelled in my face, "What's that?" "What's this, my lord? Why, this is *The Methodology of Journeying*." No, he wasn't asking about the book. "You're right. My children. They've never helped me with anything. Suleiman, for example. What's he doing in that country? Isn't there enough work here? Aren't we one family? You and I and he and everyone else? We need to work hand in hand. I worked with the kids as a boss deals with his employees, because they both deserve everything good, and because they're both smart boys. They've always been smart. And the result? Nothing! What rational person would emigrate to the Gulf?" Then the king yelled, "What's that I see?" pointing up at a specific spot in the ceiling. "That's right, my lord. Children hate their fathers. That's well known. What son doesn't want to throw his aged father into the fire or bury him alive? That's just how it is. It isn't strange or unusual anymore to find a son dragging his father through the mud. This old man, as you call him, has wasted his life for the sake of raising you! Aren't we one family? I told Suleiman I'd work with him this time just as a boss works with his employees, with a salary, rights, benefits, and all the other things an employer gives his workers. But he preferred going to the Gulf. Was all the effort I expended on their behalf for nothing? The kids didn't give me a thing. They soak up all of our sweat then leave for the Gulf and beyond. Nothing's good enough for them. Nothing will be of use in the face of children's ingratitude. Your ancestors weren't like this. Did any of them ask who their grandfather was? Take the man who walked on fire. He lived on wild plants and mustard seeds, and died of poisoning because no one wanted to hear words of truth. That's right, he died of poisoning during his first prostration of the morning prayer, or in the second sajda of the first prostration, or the second. His grandchildren and his grandchildren's grandchildren ate snakes and put hot metal in their mouths . . ." The king wasn't listening to me. He was following the ceiling's curves as he wrote in his notebook, and then he raised his eyes to the ceiling while shaking his head in disbelief. At that moment, I knew that I was doomed. I continued with my nonsense, and with that I completely washed my hands of them and the craft. "'Times have changed,' they say. Times haven't changed. People are what's changed. Now they chase after money. Believe it or not, I've been close to some important people—from Hajj Tehami Glaoui to Si Bargache, the prefect of Casablanca, may God have mercy on them both. I've been inside their palaces and eaten at their tables. I've been with them at weddings and funerals. Money used to flow from my pockets like water. But it wasn't for money, or for fame, that I worked. Or even for women. All of this comes and goes. Rather, it was because my blood required it, just like the stomach needs bread. The money disappeared when the craft was ruined and I didn't go on any further." At that point, the king's voice reined me in. The notebook and pen disappeared, but his finger remained pointing up at a spot on the ceiling. "What is that? What is that?" "That's a crack. Yes, a crack, a small crack, our lord. You can hardly see it." Hidden hands took the djellaba and slippers from me and left me standing there practically naked, looking up at where his hand was pointing, while I stumbled over some words I myself didn't understand. It was true that, when I looked at it now, there seemed to be a crack in the ceiling. Really. But between you and me, it was in a spot that couldn't be seen. It was a crack that only someone who knew the secrets of the profession could see, like us, experts in the decorative arts. Like us. Then, as he pointed toward the crack, I heard the king say, "This warp needs to be straightened, and we won't find anyone better than you, because you're one of the family, but the crack isn't as small as you say. Come on, let's climb up and take a look at it." So I climbed up. The king began to shake the ladder and shout, "This is quite a ceiling," as he shook the ladder, and shook it some more. "This is quite a ceiling. This is quite a ceiling." He shook the ladder until I fell, and I suddenly opened my eyes—the return to consciousness had made me extremely thirsty—so I closed them just as quickly. Still, I found the time to ask Outhman to fetch me a glass of water.

V

30

THE MAN SITTING IN THE wicker chair brushing the ground impatiently with his feet and listening to the strange roar doesn't notice the two o'clock train until after it has passed. He continues to follow the sound of dogs barking in the distance until midafternoon, with a feeling somewhere between optimism and pessimism that renews itself with each passing moment. According to the level of their excitement, he can tell how close to or far away from their prey they are. They might have found them by now, or will before too long, depending on how deep their grudge is. Depends on how vicious the dogs on their trail are. The man is preoccupied. Not by his wife, who is bearing the agony of childbirth in silence so as not to annoy the judge. Not because he hasn't yet come up with the joke or the entertaining and appropriate story that he will tell the judge, since the judge loves bawdy stories. In fact, the man has confidence in himself in this regard, and in his newfound ability to come up with jokes the judge will love. These stories have started to come easily to him ever since he first met the judge. They'd come to him without even having to think about it. The judge sure does love vulgar stories. These stories don't get him going on regular days, in court, for example, or at the Judges' Club. But they do excite him when he's with Najat. Really, he's more excited by Najat's reaction to them. It amuses him to see her cheeks blush, and her forehead start to sweat. The man's thoughts are jumbled, though, because he's thinking about the two lovers and the mistake they made that had led to their discovery. Perhaps they hadn't been careful enough. Or perhaps they hadn't made any mistake at all. The smell of desire is strong. The body isn't strong enough to bear it or hide it. If it doesn't come out of your mouth, it'll come out of your eyes or your pores, sometimes from every pore in your skin. He follows their perilous journey. They climb mountain paths or crouch inside caves. The dogs' barking is his guide, as is the particular quality of barking. Sometimes there's a long, mournful howl and other times a sharp, broken, vicious growl. Sometimes it fades off in this direction until it just about disappears and the man thinks they've been saved, only for the barking to rise up again from another direction. He listens for what they might be saying too. What could two fleeing lovers possibly be talking about? They blame one another. They blame their luck that betrayed them. They express a little regret. One of them strengthens the resolve of the other as they look to tomorrow with greater optimism, and then they put their heads on each other's shoulders, comforting each another as they hum a sad song the woman had heard when she was a little girl playing in front of her house in a distant village. The judge isn't thinking about them or about the dirty stories that haven't yet come to the man, because at that moment the man hears the judge ask him if he has prepared the fire.

The judge's car is large. An American car. An Oldsmobile. It's like a closet. It has everything a judge and his lover need to pass a pleasant Sunday afternoon. There is meat and the cookware to cook the meat. There are drinks and glasses to pour the drinks into. There's charcoal too. The man takes out two sacks of charcoal and arranges it in the grill. His movements are mechanical and clumsy because he's thinking about the two lovers. He pours a little oil onto a piece of cloth and lights the fire. He wipes his hands as he watches the flame exuberantly consume the cloth. Tongues of flame trace the shapes of upright fingers—dancing or praying for rain. Then horses crane their necks, running from the flames of hell, rising to the sky. And what is the judge doing right then? What is he doing while he waits for the charcoal to light and the bolting fire horses to die down in the grill? He has disappeared into the house while the man is occupied with preparing the fire. The house is his house. The beds are his beds, as are the covers, towels, water, and soap. He has withdrawn to one of the bedrooms with his lover. The judge respects the family. He doesn't want to annoy the woman, who is on the verge of giving birth. That's why he chooses another room. Usually the judge and his lover, Najat, sleep in the bed of the man and his wife during the late afternoon. The judge respects the man too. Rather than use an izar cloth he wipes his cum on the bills he finds distributed among his many pockets. This is really what happens, because the man often finds the bills underneath the bed. Bills that are wet from the judge's semen, but they're enough to cover three days' expenses. He wipes them off, folds them, and puts them in the armoire, because whether or not there is semen on them, he can always use the cash. The man goes back to the car and removes a leg of lamb wrapped in a piece of cloth that's stained with the color and smell of meat. He sits at the table and cuts it, loading the aluminum skewers with small pieces of flesh. The judge doesn't eat lamb because of the cholesterol. However, Sunday is an exception because he's with Najat. The man hears the lovers laugh through an open window. Women can feel joy at a single tiny word, even if it's meaningless. He wonders how men manage to snatch women's minds so easily. Two words are enough to tear down the defenses that have been erected since the day they were born. They remain preoccupied with these defenses and the man who will destroy them, because they've been preoccupied with men since they were born. As soon as women reach fifteen years of age their bodies change. Another soul inhabits their wombs. Their wombs are afflicted by something akin to a fever. They lose their appetite for sleep and food. At this age, another craving inhabits them. They smell men everywhere. They see them in every shape and form. They can smell them whenever they get even remotely close. They smell men whether they're nearby or far away. Even before they can be seen. They smell men even when they're not there at all. Just like what happened with my sister Khadija.

And like what happened with Farah. The fever took over her mind rather than her body. It wasn't exactly a "male fever," although it was something like it. Something else like an illness took her over. She didn't know where or how she got it. Her weakness was singing. It lodged itself in her when she was young. Whenever she passed by the radio repair shop, soothing music, or dance music, or music accompanied by singing came from inside the shop. She was young and didn't realize that her second soul had been awakened, that the malady had brought its pickax and begun its work. She didn't know that it was the music that made her swoon, or that it was the singing coming from the shop that made her dizzy. It was enough for her to pass by in the morning, completely unaware that the songs were what had brought her to that street, and that the music that came out of the shop rang in her ears all day long. At home, she would say to herself, "If you open your ears, Farah, you'll be able to hear Fairouz from here, singing from deep inside the shop." It didn't stop until late at night, as if it rang out just for her. As if calling out to her. It wasn't just music. Rather, it was an illness that overpowered her the moment her body was least able to fight it. It continued to pull her with it. Sometimes surreptitiously. Other times announcing itself out loud. Guiding her steps without her realizing it. Suggesting that she leave her parents' house. Taking her by the hand and showing her how to dispose of her father's money without his knowledge. Then, after she left Naima's house, it crammed her into a small room no larger than six square meters. She was just at the beginning of the road. The man sitting in front of skewers of meat knows all of this.

The perfume shop was located far from the small room where Farah was staying, in one of the city's European streets. She saw him as she stood looking at the beautiful little bottles of different sizes and colors displayed behind the glass window. She saw the lawyer coming out of the store beaming and walking toward her with open arms, a string of black prayer beads dangling from his fingers, as if he had been expecting her to appear there standing like that, like a person waiting on someone they had an appointment with. In life, things happen that are there and aren't there at the same time. The lawyer whom she had met at Naima's place was there. But he didn't live at the perfume shop. To Farah, he was no longer there, or rather, he was there as a memory, like a person who had passed by and remained in her thoughts. No more than that. He frequented the perfume seller from time to time to purchase his special cologne, as he told her. Why did she stand in front of the window every day? There were all those fascinating bottles with their exciting shapes. Bottles shaped like naked women, or pursed lips, or a head without hair. But was that enough of an explanation? Why did she stand in front of the window every day, then? Farah didn't know the names of the perfumes. She didn't know that they came in such a range of delicateness. She didn't know that every perfume had a taste and a flavor. Light, scented ripples came to her from inside the shop in bursts, bending and twisting like soft breezes. All of them smelled alike; all were delicate and intoxicating. That wasn't enough to explain why she kept standing there, though, and why she returned the following morning, as she had time and time again with the radio repair shop. As if this image— the image of the lawyer—was only there in order to appear again, moving away only to draw closer and assume an irrevocably concrete form. And everything that would happen would depend on him showing up, which seemed unlikely up to that moment, but could occur at any time. When the lawyer showed up, his wide smile and black rosary beads preceded him, and when she heard her own voice apologetically say to him that she was standing here in front of the colored display window only because of the perfumes, the beautiful little bottles with the dizzying scents had disappeared.

She no longer remembers if she had been looking for him, or if it was him who had been looking for her. He had made her a promise when she was at Naima's house, right? Farah doesn't forget that he had promised her. And lawyers never forget their promises. When he goes up to wish her a good morning in her small room, he doesn't walk through the door, because it's not Naima's doorway, nor is it her house. This is the house of a singer who will enjoy some renown one day. He visits her on business, nothing other than that, wrapped in a smile. The rosary with the black beads clicks between his fingers. That's because he has renounced drinking, which he exchanged for a love of God, according to what he told her. He also says that the contract with the studio would be ready in about two months, and that he'd go on the hajj pilgrimage this year, God willing. Farah won't sing in cabarets like Naima. He tells her that while standing in the doorway of her room wearing a loose djellaba—his orange djellaba—with trimmed beard and moustache and a green cap on his head. Sometimes the sound of his steps reaches her even before he turns onto the block because she is waiting for him. Her daily task is to wait. She doesn't eat much, so that her money will last until she receives her first paycheck—a paycheck for singing—or at least until she signs the contract. So she waits. Milk and bread, or tea and olives, or some vegetables. Boiled potatoes with salt and cumin make a delicious meal while she waits to hear his footsteps. She tells herself that maybe this time he'll bring good news. Then she hears him at the front door of the house saying "Good morning" to the blind woman who owns the

place. All that's missing are his footsteps on the stairs. When
he comes up, the lawyer doesn't cross over into the room. The
time for him to enter hasn't come yet. When he tells her that
in order for them to sign a contract with the record company,
before recording, in order to put together the orchestra, and
before putting together the orchestra, to find the right lyrics
and the right tune . . . she realizes it. Even before the sentence
is finished. Even before he knows that she's realized it, she puts
her hand under the couch and takes out a green plastic bag.
Then, as he counts the bills one by one, mopping his brow in
disbelief, not sure at all that he is looking at such a large sum
of money—more than twenty thousand dirhams—he wipes
his hands and raises his head to see whether she is having
second thoughts, not believing it at all as he puts the bag in
his pocket, mopping his brow again, finding himself talking
to her about the words she'll sing and the famous songwriter
who has already started to write the melodies, even before the
words have emerged from the head of the one who's writing
them. Then he takes the bag out, counts the cash, hands her
the green plastic bag, and put the bills in his pocket. The next
day Farah remembers that she doesn't know his name—the
lawyer's name, not the songwriter's or the lyricist's. Perhaps
she'll find out later, when it is no longer of any use. In the
days that follow, it is enough for her to wait for him to appear,
knowing full well that he is long past due. Some sort of image
of the lawyer who has pounced on her in her modest room is
forming in the mind of the man sitting in the chair. The girl
was practically in his grasp, so how had he lost her? The room
had a bed and a faucet. No windows. A room just the right
size. Prepared just for him. He has stood in front of her door
numerous times, and when he goes in, he knows that it will be
the first and last time. Given a second chance, her desire to
sing wouldn't cause her to lose her bearings. She knows there
won't be a second chance. If given another chance, she'd be
more careful and wouldn't give her money to just anyone,

especially if he were a lawyer or someone who resembled this lawyer. She knows she isn't going to meet the lawyer again. She had been blinded once, and that was more than enough. She isn't going to find herself in a similar position. But for now, she doesn't leave the room out of fear that he'll come and not find her there. A prisoner, more or less. Her money has gone up in smoke. She doesn't even have to find the boiled potatoes tasty anymore. She eats when the blind woman or her granddaughter brings her food. And she fasts when she doesn't have enough money. Farah didn't have waves crashing down on her that night years ago when he searched for her all up and down the beach. She wasn't a shark's feast and she wasn't entangled in seaweed at the bottom of the ocean. Rather, she had merely gone back to her miserable room to wait for the lawyer who hadn't shown up in front of the perfume store. She had predicted it. She saw it, even though it hadn't yet entered the realm of possibility.

She hadn't yet given him her money. She hadn't encountered the lawyer at all since leaving Naima's house. But she continued to wait for him. She may have spent the eleven days of her second visit running away from a wait that tired her out and destroyed her. That's right, she was waiting for him even when she was at the workshop, although not as he had appeared before, coming out of the perfume shop, his black rosary beads shining between his fingers. His promises continued to fill her head even after she left her friend's house. She remembered them that night on the beach. Sitting next to him and watching the waves as they traced silver lines that danced on the edge of the water. She didn't come to Casablanca to roll around in the sand or to look at the stars. She came to sing, and she had wasted enough time. The man doesn't remember the details. The details have faded away. Scattered in the winds of time. If he had looked closely at her face that night, through the darkness, he would have seen the fever of the call tearing at it. The man also sees the moment when he stumbled upon her, when the flood had inundated the old city and a five- or six-year-old child guided him to her in that room she rented for fifty dirhams a week, where she remained a prisoner for more than two months thinking about the lawyer's promises, then about his coming, then about his hesitation in entering the room, then about his not being there anymore. Yes, Farah had drowned. But she didn't drown in the ocean. She drowned in a small room—six square meters—owned by a blind woman.

Right then, the man gets up. These are the most beautiful moments of the day. Right before sunset, a cool, refreshing breeze blows from the west. He needs it. The breeze runs through his hair and down the back of his neck, then passes under his arms. He crosses his field, walking alongside the fence. He looks at the beetles that have fastened themselves to the wires, arranged like bunches of grapes. The beetles have ended up here. After a life full of danger and adventure. Now they're nothing more than dried shells being consumed by the sun. The magpies have emptied them of their lives. They have sucked out everything inside them and left them as empty shells. This is a more exciting story, one that's worth telling to the judge. But the judge doesn't like stories that don't cause Najat to blush. The beetle had emerged from under the ground and didn't know how its day would end. It didn't see the magpie perched on top of the pole that didn't have the slightest idea of the feast awaiting it. He himself didn't know of the beetle's existence. They met quite by accident. Defending itself, the beetle moved its legs with all the life it had in it. The magpie understood what was going on. Perhaps the feeble, ignoble resistance made it laugh. Its legs moved about in the air long enough for it to be known that it had put up a fight. The bird allowed itself a few moments to watch the beetle as it rolled over onto its back like a little turtle. The magpie took the bug and stabbed it onto the sharp wire in one sharp blow.

Short and quick. The beetle felt the wire pierce it through. And at that very moment, it knew its life's purpose. Only then did it know that it had been found not to be eaten by the magpie on the ground, but rather for it to be sucked on like a fresh piece of candy. The beetle was a fresh piece of candy. Its legs slowed down as it came to understand the situation. It wouldn't annoy a bird that was just doing what it does. Why should it annoy the bird when it considers the beetle a piece of candy, and not just a silly bug? The magpies were perched on top of the train and electrical poles, looking at the museum of curiosities they had created. And rather than sing, they watched the day march toward its end. Usually they came after evening fell, just before the beetles left their hiding places.

Then the gendarmes' car appeared.

31

The Flood

I'M THINKING ABOUT THE MUD and all the water that fell from the sky for three days straight. I'm standing in the middle of my unlit room, in front of the mirror covered in mud that had dried during the night. Thinking, first of all, about why there isn't any light in the room, or rather, about why the light stops at the window, unable to get through. Darkness comes from the room itself, from what the room came to look like after the storm had passed. Mud covers the sofa, the armoire, and the walls. It covers the window shutters and the empty cage hanging next to them. I'm also thinking about my clothes, which have dried mud on them. Three days submerged, immersed in muddy water. Without sleep or rest. Then I think about Mother. No sound comes from the foyer or the other rooms. Everyone left two days before. Family, friends, neighbors. Right after receiving their new apartments. There is a new stillness in the air, so strange that it's unrecognizable. No water seller calling as he passes. No old furniture buyer with the annoying voice. No pottery mender insistently calling out. All those calls had stopped just before this morning. No sound comes from the house or from outside except for the peal of a distant ambulance, the song of widespread destruction that has settled over the old city in the flood. A thick layer of mud covers me and everything around me—the mirror, the sofa, the armoire, the walls, the door, the ceiling. It's as if an unskilled painter has set out to paint the room and everything in it with dark brown paint. More mud drips from the ceiling. The same color. The floor is buried under a thick layer of mud. Underneath these layers of mud that have accumulated on my body and even seeped into my veins, my soul having been enveloped by a layer of dirt, there's no doubt I have changed, just as everything around me has changed. I am also thinking about the mosque, and about the past few days. During the three days of flooding, I didn't go to the mosque. I continued to watch it from a distance from up on the roof. Up till now, I don't know what happened there. Never before had I been away from it for so long. No doubt it had changed, too. The past three days have changed all of us. It is as if I had been traveling somewhere far away only to return to a place I no longer recognized because of how much everything had changed. I too had changed during that three-day journey. Does a traveler ever return the same as when he left? What do I look like now, on this, my fourth day since setting off? Before leaving the room, I turn to the mirror and draw a circle and two dots on it for my face. I draw an upside-down arc. I leave the drawing of the sad face behind as I leave the room. I leave without a face.

Water. I walk through brown water. All there is around me is water and mud. It has receded considerably compared to where it was yesterday and before that. For three straight days, the waters flowed and came together and encircled the old city. After three days, the sheets of rain still hadn't stopped. Then, on the fourth day, it stopped, just as suddenly as it began. Stunning purple and silver rays shine through, between the gray clouds. The waves that had crashed against our neighborhood's walls now gently withdraw. What is left of the water softly, yet maliciously kisses the walls that had stood so firmly against the storm, as if a flood hadn't passed through our neighborhood leaving widespread destruction in its wake. The mosque rises above the water around it. The last time I looked, the minaret was still obscured from view. I couldn't see it from our roof or our neighbors' roof. I couldn't see the minaret or the mosque. The wall of water that fell from the sky had completely swallowed them up. Now I see it as I stand on the edge of the ruined neighborhood. It is the same as it was before. It hasn't lost one bit of its majesty. The sky's fury hadn't defeated it. It floats comfortably above the brown water. The mosque has been separated from us and lives its own special life on its island.

Kika looked at me from behind a door that didn't work anymore. He stood in the emptiness. No one entering or leaving. No hands opening the door or feet passing through it, as if it had been brought by a merchant who loved to show off his trinkets in strange museums of curiosities. The destroyed remains of the many collapsed houses were visible behind Kika. His eyes were red. It looked as if he hadn't slept the whole time the flood was completing its destructive work. His face was muddy, as were his clothes. He looked just like he had yesterday as he moved against the rushing torrent carrying a woman on his shoulders who no longer had enough strength to move. At the peak of his strength. He held onto the woman's waist with one strong hand while he used the other to remove obstacles in his path. I remember the small frog that had emerged from his shirt collar chirping in fright. He stood in front of me a complete wreck, but his determination to help the flood victims still gave him strength and pushed him forward. I reminded him of the frog and we laughed in spite of how pathetic he looked. He seemed really exhausted. Should I ask him how he had spent the past three nights? I didn't ask him. He didn't give me the chance. He said that he had seen the girl. "Which girl?" "Farah." "Where?" He didn't respond right away. I heard him say it from behind the unhinged door, beckoning for me to follow.

32

It BEGAN AS A SOFT hiss. Not the least bit threatening. I got up
and looked through the window, unable to tell whether the rain
had stopped. I fogged up the glass with my breath. I traced a
circle with my finger and wiped away the inside of it so I could
see. The sky was gray, practically white, and whatever was falling from it was invisible. The air was unusually warm. I stuck
my hand out the window and waited for a while before feeling
the raindrops, as if it were some sort of mysterious water flowing in me. I returned to the sofa and stretched out on it. I stuck
my legs up and rested them on the wall, making myself comfortable. The rain didn't stop falling for more than two hours.
Constant. I didn't stop thinking about the rain, or about the
mosque and the crack that had appeared in the ceiling. About
Father. About the minaret. About other things as well. I left the
house through the window as I had done ever since Rihane
showed up. The wind was blowing at full strength now, howling mournfully. All other sounds disappeared. No water seller's
voice. No traveling salesmen's calls. No children's shouting. The
wind's howling would die down for a moment only to pick up
again with even more strength. Sometimes it sounded like a
thunderclap that could be heard everywhere. Things around
me fell over and broke, even inside the houses. All of a sudden,
the sky began to empty itself of all the water it had in one burst.

On the second day, the room darkened. At least this
change brushed aside the crushing routine of the rain that

had been persistently falling since yesterday. The rain didn't stop all night. Violent and angry. Sometimes it sounded like something creeping along the ground—a light swishing like pebbles falling on sand. Then its rhythm changed. It started to reverberate. The rain that had begun like a light tapping on my window, like a passing hiss, had now, at dawn, settled above our heads, as violent as could be. Now horses were charging down, their hooves thundering clamorously. Drums pounded relentlessly. I hurried to the window, waiting for it to let up a bit, or come down a bit harder. Had it become more severe this morning? The asphalt sparkled with the raindrops hitting it. Water gathered in holes in the streets to form little puddles or thin rivulets flowing along the ruts left by carts that had been coming and going for decades. A short while before, when I looked out into the central courtyard of the house, the prevailing mood was almost normal, except for Mother's glasses and the gray hair that had invaded both sides of the part in her hair. Then, while I was heading back to the kitchen, something seemed to change. They went to huddle together in a corner of the courtyard and stared at the ceiling, focused on a specific spot. What were they looking at? My sister Khadija was shaking. Her eyes darted around. Her nerves wouldn't bother her because Abdullah was busy outside the house. Father was in his wheelchair. It didn't seem like he was aware of what was happening around him. Perhaps he didn't even realize that his mouth was sagging a bit. The light fixture above shook, then a drop of water that had been circling it fell. With a ringing sound, the second drop fell into a copper bucket. All eyes followed them as they fell. There was bread, oil, and tea on the table. No one walked toward the tray or reached a hand toward a glass. We were all together in the foyer, so close we were practically stuck to one another, intently following the drops as they fell into the bucket. *Taf . . . taf . . . taf.* Mother, Habiba, and Khadija. I was standing farthest away, as if they had already moved beyond anticipating disaster, and were prepared for the inevitable. Abdullah was at the mosque with the neighbors, reciting the Latif prayer and composing a letter to the royal court. Habiba said, "Good God, disasters only strike at night." It was only then that we realized it was night, not having noticed before because of the black clouds that had blocked the sky. We had moved into nighttime all at once. Mother looked gloomier because of her glasses. She had aged. The glasses and the black abaya weighed her down with additional years. The lamp flickered for what seemed like a long time, and then its light dimmed, fading and fading and fading until it almost went out, and then the flame rose up again bit by bit, like something that's dying but, with a last gasp, returns to life. Everyone's eyes sparkled. They shone with a little bit of joy, albeit fleeting, because it wasn't long before the flash came back. The rhythm of the water quickened as it dropped into the bucket—*taf . . . taf . . . taf*—becoming violent. It seemed like the first hints of horror had settled into our eyes. We looked anxiously at one another. Suddenly, the light went out. Now the night was even darker. A strange silence prevailed, as if we had never seen night in our lives. As if we didn't know what darkness was. We all remained where we were, silent, as if waiting for the spirit to return to a broken body. Stupefied, scared. Waiting for the light to come back on. Then the confusion began. Things and bodies crashed into one another. When I went back into the bedroom, the light there was out too. I didn't need a light. The streetlight was enough for how little I was moving. The crashing out in the courtyard went on for a little while and then the house returned to silence. From underneath the door, a faint blinking light appeared. They must have found half of a forgotten candle. Then a frightening scream rose up in the house. Water had begun to flow in under the door, flooding the foyer and threatening to rush into every corner. There was a lot of commotion in the surrounding houses, the neighbors' houses. When dawn was about to break, we couldn't see it because it was a dawn we could only imagine on account of the black clouds completely obscuring any light there might have been. One edge of the night folded into another, leaving us floating in an endless darkness.

We went up to the roof when the first floor of the house flooded, as did the rest of the neighbors. It took a long time to move Father in his chair, which we had to do before we could move anything else. The neighbors were also moving up those who were sick and their precious items. I could see them looking like ghosts on the adjacent roofs under the lamplight, or like shadow puppets on a screen, yelling to one another as they moved the expensive furniture before it got ruined. We huddled under a cloth cover my sister Khadija and I had thrown over our heads to protect ourselves from the rain, which had intensified. Mother stretched out on a mattress, a complete wreck after the previous night's sleeplessness. She wondered again about the fate of her daughter Khadija, who had been deteriorating rapidly until Abdullah had started to pull her into his room. We all knew what Abdullah was doing with her in his room. Even Habiba knew, but she didn't say a thing. Large raindrops fell hard on the cloth. It didn't seem like it was ever going to stop. I couldn't hear what our neighbor was saying on the roof facing us, nor could I make out clearly what he was doing. Was he pointing to me with his cane? Was he saying no to his children who wanted to go down into the street to swim in the water that had started to flow like a river? Was he threatening them with his cane so they'd stay where they were? He was pointing to the wall of our house, which had started to crack. I walked to the edge of the roof. I followed the line his cane was tracing and saw the crack. I wondered, as he did, whether our house would hold up until tomorrow. Now every family was staring at their own crack. I pointed to the wall of *his* house, which had the same crack. Neither we nor our neighbors knew whether we would leave our houses, or how.

It seemed that the rain, which had been falling nonstop through the night, had taken its time to seep into all the crevices there, helping the other houses that hadn't yet fallen to quickly crack. As I swallowed my tears, the alleys I walked through seemed unfamiliar, as if I were walking there for the first time. The vendors' carts where card players had sought shelter from the rain were upside down now, their wheels spinning in the air. The card players were gone. Furniture was piled up in front of those house walls that remained standing. And floating in the puddles were the gold frames and certificates of those who had contributed to the mosque. Children and cats were on top of mounds of garbage searching for loot that the mud had buried, or were sinking in it up to their necks. The awful smells wafting around them didn't seem to shake their morale at all.

I didn't hear it until the procession appeared from behind a hill of garbage. *To God we belong, and to Him we shall return.* They were carrying three boards draped with green coverings, with Abdullah in front, even though he wasn't contributing a dead child today. The three biers didn't affect me as I walked behind them. Their small size didn't affect me at all. It was as if they were going to the neighborhood oven with trays of bread dough on their heads. The sound of the voice didn't affect me the way it had before, either, so full of sadness and pain when I first heard it in the middle of the night. It didn't have same mournful tune or sad melody. The anger it held was overwhelming. A pitch-black voice, savage, a black that tore at the soul. In perfect harmony with the anger I was feeling. *To God we belong, and to Him we shall return.* A voice that left no room for light, for any rays of hope. A pure anger. Black clouds gathered behind them as if the door of return were being closed in the faces of the three small corpses, preventing them from returning to life if ever that possibility existed.

The procession came to a stop outside the walls on the narrow stone path. The National Department of Electricity employee was the one who stopped the procession right in front of the empty mosque, using improvised gestures to prevent the funeral procession from moving forward. He was stuffed into a green rubber outfit, wearing knee-high boots of the same green. Over the outfit he had on a dripping yellow raincoat. He was coming back from fishing. The National Department of Electricity employee was carrying his long pole and basket, which smelled strongly of the rotten sardines he used as bait. The procession paused for a moment before coming to a complete stop. Torrents of rain poured down all at once, as if it had been waiting for us to be standing out there in the open. A narrow stone path ran between the water and the mill. Neither standing completely still nor walking, we held onto one another so as not to fall into the water with what we were carrying. Large waves crashed down on the rocks, sending spray above our heads, and the wind was so strong it would have prevented the funeral procession from advancing even if it had wanted to; like the whistle of a runaway train that isn't going anywhere. The mourners raised the funerary biers up high, as if they had found the appropriate talisman with which to face the employee and his threats. Then everyone recited the Fatiha out loud in order to strengthen their resolve. *Glory be to thy Lord, the Lord of Glory.* This was followed by spontaneous entreaties in one pure voice. "May God aid us in our lives. May God vanquish those who rule over us and punish traitors and thieves who steal our money. May God unify our word. Amen. And guide us and accept our prayers. Amen. And forgive us our sins. And destroy the houses of those who do not want the best for us, and who kill our children, and deny us respectable dwellings. And who watch our houses as they fall on top of our heads. Amen. May God disperse them." Their enthusiasm was infectious, and I too began to yell all sorts of insults at the employee, insults that were swallowed up by the collective din before they could reach his ears. What would the National Department of Electricity employee say now? Would he get up on the low wall to tell them about the new homes the state was going to give them once they finished building the mosque, and explain to them the advantages of affordable housing? There was no low wall near him. Then we saw him remove a large, wet piece of paper from the pocket of his yellow raincoat and affix it to the wall of the mill in front of the mourners, in the rain, then wipe his face while looking at the faces around him. It was the plans for the new houses that the state was going to grant us. "Here they are, three hundred new apartments. Each apartment has three rooms, a kitchen, and a bathroom with a bathtub. The houses have been built for a while now and we're just waiting for the work to be done on the mosque so their doors can be opened up to everyone. This is the park that's located in the middle of all the houses. This is the school, and this green here, that's the hospital." They put the coffins down under the mill's roof and gathered around the National Department of Electricity employee. "And this red part, what's that?" "That's the kindergarten where your children will play around while you're rolling around in bed with your wives. But, because of the flooding . . ." He put the basket down on the ground, revealing the fish he had caught, and took out a bunch of keys. We all lost our bearings because of the jangling keys. The three small coffins disappeared among the crowd of mourners, who were no longer acting like mourners. They were on the verge of becoming new property owners. True owners. Three rooms, a kitchen, and a bathroom. Out of an excess of enthusiasm, some of us yelled, "Long live the king!" We walked over to the mill wall so we could see and confirm that it was true. The employee went back in front of the large piece of paper, asking us not to ruin it. He stood in front of the plans he had calmly affixed to the wall, pleased with himself, showing us his goodwill, generously looking out over our faces as if he were distributing his own properties to us. Not angry, because work on the mosque was stalled due to the floods. Not angry at all. He turned toward us like someone addressing his dear children. "Life will change once you take up residence

271

in your new homes. Freestanding, and with everything you need—water, electricity, a bathroom, a salon for receiving guests. And television, especially for the children who love to watch cartoons. Family movies about mountains, the history of the Arabian Peninsula, sailboat building, agriculture, and animal husbandry. You'll learn a great many things. Without electricity, your eyes will remain covered over and you won't be able to see all these beautiful things I'm talking about. With electricity will come supermarkets like the ones in the fancy neighborhoods. There, you'll be able to pick out what you want without ever seeing the shop's owner. You'll push a wheeled cart around the store, filling it to the brim without anyone watching over you, because everything is done with labels. In fact, I'm warning you, thieves. Don't steal. There are security cameras there. And doors that open and close on their own. And do you think they use pens in these types of stores? Never. You pass your groceries in front of a screen that takes care of adding up the total. *Tak tak tak.* All by itself, without anyone else getting involved, because every label has the product's name on it. Pass your label over the screen and it takes care of the rest, without any fuss at all. And all of this at low prices. No one will be overcome with anger any-more. Now the spirit of happy hunters that was rooted in your fathers will inhabit you too." They started to joke around with the employee, asking him what kind of fish he had caught that morning. They looked into his basket. "Is it a cherghou bream or a sea bass?" They lifted the fish up high, pressing its skin to check its freshness and saying, "Tbarek Allah, blessed be God. How wonderful!" The National Department of Electricity employee, who in that moment had become their friend, as if he had just regained consciousness, with cool composure and eloquence that had betrayed him moments before, said, "Here, you see, you sons of devils? Here are the houses, new and waiting for you. And the mosque? Where is that?" He began to punch the wall. "Doesn't the effort we're putting in for you deserve some sacrifice in return? What are your useless mortal bodies worth?" But they weren't listening to the employee. They were choosing the apartment that got the best light. They were listening to the strange, jangling sound—the jangling of new keys. Their hands were busy trying to find the right keys, before the apartments ran out. Three hundred apartments. The employee yelled shrilly, "You'll see when all this hard work is done, when construction is complete and the mosque rises high and loftily into the clouds. You'll stand in front of it, you and your children and your children's children, so proud that you'll all shout out, 'There it is, our mark that will do us proud in lands far and wide until the Day of the Resurrection. So, blessed be God, Maker of all things. All countries will have risen up to share in the glory that awaits us, more or less. Except for you, you children of Iblis . . ." And all of us said, "Amen."

33

ON THE THIRD DAY, THE water, black from the overflowing sewers, still flooded the alleys and submerged the doors and windows. A deadly river was flowing. Surging forward. Its current carrying vegetables, tables, armoires, and mice, as well as cats that didn't have the time to eat them. The flow swept them up so suddenly they didn't have a chance to pounce. Now it seemed that they were moving alongside them. Sharing the same obscure fate. All of them moving toward the ocean along with some upside-down vendors' carts. Three or four streets down there was a woman crying. Kika moved this way and that in order to gather up her belongings so that nothing would be left behind while she sat in front of the door crying. I asked Kika what she had lost that made her cry so hard. "She didn't lose anything." The woman said that it was an unexpectedly good thing that the rain had come when it did so as to hasten her move. If not for the rain, it would have been difficult for her to leave the neighborhood and part with these walls that had witnessed her birth and watched her neighbors grow up. There were no neighbors now. They'd all left. She cried even harder.

The neighbors were now living in new apartments by the edge of the forest. Lucky them. Only yesterday, they had been crammed into falling-down wrecks of houses, and today here they were, happily ensconced in three-room apartments with kitchens and bathrooms. Kika had his pants rolled up. His trousers and shirt were wet and muddy. Those who hadn't yet left were now peering down from the rooftops. Their grim faces looked relieved. They were cracking jokes now and providing commentary on the baffling spectacle unfolding before their eyes—a large cage being dragged by the current with a rooster, rabbits, and a peacock riding on top of it. The peacock didn't seem to realize what was going on as it spread its alluring, colorful feathers, turning around and haughtily searching for new admirers amid the tumult. Then came a man sitting on top of an armoire, rocking from side to side as if on a boat. The man was holding a large sign that had "Contribute to the mosque's construction" written on it. As evening approached (an evening recognizable only by the changing colors), there was a crack of thunder nearby. Purple and red streaks poked through gaps in the black clouds that had been opened up by the continuous thunder, as if the world were preparing for the Day of the Resurrection. A human voice drew closer. This time the current had uprooted an enormous tree; some of its branches were being consumed by flames, while at the very top, a man sitting cross-legged, completely covered in black, was yelling, "*Say, 'He is God, the One and Only; God, the Eternal, Absolute,*'" and raising his hands to the sky. "This is a glorious day; this is the Day of the Resurrection. *A day on which neither wealth nor children will benefit.*" The voice became stronger and more confident now that the hour had come. "Allahu akbar! God is great! There is no god but God!" A thick black beard covered his face. The night, which wasn't really night at all, echoed his voice, which was transformed into a hoarse scream as he moved away. Then, after the painful silence that followed the man on the tree, a small child started screaming when the house in front of ours collapsed. I turned toward Kika and he looked at me, terrified. I think the same thought had occurred to him as well, that the child's family might have forgotten him in the chaos of getting hold of the keys. We left the crying woman's doorstep, him in front with me right behind him.

We plunged forward into water up to our chests, searching among the kitchen utensils and miscellaneous items that had settled on the bottom, deep in the mud, in complete and utter darkness. We put one foot down as we lifted the other up, feeling our way, bumping into indistinct shapes that were as discombobulated as we were, moving in no particular direction. All we had to guide us was the child's yelling coming from the destroyed house. We tried to move on in order to get to him, but without success. Torches and candles burned on the roofs above us. Rather than lighting the way, though, they caused the alleyway to sink into an even darker gloom. The flickering yellow light of the lanterns caused thick black shadows to move indifferently across the walls, as if the alley were inhabited by nonhuman beings that had come for the sole purpose of adding their chaos to the general mayhem. I managed to remove some pieces of wood and stone, and some of the furniture that was blocking up the opening, and, as I followed the weak moaning, I squeezed inside. I cut an uncharted path toward a life hanging in the balance. With searching steps, I ventured forward. Then the moaning stopped. I stood still and waited, expecting the moaning to come back to life as if by instinct—life is precious and isn't blown away with the first gust of wind that comes along. I waited, but no sound came. Small frogs emerged from Kika's shirt collar and hopped away terrified in every direction—some of them diving into the mud and making a funny sound—*blouf blouf blouf.* "Do you hear anything, Kika?" I remained standing in the darkness, clinging to the hope that the moaning would start up again. Then I repeated to Kika, "Listen. A faint moan. It came from over there. Do you hear it? It sounds like a person breathing, coming from underneath the dirt." I turned around but didn't see Kika behind me. The darkness intensified, as did my fear of going the wrong way. I turned and paused there for a moment as I took stock of my situation—the dark, the night, the water—hoping that life had found its victim, that it had held on tight in its untiring attempt to bring people back from the dead against their will. No, it wasn't a moaning sound I was hearing. It was just the sound of mosquitoes buzzing. Day or night, these horrible creatures can only be seen by the bumps they leave on your skin. Buzzing rose up everywhere and the parasitic insects swarmed in from every direction; as soon as one flew away, another swooped in like a dive-bomber. These creatures had found the optimal place for their treacherous attacks. Just from their sound, you'd almost swear that they were larger and deadlier than a silly little mosquito. Or maybe they'd had sufficient time during these past two days to grow larger and bulkier, to become such a deadly threat. As for the sound of the child's voice, it had completely disappeared underneath the rubble.

I rushed outside waving my hands all over the place, trying to shoo away the annoying insects, and then I made my way toward the rushing water. I caught sight of Kika and another person walking upstream carrying a dripping corpse on their shoulders, a person not quite saved from the disaster. Others were making their way behind them carrying other victims, corpses freed from the compulsion to moan or scream. Freed from every desire. And the cemetery? There are no cemeteries on the water's surface. The dead won't find their graves tonight, despite the efforts of Kika and the others. I meant to call out to Kika when the waves swept me away. So rather than call out to him, I found myself shouting, without even being aware of it, for my mother, so strong were the waves on this side of the disaster. The waters, rather than receding, continued to surge in from every direction. Luckily, Mother had left. Kika went the other way. He may still have been searching for graves for his dead. The place was unrecognizable. Was I close to the alley where I lived? Nothing indicated that. All signs to that effect had disappeared. The cobbler, the barber, the night watchman and his dog, the line of mopeds, the vendors' carts, and so on. And Mother and her sewing machine?

And my sister Habiba and her husband? I remember them all in a rush of nostalgia, my eyes brimming with tears. All of these lives would have been submerged underwater if not for the mercy of the employee who had saved us in the nick of time. I also thought about Father in his chair, and the crack that had appeared in his ceiling. I was thinking about all of this when I saw the dog coming down the great river that had been formed by the torrents of water. I thought he was playing, but the strength of the water's flow made me realize that the current was sweeping him away. It was the cemetery dog, no doubt about it. Or his cousin. All dogs look alike. The look in his eyes convinced me even more that he was the cemetery dog. He was looking at me with pleading eyes. Should I rescue him? I grabbed a rope I found lying next to me, but something stopped me just as I was about to throw the rope. Why not leave him to his fate? Why not let the fourth or the tenth office where he worked rescue him? Rather than move forward, I took a step back and let the current drag him away. I followed him with a sense of relief as he bobbed along the water's surface, his ferocity doing him no good there—neither his sharp teeth nor his disgusting tongue nor his supposed viciousness did him any good—until he disappeared under the water. His limbs continued to flail around in the air for a bit before disappearing as well. My happiness knew no bounds. A joy inside me ignited like a flame. A child hanging out of one of the windows yelled exuberantly, "Hey, hey, the dog was swallowed by the crocodile!" I turned around, but didn't see any crocodiles. All I saw was water. The child was only joking with me, but picturing the dog's fate as the crocodile ripped him apart and then swallowed him caused my joy to flare up even more, until for a moment I was embarrassed. And now? Now we were surrounded by water on all sides. Brown water. Black water. Everything around us was water.

34

KIKA SAYS HE SAW FARAH, because he doesn't know that the ocean swallowed her up. "Where?" He doesn't respond. He's all mixed up. This is what I keep repeating to myself after I hear him say "Follow me" four days after the flooding. After four exhausting days, he's mixing up faces. We see that we have made it through the flood safely, despite it all. Even as we set off trudging through the muddy street, I continue to wonder why I am walking at his side, knowing full well how things will turn out. Maybe he had seen her sister, or someone who looked like her. How many times have I heard someone say they saw their father who had died ten years before? Or someone who saw his wife crossing the street with camel feet instead of her own? This can often be attributed to a lack of sleep. Three sleepless nights would be enough to cause Kika to see Farah in the midst of this fever of face confusion. One thing for sure: He hasn't stopped thinking about her as I thought he had. I didn't tell him she'd drowned. But he is thinking about her. I leave him to his blindness and walk next to him beneath sunbeams that seem complete, fully formed, and warm for the first time. So much so that the day seems new. Youthful. Washed clean. The shivering that overwhelms me isn't caused by the cold. Rather, I am shivering because of a forgotten spring that has crept up on me. Spring had started while we were preoccupied with other things. I haven't seen a day like this for some time.

There's a procession of several families leaving the neighborhood. The women walk behind squeaky carts, carrying bundles on their heads. The men are eating. Eating their breakfast as they walk to their new apartments. A day or two behind schedule, but despite that, they see—with a sort of misguided or deviant logic—that they'll be the first to arrive. It's a long way and Farah's image is lodged deep in my mind. Is it the same girl Kika is thinking of? It might be her, or it might not be. Most likely it's someone else—her sister, or someone who looks like her. Farah drowned. The ocean swallowed her up. Maybe she was picked up by a fishing boat or she got up onto the back of a dolphin swimming by. It might be her, or it might not be. I'd like to think that it was her. Little kids climb up onto the carts. They yell and shout joyfully at one another, happy to see the world from so high up. They stand on top of upside-down tables and clap. Then again, people do look a lot like one another when you look at them the right way. Farah. I had erased her from my thoughts, and here she is now, rising up from the forgotten corners of my mind, laughing as she had that night under the stars. I'm back lying on the beach, watching the bright laughter shine in the darkness before she's swallowed up by the silence of the night and the crashing of the waves. The entire night I crossed the ocean, the darkness, and the waves, but I didn't find her. Then I told myself that there's no girl in the world who looks so much like Farah that you could confuse her with someone else. There is no one else.

The street we're crossing now is completely deserted. The people who used to live here left early. They slipped away during the night so as not to get caught in traffic along the way. The doors are locked. The walls breathe, relaxed finally, drying to their hearts' content in the sun. And what am I supposed to do with that night? There, on that night, I watched Farah dive into the water and disappear. I was a witness. That's right. It happened right under my nose and I was a witness to it. Another part of my mind tells me that, because it was night, I didn't see her drown at all, and although it might have been her, it might not have been. I'd like to think it was someone else. I'd like to think it was her that Kika saw. I walk behind him counting the collapsed houses so as not to think about her. Seven houses had been destroyed, not to mention the others in varying states of ruin. And Farah? I try to avoid thinking about her, but I can't not think about her. There are other carts in front of other houses, with furnishings forming small mountains on top of them. People go in empty-handed and come out loaded with possessions. Running in and out. Disappearing underneath their burdens so much that you don't know where their words are coming from. Armoires, wet mattresses, pots and pans, empty cages, televisions, and children. A chicken hanging upside down by its feet. An old woman sits on the edge of the cart spinning tales of a journey that hasn't yet begun. The road is long and the houses are far away. Why did they build the affordable housing out in the middle of nowhere, twenty kilometers away or more? A skinny horse is tied to the cart and stomps the muddy earth with its hooves, not because it's in a hurry to leave, but rather because there are flies biting its legs. The horse is relaxed standing there, unconcerned with the affordable housing, or with anything else. A woman asks her husband where he lost the key as he runs around the cart searching his pockets and socks, then in his belt. Farah disappeared three or more months ago. She left her sandals and her laugh on the beach, along with a lit flame. I lost the sandals. The flame went out. But the laugh? It has come back to ring in my ears like a set of silver bracelets. Its sound is what drives me forward. I walk behind Kika to its rhythm. I'll find her. I won't find her, because she disappeared. We go up the last street twice. I won't find her because Kika said he lost the address. The green door. We go up the street a third time. Kika doesn't find this green door. There's no green door on this street like there is on the other ones. Yesterday the door was green. Did it change color overnight? There's no other street in front of us. The alleys, houses, and doors have all come to an end.

The sound of a stone being tossed on the ground. The sound of a foot scraping the dirt. Numbers being sung: "Un, deux, trois." A bare foot pushes the stone around inside some rectangles drawn with a piece of charcoal by a small hand. A young girl no more than six years old jumps across the rectangles calling out the numbers drawn inside them. The rectangles are wet because the ground is wet. The other foot is also bare. When the girl jumps, the edges of her short skirt fly up around her. The numbers fly cheerfully all around her because of the soft ring of her voice. There's a woman sitting on the doorstep of her house. She has put a piece of embroidered cloth on her head. Traditional folk music plays from a small radio next to her. It doesn't seem like either of them are going anywhere. The woman's eyes are open, but they aren't looking at the girl jumping in front of her. They aren't looking in any particular direction. Rather, it's as if they are following a bird flying overhead. Kika stands in front of her. Finally, he finds the sign he was looking for. I shivered. This is what happens when you get close to what you're looking for. A slight shock that causes the breathing to stop for a few seconds. My heart feels like it has shifted. Is this the door that Farah disappeared behind? But it isn't green. Kika holds his hand over his mouth. He seems unsure as to whether he should walk toward the door. No, he isn't convinced that this is the right door. The girl stops playing. The woman leans her head slightly to the side. She looks at us with her ears because she's blind. She gropes around for the radio and places it on her lap. The music's volume goes down a notch. We walk past the woman. Disappointed, I continue to hear the small foot scraping the ground behind me, and the numbers cheerfully being called out. "Un, deux, trois." Unaware of us and what we're looking for. The girl's legs are skinny, like two cold stalks. Some of the houses on this street are in the sun, and some are in the shade. We walk on the sunny side. I can't read any-thing clearly on Kika's back. As he walks in front of me, his movements remain ambiguous. Then Kika stops in front of one of the doors. Finally. The door is broken and the interior of the shop is destroyed, as if it has been looted by thieves. Kika looks at me. Not like someone who has found what he was looking for. Not like someone preparing to reveal a secret he knows I'm waiting for. Rather, like a horse that has been spooked at the last moment, no longer wanting to move for-ward or backward. He says he doesn't remember where he last saw her. No sorrow. No regret. With an indifference that is closer to disregard. After two hours. After all the alleys we have walked through. He says it like someone who knows but doesn't want to reveal that he knows. His eyes show this, and then some. His eyes contain all the wickedness he has stored up inside him, all of his ill intentions. What I want to do is slap Kika on the back of the neck to make him remember, but he is determined *not* to remember. We walk back down to the end of the alley. Then we turn around as he counts the houses. He counts them like someone passing the time, distracting him-self. He knows that I know that's what he's doing. Then he says that he only heard her voice, and that he isn't even sure that the voice he heard was hers, or whether the alley was the same alley. The alleys have all come to look the same after the flooding. What I want to do is slap Kika on the back of the neck to make him forget about the flood and remember where he saw her or heard her voice. But he doesn't remember. The alleys are still the same alleys. And besides, we are in the part of the neighborhood that hasn't suffered much damage. Why would the alleys change? Would they change simply because we were searching for Farah? Kika's chitchat doesn't convince me. I walk behind him, wanting to find her more than ever. But the more enthusiastic I get, the less hope I have of finding her. That's how it goes. But there is still hope, at least as long as Kika remains so stubborn. What does someone like him hold on to? Both of his parents abandoned him, each in their own way. His mother is a whore who went to sell her fruits to the Spanish; does she even still have fruit that the Spanish could want? And his father—if he ever really had a father—was thrown into some prison abroad. But I don't lose hope. There's still a thread that ties Kika and me together. I hold tightly to this thread for a moment, then I stop. This whole story seemed suspicious from start to finish. And now? As he stands in front of me, I recognize Kika up close, with all the evil that runs through his veins, as he tells me that he saw her. I doubt absolutely everything he says. It's too bad for Kika that the visa made its way into his mother's passport. He no longer has anything else he can boast about. And I don't care. All I think about is why he's hated by everyone. I discover this for the first time as well. And Farah? She isn't there, neither on this street nor any other. She's at the bottom of the ocean. All of this has afflicted Kika's sick imagination. Why not? I have to consider the situation in this new light. The end result is that Farah drowned. We're done. I'm no longer paying any mind to him or what he says. From this point on, I won't concern myself with what he conceals or what he says out loud. I'm no longer interested in the hostility, bitterness, malice, and negativity that show so clearly in his eyes. Kika is no longer a friend, and this is something I won't go back on. Although I'm fully confident of this, I try to suppress my desire to cry as I watch Kika going back up the street, shrugging, with his hands in his back pockets. I have no desire to catch up with him, to walk next to him, or to follow him for another minute. This, too, is a story that's done.

I stand close to the blind woman, watching the little girl push the stone in front of her as Kika recedes from view and disappears from my life forever. I think about the stone that moves from rectangle to rectangle. Comfortable with its short journey that's defined by the lines of wet charcoal. It doesn't take its thoughts any further than this, and for thousands of years it won't have the desire to go any further. I also think about the numbers that fly around me. Un, deux, trois. They play their part in moving the stone along from square to square. Everything has its small, humble task that it seeks to fulfill and doesn't care to move beyond. I hear the woman tell me to come closer, so I do. She clears a space next to her. The fringes of her decorated headscarf fall over her forehead. This makes her look not so old despite her deeply wrinkled face. She doesn't look like Mother, who covers her hair with a black cloth—always black, and without fringes. The trace of a hidden smile never leaves her lips. She tells me that she knows what's making me so sad. Her sadness should be greater than mine, but that's not how it is. Her children and grandchildren had left during the night so they wouldn't have to take her with them, leaving her as she is now—blind and crippled. She was born this way. No sight to guide her and no movement to carry her along. She doesn't know why she was created, why she continued on, or how she will leave this world. She's never harmed or been of any use to anyone. She couldn't have even if she had wanted to. This is why she stopped praying years ago because she didn't know who she should direct her prayers to, or why. Her children and grandchildren had slipped off, tiptoeing away one night after another. She hadn't been asleep when they left. She pretended to be asleep so they could leave with clear consciences. Her only daughter didn't turn back to look at her as she locked the door and fled. The little girl stops playing when she hears the woman talking about her mother. She comes closer. The woman places her hand on the little girl's head and says, "As for this child, she was hiding in an armoire in one of the destroyed houses so she wouldn't have to go with them." Then, with the same calmness, she asks me if I want to see. I have no desire to see a room, destroyed or not, containing an armoire in which a child no older than six had hidden. She says she is talking about the girl.

"What girl?"

Farah. I stop asking, looking, and even thinking as I sit there next to the old woman. I am a long way off from thinking that just a few steps are separating me from her, and that Kika had been standing in front of that same door. Rather than go in himself or invite me to go in, he had continued down the street in order to lead me astray. The little girl grabs my hand and leads me to the first floor. Yes. Her thin hand makes this miracle happen; a cold, thin hand forgotten in a forsaken alley, with such power to infuse you with so much happiness without you even realizing it. I let the little hand take me up, leading me without question. Trusting. Surrendering. As if I were finally grabbing onto proof that she is there. The child's hand trembles between my fingers, as if I were holding a day-old chick, able to feel its heartbeat between my fingers, trying not to let it fall. I placed my hand into hers without the slight-est thought—without hope, for Kika had left none—or rather with the only thought that had any control over me. In the state I am in now, I prefer to think only about my steps as they imitate those of the child. Do the prints left by the girl's bare feet bring me any closer to her, or do they help widen gap between us? I couldn't have thought of anything beyond this even if I tried. Farah's image is alive, yet unable right then to invade my thoughts. Even when the little girl stops in front of the door, I don't know what's going to happen. Farah isn't going to enter the realm of possibility again after all that has happened to me—with her and with Kika. With her primarily. As if there had been an opportunity before her and she had lost it. Even the door can't reveal all the surprises caught up in there. It is nothing more than a falling-down door that makes you back up rather than invites you to go forward. I stand at the doorstep while the girl sits down on the top step. She takes out the small stone she has been playing with and begins to tap the wall with it—un, deux, trois—while I stand there hes-itantly, unable to move beyond where the girl has taken me. I turn toward the girl. The small, thin, beautiful hand is tapping the wall while I, like someone spelling out words in a new language, knock on the door three times, imitating the same rhythm the little hand is making—un, deux, trois. The door to the room opens on its own. I take a step forward, accompanied by the rhythm of the small stone in the little girl's hand.

35

Mother

I HAD BOUGHT A HALF kilo of meat for the couscous because tomorrow was a Friday. I also bought vegetables and a lot of tomatoes. I like tomatoes more than any other vegetable. The meat cost a lot. The neighbors say I make the best couscous in the neighborhood. Abdullah came at night with the keys in hand. Abdullah is Habiba's husband. I told him, "Abdullah, I'm making couscous first," to which he replied, "We don't have time." Abdullah's in a hurry because he wants to pray with the people in the new neighborhood's mosque. Abdullah was forced on us. Like life. We put up with him so God will do what's best. So, we left before dawn. Habiba, Khadija, and Si Omar in his chair. The little one, Karima, jumped up onto the cart and went back to sleep. Ever since he fell in the mosque, Si Omar hasn't gotten up from his chair. We carried as much as we could with us. Abdullah went empty-handed so as not to be late. Khadija said, "Let's take turns pushing the chair because it's a long way." Because of her pregnancy, Habiba wouldn't be able to. I put the meat and vegetables in a plastic bag and tucked them underneath the chair. We placed what remained of the furniture and dishes (still dripping wet) on the cart, along with the black rooster we would slaughter before crossing the threshold of the new house. Friday is always a blessed day. Our neighbor, Kulthum, was in front of her house washing her old dishes and putting them in a green plastic pail. When she buys a pail, she always buys a green one. Abdullah forbade us to tell anyone about where we were heading on account of the evil eye, even though everyone was heading in the same direction. I told her anyway. "Shame on you. God entrusted us with neighbors," she said. "May God bring you health and wealth, amen." Abdullah didn't know that her family left before we did, also because of the evil eye. People don't like to move. Even me. But for the sake of a new place to live . . . Besides, the flood didn't leave anything standing. This house came at just the right time. In the new neighborhood, our lives would continue as they had been, with family and neighbors, because we'd known one another for ages. Good God, the street has never been so quiet! A sort of gloom envelops the soul before wrapping itself around a place in its entirety. The moment one leaves one's neighborhood is difficult, and it leaves a mark on the soul similar to being orphaned. The cart was small. Khadija wanted to take her bed with her. The cart's owner asked that we not burden the animals that were pulling it, but Khadija insisted on the bed. It was a new bed, not the bed she'd left at her husband's place. Most of the bed hung off the cart. Habiba said, "Why don't we tie Father's chair to the cart so the donkey can pull them both together?" Si Omar wasn't sold on the idea, indicating this with his eyes. As we passed in front of the mosque, I asked him whether he wanted to stop for a bit so he could look at it at his leisure. Tears glistened in his eyes. I handed him a handkerchief. He has started to speak with his eyes. Health is the most important thing in life. Once you lose your health, no amount of money or power will be of any use. That's what I think.

The chair was purchased at the flea market. It cost us what we spend in a whole week. All of life's necessities are expensive—water, electricity, even bread at the public oven. We eat a lot of eggs. The children don't help at all. I had hoped that my daughter, Khadija, would have been luckier than I've been. That she would have found a job or traveled. That she would have found some enjoyment in the world and not think about marriage. Our ancestors used to say, "Marriage and death, there's nothing else left." The day he went off, Suleiman didn't change his clothes. He didn't wear any extra clothes. He hadn't yet made up his mind about going. He ate his dinner, went off to bed, and fell asleep at his usual time. I woke him up in the morning so he could empty the trash can. That was how it went. He found the kids all gathered together. They said to him, "Will you split with us? This time it's guaranteed." He went to the port in his pajamas. No pants or anything. When his brother, Outhman, came back that evening, he said that maybe he'd done it. Maybe he'd found a safe place to hide in a truck. Regardless, when he got there, he'd take care of himself. Then news arrived that he was working in the Gulf. Suleiman could always take care of himself. Outhman is just like him, but he's still flighty. He doesn't do anything useful. Except for when it's time to eat, he's never at home. No doubt a day will come when he'll join his brother and I can rest assured that he'll be okay. He's always thinking about when he'll leave for the Gulf. Everyone who goes to Europe comes back in the summer strutting around like a pharaoh—cars, money, swagger. But they don't tell the truth. They don't say they're doing hard labor. They say, "Everything's beautiful. There's work. Money's there. Cafés are open day and night. Your rights are guaranteed. And if you marry one of their daughters, it'll make finding work even easier. Even without work, you can live your life on unemployment. Then you won't need a job. You won't have to wake up at dawn for any old job." Others say, "There's work in the Gulf, not in Europe." That's what I think too. We haven't always lived in the old city. Our first house was like an inn. In fact, originally it *was* an inn. Even after it became a private residence, it still looked like an inn. But it was old; so old that the stable wasn't even fit for livestock anymore. I begged Si Omar to move. I refused to stay there because it was so old. Its roof was falling in. It was more than a hundred years old.

It had been an inn for livestock and people before my father bought it when he arrived in Casablanca, turning it into a woodshop and a place to live. I told him, "Let's sell it before it collapses on us," but Si Omar doesn't think the way I do. I saved some money, which I used to rent a house, and we lived there up until yesterday. Ever since I moved into this house, Si Omar hasn't spent anything on his children and I don't say anything to him when he visits us. He comes and goes as if walking around the bazaar. The kids don't need him now. Suleiman left for the Gulf and Outhman will join him there. Khadija's health improved thanks to Abdullah. It seemed that the epileptic fits paid off. They agreed with her. She didn't fall down and faint anymore. Nor did she tear at her clothing. She had almost become happy. And when she marries again, if God smiles upon her and grants her a respectable husband, my work will be done. I'll be able to say that my ship has arrived safe and sound. The girls insisted I sit next to the cart's owner. The cart's owner loves to rent out his cart, but he doesn't like burdening his animals. I sat in back so as not to hear him grumble, and to be able to see the road as it stretched out beneath my feet. Karima came and sat next to me, happily swinging her legs in the air. I took her into my arms and kissed her hair. People change when they move from one place to another. As I swayed from side to side atop the cart, I found myself humming an old song I had always liked: "The blanca, mon amour. I'll marry her without any magic allure . . ." There was still a long way to go. Those who knew the city better than I did said we'd get there in the afternoon. Habiba got tired of pushing the chair. To protect her head from the sun, she put a cloth over it. We needed the sun a day ago, during the flood. We didn't need all that rain, and we don't need all this sun now. Where were the clouds that had been floating by up above? We don't have fields or farms. The rain left the lemon and strawberry farms alone, but attacked our poor houses. The road we were traveling on was long and wide. There were brightly colored billboards everywhere, rising up all along the road. The flood hadn't damaged them at all. Naked blondes laughing with their full red lips. Khadija dragged her feet as if on a forced march. Advertisements for luxury apartments. Were those the same apartments that were waiting for us? Complete with bathrooms and windows that looked out onto the forest? I didn't know a thing about the new neighborhood. It wouldn't be as grand as those on the posters, but at the very least we'd be moving from the misery where we had been to life as it should be. That was how I saw it. Still, and may God forgive me, moving to the new residence will keep us from the only thing that had made us feel that we were alive—the ocean, the beach, and the wind as it carried the smell of seaweed into our houses in the morning. Being able to see the ocean so close to us had allowed us to feel that life was worth living. It was no accident that they built the mosque beside it.

The kids grew up with nothing to fear. I used to be scared for them when they were younger. I didn't want them to be raised badly, even though all neighborhoods are the same now—dope fiends, beggars, and drunks everywhere. I worked for the sake of the children. If it hadn't been for the children I wouldn't have thought about working. I always bore my responsibility inside and outside of the home because Si Omar was never around. When we were living in the stable— that's what I called it—he worked in a carpentry shop in the morning, and in the evenings he'd go see his friends at the café, not coming home until after midnight, smelling of kif, sweat, and all the other smells that accumulate in cafés. I was born and grew up in that stable. When he was still alive, my father bought it and turned it into a large woodshop. People would come from all over Casablanca to buy tables, armoires, doors, and all the other things they needed for their houses. As for my cousin Si Omar, Father brought him from Marrakech because he had no job, and taught him the craft. He got so good at carpentry that now it was like he was born with it. But he could never hold onto money for too long. By the time my father died, we had already gotten married and replaced him in the shop. When Si Omar's business flourished, he began to spend indiscriminately. Men are all the same. They only spend money on themselves. He never bought me a gift, not even when business was booming and he was making lots of money, except in those first days of marriage—except for the necklace and the two rings. When we got married he bought me a necklace made of regular silver and two rings made of Saharan silver. He took me on the back of his motorbike to Sidi Abdel-Rahman Beach. My hair, wrapped in a silk kerchief, blew in the wind—he also bought me a silk kerchief. At Sidi Abdel-Rahman Beach he bought me some shaved iced. It was the first and last time. He bought me a scoop of shaved ice because I asked for it, and because the idea had never before crossed his mind. That time has passed. Our share of fatigue, worry, and ennui has caught up with us.

Then we arrived in a neighborhood called "California," which I had never heard of. It had trees of every sort, both inside and outside the houses. Over here, the houses were like palaces, complete with guards, green roofs, and arched windows. We sought shade beneath the trees and asked a guard for some water. The families on the road with us were tired. We left them behind. We had covered half the distance. We were tired too. Before we started to walk again, Karima said she could walk on her own two feet to the new neighborhood. The pain, which I had forgotten about, returned to my knee. The cart's owner said, "The cart would've had enough room for everyone if it weren't for Khadija's bed." I asked Khadija if we could get rid of the bed, for Habiba's sake, who was pregnant, and who wouldn't be able to go on if she had to keep walking. For the little girl's sake too. For everyone's sake.

When I was first married, I used to get up at seven and perform the morning prayer. Then I'd prepare breakfast, sweep up, wash the floor, and straighten up the house. After that, I'd make dough for the day's bread before starting to prepare lunch. After lunch, I'd wash the dishes and plates, then take a short nap to get ready to start the last part of the day's work—washing up, and rinsing the wheat (if there was any) then drying it. At five I'd go out to the souiqa street market, which was an opportunity to forget about the house and its tiring chores. By this time of day, the prices of fruits and vegetables would have been reduced—I just needed to be careful because the quality was rarely very good by then, but I can tell fresh vegetables by their color. Then I'd return home to prepare dinner and wash the dishes. When I was first married I'd spend summers in the country at Si Omar's family's place. I stopped doing that when I moved to the old city and began to work, thanks to God. I bought a sewing machine just like some of the neighbors had done. Working at home is better than working somewhere else. Sometimes my knee hurts and I feel as if my life is slipping away from me. There's no city like Casablanca. "The blanca, mon amour, I'll marry her without any magic allure . . ." I already miss it even though I've just left. I don't know why. No one dies of hunger in Casablanca, unlike in Khouribga or Settat, where you don't always find what you want or need. Not so in Casablanca. Rich and poor alike—everyone finds what they want there. One time, Si Omar suggested we sell the house my father left me and buy a house in Berrechid, but I refused. Despite the drunks and homeless beggars who give it a bad reputation, not to mention the overcrowding, the thieves, the black-market alcohol dealers, and the criminals you find everywhere, Casablanca is still the most beautiful city. I started to sew at home to meet the household's daily expenses, and God did not disappoint me. It was as if you had said, "Wealth came right to my door." Because Casablanca is just that. What you need to live on appears right there in front of you. All you need is a little positive thinking. Washcloths, headscarves, children's clothing, and long women's shirts, as well as the many products from the north that I added afterward. Women like the clothes I sell, and they buy them in bulk because they're cheap. They can wear many of them in a single day. From this angle, I can say that I'm lucky. I believe in luck. The lucky one always moves forward. Lucky because we were born in the right place. This is the only place in the country where you can feel secure in life. I say that if you don't make it here, you won't make it anywhere. Not in Europe and not in the Gulf. But the kids, kids in general, are always looking to far-off places, wanting things they don't know anything about and have never seen in their lives. As if they're living in a perpetual dream. In any case, we're all prisoners of our own fate, which we cannot escape. That's how I see it. The neighbors are jealous of me because my business is profitable. We have to praise God because the neighborhood gave us what any person would hope for—work, family, neighbors. This is the right place. The problem of thieves will, no doubt be solved because people are convinced, even without having to say it, that honest work is what will keep one's reputation intact. Misfortune won't touch you as long as you carry goodness in your heart, because God will never be satisfied if evil triumphs. Also, the police are around at all hours of the day and night. I hope there are as many in our new neighborhood. The police are evil, there's no denying it. Their operations are bad for business. Especially when they're overwhelmed by greed and seize our neighbors' merchandise only to sell it on the next street over. Working for the police is also a profitable business.

We arrived following the afternoon prayer, as the neighbors said we would. We pushed the cart up the hill with some difficulty. We were also pushing the donkey, which was exhausted by the trek. At the top of the hill, the buildings came into view. Our new buildings. Bright white in the sun. They remained bright as snow until we arrived. Karima jumped down from the cart and started to run between the ditches. Everything was brand new. We had arrived in the new neighborhood, but it seemed like there were a lot of things missing. The road running between the houses was all dug up, with large stones sticking up from it and metal poles coming out of the holes. Some of the walls were whitewashed—the front walls. Splotches of cement and cement color dominated the rest. The white that had blinded our eyes as we gazed at the neighborhood came to an end as soon as we entered. Cables and pipes were stuck into the houses, forming a bridge over the structures. And there was no sidewalk, or rather, it was a work in progress. The line of stones that would form the edge of the sidewalk was there. And it was nearly straight. As for the sidewalk itself, it was not there at all. The dirt extended right up to the houses' doorsteps, filled with holes, metal, and pipes. Then there were the windows, side by side in a harsh-looking line. Small and dark. Forming a disturbing scene along with the sky up above. Anything can be fixed. After some weeks, life will change here. Much work awaits us. Work is necessary, and it's the only thing we won't lack. Today, tomorrow, and in the days after that. Everyone will find a job and a livelihood here. God won't disappoint us. Good things lie ahead. The glory days are to come. Great days will come when our new neighborhood will be even whiter and more spectacular—thanks to our work and our efforts—and the peach and pomegranate trees that we will have planted will blossom. Parks and fountains too. In the evenings we'll sit around the table in clean clothes eating food that we deserve, exchanging stories of those desperate days that are gone, never to return. The days of hard labor are done, leaving behind plenty of money that will be enough for the lean years, and good memories, and something magical floating in the air like everything the soul yearns for. Bread, honest work, a roof over our heads. Tomorrow will no longer be uncertain. Glory be to God! It is truly a gift from God that we've found a place to live so soon after the flood. "The blanca, mon amour, I'll marry her without any magic allure."

VI

36

THE MAN SITTING IN THE wicker chair, brushing the ground impatiently with his feet and listening to the strange roar, had noticed neither the two o'clock train, even after it had passed, nor the fog that had begun to obscure the horizon in a light purple veil a short while ago. He sat gazing at the gendarmes' car approaching in the distance, not taking his eyes from it the whole time it traversed the distance, slowly and without a sound, as if it wasn't approaching at all. It appeared small from so far away. The man stood up now and craned his neck as if to encourage it to move faster, but the car neither sped up nor slowed down. The man forgot about the skewers of meat on the fire. Perhaps the car was weighed down by its troubling cargo. The two lovers who had disappeared from his thoughts reappeared now. Was the car carrying some of their complicated story with them? The car didn't say anything, nor did the two gendarmes. They were still far away. What was the young man thinking about right now? And the older woman? Were they thinking about the disastrous relationship they had stumbled into against their will? Did it warm their cold night as they were grabbing onto the embers of love for the first time? It wasn't like the animal attraction that compels a man get up on top of a woman to empty himself into her, while he wonders whether the being that will come will be a criminal or a religious scholar. Rather, it was more like a one-time adventure with no past and no future; one they were forced to plunge into, knowing full well they wouldn't emerge fully intact. The pure call of the body. The body has its own special rationale. Desire has its own timing, and it will always be that way. Children or no children. Marriage papers or no marriage papers. Despite the patrols, guards, husbands, wives, and judges, the forbidden and the permissible, laws and prisons, faqihs, astrologers, soothsayers, and pimps of every type. Even when it drove past the barbed-wire barrier, even as it got closer, even when it stopped and the two gendarmes got out, the car remained cloaked in secrecy. The man continued to wonder where the magic this car practiced sprang from, even though it was empty. Where were the two lovers? Had the gendarmes killed them and tossed them into the wild, or had reckless Bedouins killed and eaten them? No trace of what he was thinking about appeared on the gendarmes' faces, or on the car. The man didn't walk toward the car, nor did he look through its window to still the thoughts that had been burrowing into his mind for hours. He would have preferred another ending. Perhaps the two lovers had been saved, having found themselves quite by accident on a road rather than at a roadblock, and a truck passing by at just the right moment had carried them off. At just the right moment, they sat in the truck's cab as it tore up the road, driving off into the distance, taking them away as they wiped their sweat away and smiled—the smile of someone who has been saved at the last possible moment. The young man would say to his lover, "Remember this moment. Remember that we got through this too." The smile of someone who has been saved at the last possible moment—a moment infused with youthful thoughts. The smile of someone who has been saved at the last possible moment, which always had tucked away inside of it a little bit of pain that quickly turned to tears, burning tears of joy.

The two gendarmes greeted the judge but they didn't greet his companion. They asked him about his family and children—about the one who works in the bank and the one pursuing his studies in America—about his wife who went on the hajj pilgrimage last year and who is thinking about doing the umrah pilgrimage this year, inshallah, and whether he will accompany her, God willing. The man stepped up to the grill and turned the skewers over, blowing on the flame. A cloud of ash rose up around him and got in his eyes before settling down on the sizzling meat. The meat started to crackle again on the fire. The smoke rising from the grill carried the smell of grilled meat to the two gendarmes. The scent rose to their nostrils. They grabbed the skewers and bit into the charred meat, lips parted, biting like animals, trying to avoid touching the hot metal. They chewed for a while as they held the skewers up in their hands. The gendarme with the yellow epaulettes on his shoulders turned to the judge. "D'ya wanna see them?" The judge didn't understand what the gendarme was talking about, thinking that the meat in the gendarme's mouth was preventing him from speaking clearly. The gendarme repeated, "D'ya wanna see them?" "Who?" "The boy and the woman." It was enough for the judge to twitch his nose. As if a fly had just bitten him. The gendarme with no epaulettes on his shoulders went back behind the car. The man was no longer interested in the two skewers, or in his eyes, which had been blinded by the ashes. The judge let his companion's hand fall. The young man stepped out of the car first, his clothes dirty, but not torn as the man expected, and you couldn't even see the dirt unless you really looked closely. Then the woman. A story that wasn't worth all of this anticipation and waiting. It seemed as if the man's expectations had been dashed. Disappointment first. Then hatred—not blind hatred, but rather, blackness. That was what was pressing down on his chest. He felt as if he was going to cry, because hatred contains its share of gloom. The young man had lost the opportunity to save what could have been saved, and there wouldn't be another opportunity. These sorts of opportunities don't come around too often. All of this happened before the woman stepped out—between the moment when the young man emerged from the car and the moment when the woman appeared. Her coal-black hair fell down over her white forehead. Her white skin was clear. A high chest, generous, with curves that made the man's mouth water—would make any man's mouth water—as soon as she appeared, strangely unhurried and confident, as if she hadn't just spent the night being chased by dogs, gendarmes, children, men and women, old folk, and bad luck. Her bright, beautiful wide eyes were milky white, their lashes blackened with kohl. There wasn't a trace of sleeplessness, fatigue, or regret in them.

A black butterfly with red, orange, and yellow spots fluttered in and out of the threads of smoke rising from the grill, darting toward it and then away again, flying up and down. It flew away from the smoke until you'd thought it had flown away, escaped with its skin intact, and then it reappeared, making the same dodging circles to get even closer to the fire, its fragile, brightly colored wings penetrating the smoke in a game that entertained both of them. The smoke and the butterfly danced with one another, touched one another, each tickling the edges of the other, embracing one another and then pulling away. Laughing together from afar then touching each other once again. Neither the smoke nor the butterfly knew how this deadly game would end. Would the butterfly end its life far away in a bird's beak, or on top of a carnivorous flower, or would it end here, on the grill? Instead of swooping down into this blaze all at once, it tried to become one with it so it wouldn't be struck by the flame. The woman who got out of the gendarmes' car in bare feet continued to follow the butterfly's flight. Her feet were clean, the toes slender, nails painted a light rose. The color made her walk look more feminine. Her feet showed no traces of dirt or wild berries, nor of stones or thorns from the road. Her feet looked as if they walked only on rugs, to melodies that rang in her ear all night long. An image of Farah passed by like a summer cloud as he watched the woman walk proudly toward him, sit down, then rub her right temple and kiss her finger as if today were her lucky day. A butterfly lives for one day, but it's a full life that contains all possible happiness, all possible pain, and whatever else might come along to furnish the memory. The butterfly flew around some more, down, down some more. It was swallowed up by the smoke and didn't reappear. In a little while, the judge and the two gendarmes would eat it in the grilled meat, and they'd smell it in the smoke that was making their mouths water. They wouldn't know, nor would it interest them to know, that their lives were extended for a minute or two thanks to a butterfly that was just passing through. Farah had passed through just like the butterfly. The man didn't think about whether Farah had any regrets when she left her small city to sing on television, or in front of a huge crowd in Honor Stadium, or in front of the cameras in the United Nations Plaza. All she had was this one choice. All she had was the few months she spent in Casablanca. Eight months, maybe nine. Whether it was a little less or a little more didn't matter. During that time, she had gone from house to house, season to season, person to person, and passion to passion. But she didn't sing. Maybe she just came to see what summer was like in Casablanca. But she didn't get to see it. Maybe, for her to go away happy, all she had needed was that summer. She left before summer had begun. Despite that, perhaps her short life was enough. Full enough of love—and disappointment—to go away proud and impervious like the woman sitting next to him right now on the sidelines of the fury all around her, following the flight of a butterfly fluttering close to the fire that would swallow it, or that had swallowed it already.

Nothing changed. Things have desires too. What would have been different had Farah not entered the Saâda Cabaret that night? That young man with the tattooed arms, the one wearing the red leather wristband, blocked her way numerous times, trying to prevent her from entering. And in the end, he looked the other way, not knowing that she wouldn't come out the same as when she went in. The mistake wasn't so much his as it was in his unfortunately timed lapse of attention. Perhaps it was the mistake of that other young man, the anonymous one, unknown by anyone, no one knowing his address, face, voice, or clothes; that young man who had called for the waiter, called him over just to ask the time, providing the opportunity at just that moment for Farah to slip inside the cabaret after having come back from her room. He sat in front of the work-shop drawing circles in the dirt, asking himself what he was going to do. The circles he drew were no longer done with the same expertise as before, and for the first and last time he spent the night writing a poem. Half a white sheet of paper with a few lines in blue. The next day, early in the morning, he went back and stood in front of the house with the folded piece of paper in his pocket, in front of the blind woman who was still sitting in the same place. Maybe Farah had woken up. Should he go in? He didn't go in. He stood for a full hour in front of the old woman's house, telling himself that he'd take out the piece of paper and read what was on it, but he didn't. All of this seemed ridiculous. The poem wouldn't change a thing, neither in his journey nor in hers. He imagined that he was married to her, that they had a child, and that the happy family was traveling to the south in the summertime. They continued along side by side, forming memories—that trip to the south, their son burning up with that fever on the first night, and them rushing back home. The following New Year's, rather than going south, they would go up to Ifrane to ski, throw snowballs, and shout out at one another. Nothing like this happened, though. Because he wouldn't equal the smallest bit of the afternoon during which he remained fixed in place in front of the old woman's door, not knowing what to do, hesitating about whether to go up, the short poem in his pocket burning his thigh. Because basically what he wanted to do was say the words he didn't say, and wouldn't say. The words that he wrote down in the form of a few other words that contained only that meaning. Would the door be open if he went up the stairs? It would be better if it were closed so he could slip the paper underneath and run away. He was intent on *not* barging into her room as he had done the day before. The old woman didn't see him. Or perhaps she saw him with that additional sense that only the blind possess. In her traditional clothing, embroidered straw taraza hat on her head over her finely wrinkled face, the black-and-red-striped haik around her waist. The little girl wasn't there. If she had been there, she would have taken him by the hand and gone up with him to the door. Why not sit next to the blind woman and wait and make it look like he wasn't waiting for a thing? He didn't do this, or that. And this old woman, what was she waiting for, sitting here all the time on the doorstep? Why wouldn't she be like him? Waiting for the man she loved? After all these decades, she could still love. The man would come. He'd say the sweet words she'd been waiting for, the sweet words that would cause her to let out a loud, flirtatious laugh, unconcerned with the street and who was passing by. She'd be expecting a gift. The man would take a bottle of perfume out of his pocket and hand it to her, and she'd smell it as she looked to him with all her heart, captivated, enchanted. She'd expect a kiss, so the man would lean forward and kiss her on the lips, long enough to quench the thirst of all the years that had passed. Then she'd get up and go back into her house—light, radiant, happy—and she wouldn't come out again.

37

An Iris Bloomed

AFTER TWENTY-EIGHT DAYS, WHICH I marked off on the work-shop wall, she left her room. In a dress embroidered with flowers this time. That's why, as I looked at her standing in the workshop, I found myself thinking about the flowers as she walked. The slant of the flowers on the dress caused her walk to lose much of its radiance. Usually, when a tailor sews a piece of clothing, he makes it so the flowers stand straight up, rather than lean over or point downward, so as not to have the young woman's future imitate her upside-down or slanted flowers. She took a few steps toward me, hardly making a sound. Her dress rustled lightly. The flowers appeared in its folds and weren't altered by how she walked. She hadn't put perfume on, which would have let me know it was her before she entered. I don't really like perfume.

I knew that she had emerged from the workshop with-out even seeing her or her flowers, especially since I had been waiting all this time, hoping to hear her footsteps, waiting for some sort of movement in the air that would tell me she was approaching, on her own. Without perfume or fragrance. Even without hearing her footsteps, I imagined her now look-ing from afar at the carvings I etched into the wood. My hand was proud of this small victory. The look on her face showed that she didn't like my drawings too much. She wasn't affected by them in the slightest. Whereas, just like I had been during the first week she stayed in my workshop, I was plotting to get her close to me. Nevertheless, Farah was still distant. During that first week, she barely left the spot where she was sitting. We ate and exchanged bits of conversation. We didn't spend too much time on the topic of the lawyer who had blinded her, and who she had agreed, voluntarily, to let rob her—because of his occupation, his new clothes, his cologne, or his lying voice; or because of things I didn't understand—but it was a story that subsequently made us laugh. She told it without bitterness, as if it had happened to another girl in another town. There were other stories similar to that of the lawyer, meaningless ones, which also made us laugh when we told them to one another. But she didn't stray far from the workshop's interior. This was her place, where she sat the first time she came in. Because of our previous experience, I rejected the idea of going down to the ocean to fish. My red drawings would attract her and draw her out of her isolation. This was also what I told myself. By the end of the first week, she began to move toward the decorated pieces of wood without actually getting close to them. I was amazed that the color red—Casablanca red, Father's color—didn't attract her as I had thought and hoped it would. Everybody likes red, except for Farah.

The dress was white with purple flowers. I had noticed it as soon as she stood in the door of her modest room. She stood there as if waiting for someone to show up. Her face was pale and it was difficult to recognize in a room with no windows. As if her real face were hidden underneath a temporary mask that was preparing to surprise me with its previous freshness. Farah's current situation, like that of anyone who has been saved from a disaster, didn't concern me. Barging into her room without permission didn't concern me. I was encouraged by the child's tapping on the wall. Un, deux, trois. I stood there unable to speak, as if the time we had spent apart had created a chasm that was difficult to jump over. How had she been saved from drowning? That was the only question that concerned me. I had spun all sorts of tales about her disappearance that night, each stranger than the other—a ship or fishing boat had pulled her out; she had spent a night, or many nights, clinging to a board that fate had placed in front of her at just the right moment; the tide had tossed her onto a distant beach after she'd spent the night lost, with no moon or stars or even the slightest light to guide her—as I pictured the extraordinary efforts she must have made as she struggled with the waves and the night and the sharks, using all of my mental faculties to avoid picturing her breathing her last breaths underwater. There was nothing more horrible than drowning, which I'd always imagined to be an accidental death. As if the drowned person had slipped or gotten distracted, and here she was now, stumbling over her mistake, thinking she could correct it, a simple mistake. After all, water is merciful and doesn't kill. Making fun of herself, her mistake, and her foot that slipped. Until the final moment, the drowning person thinks she has made a simple mistake that she'll be able to correct, until she sinks to the bottom, until the water brings her back up to the surface emptied of all meaning except for the meaning of being on the water's surface where people don't usually sleep. Death by drowning is always a humorous calamity. I was also thinking about how she arrived at this house, moving between the darkest of thoughts and even worse expectations, as if preparing myself for her fickle moods and strange disappearances. I stood in front of Farah in a room with no windows, without even the smallest peephole you could look through to see the world. Farah's face was pale, drained, the face of a girl exhausted by lack of sleep, or hunger, or both. It was as if I had found her on a boat long lost at sea. Her eyes were filled with doubt and suspicion, at least for the first few minutes, as if she were taking her time to recognize me and what my intentions were. All I remember is that I pointed toward the door, as if inviting her to take a walk around the neighborhood. She responded as if she were saying that she was busy, unable to go with me right then. Maybe tomorrow, or the day after. What was bothering her? What was it that she had been doing before I had barged in on her isolation? What could a young woman possibly be doing in a small room six meters square? Not now. No, before now. Before I went in, this morning, yesterday, and all the time she had spent locked up in this suffocating room. If there had at least been a window, I would have said that she had been spending some of her time watching the girl move her stone from square to square, or watching the birds if her window looked out over the garden. The second time I burst into her room, she categorically refused to accompany me, even when I insisted (when I felt bold enough to dare). As if the room were my room. As if it were just a passing stubbornness that would neither listen to nor accept any advice. I was also a bit pleased with myself, even feeling a little cocky seeing her apologize, saying she was sorry, completely at my mercy. At my mercy, but refusing to take even two steps outside of her square. She was waiting for someone. He'd come today or tomorrow, so she had to wait. She couldn't go anywhere. He could come anytime. Her life depended on him coming.

For days I sat in my workshop waiting for her to come. I was certain she would show up one day. As if she were sitting on the mosque's wall and might come in at any moment. I was even picturing the way she walked and the dress she would be wearing. And she really did come to visit me, *two* times, then went back to her room. She came in hesitantly, as if setting foot in my workshop for the first time, standing close to the door like a stranger, watching me draw on the wood (or at least pretending to). What could I have been drawing? Circles. Then more circles. Each one less complete than the one before. After Father fell, work ended. Lines, circles, and muqarnases with their bright colors all came to an end. The red that he was so proud of was done. For the most part, I was pretending so as to give her the chance to become reacquainted with me and the place. But she didn't leave her spot by the door. She didn't say a word. She just stood there watching what I was doing, and I wasn't doing anything of any use. I wasn't going to make any move that might drive her away. Like you do when a dove lands close to you and you think your heartbeats would be enough to scare it off. Even when I heard her voice saying hello to me from behind, I returned the greeting without turning around, or rather, I turned as much as necessary to assure her that I was returning the greeting in my own way. Then, after twenty-eight days, she handed over the keys and left her room for good, and she agreed to stay in the workshop temporarily. I think it was because the old woman was no longer able to feed her. I also think that she came to stay.

38

BEFORE TOUCHING HER OWN BRUSH, Farah sat down to watch me and what I was doing. I wasn't drawing circles this time. I was struggling to draw her into the world that I loved, one that had dominated my thoughts ever since I was little, when I would run through the thicket of wood in our old house. I brushed the colors I had just prepared—blue, yellow, orange—over the piece of wood. Farah loves the color blue. Red doesn't make her think of anything pleasant. Farah turned toward the pieces of wood and picked up the brush. Contrary to what I thought she would do, she plunged the brush into the red paint, as if to try her luck with this color I had talked with her about for so long. Maybe ten minutes went by before I went up to her again after having left her with her pieces of wood, along with pictures and images that might inspire her, although I hadn't left her completely. A bell inside me rang to the rhythm of my newfound excitement. I was with a young woman for the first time in my life. A young woman made of living flesh and blood. Her name was Farah. A real name. She moved like someone who was used to places like this. She was meandering her way closer to me. I sensed this in the way she looked around. My proof was that she was moving closer to the color I loved.

So I drew closer. I didn't have to tiptoe. That's because Farah was completely immersed in drawing whatever she was assembling in her head, crouching in front of the vibrant colors, her bright smile shining in the darkness of the workshop. She hadn't yet drawn a single line. But she was ready. I sat down next to her. Then I remembered the golden spotlight that had fallen onto her rounded breasts that night when we were at the cabaret as I sat next to her without the need to speak at all. I smelled the scent of cloves in her hair and said to myself, "This time she's come to stay." Then she said she'd draw a cat. "In mosques and mausoleums, they don't draw living things, Farah. They only draw things that are dead. Like letters, shells, circles, and squares. They don't draw humans or animals." But Farah insisted on drawing a cat. A red cat. "In mosques and mausoleums, they don't draw living things." She replied that *her* cat wasn't alive. That it was neither living nor dead. A red cat doesn't even exist. It only existed in her head and in her hand, and it wouldn't become any more alive once it was transferred to the wood's surface. Farah is beautiful, with her Asian-like eyes—amber, almond-shaped, narrow, and cheerful. Here she was, having brought back her laugh and her vigor. Here was Farah, just as I'd like her to be, always. Farah was beautiful, with or without her red cat. I watched as she drew her first lines on the wood panels.

I brought her food from Mother's house. Or I stole it from the big restaurants that run the length of Boulevard de la Résistance. When Farah showed up, my enthusiasm for bringing tasty treats like the ones Kika and I used to steal was renewed. Even more, I wanted to surprise her every day with a new story. Even if it was only a story I had made up so she wouldn't get bored. I also brought her a book I bought in the flea market—*How to Preserve Your Beauty*. Then I took her out to look at the luxury car of one of the tourists who had stopped there to check out the nearly completed mosque. I opened the door for her. My excited mind had cooked up this idea too. Farah looked pleased as she sat in the back seat. Thin and fragile as a twelve-year-old girl. She loves everything she touches and lays her eyes on. I don't know how long she has loved cars. Farah didn't strike me as the car-loving type. But she loved them as something that went perfectly with singing, as she once said. As if she couldn't picture singing without all of the pomp that went along with it. Her laugh was resplendent. The imaginary hum of the car swallowed her laughter. Her hair laughed too because of the imaginary wind that reached us, even inside the car. Farah's confidence and vitality had returned to her. And next to her I was happy, filled with joy. We got out of the car and I offered her an imaginary flower. She asked what it was called. I didn't know. She didn't know what it was called either. It wasn't important that this flower have a specific name. We called it an iris, or a water lily, or a red cat. Delightful days, during which I came to love the mosque and yearned to see it every day because Farah loved the mosque. When the sun went down and its rays reflected off the floor mosaic, spraying a joyous celebration of colors everywhere, she loved to walk between the mosque's pillars at dusk while she hummed her special tunes. And I came to love the workshop because Farah said she loved her new home. Sometimes, when there wasn't any work to do, we'd walk around the mosque. Farah and I would dress like the tourists who came after the dedication, and we'd strut around, amazed by the height of the structure, gaping at the ceiling decoration, pausing for a long time under Father's ceiling. The guide (who wasn't there) would ask us if we knew the artist who had created all of this magnificence, and we'd reply that we didn't know who he was, but no doubt he was a great artist. We'd laugh loudly. We'd continue our tour, amazed at the beauty of the zellij tiles on the walls and the rows of pillars. At the end of our visit we'd go out and pretend to stand in front of the imaginary ticket seller to buy a small replica of the mosque, which we'd hang on the keychain that held the keys to our big black car, a grand memento of our visit to this historic site. Then there were those Friday afternoons when the mosque was empty and the few workers who remained had gone to the hammam or the movies. We'd sit in the main plaza listening to the crash of the ocean as it echoed throughout the mosque. As if we were sailing on an enormous ship taking us across the ocean. There was no night, no day. There was no need for food or drink. We were full. Satisfied. Overflowing with calm. A fountain burbled someplace in the mosque. Its music added to the overall rhythm of the place. Or we'd stand on a hill to look at the mosque from another angle. The mosque towered over the ocean. It seemed to glide across the water with an unparalleled loftiness. Rising above the minaret were the three spheres of the jamour. They had completely changed the look of the minaret, giving it a rare dignity. They gave it the life it was missing. It didn't look like any minaret we had seen before. In the fading light of the evening, the mosque was transformed. As if renewing its own shape. A sailboat was visible on the ocean's surface, its towering mast piercing the sky's vault, and when night fell, the stars came right up to the edge of the minaret and stayed there for the entire night. Farah said that she had loved the mosque from day one. That she came from Azemmour to sing. She didn't sing that day, but she did see the mosque. Perhaps she had only come to see the mosque (it seemed that way to her now in the magic of that moment), and to forget what had happened with the lawyer. She loved to watch the changes that happened to it throughout the day. In the evening, when the sun touched the surface of the water and what looked like mist rose up from the ocean, the mosque appeared to be floating in a translucent purple mantle of light, while the top of the minaret disappeared in a light cloak of azure and orange fog. These were moments when the building was like a dream. Yes, they were pleasant days.

We considered ourselves lucky—Farah and I—being so captivatingly close to the mosque. Except for the days when I brought food from Mother's house or from the restaurants on Boulevard de la Résistance (when I earned some money selling pieces of metal and cardboard left behind by the workers, or Father's wood that was no longer of any use), we had bread and tea, and sometimes eggs. At night we put cardboard underneath the blanket to keep the dampness out, or at least to keep some of it out. We dreamed of the mosque rising high into the air with its tall minaret, its green zellij, its wide doors, its ceilings, chandeliers, and mirrors. The unique green light of its minaret that would guide those passing by on land and by sea, that would guide passing ships to the far corners of the world so sailors wouldn't get lost at sea. And its numerous fountains with water that sang. As we slept deeply, we heard the muezzin raise his gorgeous voice calling out the prayer. Even those who had died as a result of their overenthusiasm, those who fell into a hole or from way up high—we started to see them rising from their graves so as not to miss such a blessed prayer. Glory be to God! It was truly a gift from God to be so close to such a grand mosque. There were other nights when we didn't sleep at all. We lay down next to one another, my hand in hers, without any need for words. The only sound was that of the crashing waves that sang out down below. And when she was happy—for no apparent reason—she got up humming melodies, and drew what she believed to be her red cats on the wooden boards.

I took a chair and pulled it over next to her, our shadows becoming one. She wasn't smiling. She was serious about what she was doing. I asked her to get up on the chair to grab a brush from the shelf. She laughed, then got up and lifted her dress a little bit. In those moments I examined her white legs and her perfectly arranged toes. We painted and painted and painted. Each one in their own square. Each one with their own colors, their own ideas, and their own unspoken desires. A moonbeam slipped in through the window. It landed on her face. I felt it on my face before seeing it settle on hers. It gave the impression that we were on the verge of a clear night, the likes of which we hadn't seen for a while. A feeling of optimism swept over me, like a rest after feeling tired. I said to myself that tomorrow was going to be a beautiful day. Exceptional. No workers banging their hammers or dragging pieces of metal large enough to cause the ground to shake. No bosses barking at their employees. Her shadow danced in the candlelight. Then her smile returned to dance around us once again, shining in the workshop's darkness as she got up and stared at the color-spattered fingers, her fingers. She said she had only pretended to drown that night so I wouldn't be too sad for her. A few hours or days of sadness, and she'd be counted among the unknown dead. She also talked about how the lawyer knew how to corrupt her soul because she thought so much about the happy life that singers lead. She thought about singing first—because she always loved to sing—then about herself and her future, and about the money she took from her father's pillow. It was her right to think as other people do. Her spirit was just like theirs, easily corruptible. Then it was as if she had entered a period of quiet reflection as she moved away from the window, as if the moonbeam that had settled in her square was pulling her, just like Father when a thought eluded him. I was amazed that, at that moment, I was thinking about the future. Our future. This was something completely new to me. I forgot about the Gulf and my brother Suleiman's promises. Azemmour is a small city, but it would be enough. Down alongside its walls there's a river called the Oum Errabia. Farah's face was bathed in the purple moonlight, weaving her small desires into mine. Her father, the retired solider who, once upon a time, had been preparing her for the life of a soldier so people would respect her, was now sapped of all strength. He walked on one leg so people would respect what he had gone through. In our imaginations we saw that we respected him because of how much he did for his daughters. Despite this, he ended up on a riverbank waiting for a fish that had gone extinct decades ago, stretching his one remaining leg out in front of the doorstep. We would jump over it and go inside.

Marriage isn't a good idea. Marriage in general. Because the married man forgets all about the desire he once felt—the passion, the sleepless nights. He no longer waits impatiently for that appointed time that comes around every day or week when he'll see his beloved's face. He no longer waits for anything. That possibility has disappeared from his life altogether. He won't be going to the hammam, putting on cologne, and donning his finest clothes. He won't be watching the clock hands, which seem to stand still rather than move toward that appointed hour, because the face of the woman he will have been waiting for has now become familiar. In front of his face when he opens his eyes in the morning, and there when he closes them at night. He might even start looking for another woman as soon as he gets married. No sooner does a man sleep with his wife than his respect for her diminishes. He no longer cares whether she stays or goes. She becomes extraneous. A hidden tingling sensation (like that of creeping ants) shamefully struck the lower part of my body as I thought about all of this. Other than Azemmour, what more was there for us? If only a person were like a mountain goat in the forest, waiting for spring to come and spark his appetite. Once a year. One time. Satisfied. Enough, and then some. Afterward he roams around the forest filling his time by climbing trees and diving into lakes, rolling around on his horns (rather than walking around on two legs) until the following year, and then, at the end of his life, climbing a mountain to die there. With peace of mind. No scars. No missing leg. No funeral or mourners. No crying or weeping. No mourners faking their sadness. Why don't we do as doves or cats do? Life would be less tiring. I saw her grab a piece of cloth as if getting ready to wash the floor. I tried to prevent her from doing so, but she ran away with the cloth in her hand, and I ran after her. We ran as far as the beach. She stopped for a moment, panting as I approached. Our breaths mingled and she asked me whether her breath smelled bad. I laughed because I hadn't thought about it before. She blew into my face and ran off, while I remained standing there thinking about the stolen kiss she had planted on my lower lip. I stood there thinking about the scent of that kiss, wondering how I hadn't yet tasted the scent of her mouth! Then we came to do something else impulsive, not knowing how we found ourselves rolling around in the sand, her grabbing my head and putting it on her chest. I imagined rather than actually saw her chest. Two ripe oranges rising up underneath my head. A delicious dizziness seized me. She pressed down on my head and let out her resplendent laugh, insisting I listen to her heartbeats. "Do you hear it?" But up until that moment I could only hear the beating of my own excited heart. Then my head started to pound violently, so I went back to where I had been lying before. I didn't like playing around like this. I lay down on the sand. She seized the opportunity to run away again. I let her run away toward the mosque so that I'd miss her. I wasn't missing anything, now. Now that I'd found her. Farah whom I loved. Just as she was, and just as I had wanted her to be since the first day. Exuberant—exuberant in the way she lived, drunk with life, light as a butterfly. Then I heard the singing. By the time I heard it, it may have been wafting over me for a long time while I was stretched out on the sand. Her voice. I lifted my head a little and turned around. The voice was coming from the direction of the mosque, pure and trembling and wounding, filling the night, flooding it.

> There's no one there
> Don't call out
> There's no one there
> There's only darkness, and a road, and a bird that
quietly flies . . .

Never in my life had I heard a voice like the one I was hearing now. Sure, I had heard her sing before—singing that wasn't too exciting. Closer to humming. Now all of my extremities trembled. My blood roiled and a deliciously intense tingling washed over my skin as I watched her in her white dress sway under the beams of light shining in through small openings in the ceiling.

> Who do you want to return with in the darkness
> of the road?
> You haven't lit a fire and you don't have a friend . . .

She was like something not of this time, surrounded by her purple flowers. I know the voices of many singers—Oum Kulthoum, Muhammad Abdel-Wahhab, Najat al-Saghira, but that's not what I was hearing now. Not even close. I even knew the voice of Fairouz. But Fairouz at this range? Open and closed at the same time, between the marble columns, under the silver moonlight coming in from the dome and the sides of the mosque, all of which enriched and infused the voice with a magical echo. I felt nothing except for my eyes filling with tears.

> I wish we could have lit the old lamp in El Kantara
> Maybe someone would have found their way.

I knelt and remained frozen there.

Two wings fluttered above us, causing her to jump in fright. She came close to me, her face having changed color. "We're not alone." "It's just us, you and I." "No, we aren't alone. There's someone watching us." Why someone would be watching us, I didn't know, but some person or people were watching us. The magic was gone. The sweetness of the song evaporated. Two kids were standing outside the mosque. In the courtyard. Under the light of the moon. You could only tell that they were children by their shapes. I walked toward them and saw that I didn't know them. Perhaps they were children of one of the families that hadn't left the old city. That was my guess. They hadn't found me in the workshop. What did the two kids want? A man came asking for Mother. Where is he? Carrying a letter for her. Where is he? He asked for her at the old address.

"We have a new address."

"He doesn't know it. He only knows the old address."

"Where is he?"

"The man? He left." But, before leaving, he said that my brother Suleiman was on his way, but that he didn't know our address in the new neighborhood.

"Suleiman?"

"No, the man."

39

THE SOIL IS BLACK, CHURNED up by the machines. The new white buildings appear behind them and the fields like a forest rising up from the ground all at once. Gigantic spools are rolled and black wires are strung by workers over an open space the size of a football field. There were more of them than there were the last time I visited the new neighborhood. They came from surrounding villages. Working for twenty dirhams a day. They didn't know what was going on inside the heads of the men lined up on the edge of the field, watching them. Angry. Furious because of the unsuitable new housing. The doors fell apart the first time you knocked on them, and the sewage lines were blocked. The shoddy walls had cockroaches coming out of every opening. Same with the locks and the zellij tiles. The window frames were lopsided from the get-go. The faucets provided no water and flicking the light switches did nothing. The smell of deceit oozed from every hole in the walls. The new residences wouldn't do at all, Mr. Employee. They'd rather go back to their old homes, despite how rundown and dank they were.

As soon as I got there, the angry men lined up on the edge of the field stopped watching the bulldozers. Now that I was standing there they no longer needed to protest. They weren't angry anymore about the new and unsuitable housing. They had a look of indignation they didn't know how to express. Take, for example, the young man who asked me about whether Suleiman had come back. He wasn't actually asking me about Suleiman at all. And I wasn't going to respond to his question anyway, even though he waited for a response. Just as I wasn't going to respond to the others who walked toward me with the same hateful looks. Perhaps they were waiting for me to enumerate the gifts Suleiman was bringing with him, or the fortune he had stuffed in his bags. Perhaps they were expecting me to count out their share of it. Instead, I disappointed the mob that was forming a circle around me when I didn't answer at all. I had the same hateful look in my eyes. For a moment I thought they were going to pounce on me. These things happen every day—in markets, at weddings, and even at funerals. Just standing there can incite a deeply buried anger in people, or at least a desire to cut you down to size. Without the slightest provocation. Just because you don't hold the same views they do, or wear the same clothes, or walk the same way, it puts them into this incomprehensible tribal state. They forgot all about the employee. They forgot about the unsuitable housing and the faulty doors. They forgot about the blocked sewage pipes and the crummy walls and the cockroaches that had begun to nest in the cracks. Instead of berating the employee, they proceeded to pour their anger onto the newcomer, whom they hadn't taken into account just moments before. And when looks were no longer enough, and asking about Suleiman was of no use, they remembered the mosque. The mosque was what really concerned them. Everything else was just a distraction. They continued to discuss at length the work they had done, the efforts they had expended for the sake of the mosque, and their friends who were buried beneath its rubble. And these machines were witness to it all. These same machines. With their bright yellow color, their noise, and their murky plans. Machines operated by these very hands for five years. They were with these people the whole time. They listened to their complaints and took short naps next to them in the mosque's courtyard. Years that were neither too long nor too short. Just enough time for a mosque to rise up over the water; enough time for the toil, the sweat, and the blood. And the result? They never imagined that they did all of this work and made all of these sacrifices, only for prostitutes to sing in it!

I turned toward the machines, my mind burning with anger, disregarding their talk about the mosque and the singer in the mosque. The young man who had asked me about Suleiman—but who didn't really want to know about him—said that he knew her. A girl who stripped in cabarets and danced at weddings. She came from a broken family. Her father was a drunk, and her mother a witch who spent her life separating men from their wives, and fathers from their sons. While scoffing to myself and turning away from them toward the machines, I said that this wasn't the Farah I knew and surely they were talking about some other girl. Facing their hatred with an even greater hatred. And rather than think about them, I started to think about Rihane. Would he have stood idly by in the face of all this insolent behavior? Would his reaction have been anything other than violent? A pit bull's reaction never conceals how much it loathes something, and it seizes any opportunity to show its hatred for this sort of person. Even when they went back to the bulldozers, forming a circle around them, the hateful looks didn't disappear completely. Shards of that hatred remained scattered here and there. I think my stern stance was what pushed them to retreat and hunker down behind their previous worries and questions about the affordable housing. Their eyes, which had spewed such hatred for a girl they didn't know and whom they had never even seen in their lives, came back to stare once again at the machines and the National Department of Electricity employee.

The National Department of Electricity employee wasn't bothered by them standing there, nor by their silence, which was louder than the clamor of the machines. Their unasked questions didn't bother him. This was his field of expertise. His new workers rolled a large spool over and flipped it on its side so that the employee could be higher than them and prevail over their silence. The employee knew very well what went on in the minds of the poor. Poor people didn't produce a single sound thought. They produced nothing but tricks and ruses, and if you gave them free rein, they might carry away the bed you slept in. That was why the employee asked them to calm down. Better to calm down and think about things that are useful. They weren't looking at him now. They were staring at their feet, which traced their vague intentions in the dirt. Up on his improvised podium, the employee told them there was damage everywhere, so why wouldn't it also be so in this neighborhood after all the rain they'd had? "The electricity was cut off, but it will come back. All this work we've been doing for the past two weeks, that's so the electricity can come back on. Don't you see those high poles coming from the Sidi Said Maachou Dam? Or the Massira Dam? That's high current. Higher than what your small minds can imagine: twenty-two thousand watts." Their eyes turned, glaring unconvinced at the high poles. Did they even know what twenty-two thousand watts meant? "It's enough to burn down the entire city. And when the new transformer arrives and is erected on this piece of land we're leveling out right now . . ." Eyes moved back and forth between the high electrical poles and the transformer, which right now only existed inside the employee's head. Their feet hadn't decided yet whether to storm the field or wait. "Do you know what will happen when the electrical transformer is put up on the edge of where you're standing? You'll see the electrical current transformed into a standard current with your own eyes. It'll run before your very eyes like a dependable stream. After that, the thought of going back will never occur to you. Once you're able to store your meat in the refrigerator so it doesn't rot. That's right. Electricity is good for that too." What did the angry men do now? They walked back and forth along the edge of the field, satisfied to watch the machines smoothing the dirt, and the high black poles with the electrical wires stretched above them all the way to the horizon. In a final episode of anger, they fixed their hostile glares on the National Department of Electricity employee. Not everything was going as it should, Mr. Employee.

40

FATHER'S CONDITION HAD IMPROVED AND he no longer sat in the same chair. He was delighted with his new decorated chair. But in fact it was the same chair Mother had bought at the flea market, the one he had been carried in on, but now it had drawings on the back and sides that made him think he was still sitting cross-legged on his old throne-like chair with its two snakes descending to the ground and its high back resembling the wings of a soaring eagle. Father looked like a general in exile after losing his final battle. His entourage, which no longer understood what he wanted, circled around him like out-of-control animals. They were imprisoned in an apartment that resembled a cell. He himself looked like someone who no longer had any desires. His last wish was to get a haircut so that he could welcome my brother Suleiman, like a general receiving the last soldier of his defeated troops as he sits on his throne. His desires had been soaring above our heads for years like birds of prey. No one worried about or was proud of them anymore. All of this was over. They no longer interested anyone. He didn't have anything else to take care of, except for this single desire—to get a haircut—in order to forget about the crack that had been left behind, stretching across the entire length of the mosque's ceiling like a viper in clear daylight, like a sword threatening to come down on his neck at night while he slept. Khadija and I looked at his head. The razor was in my hand. Khadija was a bit too enthusiastic. She wanted to shave his head for him. Like a child wanting to play. The anxiety I was feeling didn't come from the razor blade in my hand, or from the sight of Father looking like someone getting ready to shave his head for the last time before descending into his grave. The anxiety I was feeling emanated from this very place, from its suffocating atmosphere and from the depressing thoughts it evoked. First and foremost, it came from the new neighborhood. When I walked through it, I saw that the women—the same neighbors from our old neighborhood—had spread their covers out over the rocks, sunning them and their brittle bones. They sat on the sidewalk that wasn't there or on the hills formed by dirt and rocks that no one had gathered up. They warmed their bones, which had been penetrated by the moist air of the previous rainy nights, while at the same time looking at the shadows being traced by the sun over the holes left behind by the construction workers. The walls were still dripping and they had holes in them here and there. The sun's heat heralded an early summer, as if these places have only two seasons, as if in places where the poor settle they only have a choice between a rainy season and an extremely hot season. The children emerged from the ditches, brandishing pieces of metal and yelling at one another. The houses' stairs were too narrow. Long, bare hallways echoed with the sound of the wind and children's shouting. Then there was the house itself. One bedroom, a salon—square like a box—with two small windows that looked like those of a prison cell. The sewing machine was gone. There was no bazaar where Mother could sell her goods or buy things from the north, so her hands sat practically idle. There were no customers. Instead of buying and selling, her hands satisfied themselves by monitoring Father's head (the same desire that ate away at the other hands ate away at hers). Everyone had a score to settle with the head—Father's head, which he generously offered to us with a sudden, never-before-seen humility. And finally, perhaps most essentially, there was the thought that hadn't left me since I had first looked at the neighborhood: that I would run into Kika. I remembered him prior to this moment. My heart seized even before looking at the neighborhood, when Kika was nothing other than one possibility among many, like a project, like an image that passed by while I faced the hateful glares that united the people who were angry at a girl they didn't know, who protested against singing they'd never heard; a girl who made my heart flutter—it started to beat embarrassingly harder. When he heard the news of Suleiman's return, Kika came by the house asking about him too. He asked many times a day. But, really, he wasn't knocking on the door with the intention of asking about him. Rather, he hadn't forgotten about Farah. He came to add his wickedness to that which had spread out all around the girl who sang in the mosque, because what did Suleiman have to do with a girl singing in the mosque? It was the same spite he had been carrying inside him ever since he first saw her in the cabaret. He wasn't given the pleasure of a single nice word from her mouth. That's why. Farah had ignored Kika as if he were a mosquito. Then he talked about her everywhere. It was best that I avoided Kika. Really, he was no more and no less than a mosquito. Relinquishing Kika came to taste like deliverance. It didn't matter that Kika had once been a friend. A friend, yes, but not like being friends with the color red or cedar wood, for example. Those are true friends; friends you can rely on and be a companion to without question. Without feeling an anxiety you can't respond to. With some joy, I remembered that I had forgotten him these last few weeks, and I felt even more joyful and reassured when I didn't see Kika among the young men leaning up against the walls all day, watching the sun and the moon go around in the sky. I didn't care about the fact that he'd gone, nor did I have any desire to know where he went or what happened to him after the visa fiasco. I could picture him anywhere. At the port waiting for a truck he'd never find to take him away.

In front of an embassy where a policeman stood at the door threatening him with his truncheon. But always without the visa. Why would he deserve the visa? Why did he want to emigrate anyway? Just to copy Suleiman? And why would he get to Spain or somewhere besides Spain? Kika didn't deserve to go anywhere.

Or perhaps this feeling of anxiety stemmed from the message that arrived from the old city, casting its pall over the entire household, sowing childish desires in Father's heart and invigorating Mother's broken hopes. A message from Suleiman. Finally. But it wasn't a message like other messages, just a bit of news transmitted by a man we didn't know. The house was suddenly and radically turned upside down. And the man who brought the message, where was he? He contacted us at our old address, but the old address was no longer there. An unwritten message. But that was unimportant. The important thing was the piece of news, which was that Suleiman was en route, although it would take some time for him to arrive because Saudi Arabia was far away. I didn't see the man who carried the message. The ones who saw him were two kids who stayed behind in the old city because they weren't lucky enough for their parents to have gotten an apartment in the new neighborhood. Why Saudi Arabia and not Abu Dhabi or Oman? No one knew. They're all distant countries located in the east, as far away as one can go. And the man? He hadn't gotten in touch before because he didn't know our new address. But thanks to airplanes, all points on earth are now close to one another. Saudi Arabia is still far away, though. The news came at just the right time. Mother figured that a reasonable amount of time had passed. "There's nothing better than for a person to remember his kin after being away for a year! We don't know how many days Suleiman will spend with us." We bet that it won't be more than one week. Then we bet that it will be longer. Two weeks. We had never seen a migrant worker return to his job after less than a month, especially if he was working in wealthy and far-off countries like Saudi Arabia or the Emirates. People didn't need to work too much there. All the money he might be bringing back with him would be useful. Mother said that the best that could happen would be for us to be done with this cardboard box of a house before it was ripped from above our heads by the wind, and to go back to our old house and fix whatever could be fixed. All things considered, it was a fine house with four rooms where we couldn't hear the embarrassing things the neighbors were doing in their houses on the other side of the thin walls.

The razor passed over his head, shaving it bald as his eyes followed its movement. The blade mowed down the white hair, leaving behind red skin like that of a plucked rooster, along with some shaving cream. Khadija asked for the razor before the hair was completely gone. The head shrank. Mother demanded the razor back before the head shrank to the size of a pomegranate and became too difficult to handle. Mother wanted to have her share of the fun with Father's head before it disappeared completely. It might be gone at any moment, then we'd be left without a head at all for us to empty our old hatreds into. Father's physical condition had improved, but the ceiling and the crack in it came back to trouble him. Karima rubbed her small fingers in shaving cream mixed with hair. She was playing too. Father asked whether Suleiman was going to come in now, and we told him that he was en route, as we had been told. Then he immediately forgot about Suleiman. He went back to asking about what was still worrying him: Would the king see the crack in the ceiling on Dedication Day? He was no longer worried about his shrinking head, or about the hands tracing all of their accumulated anger on it. He was no longer worried about whether his son Suleiman was coming back. Rather, for every single ticking second, he was hoping that in the coming days the king wouldn't notice the damn crack. Father didn't get up from his chair, but his health had improved, as Khadija said as she rubbed his beard. His wrinkled red neck had grown longer, and his head had shrunken as much as it could. His speech seemed heavier as he talked about the mosque and Dedication Day. He asked when it would be. It wouldn't do for him to miss a day like that because he had contributed to it mentally, and his health had suffered for it as well. Dedication Day would be memorable, and the hairline crack wouldn't be visible to anyone. Do you think the king is going to worry himself with something so minor as a small crack in the ceiling ten meters up? And about the crack, he also told us that he'd discuss the matter directly with the king in the event that he did see it. If the king saw it, there was no doubt he'd demand that the one responsible for the ceiling be brought before him. And that was what Father was anticipating with all of the former enthusiasm we recognized. As if the thought of the dedication returned him to his old vibrant self. Then, this question: If the king doesn't see it, what if a member of his entourage does? These guardians of hell don't allow anything to go unnoticed. That was what worried him. What would happen if that were to occur? Then he forgot all about his question and told little Karima that he'd take her with him to see the mosque he helped build. He wouldn't say anything to her about the crack, though. He'd let her discover it for herself. And she'd tell him that she saw it because she's young and doesn't know how to lie. All *she* wanted to do was pluck one of the hairs from his head, but the hairs were all gone. We all still harbored a hatred inside us that had not yet been slaked. An unsatisfied anger.

Abdullah wasn't at this party, which seemed more like a funeral. Absent from the shaving ritual, which seemed more like a farewell rite. He was working in the new neighborhood's mosque. It wasn't really a mosque. They forgot to build the mosque in the new neighborhood. It was more of a cellar underneath one of the houses. Abdullah was the one who suggested converting it into a mosque. And he was the one who led the prayers and delivered the sermon. This job had completely transformed him. He spent his days repairing the floor. He patched the holes that appeared on the walls after Father constructed a mihrab for him out of wood left behind by the construction workers. And for the occasion, he also put in an arched doorway like those found in palaces. Abdullah repainted the mihrab and door once a week, as if intentionally not allowing himself a minute's rest so as not to have to make an appearance at home. He redid the mosque's straw-mat floor coverings. He searched among the pious for new Qurans, incense burners, strings of prayer beads that could be seen in the dark because they were lit only with the light God planted in them, and anything else that might be appropriate for his mosque. Yes, Abdullah had changed considerably. So much so that I had to admit how wrong I had been, and that I had judged him too harshly before. In the evening, he brought home whatever food the other residents brought him—bread, sugar, large bowls of couscous, and sometimes mouthwatering dishes such as soup with local chicken in it, some of which I took to Farah. It was as though Abdullah had become indispensable for sustaining life in our household, and outside of it as well. Even Khadija was touched by the same healing hand. Her face became noticeably fresher. She no longer complained about her old pains, and when she was afflicted by one of her spells, Abdullah took her into the only bedroom, which had become his, and after a quarter of an hour she would be cured. Habiba was the only one not happy with the situation because the room was hers. She didn't want Khadija or anyone else in it. When the arguing between them grew fierce, Habiba accused her of stealing her husband. And Khadija responded that she didn't understand why she was making such a fuss for no reason. "No reason?" And what was the harm in their sharing the same man? Habiba was being selfish, because men were created to sleep with many women, four at least. She went on to explain to all of us in scientific fashion that the total number of men was decreasing in the world. They were dying in wars, on the roadways, and at work in the mines. Even those who were still living didn't live for very long. So, in order for women to fulfill their duties, and in order for life to continue so that the human species wouldn't disappear from the face of the earth, each man needed to have a number of women. It was just envy gnawing away at Habiba's heart. "Envy? What envy?" At this point, when the yelling between the two sides reached a fever pitch, I no longer understood any of it; perhaps no one did. But there was still that dangling question: What did Abdullah and Khadija do in the room? After spending a quarter of an hour with him, she emerged rosy-cheeked, in full health, walking and stretching out her arms like someone who has just woken up, fresh, new, cured, completely cured. Then we heard Father demand his gold-embroidered selham robe. When we smoothed it out over his shoulders, he said, "Now I can receive him." We realized after a moment that he meant Suleiman and not the king. Before leaving the house, I heard Mother ask about the girl who sings in the mosque. She was holding a pot between us, and the steam rising from the pot smelled delicious—saffron, olives, and preserved lemon. The smell didn't dissipate when she put the top back on and handed it to me, without adding anything else. Without waiting for a response.

These annoying stairways, twisting halls, and narrow windows looking out over the debris left behind by the construction workers didn't help me know whether Kika was lurking in some corner waiting for me. Because of the buildings, because of the evening sky weighing heavily over them, because of the toxic news that had been spread about Farah, the threat of Kika seemed more imminent than ever before. Not because of the question Mother asked about a girl she didn't know; not because of the number of times he came knocking on the door; not even because of how long he had been gone before suddenly showing up and spreading the

340

word about the girl who wasn't interested in him. It might have been because of the way he had stood in front of me, with all that malice coursing through his veins, the day we went searching for Farah and he had left me out to dry. Still, to this moment, just remembering that hateful flash in Kika's eyes gives me the impression that a nasty wind is heading my way. It might even have started before that, from the looks he had given Farah the first night we met at the Saâda Cabaret, and then afterward on the broad, dimly lit avenue as he walked around her, first as a victor in a battle that hadn't yet begun, then as a wounded animal that had fallen in that same nonexistent battle. If I ever emerge from this maze that is the new neighborhood, with its dark alleyways and dug-up streets, I'll never come back again. I can't walk through it without thinking about Kika, and about Farah.

I passed through a grove of jacaranda trees, putting some distance between me and the new neighborhood, the machines, and the men, who hadn't moved from where they were standing. Small, purple, bell-shaped jacaranda flowers continued to fall as I moved through the trees, stepping on the blossoms as so many others had, and would. When they'd been stepped on and dirtied, and had lost their color and scent, when they were completely obliterated, new flowers would bloom. Other purple, bell-shaped flowers would fall to earth, fresher, more welcoming of life, even more ready to be stepped on. Before continuing along the road, I stood there for a while smiling at the purple field. A small bell-shaped flower fell onto my shoulder and filled me with a fleeting feeling of intoxication. In order to forget about Kika, I thought of Farah. Would she stay? As sure as I was of the generous, eternal life that filled the flowers of the jacaranda tree, my conviction faded when I thought about Farah. I have little patience, and this causes the fires of disappointment to flare up. I wish my mind would allow itself even a brief moment of relaxation, but it can't. My mind needed some time to not think about Farah, but that was impossible. Would she stay? How long would she stay? Last time I counted up the days, hours, and minutes. She's been here longer this time. Did that mean anything? Would I find her there when I went back? I was seized with the feeling that there was some sort of threat out there that would continue to pursue her. The danger still threatened her.

41

THIS LIGHT HAS ALWAYS BEEN here. As far back as I can remember, I can't recall a single night when this yellow light wasn't flashing. Never was there a night when it didn't penetrate the bedroom window and even get into the bed. Even when it didn't come in, it would reflect off of the window all night long, every night, blinking at regular intervals like eternal flashes of lightning. The guardian said, "That lighthouse has been operating for more than seventy years without a shipwreck," and the guardian knew because he has always been at its side, day and night, in the heat of the summer and during the coldest days of winter. He stays up late at night with it, cares for it, and keeps it company. The guardian talks about the lighthouse like someone who spends all night worrying about a family member, with all the tenderness that has been stored up for decades, so that I imagine tears of compassion shining in the corners of his eyes. Perhaps the lighthouse is his entire family. He's always been here. Even as kids we would always see him from far off while we were playing ball or swimming between the nearby rocks. We would pass by to watch him washing his hands, not getting too close to him, though, because he was a medic in the Royal Navy. He started guarding the lighthouse when he wasn't really needed anymore. But he was a medic by profession, and maybe this extended to the lighthouse as well. When we watched him washing his hands, we imagined he had just finished treating the wounds of one of his patients.

We were always afraid of him because of that, just as we were afraid of the lighthouse. This guardian and his lighthouse resembled one another—in their isolation, their old age, their loneliness, their seclusion, in how content they were, and in the mystery that surrounded them and their roles. Lighthouses aren't anything without the mystery that permeates their lives. If it weren't for the round light that slowly moved up above at night, we would have always wondered what went on way up there. How many mythical beings lived inside it? Did everyone who went up come safely back down? It was perhaps for this reason too that the idea of going up had never occurred to me before that day. The idea of going up hadn't occurred to any of us because we had known since we were young that no one who went up ever came back.

Two hundred and fifty-six steps spiraled upward, and the whole time we were going up, I couldn't see the guardian who kept walking ahead of me until I entered the high raised platform where the lamp and its notched mirrors were. All I could hear was the sound of his footsteps on the white marble—*taf taf taf*. As if the sound of my steps preceded my feet. The sound of the guardian's footsteps brought to mind images from my childhood. A chronicle filled with fantastic beings wrapped in fog, mystery, superstition, no small amount of fear, and a desire to go back down as Farah had done. Halfway up the stairs, I heard the echo as she stopped suddenly, then the echo of her laugh as it rolled down behind her. The farther up I went, the farther her laughter got from me, and the more violent the sound of the guardian's footfalls sounded in my mind. Going up is always dizzying. I arrived at the last step exhausted and sweaty. Not because of the 256 steps I had climbed, but rather on account of thinking about her the whole time, along with all the arresting images that accompanied those thoughts. The guardian went up nimbly, talking nonstop, as if he were walking on level ground, or as if it were his way of dealing with all forms of fatigue. Farah decided to go back down after the first hundred stairs. Would I have climbed them all if it weren't for her insistence on doing so when we were at the base of the lighthouse?

That day in the late afternoon, I returned from Mother's house in a bad mood. That house is a trap. Same with the other houses that were like confined boxes. Same with the dark passageways, the blazing sun, the deep-blue sky, the old and new workers, the employee and his machines, and Kika, who spread rumors wherever he went. This neighborhood was a great big trap. Best to get far away from it as quickly as possible and be rid of it altogether before getting caught in its snares. Then, as I thought about my brother Suleiman and his imminent return, I realized that going back to the neighborhood once a week wasn't as dangerous as I imagined, especially since the matter of coming up with money was never more urgent than it was now. My thought was to buy Farah a red dress. As if her staying longer depended on this color. No doubt she had gotten used to it as she drew her red cats. At home, out in the streets, and in markets there was nothing to sell. The sewing machine had been sold by Mother. The only thing a man could find to sell was another man. Suleiman might come tomorrow. Why not? From Saudi Arabia, the two kids said. Not from Abu Dhabi or Oman. Saudi Arabia is a rich country. People there don't work much, but they earn a lot. He'd bring more than enough money with him. As such, the news came at just the right time. I found the door to the workshop closed, and on it was a sign with "Do not enter" written in red. This delighted me even more than the sound of splashing water. I sat beneath the window listening to the sound of water pouring inside. Thinking about Farah bathing and humming didn't help at all. Some other time, it might have been possible for the same happy tune to flow through my veins. Instead, I felt a feverish wave wash over me, reaching my temples. Could this be traced back to the sadness and worry that had been overwhelming me since this morning?

I also thought about the previous night, about all the things we had discussed, and the other, more exciting things we had stayed silent about. One question stayed with me for part of the night and during part of the long walk I had taken this morning: Was there any place Farah and I would be able to find refuge? An island, or a forest, or a cave suspended in the sky that no human hand could reach? The thought of going to Azemmour wasn't pleasant, because she said that if we found ourselves in Azemmour, we'd be going up the river ourselves to fish for North African shad. We laughed because this fish no longer existed. It's really frustrating when you can't find money when you need it. What's more frustrating is when you can't find anyone to go to for help in your whole entire family that's spread out across the country and over history, as Father would say every time he recalled his notable forefathers. Or maybe it should be like that. Maybe we shouldn't be able to find a relative to go to. Not in this city or in any other. Not in an adjacent village or in one far away. Nowhere in this country was there that relative who once said to me, "If ever you need a roof over your head . . ." or "The house is yours, you can count on it." No aunt on either my mother's or my father's side. My uncle Mustafa was in prison. He might have died by now. A bullet like the one that pierced his thigh could kill a camel. As for Suleiman, whose return had been announced by the two kids, no one could confirm the news. No one knew when he'd come back, or if he'd ever really decided to come back in the first place.

It seemed to me that I had been lost in thought for quite some time as I sat beneath the workshop window. It was as if I had woken up from a nap. I got up on my knees, grabbed the edge of the window, and looked in. I felt like my brain had jumped out of my head, like someone who had thrown himself from a window without knowing what was out there. It had nothing to do even with that. It had to do with the suddenness with which it had happened. Farah was naked, standing in the middle of the room pouring water over her head as she sang. She moved slowly. As if she were pouring rays of the setting sun over her body. Before that, too many times to count, both awake and in my dreams, I had pictured naked bodies. The images had always seemed far away, not really there, like abstract images, like a dream someone else was having and telling to a third person; you listened comfortably, as if listening to a story about a deadly disease you wouldn't be struck by, and then, lo and behold, you found yourself wandering into its furnace, caught in its inescapable web. Farah wasn't as thin as I had imagined when I pictured her body underneath her clothes. Her slight chubbiness awoke a certain craving. The kind of embarrassing and captivating craving that makes the water of desire flood your entire being without you realizing it, without even being able to taste its sweetness until after the magic has passed. Her breasts were full. Just yesterday I had asked her, "Can I see your breasts?" and she had answered, "You'll see them someday." At the time I didn't know that day was so close. They were pert and jutted out, and water dripped from her nipples. The translucent water fell over her belly like a small waterfall flowing over soft rocks. She had a good body, with full buttocks. The water stopped for a moment at the sloped knoll as if surveying the area that had all of a sudden appeared, then flowed over the pubic hair to fall, drop by drop, into a small pool that had formed around her small, calm, beautiful feet. For a brief moment, I imagined that she knew I was there, and that she had even thrown me a cunning, stolen, sideways glance; that every one of her movements was meant for me to see. Rather than pleasing me, however, this notion caused me to take a step back. Terrified. As if I had caught myself in the act. So, I went back to sitting and waiting. Waiting for her.

A light creak. It was her. She opened the workshop door and stood there, as if reading signs of her youthfulness on my face. It looked like she had just come out of the hammam rather than pouring a miserable bucket of water over her head. A halo of intoxicating steam danced around her face. Damp hairs were stuck to her forehead. Her dark eyes were even blacker, shinier, wider, brighter than they had been. Eyes that had been cleansed. There were droplets of water on her lower lip and the bottom of her chin. A bit of water still dripped onto her bare shoulders. Today's dress was new to me. It had a wide, rounded neck. A blue-and-white-striped dress with sleeves that came down to the elbows. She stood there in her sailor's uniform, smiling, ready, like the captain of a ship whose departure time had come. She leaned over. Her damp neck shone the whole time she spent tying her shoelaces. Then she reached her hand out toward mine. We walked in silence over ground that had just started to be covered by grass, not yet having come into full bloom even though we were well into spring. It spread out between us without us even noticing. The silence that wrapped itself around us was deafening, replacing the roar of the ocean that stretched out beside us. We took pleasure in what was being said about us. My hand got sweaty a number of times before we got to the lighthouse. More than once I thought about taking my hand from hers—if only for a minute, to wipe it off—but I didn't want to let go of her hand, scared that she might run away. I didn't know that we were heading toward the lighthouse until we had stopped at its base. The entire time we were walking, I remained preoc-cupied with the hand, with the meaning of the small, delicate hand nestled between my fingers like a bird in need of protec-tion. I held onto it tightly. The heat of her hand flowed into mine for the first time, an actual heat moving into my hand, a migrating heat flowing into my arm and rising with my blood as it saw fit. This was no small thing. Sometimes I squeezed her fingers a little bit, and other times I relaxed my grip to see if she'd remove her fingers on her own. Farah's hand fell into a rhythm with mine. A shaved-ice seller had parked his cart against the base of the lighthouse. Before walking up behind the guardian and his explanations, which had begun even before we could see him, I ordered three scoops of berry-flavored ice for her. My mouth watered as the taste of the berries flowed over my tongue. The vendor wielded the scoop in an exaggeratedly lewd manner that made him laugh, and made us laugh too. He winked. His rude behavior wouldn't have made us laugh at other times.

The guardian was still providing commentary, but I could only hear the most obvious parts of what he said. "The French built this lighthouse in 1916." He had no teeth and his coveralls were blackened from going up and down the stairs so much, and from the amount of talking that had flowed over them. "This glass is the same glass they'd brought with them that first day." I listened, but didn't really hear what he was saying, preferring to stand and take in this wide-open expanse laid out before me for the first time. I'd rather think about Farah in her absence. She was waiting at the bottom of the lighthouse. Maybe she was waiting for me to look down at her. What was I doing here? The sun was a red ball suspended over the edge of the water. There were ships that looked like small cities anchored on the horizon. The purple twilight colored the water and sand. Things looked different from up here—different colors and different sizes. The Royal Navy building, the insane asylum, and the Auxiliary Forces' barracks had all acquired the same unreal color, as had the green bay that separated the mosque from the lighthouse. The girls boisterously swimming there splashed each other with purple water. Their laughter was purple. From this height, the world looked thrilling. I searched down below for the blue-and-white-striped dress. I looked for Farah so I could use my hand to explain what I was unable to with words. Using my fingers, I told her that, for the first time, I was seeing the brown backs of seagulls rather than their white bellies. I explained to her how happy I was as I watched the seagulls flying below me rather than up above, small, the wind practically sweeping them away by their wings. But it was difficult to see because of how high I was and how strong the wind was knocking against the door, not to mention the echo of the guardian's constant prattle. I walked around the mirrors, but I didn't see Farah. Then I saw the shaved-ice vendor's cart. I remembered the colored scoops drawn on a piece of wood on the side of the cart and their vivid colors. Their flavors were also drawn there—lemon, berry, and apricot. It was as if I were sensing something before it happened when I looked down to the foot of the lighthouse, or more specifically, when I saw people rushing toward her. I felt the sudden danger before that moment when Farah screamed—a long, painful scream. It went on for a while longer, during which I couldn't see her at the base of the lighthouse. Then I saw her raising her hand to me, or to the sky. Her hand had been in mine just a short while before. She was spinning around in circles, reeling like a drunk. She turned and turned as if she'd been blinded. She turned, disappeared, then reappeared. I heard her scream despite the glass barrier—or I imagined I could hear it—before it got lost in the tumult and the more thunderous screaming that occurred inside me. Getting down took a few minutes. People had gathered around her. I began to walk around the growing crowd, not knowing what to think. They came from every direction, out of nowhere. Women who had been swimming, and teenage boys. Nothing had brought them together before. They began to cluster, suddenly united, forming a fraternal group, coming to a mutual understanding around a calamity they didn't yet understand, partners in something that had yet to be defined. They were brought together by an anonymous roar let out by unknown mouths. I could see the men and their mysterious dance. With difficulty I cut a path between them. Finally, I was looking at Farah, lying unconscious at the base of the lighthouse. Looking at her burned face and neck, and at the police officer asking what happened. A young man had thrown sulfuric acid on her and ran off this way.

Or had he gone that way? No one knew where he had come from or where he had gone. Then the police officer asked who among us knew the girl. I tried to respond to his question. My mouth opened but no sound came out. The policeman studied our faces. "Who knows this girl?" My old fear returned, after having thought that I had put it behind me when we stole the copper pipes, or when I met Rihane. I wasn't sure whether to say something. Standing in front of Farah, who was lying there unconscious with her burned face and arms. The threatening voice of the policeman. The ambulance that came to a stop without turning off its siren. A man leaned over her and covered her bare knees. Then a young woman came and threw a clean towel that had just been on the sand over her face. The insistent questioning of the policeman—"Who knows this girl?" Then the ambulance door closed, and Farah disappeared. As if there was nothing more to be said. As if her disappearance from the scene absolved me of any need to answer. For a moment, I wasn't concerned with the ambulance as it drove off, or with its siren gradually fading away, or with the crowd that was beginning to leave to attend to other matters. I remained standing in the same spot, as if still checking on things. I took a few steps back and reconstructed the scene from the time I was looking down from the top of the lighthouse to see if there might have been something wrong with what I had seen, to determine that, in fact, what had happened didn't have anything to do with Farah. I could see her going up halfway, then laughing as she went back down. With the flavored ice in her hand or without it. I imagined another girl had been taken away by the ambulance. As for Farah, she was still walking down the lighthouse steps, and she'd appear at any moment, sucking on her little flavored scoops of shaved ice. I continued to look for her after the ambulance had left, after the cars that had been blocking the street were gone. Could she be hiding among the fruit- and ice-vendors' carts? I kept looking for her after the passersby had all dispersed, still believing that a miracle could happen. As if maybe Farah had been held back in front of the lighthouse door because she had been listening to the guard's chitchat. Maybe she had gone down to the beach, and now she was lying on the sand, and in a little while her voice would surprise me.

> If only I were a tree towering over the world
> And our only neighbors were the sky and the horizon
> Besides them, there's no one . . .

The berry-flavored ice having melted and dripped down onto her hand as she waited for me to show up and surprise her.

42

Suleiman

IT WON'T DO YOU ANY good now to chew on your fingers or pull your hair out, because the head has been thrown to the other end of the wooden box. Do you still love wood as much as you used to? And the color of wood? And the smell of wood? Or have you come to hate it forever? From the outside of the box, rather than smelling like the forest, the wood smells like a perfume shop—a combination of rosewater, cloves, and preservatives so you won't decompose too quickly. I'm not sure what it smells like from the inside. Would you like to put your head back where it belongs? I'll think about it. The box arrived at six, from a country without forests. It arrived as expected, firmly locked. Four people came in a light black truck, put the box down on the doorstep, wondered what time it was and whether there was a place nearby that served coffee, and left. It might have been six in the morning since they were asking about breakfast. Right then, it had occurred to me to whisper to them to tilt the box a little bit so as to roll the head close to where it should be rather than leave you in the ridiculous spot you're in right now. Then I reconsidered. Why shouldn't the head be down by the feet? Why are you insisting on putting the head back where it should be? It doesn't matter anymore. Just as it doesn't matter anymore whether time moves forward or backward. It doesn't matter anymore whether it's night or day. This is one of the good things about the hereafter. You're no longer faced with a day on which you need to wonder whether the sun deserves to rise, or whether the earth is rotating in the opposite direction to what you had thought. Your whole life, you'd imagined day to be nothing more than a veiled night. So, the door will open and the family will look down humbly at the box. It will be five rather than seven o'clock, then it will be tomorrow rather than yesterday. And so it has been from the very first drop, from the very beginning. The mother's uterus takes back its egg, and the father's penis takes back its drop of semen. And everything goes back to point zero. And we will have rested for eternity. You wonder why the door hasn't been opened yet. I'm not responsible for the arbitrary ways in which people behave. They're consulting with one another. The entire family, except for Outhman, is here behind the door. They're inside asking one another whether they should accept your corpse prior to knowing who they're going to demand compensation from. The Makhzen? The airline company? The Kingdom of Saudi Arabia? The man who cut your head off in a fit of anger? Or everyone? They're deep in discussion. I was about to ask whether there had been a lot of rain in recent days. They'd find the question humorous because they'll think that the little girl, Karima, was the one who asked it, and they'll continue to discuss the fortune you're bringing them with your death. Corpses are valuable too, especially when they've come from Saudi Arabia. Ha! This country exports oil and corpses. What do you think? And while we're at it, I'll tell you that Abdullah is the one leading the campaign for demanding compensation. Look at him coming out all angry, just as I said. The family will follow him. First Father in his chair, then the rest of them. Here they are, lining up in front of the box. In front of you. Do you know what Father is doing right now? He's leaning on the box. His nose is what's passing over you right now. His nose has always preceded his hands because he is partial to the smell of wood. The wood is smooth and clean. The smell, although nice, is not the smell of any wood he knows. It isn't the smell of cedar or cypress or juniper. Then come the hands. Father's hands are rough. You recognize them without even seeing them. He passes his hands over the polished box with a sound like rusted metal. You hear his rough hands passing over and you wonder whether he'll lift the box up and drag it inside in order to put the head back where it belongs. But his hands have lost their strength. Didn't you know that? When you left him in the forest, when you ran off to the Gulf and left him with his wood and his project, you knew he was depending on you. Does blood run from its own? Now what do you say? Was going to the Gulf a good idea? In any case, all your father possesses are his two hands, but they'll never be what they once were. Your poor father is finished and cannot carry you himself. Until now, it's been enough for him to sniff like a rabbit, and he's not yet ready to go further than that. And what about the others? Are they ready to cry? That's what you're supposed to do at times like these. I'll let you know if a tear falls on your box without you hearing it. The placement of the head, tossed as it is between your feet, doesn't help you hear as well as you should. Just as you can't see the other faces peering at you. And you won't hear their crying either. I'll inform you of all the details if there are any details worth hearing about. Except for your sister Habiba, I don't hear any crying. She's crying, though. She always used to cry. Khadija? She's busy with the tiny life moving around inside her belly. And Mother? You recognized her from the smell of milk that never left her breast. When she looked down, the smell of milk came close and filled your nostrils. Will her milk fall onto the box and flood you with its warmth? Shall I ask her to pull the box and lift one end so the head will go back to where it belongs? It's noon now, and the situation remains the same. They're refusing to accept the box, not knowing what's inside it. Your stubborn head rolling around at the bottom of the box is angry because of this situation. Because of all situations and decisions and thoughts and counter-thoughts. There's no such thing as a sound or an unsound thought. All thoughts are correct and incorrect at the same time.

The trip began with some idea in Father's head about a wood deal. Before noon, you two had arrived in a small city called Khemisset. "This isn't the road to Azrou," you said to him as you watched him steer the truck off the road and follow a number of dirt paths. You were hoping to get to Azrou before late afternoon so you could pick up your load of wood and get back home. Father said, "We're buying the wood on the black market." He was happy. He hadn't struck such a significant deal in a long time. This scheme would generate enough profit to more than meet the needs of your family. Father was more enthusiastic than you'd ever seen him as he talked about how the dome would be made of cedar and pine. The cedar was no longer that far away. In the forests of Ifrane, which were getting close, the smells of the scented wood wafted toward you, even entering the truck's cab. That was why Father was driving the truck so recklessly. When the truck tilted to the side, you muttered to yourself that he had been blinded by his own zeal. Then, when he parked it in front of the isolated one-story house, you thought for a moment that he was waiting for the guide. Then you thought otherwise because it seemed unrealistic considering the glint in his eyes as he stepped out of the truck and disappeared into that isolated one-story house.

You got out of the truck after the muezzin called in a far-off minaret. At least two hours had passed. You took a few steps toward the door of the house into which Father had disappeared. The door remained closed. You were also thinking about the woman keeping him behind these walls. Then you went back to the truck and turned off the radio you had left on. You continued to worry: "We won't reach Ifrane before late afternoon or even after that." You resented the woman. You resent all women who run off with men. You wouldn't care under any other circumstances, even if Father had disappeared for two days or three months. It wouldn't matter to you at all. But now, in a strange city, in front of an isolated house in the middle of nowhere, you might have turned the radio on and off ten times before his face reappeared in the fading light. Bathed, wearing cologne, his white hair slicked back, the woman behind him. He didn't apologize. He didn't explain. Maybe he didn't even realize that you had been standing there for the past five hours. It was enough for him to gesture toward the woman and whisper, "This is Maymouna." And, pointing to you, he said to her, "And this is Suleiman." Without even seeing you.

Night closed in around you for a while, and then you passed through the city of Azrou and plunged into the forest. None of this was expected or anticipated. Now you were four in the car with the woman named Maymouna and the guide you picked up at the Stork Bar. Father made his way through the forest without lights, because the light would alert the forest guards, according to the guide. No light, the truck swaying from side to side because it had become twice as dark now on account of the thick foliage. The drunk guide said you can see better at night. You asked Father to turn on the headlights so at least the truck could see where its wheels were going. Instead, the guide ordered you to be quiet, while at the same time indicating that Father should stop. Then the two of them got out of the truck. The woman, intent on accompanying them, got out of the truck too. She looked like she was in her thirties. Fair-skinned with wide eyes. The guide objected. They were standing ten paces away. You couldn't hear what the two men were saying. You heard the rustling of cash. Then you saw Father hand the guide a wad of money. As he counted the bills, the guide said, "You can see better at night," and the three of them disappeared into the darkness.

You pushed the button and the singer's voice rose from the truck's radio. They might come back before midnight. You said this knowing that midnight had already passed. Then you thought that maybe the guide was watching you from behind a tree, laughing, repeating that one saw better at night. You got out of the truck. You stood next to it without lifting your eyes toward the sky because the darkness of night and the tree branches were obscuring it. After taking a few steps, you looked up and a small patch of dark-blue sky appeared above you. You too believed that one could see better at night. You spent a bit of time watching the trees move. You saw the end of a rifle aimed at you. Like a spear. Because you were scared, because it was such a dark night, your mind was making you think a rifle was being aimed at you. You took a few steps from the truck. You breathed in the strong smell of the forest and, aware of your fear as you tried to overcome it, you said to yourself, "Now we're really in the mountains." You told yourself that when you were in the forest, you were calmer because of the trees' shadows, the mist from the lakes, the smells, the rustling of birds' wings as they shifted positions in the trees, the vastness, and the scent of flowers coming from the rivers. You saw, though, that none of these thoughts did you any good, so you went back to stand next to the truck at the side of the dirt road on the edge of the forest. The forest's silence was broken only by an intermittent hum, as if the animals were dreaming in their nests. You looked toward the road whenever it seemed that a person's form appeared, but saw only darkness. Night swallowed up the road and the sky. The cedar trees were swallowed by it, leaving behind only their intense smell. They might not come back until morning. It would be best if you left. With or without Father. With or without the truck. No time for anger. It wasn't anger, nor was it rage. Something resembling a lump, like a spiky ball scraping the back of your throat. When the tears came to your eyes, you told yourself they were a result of the pain, in order to avoid feeling ashamed. When your thoughts took this turn, with all of the anger you had stored up inside, you turned off the radio and made your way into the forest, feeling your way, not knowing at all where you were headed. You looked up at the sky as if finding your way by using the small openings the trees had willingly created. When you started to hear loud music, you stopped. Then you took a few more steps and found yourself on the edge of a clearing with many trees that had been separated from their roots, lying on their branches. A lamp was lit inside the wooden storehouse. That was where the music and noise and laughter were coming from. Men's shadows moving inside the storehouse were reflected outside in dark shapes flickering around it. The scene didn't change when I walked up to the window. Men getting drunk and Maymouna dancing, with Father stuffing what was left of his money into the blouse of the woman circling him like a viper that hypnotizes men before biting them.

And now? It's noon and we're still waiting. By late afternoon it will be too late for a burial. Do you want to know what they're doing inside? They're still negotiating. Discussing what would be better for you—to be buried or to remain unburied. Do you hear them? It's the inhabitants of the neighborhood gathering around us. Do you know why? They want to carry the casket to the prefecture to protest the new houses. Do you hear how they're shouting? They want to exploit your unresolved situation. I'll suggest something to Abdullah that will get us out of this predicament. In a little while he'll take you to the neighborhood mosque since he has started to lead the prayers there. He'll collect money from the residents to cover the cost of dinner and a hearse. And when he sees that he's made enough of a profit at your expense, he'll take you to your hole. There, you see? I'm not always the way you think I am. Would you like to hear the story of the apple? It's the only story I'm good at telling. Here it is: "The earth is an apple. A person sits on top of the apple. The only person since the beginning. What does the man on top of the apple do? Does he gaze at the stars above his head? No, the apple looks good and this person is waiting to take his share. Inside the apple there's a worm. The worm makes a hole in the apple, drags him inside, and the apple goes back to the tree it came from." And so ends the story of the apple. What do you think? I understand that you have no desire to look at me, even if I were to put the head back in its place. You still wouldn't be able to see in the dark, and in any case, there's no longer anything there that would be of any interest. A man's life is merely one life divided into little tiny bits. Does this way of looking at things reassure you at all? Does it reassure you knowing that a person's life is nothing but a single life, and that the tyrant is a beggar and the beggar is a tyrant, and that any tyrant, no matter how powerful, might die by catching a cold when he is at the zenith of his power? And that the beggar who lives off of scraps might live for a hundred years? What do you think of this philosophizing (not something I'm in the habit of doing)? I forgot to ask you about the pain in your back. I just remembered it when I saw the festering marks the whip left on your flesh. Do you still think it was my idea? The idea of working in the Gulf was always a good one. The Gulf or Saudi Arabia, same thing. Maybe you just didn't meet the right man. One who would value your gifts. All lives are in God's hands, or at least that's what the man you worked for said as he handed the box over to the men at the airport and asked them to pray for him. They call him Abu Khair, because he gives to so many charitable causes. Don't forget that. He works as a delegate in the Saudi Ministry of Health, spending money on the poor, buying them holiday sheep for Eid, fasting for the months of Shaaban and Ramadan, as well as other days throughout the year. He listened reverently to the prayers of the men at the airport, opened his wallet to dole out cash to them, and said "Amen" before leaving. I'm telling you this so you'll know the man and think well of him rather than deal with him in bad faith like you do with me and everyone else. What was a man in his position to do? You should blame yourself, first and foremost. Why did you sit listening to his wife's tales? She too was a foreigner. That was what made you feel sorry for her. At least that's what you say now. As for me, I say a driver is a driver, and the driver stays outside. Even as you sat in the salon listening to stories about her travels and her previous work in the movies, and about how she had been a star in her country, you didn't realize, not even for a moment, that she was lying. Then, when she dragged you to the bedroom, I said to myself, "Ah, he'll see the sword hanging over the bed and he'll figure it out." You didn't realize what her intention was. She meant to make her husband jealous. If you couldn't understand such a simple thing then you'll never understand anything. What would you expect, after all of that, from a man in his eighties who possesses nothing more than his jealousy? And the whole time she was describing the airports she used to fly into, and the journalists who used to interview her and take pictures of her, she was sitting practically naked on the bed with a cover of silk embroidered with gold, and above it was a sword that had never been used. The image of the sword that had been hanging over the bed for years caught my eye. No doubt it was hanging there for a purpose unbeknownst to anyone before you came along, since before you were born. That's what I thought. I thought that its purpose was hidden inside it before it even became a sword, when it was just a piece of metal in the corner of a blacksmith's shop in Singapore. Just as I was also thinking about the ill-timed arrival of her husband, the delegate of the Ministry of Health. Even when he came in, whip in hand, the sword hadn't crossed his mind. The thought hadn't yet clearly manifested itself with the overwhelming strength that it eventually did. But there was one thing missing from the scene. The faint glint above your head, where the sword had been, was missing. Wasn't it still just as sharp as it was on the day it was made? It didn't take more than a blink of an eye. One blow. Like a wisp of cold wind passing over your neck in a flash. If you think good and hard about it, you'll see that you missed your chance. That's what anyone anywhere would say, whether it was the appropriate time to say it or not. All people believe they have missed some opportunity, because they don't understand why they came or went! A rose blooms at their feet, and rather than look at it they crush it underfoot. Stop! The journey has ended. A drop of sperm fell into the darkness and a handful of worms blossomed in a hole, and between those two events there's a lost cause called life. Isn't that how it is?

VII

43

THE MAN SITTING IN THE wicker chair brushing the ground impatiently with his feet and listening to the strange roar, who hadn't noticed either the two o'clock train, even after it had passed, or the fog that had begun to obscure the horizon in a light purple veil just a short time ago, didn't raise his eyes to the sky pleading for a drop of rain; nor did he turn in the direction of the newborn baby's first cry, although he did give it a barely noticeable glance. The day's sky was turning blue tinged with red, more tolerable now that the sun had lost most of its strength. The baby's first cry didn't surprise him as it did the others. After the second cry, the man looked up toward the window, an unexpected shiver shooting through his forearms. As if to wake him up, to remind him that a new being had come to earth, in case he hadn't noticed or had forgotten, like someone not expecting a baby to be born at sunset, an inappropriate time for birth. Women tend to give birth at dawn, when everything else in creation is born, or during the night, unbeknownst to it, not at this in-between hour. Najat said, "Mbarek messoud. Congratulations," but he didn't respond to her, neither right then, nor afterward. Maybe he was waiting for another cry just to be sure. The two gendarmes raised their glasses and drank without thinking about whether they were drinking to the health of the newborn baby or to the health of the judge and his companion, Najat. Or because the day had ended as they had wanted it to end, with a valuable catch in the form of a woman whose femininity incessantly wounded their masculine pride and toyed with their imaginations with every glance. The man was also preoccupied, although not as much, with the bursting femininity to his right. Her chest was full and generous. Since the moment she sat down, he couldn't take his eyes off it. The fullness of her chest moved something primal inside him that had been lying dormant; something obscure he didn't understand, imposed on him even before he thought about it. The chest is a place of dreams and comfort. A woman's chest is eternity. The third scream was loud, or perhaps it just seemed that way so he could wake up. It was followed by a series of broken cries. Something between crying and laughing. He got up from the chair and shuffled back inside, slowly dragging his babouches. He looked down at the baby. A thin, naked human bundle, wrapped up and screaming. In a couple of years, it might look like him or it might not. Not important. The man wasn't where he should be. For the first time he saw that the place where he lived wasn't right for him. He would rather have been far away, in another city, another country. He would bump into that person in the street, who would say, "Mbarek messoud. Congratulations and may God bless you," and the man would remember, with much longing, that he had left a pregnant woman behind in his country, beyond the sea, and he'd respond, "And may God bless *you*." The man would immediately forget what had just happened and continue on his way. But nothing of the sort happened. This was his place. He would have preferred a country very far away with timeworn customs, perched on a forgotten mountaintop, with another nationality, other customs, and another language. His religion would be the sky and the earth and the wind and water running in a gentle stream, and the dirt with which he'd make a pillow, and would sleep under in the end. That, too, was a distinct possibility, which he could not entirely discount. But nothing like it occurred. Rather, he was here. A new life in front of him. A small miracle, but a miracle nonetheless. A run-of-the-mill miracle that occurred everywhere a thousand times a second, but a miracle nonetheless. His mother-in-law grabbed the newborn by its feet and lifted it. It remained hanging upside down in the air, swinging in her hands. The dangling baby liked this new position, so it laughed. Without wondering whether it was a boy or a girl, the man said, "We'll name her Farah." He lit the candle hanging on the terrace wall, leaving half of it in the dark. He went back to the grill to put on some more skewers of meat in honor of the judge and the two gendarmes. He noticed that the judge had put on his splendid judge's robe. Sloshed as they were, they were preparing for the trial of the woman and her lover, and Najat was laughing hysterically because it was her idea.

A white wax-colored spot had dried on the judge's robe. The shiny white spot made the two gendarmes laugh when they noticed it above his knees. The gendarmes didn't like the judge, spot or no spot, and they didn't like his friend either. Najat looked at the gendarmes to get their attention and asked whether it was a spot of milk, but they didn't pay any attention to her question, or to the guffawing that followed. The gendarme with no epaulettes on his shoulders raised a skewer of meat high in the air and yelled, "Court is in session!" The judge fidgeted drunkenly, straightened the collar of his robe, and opened an imaginary file. The gendarme bit down on a piece of meat. The gendarme with the epaulettes drank an entire glass and offered one to the young woman. Najat clucked as she slapped her thighs and emptied the glass into her mouth. The judge didn't like this. He didn't like it when Najat showed interest in any hand other than his, or in a glass that didn't have traces of his lips on its rim. He closed the file and continued to watch her face sternly, then opened the file again and turned to the young man.

"This woman your wife? What were you two doing in the forest?" He turned toward the woman. "What was he doing to you, my girl?" Then he turned to Najat and winked at her before turning a page of the imaginary file, continuing with his interrogation: "How big is his, my girl?"

Najat didn't chuckle as the judge had expected she would. Nor did she slap her thighs.

"This big? Or *this* big? Bigger than mine? Or bigger than his?" pointing at the gendarme with the yellow epaulettes on his shoulders.

The gendarme with the yellow epaulettes added, "Or bigger than the judge's?"

"The judge's is always bigger."

The judge, who added his voice to that of the gendarme with the yellow epaulettes said, "Tell me, my girl. Don't be shy." Then he turned to watch the changes on the face of Najat, who wasn't so amused at the way things had started off. She wanted a court hearing like in the movies, with testimony, confessions, evidence, witnesses.

"There's no shame in religion . . ."

"His is the big one."

"Mine's bigger than yours."

"Mine's bigger than both of yours."

Laughter burst out from every direction. The judge kept repeating his questions while watching their effect on Najat's face. He hoped to be surprised by her reaction. Like her cheeks would turn red or desire would shine in her eyes. The gendarme with no epaulettes on his shoulders stuck his leg out and prodded the woman with his shoe. "Answer His Honor, the judge." The woman kept her head bowed as if she was thinking. Unconcerned with the shoe's poking, tickling, and prodding, she remained deep in thought for a long time, or at least that was how it looked, then a tear fell from her eye to the ground, followed by another tear, which fell next to the first one. This second tear burrowed more deeply into the dirt than the first one.

*

The wind has its ways. Cold in the winter and hot in the summer. And it has its whims. Like when it blows past when no one is expecting it. This strangely playful wind mussed Farah's hair as it would any creature's hair. As if this frivolous wind had been waiting for her at the door. Farah went back inside, grabbed a kerchief, wrapped it around her hair, and went out again. Farah was changed right at that very moment. The neighbor greeted her, kissed her on her cheeks, and congratulated her, as did the grocer, who whispered something she couldn't hear. Farah thought that the grocer's voice was as sober as the color of the headscarf she had put on her head. She didn't understand why right then. And in the street. In the café. Baffled, her friend pointed to it, to the headscarf. Farah looked all around her before realizing what she was talking about. She said it was because of the wind, but her friend gave her a look filled with doubt. What did the wind have to do with a hijab? This isn't a hijab. This is Mother's headscarf. As if one door had closed and another one had opened in its place. Noisy. Sitting in the café was no longer the same. The coffee tasted different. As did the water served by the waiter, and the look he gave. Everything was different. The young man sitting on the chair next to her, who was used to the way she looked before, said to her, "What's with you? Your hair's so pretty." She turned to him apologetically, explaining that it was just the wind, but the same doubtful look remained on the young man's face. His eyes continued to wonder: Was this the same girl who sat with us yesterday, with her short, light hair that danced above her forehead and around her face when she turned? It wasn't the same face. What happened to it and to the girl it belonged to? It was the wind. But no one believed it. When Farah looked and saw it blowing in the street, rising and falling, she went back home and wrapped her hair in the first piece of cloth she could put her hands on. That was all that happened. But the others saw it quite differently. This wind wouldn't last long. She'd take the kerchief off when she went home. The kerchief was just a temporary covering that would go away once the wind died down. Who knew—maybe the wind would continue long enough for the grocer to see that she had changed. And for her friends to see that she had changed. And for the neighbors to see that she had become rational, mature, and balanced. And her father would see. That was the most important thing. That her father would see that he no longer had to put his disability on display in front of the General Command office, all because of a form of respect that came within reach thanks to a pale kerchief his wife had used for years without him or anyone else showing any interest in it. The piece of cloth made her father happier than she had expected it would. It was just a piece of cloth, no larger than a meter square. It wouldn't even cover the dining table in their house. But it calmed his heart and put his mind at ease. Instead of the constant fear he had felt for her before, he now sat relaxed on the doorstep, smoking tobacco brought to him from the base by his friend who hadn't yet retired. In this regard, he wasn't worried about his daughter anymore. Instead, he was worried about finding a fish that had been extinct for decades. And Farah? She continued to wrap the kerchief around her neck and cover her hair—at home for her father's sake, and outside for the neighbors, the grocer, and the waiter. Even on the day she found herself on a bus that was taking her away from her father, the grocer, and the waiter. Taking her away from Azemmour altogether. She opened the bus window and allowed the kerchief to free itself of its labels, to go back to what it was before—just a piece of cloth fluttering in the wind.

Suddenly, some clouds appeared on the horizon, darker than the night that was wrapping itself around everyone. The man said they were very close. They'd been creeping toward them for some time now. As for the gendarme, he was now leaning against the clay wall looking at the stars in the clear part of the sky as if examining another earth. From between his teeth he let out something resembling a horse's whinny that might have been some sort of drunken laugh. He wondered out loud whether any of them had seen a gendarme fly, adding that gendarmes are earthly creatures, and that the ones who fly end up with their wings smashed. Then he let out the same drunken laugh that sounded like the neighing of a winged horse. Still, the gendarme with the epaulettes was an even-keeled man. He had drunk just enough to cause his head to lean slightly upward, enough to cloud his eyes so he could see that his wings wouldn't work, and to see that, whatever else happened, he wouldn't go any further than the yellow epaulettes on his shoulders.

The other gendarme shifted in his chair. "They're here."

"Who?"

"All of them." The gendarme with no epaulettes on his shoulders was as alert as a panther. Ready to pounce. The night enhanced his vision. This was part of his job. Waiting for his boss to finish the lost episodes of his intense dream, he took a step into the darkness. "You don't see them?" The man walked halfway across the field behind the gendarme with no epaulettes on his shoulders. They stoppĕd. "Now do you see them? They're here." Everyone who had been making their way over during the day. The night had been hiding them, and now, after the gendarme had spoken, their presence seemed more intense. A single cohesive throng. A single body stretching out, then contracting. Under the darkness of night, it became even more threatening and present, even more ominous. The two men went back to where they had been sitting. They were wrapped in a deceptive stillness, a false stillness resembling the roar of the lurking mass in the darkness. Eyes surrounded the two men. The fact that there was no shine to them became more threatening than if the shine had been there.

"Are they waiting?"

"They're not waiting for anything."

They weren't waiting for a conclusion because the ending was in their heads. They wanted the woman and her lover. They wanted meat. Not the grilled meat, though. They wanted live flesh. "Do you hear that sound?" The man heard the sound now but didn't know where it was coming from. Or, more precisely, it had a new, unfamiliar rhythm. It was the sound of rocks in their hands and pockets. Their hands, whose patience had run out, were moving them. Those hands had been ready since morning, since last night. Until they saw blood, until they saw two crushed heads and bones mixed with blood, flesh, and hair flying through the air, until they'd quenched their thirst for violence on two defenseless skulls, they weren't going anywhere. The man, even after going back to where he had been sitting, could picture the stones as they came down on the two, bare, defenseless heads, blood gushing out over their faces and covering their eyes. White rocks the size of a palm, maybe a little bigger, rained down from everywhere, and their two heads were stunned, not from the pain, not from the force with which the rocks struck their skulls, but rather from surprise and shock.

What were the two gendarmes waiting for? And the judge who had forgotten that he'd been wearing his judge's robes for a while now? As for the two prisoners, they didn't expect anything less than the worst. They certainly couldn't be hoping for a possible rescue. And Najat (whose name actually meant "rescue") had gotten drunk, laid her head down on the judge's thigh, and fallen asleep, which prevented him from moving. His robe lost its dignity, and the magistrate lost his prestige. The gendarme with the epaulettes turned toward the judge. Why was he waiting to issue his verdict? The judge said that he would allow the man who was hosting them to rule in the case, and whatever his verdict was, he would accept it. The man continued to follow the clouds' movement across the sky. It didn't appear that he'd heard what the judge said. One of his legs scraped the dirt for a bit. The gendarmes started to feel that it was getting late, that the road was awaiting them, and that they had to return the two prisoners to the car before the crowd lurking in the dark attacked them. Then the man said, "Let them go." Silence descended once again. It crept along noiselessly, like the clouds above. The judge removed the car key and threw it in the dirt at the young man's feet. The young man couldn't see the key because of the darkness. He didn't have to see it. The hand is what sees in situations like these. He didn't possess anything other than his hands to see. He used one hand to grab the key while helping his lover up with the other. Then they made their way to the American car. All of this happened without a movement from anyone. They could only watch, unable to move, as if it were happening someplace else and they were separated from it by a wall or a trench. And even after the engine roared and the car took off, the man continued to look at a sky that was no longer the same sky. All of a sudden, the rain started to gently fall, and the dirt took a breath. From deep within the earth the smell of forgotten grass and stored-up promises rose. Could the two gendarmes leave now that the road had turned to mud? Yes, their car was made for this. After they left, the judge grabbed his companion's arm and they went inside. The man stood there, taking pleasure in the droplets of rain falling on his forehead, tickling his nose, going into his mouth, and flowing sweetly down his throat. As he got up, he thought that it hadn't occurred to him before to get up, go into the room, take Farah into his arms, and hum to her until she fell asleep, so he got up and took Farah in his arms as if to test his emotions once again. Perhaps he expected more than he had when he passed his hand over the small lump just a short while ago. Yes, perhaps the time had come for him to change.

44

A Grave in the Water

HOW DOES LUCK ARRIVE? LUCK is life. Luck is relationships. It's
money. It's the woman you meet on the street corner—this
street and not any other street. Or on the bus—this bus and
not any other bus. And luck is *not* meeting her as well. This
little bit of luck that a person needs in order to jump to the
other side without falling into the abyss of despair. I watched
her for two days, telling myself she might get up. It was a
temporary stumble, and with a little bit of luck, she'd get back
up. Her luck wouldn't betray her again. Then, when she did
get up for a little bit and stepped outside the workshop, I continued to watch her from the window while she laid her body
in the sun not far from the door, and I wondered whether her
strength had betrayed her this much. What was missing? She
wore my light shirt so as not to hurt her injured skin, along
with my leather sandals, and she had on a large straw hat from
which she hung a translucent white veil that concealed her
face and neck, which were covered with burns. Today, when
sitting down tired her out as much as standing did, she went
back into the workshop and stretched out among the pieces of
wood. For a long, long time she didn't move. Seeing her in that
frozen position, I figured she was sleeping, which was a good
sign. I walked back and forth between the pieces of wood on
which she had painted red cats that didn't look like cats at
all; with legs like sticks and round white eyes that looked like
moons. Farah was laid out next to her paintings. Distant. Had

her strength betrayed her as much as her luck had? I looked nervously at her. I saw her chest moving up and down underneath the shawl in the shadows of this small forest, brocaded by the sun's rays at the peak of its radiance. Her burns were minor and no cause for alarm. There was no need to imagine things that weren't there. Should I take her back to the hospital? What would I tell them at the hospital? I didn't even know if Farah was her real name. For no logical reason, I continued to think that she had a name other than this one. Farah isn't a name. It could be the name of a plant or a flower. There isn't a girl named Farah in Azemmour or anywhere else. Then she moved, and hope glimmered inside me. She let out a faint sigh. She was returning little by little. She was waking up bit by bit, and the fresh burns and pains were waking up with her as well. Should I prepare the little sardine balls she loves so much? I got a sardine that had been caught in a fisherman's net today at dawn. I cleaned it and mixed it with garlic, cilantro, and a bunch of other spices, making it into a paste, exactly how she likes it. I waited for her condition to improve enough for her to be able to sit up, just long enough for her to eat a mouthful. Just long enough for me to see that her condition had improved. It had been six days since she had run away from the hospital while I waited for her condition to improve. But no sooner did she gather her strength—no sooner did she gather just a tiny bit of strength and try to get up—than she collapsed and went back to sitting or lying down for hours. From her deepest slumber I heard her say that she wanted black coffee. She moved slowly. She raised her hand, and with the same slowness removed the blackened piece of cloth that was covering her face revealing gouges and lacerations that were difficult to look at. She took off her dress and sat in the middle of the void that surrounded her. It was difficult to recognize Farah in what she was doing right then. And there was no way of knowing what I should do. Should I cry? Farah was on the other side of the world, wallowing in her pain and loneliness. I went to her and helped her lie down again, throwing a cover over her and placing a cloth on her face.

I boiled the water. I poured a bit of coffee into the glass, added the boiling water to it, and placed the glass next to the blanket. She'd wake up and remember she had dreamed of coffee, and she'd be happy when she saw the glass. A small dream come true. A little bit of luck to brighten her dark day. We always need this little bit of luck, this piece of luck that hadn't been there before. The world is made according to this incomplete principle. Nothing is complete. We'll always believe in another possibility, in second chances. But there are no second chances. I won't find the lawyer, or Naima. Just as Farah didn't find the man who was going to take her by the hand to make her a singer. No one takes anyone's hand. No one helps anyone except in fairy tales. She opened her eyes and looked around from underneath the veil. She might have calmed down by now. Her fear had conquered her pain, so she forgot everything and became calm. She said she had been sleeping, but had remained conscious of what was around her. Not too long before, she had managed to flutter her eyelids, right? I nodded. She could lift her left arm and remove the veil hanging over her face. She moved her head right and then left. I was still hesitant. Was she there or not? I heard what she was saying and pretended to understand. She said she had heard sounds. Footsteps on stairs that weren't there, and grass growing on the banks of a river. "The Oum Errabia, our house on the banks, trees, birds chirping, a car horn. I heard and felt all of this around me, but I didn't see it. Maybe next spring." She continued to babble incoherently.

After the sun set, her condition suddenly improved again. Astonishing. As if nothing was wrong with her. Not even the burns meant a thing anymore after this stunning turnaround. She threw aside the cloth that was covering her face and went out. From the window I watched her go up the sand dune that separated the workshop from the beach and sit down. Farah radiated beauty even though she hadn't completely healed. I went and sat next to her. My desire to throw my arms around her and embrace her tightly caused tears to come to my eyes. I just put my arms over her shoulders. After about two hours, night fell without us noticing. As we sat there silently, a small moon appeared in the middle of a circle of clouds that looked like colored steam. The moon's round edges shone magnificently. The water's surface shone as if there were another sky filled with stars. Farah and I counted them one by one, even though we didn't see them. In the stars, Farah saw that the days to come would be radiant. I didn't say what I was thinking, which was that I didn't know what good radiant days would do, given her condition. A light wind blew, enough to make her thin body shiver. Walking back to the workshop, she said that she felt a sense of tranquility, that her mind was calm. I slowed down, letting her go ahead of me so I could watch her walk from behind, thinking that I'd jump in through the window to beat her inside. Instead, I went in after her, again mulling over the shapes she had painted on the pieces of wood. I stood there looking at them in the candlelight. Besides the cats that weren't cats, Farah had drawn triangles linked like a chain. She said they were flowers. Flowers as she saw them. I had never seen flowers like these in my life. I turned around. She was naked. Lying on the blanket, naked.

Farah's fingers are thin, translucent. You can easily see the life that fills her veins. When I turned my face away from the candle, the fingers appeared. Then I turned my gaze toward the mosque and the fingers disappeared. I contemplated the mosque as it had risen to its full majestic glory. Then, instead of fingers, I saw her body. Her thin body. White and naked. It lay on top of the old cover in the workshop. Completely naked. Amid the panels, plastic bags, empty jars, and cats. For the first time since that day I'd looked in through the window and run away from it dumbstruck, I was looking at her naked body, lying in front of me. For the first time, I was looking at a female body, being generously offered like a gift. Was this what I had always secretly craved without having had the courage to articulate it? Wood panels stood up straight in the dark like forgotten ghosts in a thicket. She lay there languidly. When I put the cover back over her body she kicked it off, raising a cloud of dust. Then, when the beams of moonlight came in through the window and dust enveloped her exposed body in a translucent purplish cloak, a wave like a bolt of electricity passed between us and lit a flame in my chest. I went back to the window. My vision was blurred. In my eyes, desire was like fear. Desire is fear. My penis embarrassed me as it peered out from an opening in my pants and laughed, after desire had transformed itself into what was now between my legs. With it, fear settled in. Desire was the fear between my legs. What my legs were saying was unclear. They weren't used to standing so close to a naked body. My mouth was dry, as if there were a ball of wool inside it. The mosque looked at me with its many eyes. What was Farah doing? Was she showing her body to the moonlight? She opened her eyes then closed them, smiling. Her nipples smiled invitingly atop the two quivering mounds. For the first time in my life a woman was inviting me to do this and I didn't know anything about it, despite the twenty years I had been registered under my current civil status. And what did this seagull perched over my head and pecking at the tin want? There were many eyes around me. Farah's eyes, as well as those of the mosque, the seagull, the window, the wood with the many cats on it with their moon-shaped eyes. And the eyes of desire. The eyes of desire asked what I wanted to do with this heavenly gift in front of me. Her breasts were large. Heavy. Weighed down with promises. Captivating. Larger than my adolescent desire could contain. Full. The creeping sensation moved from my head to my thighs. Her nipples urged me down. I took two steps forward to become better acquainted with her body's contours. What should I do with the mosque that was watching me? Should I close the window? Would it disappear if I closed the window? And then what would the window think about this? Would it have an opinion about something as complicated as sleeping with a woman? I closed the window and sat close to her. Bashfully, I removed my clothes and lay down next to her. No need to look at her face. Not now. Perhaps I'll need to later. Her disfigurement helped me overcome my fear, and her boldness and severity. Looking at her through the lens of pity helped me gain the upper hand. In the state I was in, I'd need that disfigured face, and all disfigured faces. Had the time come for me to look at the face? Her disfigured face called out to me, but I didn't look at it yet. I didn't want to try to decode what was there. I might do that later. I didn't want to put my hand on the burns on her face because I didn't want to cause her any pain. I might do that later. My hand moved over her body's soft skin. Her body called out to me. Her face slept. The burns shone. Her eyes had narrowed and turned red, and the edges of her mouth had been consumed by the fire of the sulfuric acid. My hand passed over a world it was unfamiliar with. Here it descended a hill and stopped at a delicious crevice. It settled deep inside the cavity like a bird that had found a nest just its size. The hand rested for a little bit before continuing its jaunt, inclining toward the roundness of the buttocks. It was pleasantly surprised that the roundness fit exactly inside its palm. I hadn't been interested in her body the night I saw her for the first time in the cabaret. And I didn't think about it afterward, simply because I hadn't been expecting her. The first time you sleep with a woman, with the woman you love, it always comes as a surprise. Spontaneous. When you least expect it. The first time. That's why you find everyone talking about their first time. Because it leaves an indelible mark on them. They have eaten from the fruit and they spend the rest of their days trying to find the taste that's still there, though not on their tongues, but in their tongues' memory. A unique taste they won't find in any other fruit. The first time you sleep with a girl you love is the only time. After that it doesn't have the same taste, nor does it provoke the same intense desire or the same feeling of apprehension. It doesn't show on the father's face or the mother's. No doubt they remember their first time. The times that come after are nothing but a rehearsal for a long play of maneuvers, intrigue, bribery, deception, oppression, despotism, deceit, and what you'll later call "life." No one constructs his own life. Your life drew it that first time. And what remains are failed attempts to repeat it. Without meaning. Without pleasure. Without desire. Perhaps there are glands in the body that secrete a substance that might help you recognize the girl who will take you by the hand and lead you into the abyss. Or that will help her recognize the boy who will take her by the hand and lead her into the same abyss. My hands moved gently up to her chest. My mouth sucked the cherry. Little by little my thirsty mouth was filled with the cherry's nectar. My hands moved up to her face, fingers passing gently over it. The burned, wrinkled skin had softened. The burns had disappeared. The wounds on her face were neither ugly nor repulsive. They were just wounds, like any other wound. Maybe I saw them, maybe I didn't. I did see that they weren't defects. They were drawings that looked like crimson roses with yellow and orange petals I'd drawn many times on pieces of paper, wood, and walls. Why shouldn't I love them just like I loved the drawings I did on Father's ceiling? The wounds on her face were radiant like the drawings I loved. I loved Farah because of the drawings on her face. Small dark leaves all over her, even reaching her neck in a delicate and brilliant arrangement. I kissed the orange petals first, one rose after the other. Farah was beautiful in all her rainbow colors. The colors of the mosque's ceiling blossomed on Farah's body, giving her a unique brilliance. I moved up onto her stomach and thighs, holding myself above her chest. Between her chest and me was a gap of air where currents and smells and thoughts and discernible golden rays pulled at one another. Had the time come for my thirsty eyes to take in her face? The more I lowered myself, the greater my desire became. And the greater my desire became, the easier it was to enter her. Her body was warm, as warm on the inside as it was on the outside. She sighed without a sound. She clung to me, so I moved down. She scratched my back with her small nails, so I lowered myself farther. She scratched my back, slowed it down, sped it up, pushed it away then brought it closer, lifted it so it rose, and lowered it again. Her nails scratched my back, penetrating deeply into the skin, digging into it. When I finally rose back up her face had transformed. It had become Farah's face as it was before. Gorgeous. Radiant. Her curving waist was colored by the light of the moon when I leaned over slightly. Her body was the moon. She was tranquil now, or sleeping. I closed my eyes and opened them again. I turned toward her and saw she was asleep. I covered her body. I waited for her to move, but she didn't. She was more than sleeping. I kissed her little finger and saw that the finger didn't respond. I moved it, but it didn't move. I lifted it and it fell. I moved her, but she didn't move, and it was as if someone slapped me across the face, and darkness closed in around me.

45

EVEN IF THERE HAD BEEN enough light, I wouldn't have been able to see her. Minutes passed. Hours passed. An eternity passed. Right now, I didn't dare turn toward where Farah was lying—not how she was a little while before, but in a way that was new to her and to me. And even if I did turn, I'd wonder what this indistinguishable pile was inside the workshop. Was it a net left here by one of the fishermen? It couldn't be Farah, in any case. Farah? Who is this poor girl you speak of? Farah? Is that the name of a flower or a garden? I forget. I feign ignorance. But unintentionally. I don't understand anything about corpses. Just as I don't understand anything about crimes; in the moments that preceded this one I wouldn't have imagined that this could really have occurred, that Farah could have died. It wasn't yet time to picture it. I grabbed the candle and left the workshop. Barefoot, I headed toward the ocean, my shadow wobbling before me, as if going back to look for her again in the waves. I didn't know whether I was gaining time or wasting it! Farah didn't go up into the sky. She was still in the workshop. I needed to think about her. My throat was dry and seawater wouldn't do any good. I went back and sat on the doorstep, leaving my shadow to dance around between us. I forgot about the water. A cricket that had been chirping next to me fell silent. The mosque in front of me was cloaked in darkness. A deep hatred rose up inside me, making my blood boil, hissing and twisting its tongue like a snake. I hoped the building would collapse. The mosque was the reason for all of this. Or the ceiling. What need do people have for mosques? When we were young we used to see them performing the holiday Eid prayer out in the open. Thousands of people. Clean, happy, with no ceiling blocking the sky. There's nothing better than praying under the sun, or in the rain, or under the clouds. Even if walls are absolutely necessary, what use is the ceiling? The ceiling is the basis for this whole disaster. I hoped to wake up in the morning and see that it had collapsed, to see that the ocean had swallowed it up during the night, or that it had been struck by an earthquake. One stone on top of another. If God could see that the mosque was built with the money of the poor and the unfortunate, why didn't He send a fierce wind like the ones He had sent before? I'd wait until morning to see whether God had heard my prayer. I was sure that the sun would not rise over the mosque again. Before the break of dawn, each and every stone of it will have crumbled. The continuous plunder will have gone on long enough for the Lord of Heaven and Earth to justify demolishing the structure, or at least for my uncle Mustafa to find solace. The same went for those who had fallen from the top of the minaret, or been crushed by bulldozers. I was also thinking about the way Farah left this world. Was it because of pain or pleasure or fear? Was it as a result of the burns or the agony, or was it because of the songs she never got to sing? Then, before everything else, I needed to think about our current situation—the corpse and me in the workshop and this night. In life there are these unfortunate times when nothing you think about leads to anything. Once, Kika and I found a dead bird on the sidewalk. It might have died just moments before—the warmth of life still moved the feathers on its white belly. We were young, and it was useless for us to think about finding a way to bury it. There's no place in this city where you can bury birds. I told Kika that we'd look for a park. But there are no parks where you can bury birds. Kika kept it in his pocket. At his house we lit the fire, grilled the bird, and ate it.

Should I eat Farah? That would take some time. This was one of a number of possibilities. I'd start with the fingers. I'd bite into them to whet my appetite, as if they were licorice sticks. Farah's thin, translucent fingers. Then the arms, followed by the legs. I'd leave the rest for a midnight feast. At dawn I'd donate the innards to the seagulls because they were poor like me, and they had young ones that needed their mother's milk. Other similarly foggy and distorted thoughts came to me. For example, I imagined she was breathing and merely in a temporary slumber. I didn't go in to verify this. I thought about her breathing because I couldn't see her. Or I imagined she was crying, recalling a little bit of her short past. Heartbroken or remorseful. More seriously, I thought about the seagull that would come and take her away, because Farah had become light, and she'd become even lighter once she'd gotten rid of her bad luck. And it wouldn't come alone, this determined and hoped-for seagull. It would come with its flock, which had been fattening up over time. All of those that I'd fed since we began work on the mosque. What are seagulls good for? Especially the black ones whose peace-loving natures abandoned them, after which they began to eat cadavers. A ridiculous idea, of course, although I did turn to see if the window was open.

Then there was the matter of digging the grave. A grave to preserve the workshop's memory. It was imperative to think about digging the grave when dealing with hiding dead bodies. The easiest thing to do would be to leave it outside to decompose, like people used to do in ancient times, before graves, shrouds, witnesses, and the prayers that followed came about. I set these meaningless thoughts aside. Right now, I needed a pickax and a shovel. I got up and went back inside. Preparing the modest spot that would provide Farah's shelter wouldn't take too long. I tossed a piece of wood aside and began to dig under the moonlight that streamed in through the window and settled on her waxen face. Her face had been pulsing with life just a few hours before. Not a life as it should have been—without wounds or burns or setbacks—but life nonetheless. What had happened? I stopped digging. I walked closer to examine her. There might still be a spark of life smoldering inside her. She looked like someone sleeping. At rest. She'll get up. She was at peace. No nightmare disturbing her temporary slumber. She really needed the rest and was going to get up in a little bit. I placed my hand on her forehead and it seemed to me that there was still life pulsing under her skin. I called into her ear, "Farah . . . Farah," and waited for her to jump to her feet, laughing, making fun of me and my fears. I just needed to be sure. I stepped back and turned the pickax over in my hand a few times, to give hope enough time to settle in beside us. And then, in a moment of distraction, I saw her eyelid flutter. I walked back up to her and saw that she was breathing. I put my hand on her nose. I grabbed her by the hand and put my head down on her chest. "Farah . . . Farah." I heard a sound next to me. Was it her voice? I got up. A humming coming from inside. Then I saw that it was coming from outside, from the ocean or from inside the mosque, as if people had come specifically to see the crime with their own eyes. Wherever there's a body . . . I walked to the window and looked out. I couldn't see the faces in the darkness. Faces enjoy sneaking around, hiding themselves in the dark, licking their lips excitedly. I wiped the sweat from my forehead and prepared to get back to work. I removed some dirt with the shovel and got back to digging. Seven months of working here, and for the first time I was seeing the dirt of our workshop close up. As I brought the pickax down to the ground, I saw that we'd built the workshop on top of stone. Wherever I aimed the pickax, the only sound I heard was the resounding din of metal, sparks flying as it struck the rock. It was because we were so close to the shore. I tossed the pickax aside and sat down, not knowing what I had expected!

It would be better to wash her in seawater so the salt could treat the wounds as she went on her way, so she'd arrive in

Heaven as her Lord created her on the first day, healthy and whole. Two buckets of saltwater. It would please Him to see His creation returned to Him as He had given her to us, in full health and in all her beauty. These thoughts refreshed me and removed any distress on my gloomy face. And the shroud? Was a coffin really necessary? No. She'd go in her purple-flowered dress, and I thought that, this time, the flowers wouldn't be drooping down. I gathered the wood panels for a coffin that would fit her, all the panels that Farah had drawn her cats and flowers on. They were her panels and they'd go with her. No need to add any other drawings. The drawings that I knew, and Father knew, and Suleiman knew, were only good for ceilings. Ceilings of a certain type. Ceilings that resulted in Father falling from the top of a ladder, that resulted in Suleiman coming back without a head, that resulted in a wicked hand pouring sulfuric acid on Farah's face in front of the lighthouse door. Anguish returned to dominate my thoughts, and with it the cricket started chirping again. This time it was bloodcurdling. It was only a cricket, smaller than a cocoa bean, yet it made my hair stand on end. With its vast range, its chirping tonight was enough to awaken those deep in slumber. I stopped what I was doing. This cricket was chirping deliberately with all its strength to alert people walking by. Workers returning home from the weaving shops. Or fishermen out at sea, preoccupied with migrating fish, not having even the slightest notion about Farah. Or those who were sleeping. This damned cricket could even wake the dead in their graves. Could it awaken Farah? Better to put out the candle, because even if this insect didn't shut up, no one would imagine that a person would dig in the dark. It was just a cricket singing in anticipation of summer grapes. And, in anticipation of summer, I went out without a candle, shovel in hand, determined to finish it off. One blow and I'd crush it like any other disgusting cricket. *Baf!* Just one blow. I stood defiantly in the dark, waiting for its final chirp, the shovel at the ready above my head. It was silent. Just as obstinate. Just as defiant. We could have remained like that until Judgment Day. The cricket had all the time in the world, and could remain silent for an entire year. I went back to work, determined to finish before it chirped again. The second time, I went out with the candle in one hand and the shovel in the other. On tiptoe, inching my way toward it. The chirping didn't stop because the sound was coming from inside the workshop. I didn't make the slightest noise. No sound whatsoever. Not a peep. I tiptoed toward the irritating source. Then I saw it—black, shiny, small—on top of her chest. Like one of her flowers. It wasn't hopping, either. Rather, it was walking, matching the rhythm of my steps, as if imitating my walk, my every move, as cognizant of my presence as I was of its. Or as if both of us together knew how far this charade could go. We approached one another. When it stopped on her face, all I wanted was for it to get off her body and settle on a piece of wood, or a paint can, or under any rock it chose, promising not to hurt it as long as it moved away a little from the body. The truth of the matter is that a damn cricket will always be a damn cricket. They'll never care what we say or think about them. It continued to creep along slowly, very slowly. Then it disappeared up her nose. Silently. Without a chirp. As if it had entered its house. As if it had found the place it was looking for.

The night might have been over—most of it having moved over to the other side of the earth—when I left the workshop with the coffin on my shoulder, the shovel on top of it. The first signs of the dawning day spread out above me with a sad orange color. As I headed down toward the beach, I was still thinking about whether I should dig a hole in the sand or whether I should let the ocean take care of that. The water was somewhere between high and low tide. I didn't know whether it was coming in or going out. I put the coffin on a rock. On either side of it were blue triangles Farah had painted. And yellow leaves. And what looked like green English ivy winding its way up the wood. The coffin had all the paintings Farah had done on it. And the cricket? It was inside the coffin. Inside Farah. Its chirping might start up again in a little bit, and no one would know where it was coming from. As for the cats, with their eyes that looked like white moons, they were facing inward toward Farah. That way when she woke from her slumber she'd see them, her red cats, and she'd know that she was still close to us, and it would be as if she'd never left. I wasn't able to finish digging because the water came up on us suddenly and began to lap at the sides of the rock where I had placed Farah. I picked up the coffin again and went into the water. When I felt it at my waist, I placed the coffin on its surface, but didn't dare let go of it. I remained standing there, waiting for something to happen— for the cricket to sing, for example. I waited but didn't hear it. Then I smiled and pushed the coffin out into the water.

Clothes wet. Exhausted. Thoughts jumbled. Completely uncomfortable. As the sun came up, the mosque appeared loftier than it had before, even though it should have been the opposite. Was it destined to remain there forever? I studied it carefully as I sat by the roiling ocean, expecting to hear the cricket, but it didn't let out a single chirp. Maybe later. Some fishermen began setting up their fishing rods on the beach. The workers who came back again with the National Department of Electricity employee weren't stringing cables this time. Rather, they were hanging flags and multicolored lights, and setting up barriers. Red and green ribbons, too. New trucks began to appear. Fire trucks arrived to spray the ground and bulldozers came to tear down what remained of the workshops where unknown workers had lived and died. They had laid down their pieces of cardboard and lived on bread and tea. They left behind a bit of their sweat, their bodies, and their souls so that the edifice could rise up high. These workshops were no longer of any use. Moreover, they sullied the overall look of the place. I walked up to a fisherman to ask what was going on.

"It's the dedication."

"What dedication?"

"The dedication of the mosque."

"When?"

"Don't know."

I climbed a hill and walked away. Our workshops were no longer of any use. I didn't care one way or another that they were being destroyed. Same with the mosque, the minaret, and all the facilities that had been constructed around it. My only consolation, my biggest consolation, was the crack. It would remain there. No one would notice it, but it was there, somewhere on Father's ceiling. Only I knew the secret that the mosque concealed—except for Father, of course. But Father was now sitting in his wheelchair. There was a crack in the mosque. Yes indeed. A crack the size of a finger. No one could see it, but it would continue to get bigger. I hoped it would continue to grow until the building crashed down without anyone knowing why.

46

So, THE BIG TOE ON my right foot hurts. A pain I haven't felt before. There isn't the slightest hint of anything on the toe that might indicate what's causing the pain. A pain like quicksilver that leaves the toe and then returns whenever it wants. It moves as it likes. It stays in the same spot for two full days only to suddenly move up to the ankle—two or three days for me to be able to say that I've become accustomed to it, or that it isn't actually a pain at all, but rather a tight sock I forgot about on my foot. Then one morning, without warning, it shoots up to my left knee with a lightning-quick acrobatic flip—or to my joints, or my back—only to return to the left toe, depending on the time of day. At first, after Farah's death, it didn't move beyond this general area, and it showed up quite infrequently. Then it began to appear regularly. A reeling, chaotic pain, without any clear rhyme or reason. On the positive side, I discover with great joy that thanks to the pain in my toe, and how severe it is, I can overcome the other pains occupying my mind that would have been even worse. It gets so it becomes necessary to embrace the pain—whether it's in my toe, or knee, or back—and to nourish and protect it like a small child if I want my other pains, the ones related to Farah's death, to disappear. And so it goes, replacing one pain with another. Replacing one disappointment with another. A thought is emerging about a dear entity that had died. At the same time, the pain in my big toe on my right foot is waking up too, brandishing its deadly weapons, burning the image of a face lacerated by sulfuric acid into my memory, and then the pain leaps to my knee in a single jolt that feels like an electric shock. At that moment I clench my teeth in joy, or pain. Same thing. This grants me a bit of eventual comfort. It will last as long as it has to. I'm thankful for it. Grateful for the inner calm it grants me. Little Karima stands in front of Father. In her hands she has some cloth, some thread, and a few sticks, and she's waiting for him to make her a butterfly that flies. But he's busy. I sit on a crate that serves as a chair and watch what Father is doing. Two old men passing the time, observing each other's pain. One man older than sixty, and the other almost twenty. I lift my foot when he lifts his. I grab my leg when he grabs his. I grimace when he does. When he's not doing this, he passes his hand over a board and I pass my hand over the board facing it. We're working. Father is restoring his chair and I'm making a chair similar to it. We sit in front of one another, entertaining ourselves with our old and new disabilities. We're working without any help from anyone. We don't need anyone's help anymore. Our most recent invention, as Father calls it, depends on what remains of his old zeal. There's a fat calf lowing outside the house. The two chairs are wide, too, so we can stretch out on them whenever we please. We no longer have any need for beds or bedrooms. There's only one bedroom in the house, anyway, and Abdullah took it and gave the key to Khadija. Khadija has become his second wife. She stands behind us looking out the window and massaging her belly. Father and I are no longer interested in something so insignificant as a woman massaging her belly behind us. Everything comes in due time. We are no longer the normal human beings we once were. And no one in the house or outside it wants to understand such simple matters. The best way to pass the time with the least amount of possible trouble is to spend it at work, constructing long-lasting chairs, as long as the wood is good—pleasant-smelling cedar from the forests of Ifrane. With the texture, smell, and everything else wood needs to remain as fragrant as the day it was born. Nothing matures outside of work. With the passing of time, we'll discover astonishing things. Father and I have hellish plans for the future. People are involved in something big, and right now they don't want to understand this. One morning someone will understand this, and that's the day someone will shoot himself.

My sister Khadija is behind us looking out the window. Father and I are completely engrossed in serious work, whereas the others, all the others who don't have any work at all, are amusing themselves outside the house, including Mother, even though she doesn't like to have fun. Her hands are stained with dye. Instead of sewing, she's mixing henna in a small container and dabbing it on the calf's forehead. Farah isn't with them. Rather, she's at rest on the water's surface. The waves are moving wisps of her hair to and fro in the timeless moonlight. The moon of that night. The pain in my knee awakens. Sharp. Painful. It becomes more acute the more the hair undulates on top of the water. I stop working. I gather up all of my other pains and stand smiling at the door. I scratch my left knee, happy with the twinge of pain on that side.

I see them congregating in the street. Mother, Abdullah, Habiba, the neighbors, Karima, and the children—as many children as the street can absorb. My sister Khadija no longer suffers from her old ailments because Abdullah has added her to his first wife, without a wedding ceremony, just as Habiba had stipulated—no wedding, no joyful trilling, nothing of the sort; just the reciting of the Fatiha—putting an end to the fits Abdullah had devoted specifically to Khadija in his room. Also putting an end to the devilish sounds that used to make their way out from underneath the door. And Mother said, "Amen," when she stopped menstruating. Now Khadija is content to massage her swollen belly while she chews on cloves and watches the calf. Abdullah has forgotten all about Habiba and her pregnancy. Whatever she gives birth to no longer matters to him, whether it's a boy or a girl, a calf or a monkey. As for Khadija, this is her first child. She is in her third month, which is why she is forbidden to watch television—the third month being when creations take their final form, according to Abdullah. In the third month, the fetus might be male, then all of a sudden turn into a female, or vice versa. Or the fetus might be white, then turn black. The third month is the most dangerous month for a pregnant woman. He doesn't want his future son looking like a monkey or a camel or one of those cursed creatures that constantly appear one after the other on the TV screen. May God curse it and those who broadcast such deformed images of human beings! And she is forbidden from seeing the calf, alive or dead. That's why she's inside, satisfied with looking at us through the window, chewing on cloves. As for Habiba, she can approach the calf and grab it if she wishes. No one would keep her from doing so. And there's also Kenza, Kika's mother. She's the one who bought the calf. Señora Kentha. That's what they called her there. After five months in the strawberry fields of Spain, Kenza came back with this strange name, along with the white silk gloves that she never takes off. "Señora Kentha" because the Spanish pronounce the *z* as a *th*. My God! This in addition to the respect they showed her. The Spanish respect women. Everywhere. They call them "Señora." And they didn't respect her—Kenza—because of how beautiful her name sounded, or how her hands moved, or her silk gloves, or anything else. They respected her simply because she was a woman. On the train, on the subway, at the bus stop, and in the street. Even the Moroccan grocer would forget his Moroccanness when she came in, and called her Señora Kentha. Good lord! That was what she told us yesterday, adding, "In Spain the man opens the elevator door for the woman and says, 'After you, Señora.' Just like that. He says it from the heart. And he stands there holding the door until the lady goes in, closing the door politely behind her. Why does he do that, without even knowing her? Because he respects her. That's why. It's in the Spaniard's nature. He respects women, and that's that." Whenever Kenza saw this behavior, she said, "My God!" She suddenly remembers that she hasn't come to visit us to tell stories about how the Spanish act, but rather because Kika had threatened to slit her throat if she showed up at the door. She had given her passport, visa, and the money and papers she was carrying to Mother so Kika wouldn't tear them up. The funny part of it is that Kika will always be a criminal, that she doesn't know this, and that she has come for one purpose only, which is to be slaughtered by him. The proof is the calf. Even though she says she bought it to celebrate her return, she really bought it to atone for her sins. But she knows deep down that reconciliation is of no use to the criminal. Once a criminal always a criminal, and his hand might be gripping a knife handle right now. It might have been his hand that had thrown the sulfuric acid. The pain in my toe begins to swell. I suggest to my toe (and to my other body parts that are very likely to rise up and join in the band of pain) that we visit him, that we visit the criminal in his lair, just to see what's going on. If we can figure out how to lure him forth, we might learn his dangerous secrets. And so, just like that, when my cranky body parts and I go in, we find Kika in his room, on the bed. Clothes are scattered all about (the clothes his mother had brought with her to bribe him with) and his legs are stretched out in front of him, covered by the long brown overcoat. Sitting like someone fully capable of burning girls' faces. Next to him is a large knife, the kind of knife criminals use to slaughter their mothers who went to Spain on their children's visas. I steal a glance at the knife in a way that won't arouse his attention, and so as to not give him the impression that I have seen the knife, or that I am about to interrogate him about the sulfuric acid he had thrown at Farah's face and parts of her body. I start to think about the most effective way to extract the information, similar to the method I could have used with Abdullah to find out about whether it was him who sold out my uncle (I had been on the verge of interrogating him so many times before retreating, knowing full well that he would deny any connection to what happened to my uncle). Who would admit to such heinous acts? Whether with criminals or snitches, it's what Kika would probably say right now. With all murderers, you've got to be cunning, indirect. One needs to be very crafty and sneaky. For example, I could say to him, just like that, real casually, "You don't smell anything?"

He'd respond adamantly, "No. I don't smell anything."

Then I'd home in on a more serious question. "My nose is picking up a smell like sulfuric acid. Or the smell of burnt flesh. Or something like that." At that point I'd watch his face. A question like that, out of the blue, won't allow him to remain frozen for long. It will force his face to betray what is going on inside his head; just as I could have done with Abdullah had I ambushed him in the same sudden way. "The smell of sulfuric acid, Kika. Do you know it? And that burning smell? When skin burns, smoke rises up and the smell of skin mixes with the smell of sulfur . . ." The pain, rather than remaining lodged in the toe, shoots to my joints, rendering my feet incapable of movement, preventing me from continuing with my scenarios because it has become unbearable. Besides, what is the use of posing questions he won't answer? Just like all criminals. I limp out. Once a criminal, always a criminal. I limp partway across the street.

So anyway, our neighbor Kenza came back two days ago—with white gloves and this strange name—thinking about throwing a party to celebrate her return. Five months isn't ten years, or even four. Her return was premature. Who misses a woman who's been away for only five months, or longs for a profession no one cares to mention by name? She came back because of her son Kika. If it weren't for the white gloves, the strange name, and her endless stories about the

Andalusian fields, we would have said she had never left her house. But she came back. That was what was important. The banquet always comes when it should, no matter what. The tent was erected amid the rubble of our new street. The calf was here. He spent the night tied tightly with a thick rope to a metal pole. All we were missing was Kika, but Kika wasn't even thinking about leaving his room. We had to listen to Kenza go on and on about the Spanish strawberry fields she had left behind for us to realize that she had come back on account of her son Kika. Why else would she come back at the height of the harvest season if not because of her son? No one knew what had come over him. She had come back at a bad time. That's all there was to it. That's the reason our neighbor didn't announce it, although we all knew it as we listened to her tell about the vast fields, about the fruit that ripens in no time, about the work that begins at six in the morning and doesn't end until the sun goes down, and about the calf tied up since yesterday to one of the extra metal bars left over from the construction. She herself didn't know whether she was slaughtering it to celebrate her return or to make Kika feel better. The banquet always comes when it should, no matter what. The men in Kenza's life came and went. Kenza had no man to buy her a celebratory sacrificial animal or offering. And Kika's condition had changed. Father and I told her that our specialty was wood, not buying calves. We didn't go with Abdullah to the market. Besides, we were busy with our new chairs. We had no time to waste. Two chairs unlike any chair humankind had ever known, and the likes of which would never be known again. The children spent the night offering the calf Abdullah had bought everything they could lay their hands on—bread, olives, mint, carrots, dry cookies. Karima gave it an orange, and stayed up all night waiting for it to eat it. When it finally did swallow it, she was sleeping in the street. She might have been dreaming that she had gotten her orange back and run away with it. The other children didn't sleep. I came back from Kika's room and found them waiting for the moment the calf's blood would flow as Abdullah grabbed its modest horns and twisted its neck with a surprisingly quick move that the children didn't expect. The calf's eyes widened as it fell. The move was violent and sudden. The pain transformed into a prickly feeling in my ankles, like pinpricks on lacerated skin. The calf wasn't expecting it either. It looked at the children with the same shock that was in their eyes. But where was Kika? Our neighbor Kenza said we wouldn't slaughter the calf without Kika. Kika was in his room, and he wasn't going to come out just because Señora Kentha wanted him to. The pain that was shooting back and forth between my ankle and my knee moved to my back. A child shouted toward the window, "Kika! Your mother's telling you to come down to watch them slaughter the calf!" Kika wasn't going to leave his room just because some kid was shouting. He had a big knife. He was waiting for his mother to show her face so he could slaughter her. The kids shouted, "Kika! Your mother's telling you to come down to watch them slaughter the calf!" Kika wasn't going to leave his room just because they were in the street shouting. He held the knife upright, at the ready. Kenza turned toward the men leaning over the calf, intent on finishing it off. What would her son do in Spain even if he were to go? Would he work in the strawberry fields like she had? He wouldn't be able to stand one day under the brain-frying Andalusian sun. And anyway, he can't do manual labor. He'd never done anything with his hands except steal from God's children. Would he be happy when his hands turned into something that looked like rotten tomatoes? When she took off the gloves and tossed them aside, I couldn't make out the fingers. Swollen and red like little sausages. And the palms? They weren't the same red as Andalusian strawberries. They were a rotten red, more like that of rotten eggplant. A dark, gloomy red. Depressing. Staining her hands and arms. Staining the road you take during the day, and staining your dreams at night. You wake up with the same rotten red color covering your eyes. It's nothing more than the exhaustion that remains from the previous day. Kenza was the one who burst out crying. The little kids saw her crying and shouted again, "Kika! Your mother's telling you to come down to watch them slaughter the calf!" Even if I had wanted to, I wouldn't have been able to go back to his house because I would have fallen down in the middle of the street after two or three steps.

47

It's a long way to the mosque. If it weren't for the letter, if it weren't for the chair I was pushing with Father sitting in it, it would have seemed shorter, and the weather would have felt less hot. Would this weather have hummed a different tune without this oppressive, feverish heat? And it wasn't even ten in the morning. Those walking ahead of us and behind us were untroubled by it as they were thinking only of the road and what would happen at the end of it. First of all, there were the chergui winds from the east that had been blowing for three days, bringing hot nights that seeped into the skin. They wove a diaphanous, steamy cloak of air, putting our sticky bodies into a daze as they floated along. During the day, rather than walk, they just moved along, floating. Then there were the cockroaches that had driven Khadija wailing out of the house in the middle of the night like someone stricken with rabies, barefoot, with her hair flying every which way, and the others following closely behind. Khadija has always been afraid of mice and cockroaches. These creatures have always been an abundant part of our lives. Then there was the dedication of the mosque. This coincided with the heat and the cockroaches. And it was what prompted everyone to leave the neighborhood before dawn, among them Abdullah. He was the one who had written the letter, although he left out the cockroaches. A polite letter about our suffering in the new neighborhood, about how far the neighborhood was from all of life's basic necessities—the hospital was far away, the market was far away, even the prison was far away. And the buildings we found when we got there were full of cracks! That's right, full of cracks. The sewage pipes were broken, the faucets had no water, and the roofs were falling apart after the recent torrential winter rains. Abdullah suggested that the children carry their tablets with Quranic verses written on them. This was the time for it. So that the king would see that we preserved our customs and were raising our children according to necessary religious upbringing. And don't forget the certificates. The certificates are important. *His Throne was on the water.* A neighbor suggested that the children wear the new clothes they'd been saving for the upcoming Eid (which was still a ways off), at least for the children carrying certificates; and red tarbooshes and white djellabas for those carrying tablets; and that they should memorize the national anthem. Our neighbor Kenza suggested buying colored balloons and pictures and banners like the ones fans hold at football matches. She said that this was so we wouldn't look like shameless people whose only purpose was to present their letter to the king and leave. True, their ultimate goal was to return to their old houses, but the best way to achieve it was to not look like someone who wanted to do just that. Rather, they should look as if they had come primarily to gaze upon His Majesty and yell out, "Long live the king!" Essentially, what they needed to do was to *not* look like someone with specific demands. Otherwise, they wouldn't gain a thing. That's how kings are. They give you things when you don't ask for them. That's just how it is, and there's no need to go into it any further. And the letter? Why did they write the letter, then? With all of those details. Our neighbor Kenza stipulated that for buying the balloons, they include her name in the letter. But all those who were so enthusiastic about the colored balloons at first were now wondering how their children would carry flags, tablets, certificates, *and* balloons, all at the same time.

Even if they had four hands and luck came to their rescue as they carried all of this stuff, where was the fifth hand they'd need to wave to His Majesty when he passed by? In the end, they decided that the balloon idea didn't make sense.

Father would present the letter to the king. He'd hand it to him personally. First, because he had contributed to building the mosque, and second, because he had paid the price with his own flesh and blood so the mosque could stand as loftily as it did today. Abdullah didn't agree, given the long line of his children who had been martyred so the mosque could stand on its two feet, and so the king himself would come to honor its dedication. The argument went on for a while. Everyone mentioned the ceiling and how much of father's money and body it had cost. "And don't forget that we're from the same family. Don't forget that," said Father. Don't forget that he had spent the night dreaming that he was speaking with the king, the two of them strolling along the corniche, deep in a conversation only they could understand. Who else could talk to the king about perforated wood decorated with Casablanca red? About brocaded colors, multilobed arches, muqarnases made of ornamented, polished, cut cedar, and the eighty corners? Yes, that's right. Eighty corners, no more, no less, and Your Majesty can count each and every one of them. And after Father was done, nothing more could be said that would be so glorious. After that, every form of eloquent speech would be superfluous. His monologue and the argument that followed took up many hours of the previous night and a good part of the early morning too—a completely ridiculous idea. This old man who looked like a piece of old frayed cloth was still dreaming of the glory to come—before we headed off to the mosque, to our old houses, at about seven in the morning.

The way back never looks the same as the path you took to get there. It's always different, as if it were a completely different route than the one we'd taken before. I pushed the chair, remaining close to Father, so that the letter in my pocket would remain close to him and he could hand it over at just the right moment. I thought that maybe I wouldn't take it out at the right moment. I was still debating with myself. I might not remember it because the letter had to do with the mosque. And the mosque had consumed a good portion of my thinking, as well as that of Father's; it put a hole in my uncle Mustafa's side, and it made off with Suleiman's head. And then there was that young girl who used to sing in the mosque. There was no doubt that what happened was written down in one of your files, just as Rihane told me. Your Majesty doesn't know Rihane? The pit bull that used to work in one of your police precincts? Where is he now? In Heaven. Or Hell. Depends on the file. Ha! It pleased Father to see me laughing, so he laughed too. It was the first time I'd seen a sign of cheerfulness on his face since he was confined to his chair. I stopped, not because of Father's cheerfulness, but rather because the pain had returned to dig into my toe. The crowd continued to surge around us.

As we passed through wealthy neighborhoods and looked out over the houses of the poor, a large group of people joined us. I didn't notice them until their smell (which resembled an old stale dinner) wafted over us. The sharp smell of sweat and mildew. Unfortunately, they were going to attend the dedication without having bathed. When we arrive, the ocean will have swallowed up the mosque. My brain was trembling. My entire body was shaking with excitement. Kenza didn't buy colored balloons, but she did allow the children to bring the calf with them as long as they didn't lose it in the crowd. We'll wait for Kika to come out of his room—he has to come out of his room today or tomorrow—with his brown coat and his suitcase, and we'll slaughter the calf when he does. Ha! Kika will have turned into a skeleton by the time he leaves his room, and he'll go to Spain in that ridiculous form. The letter in my pocket burned with anticipation, because it too was waiting to see what would happen.

In order to distract myself from the road and the heat, I watched our shadows stretched out in front of us—me and Father in his gold-embroidered selham and the chair that shook underneath him. Sometimes I saw him in front of me and other times he disappeared completely, so I looked around for him. As more time passed, I found a Coca-Cola cap that helped me continue along my way. I cheerfully kicked the cap, completely confident in myself. The letter held no importance because the mosque was destroyed during the week I was gone. I had given the Lord of Heaven and Earth a full week to crush it. Then I started to listen to the hair on my head. I heard it growing as if it were a small garden. I was pleased with the thought that no sign of the mosque would appear, and we had already covered half the distance. Excited and giddy, I was surprised with myself. How could I explain the incredible happiness that had taken hold of me these past few days, all the while feeling like I'd been pricked with a needle or stabbed or had banged my head on a door or wall, or even been stung by the pain in my toe or ankle or knee? Things were no longer as they had been. That was the reason. Nothing was the same. Next to me, Karima played with her kite. A huge, brightly colored gazelle made by Father out of paper and thin sticks. Her gazelle didn't want to go high enough. I told her, "Let's wait until we get to the beach so we can all have fun . . ." She with her gazelle, and I with my premonition that grew even stronger when I saw *Le Matin* on the sidewalk with its headline—green, prominent, provocative. The headline still occupied the uppermost part of the page even though construction was finished and work was done. "Citizens! Contribute and pay your share in building the mosque." Even on Dedication Day they were asking for contributions! Now these mercenaries were stealing for their personal gain. Wasn't that enough of a justification? These thoughts only strengthened my belief that the time for its inevitable fall had come. I felt sorry for these impetuous souls, so enthusiastic, so unaware of the consequences of their contributions, with a sort of pride as a member of a small gang of insubordinates who had shirked their patriotic duty—me, my uncle, Suleiman, and Farah. "Citizens! Etcetera." Ha! That was how it was. The mosque had collapsed during the night while everyone was sleeping. There wasn't a shadow of doubt in my mind, even though, between steps, I wondered whether it was still standing right now. Thinking is sometimes a sort of luxury, nothing more.

These people, the residents of our new neighborhood carrying their worthless baggage, nothing of any value whatsoever, weren't driven out by the paper-thin walls of their houses that allowed all of their intimate secrets to be heard even in their neighbors' beds. This didn't frustrate them or cripple their resolve. The heat of the chergui winds that blew all day and night didn't drive them out either. They hadn't even been driven out by how far they were from the great mosque that they had contributed to. They were driven out by the cockroaches. I had woken up in the middle of the night to a strange crawling sound. What I mean to say is that I sat up in my chair when I heard the crawling—I hadn't actually been sleeping. At this hour, when most people would say that tomorrow will never come, I'm usually sitting and studying her face—Farah's face—in a mirror of moonlight to see if she's still with me, after the sharpness of the pains in my knee and the rest of my limbs have subsided. I don't think the smell came before the crawling—an awful smell that wasn't coming from the kitchen or the toilet. Nor did it come in through the window. Its source was unknown, as if its stink were something new, unrecognizable. Secretions that smelled like rotten eggs or something of that nature. Even when you finally notice the crawling sound, you think it's the smell that's crawling because of how much it overpowers the nose and eyes. So, I didn't find it strange when I rubbed my eyes. I *did* find it strange that it didn't wake up the others who were sleeping next to me—Father in his chair and mother on her blanket. They didn't even wake up when the sound began to move through the walls, changing from a light hum to this continuous crawling sound like bees buzzing. Then the walls began to crack. All at the same time. A small earthquake was shaking our new house. The cracks that had merely been lines meandering over the walls now widened and filled in what was left of any blank space. An intertwining map of grooves, crevices, pathways, and holes formed in a few seconds, and then they appeared . . . first, their antennae. Thin as hairs that had grown in the cracks' openings. A wind that wasn't in the room made them move. Fear kept me glued to my chair for a moment, and then I managed to get up and walk toward the wall, because I realized that this was really happening in the house, and not in my head. I wasn't imagining these frightening things. Should I touch the insects just to be sure? They were coming out from everywhere. Not small insects, like those we were familiar with in our old house, that crawled around among the cooking utensils and over the plates. These were huge cockroaches as big as chestnuts, and the same dark color. They were crawling around in every direction, sniffing their way toward us with their wings and their antennae. Cockroaches are not like mosquitoes. Cockroaches don't suck blood, but it's enough that they give off that smell and swish their wings the way they do. Just as bad. Black. So many of them. On the ceiling and walls. Crawling, flying, bumping into the walls or into one another. They fell to the floor. They crawled all over it. They took off again. Their wings were huge. All they were good for was causing fear. The door to the bedroom opened and Khadija ran screaming and wailing into the street, barefoot and in her underwear.

Then the mosque appeared with its huge frame, its green sloping roof, and its enormous minaret decorated with colored lights all the way up to the top. The closer we got to it, the higher it rose and the larger its shadow grew. Its magnificence was overwhelming. The light coming off of its lanterns became even more luminous as they flashed off and on to the tune of music being played nearby. Soon its shadow would obliterate us completely. I looked up at the minaret rising before me in all its splendor, rising high in the middle of a cloud of smog. And as the mosque rose even higher, when I saw it standing there, I felt a buried hatred welling up inside me that made my blood boil. I was the one who was hoping for the building to collapse as a form of justice. Completely fair. To crumble to the ground. Was it too much to ask to see it collapse? As long as God saw how His mosque was actually built. Perhaps it would take longer than I had imagined. There were still people who needed to be robbed and plundered and flogged and thrown in prison. They still needed a chance to beg for a piece of their lives and to buy another piece. They needed more persecution and oppression and misery and humiliation and poverty before God would come to a decision about the mosque and send His raging winds down to it. He needs a justification in order to be fair. This was the only way to explain all of this delay. He still saw that people need to be plundered, so until the Lord of Heaven and Earth found sufficient reason to bring the mosque down on top of us, He'd leave us to wander on the margins of life from misery to misery, from blindness to blindness, from nakedness to nakedness, from nightmare to nightmare, from wasteland to wasteland, our bodies trembling in fear, our skin turning blue with terror whenever a seed of life blooms underneath our feet. We'd rather crush it underfoot than see it. Amen.

But what were people's eyes seeing at that moment? Do you think they were seeing the minaret? Or that they were even looking at it? Do you think they were watching the National Department of Electricity employee sitting at the base of the minaret, in front of his control panel, happy that his colored lights had finally found a proper use? No one's eyes were looking at him—neither Mother's eyes nor those of the others; not those of neighbors and family members, or women and men, or old folk and young. He hadn't yet entered their field of vision. They were staring at something that wasn't there, far from the minaret in the other direction, where there was no minaret or mosque or employee or control panel. Their eyes didn't recognize the place, as if they had descended upon a place that wasn't theirs. Standing together in the middle of dust clouds that had been kicked up those walking by. Over there, where we all turned now, there wasn't anything at all. Just a wide strip of asphalt. Wide and stretching off into the distance. Our houses had been replaced by the wide avenue. Those of us who hadn't seen the ocean from this angle before could certainly see it now, but we didn't see our old houses. The ocean. Ships along the ocean's surface. The horizon behind the ships. And our houses? There was no trace of them. They'd been leveled. Mother sat on the ground and stretched her legs out in front of her, staring at the emptiness left behind by the bulldozers. She didn't turn toward the minaret. She was still looking for her old house among the bits of dirt. Mother didn't raise her head up to the National Department of Electricity employee who walked toward us, pushing his control panel in front of him; in his official uniform—the jacket, the dark cap, and the sky-blue shirt. He had never looked more official than he did at this moment as he pressed the buttons on the panel. The minaret changed colors, as did its shape. Would he comfort her with words? In any case, he possessed nothing other than that. Father touched his pocket as if asking me to hand him the letter. I told him that this wasn't the king, that he was the National Department of Electricity employee. And as he pressed the buttons, the employee said, "There's no dedication today."

"And the king?"

"The king isn't coming today. And he won't be coming tomorrow."

And when would they be returning?

No one knew. And anyway, they weren't listening. They were preoccupied with sounds they could still hear even though they had disappeared weeks ago—the clinking of dishes while breakfast was being prepared; the shouts of children as they gathered around the table. The bulldozers had crushed all of it. It was as if they had entered a maze of nightmares and couldn't find their way out. My thoughts began to move away from them and toward the mosque, a bitter taste on my tongue. I listened with one ear to what the employee was saying about the new street that cut through the city and that allowed the minaret to be seen even before you'd entered the city limits, no matter what direction you were coming from. "The minaret has green zellij that the tourists will be able to see from the capital; from Agadir, even. How can your little hovels compare to this achievement, my children?" Without any warning, they threw themselves all at once at the employee—a huge, heavy throng—shouting angrily and thirsting for blood, and after a moment there was almost nothing left of him. That was the scene. Just like during the mawsim festival of Saint Hadi Ben Issa when the baby goat flies through the air and is grabbed by hands, fingernails, and claws of disciples and eaten by them before it falls to the ground, before even a single drop of its blood hits the ground, before the baby goat realizes what's happened to it. That was the scene. The National Department of Electricity employee was gone except for his hand. Not even a single drop of his blood had fallen to the ground. Even his official clothing was gone. As if they had swallowed it along with the man wearing it. The attackers disappeared, dispersed, while the National Department of Electricity employee's hand remained behind, planted in the soil, its fingers moving haphazardly as if they were still operating the control panel and moving along with the minaret's colored lights.

The smell of cedar wood. Then fresh cashew. Was it Father's wood that was singing over my head? These were parts of the mosque I hadn't seen before. The surface of the prayer-hall ceiling was adorned with small, oval glass windows that looked like a flying wild duck, its crystal wings outstretched. Other small glass windows were shaped like red plants, with generous branches so weighed down with fruit that they could fall on my head at any moment. The molding with its green writing encircled the hall like a soothing headcloth wrapped around the head—the ninety-nine beautiful attributes of God. Its green color was calming, causing you to let out a deep breath. Would I be able to make amends with it someday? I wasn't aware of the two tears that fell from my eyes until they came to rest on the edge of my lips. Two salty drops. I began to weep as I broke into a run, leaving the mosque's courtyard behind, bolting through the endless domes, afraid that it would come down on my head. Essentially afraid that the voice would emerge. Because the singing I heard wasn't that of the wood, or the gypsum, or the crystal. The voice was hers. The singing was hers. I turned all the way around as if to regain my balance, drawn into her singing. The colors of ivory fields and copper intertwined before my eyes and mixed with the singing that was resounding in my head as I went around behind the mosque. I walked along the stone ledge that separated the mosque's wall from the ocean, like we used to do before—Kika and I. I hadn't yet freed myself from the effects of the images that the mosque's serenity had placed in me—its fatal beauty, gilded lobes, smooth bricks, polished marble, rose-shaped ornaments, and calligraphy done in gypsum—when I saw the coffin's panels floating across the water's surface. It was being tossed by the furious waves and crashing into the rocks. Farah's red cats disappeared underneath the waves, then reappeared on the water's surface, rising and falling before coming back to crash violently into the rocks, as if banging on a locked door.

I gathered my pain and went down to the beach. Behind me the gazelle appeared. It was Karima playing with her gazelle kite. The gazelle rose and dipped erratically. Sometimes it would scrape the sand until you'd think it had fallen for the last time, only to rise up a little, enough to make you think it had returned to life. The child ran along the sand raising her hand to the sky. The gazelle was happy with its new life, as if it hadn't been expecting everything this child was doing. She moved her hand and it did a half-turn as if evading the wind, and she laughed. The gazelle danced and stared at us, its bright colors even more brilliant under the azure sky. The child's laughter resembled the laughter of the colored gazelle that followed her, trembling violently because of the wind and the running and the string that pulled on it whenever it seemed to behave of its own accord, in a constant back and forth. Then the gazelle opened its wings and flew high, without the slightest effort. Its colors were vivid—light green, pink, and yellow. These resplendent colors would have made me laugh if it weren't for the pain that had come back to afflict me. This time it was pounding deep inside my head. This was where Kika and I had sat, Kika throwing rocks at the old seagull that couldn't fly. Farah wasn't too far away. She was sitting some-place underwater, looking at the mosque. Half human, half fish. I'll leave the matter of the mosque's destruction to her. She'll do her part, underwater, eating away at its foundations little by little, like an army of trained sea mice gnawing away at it pebble by pebble. After a while there won't be anything left. The beautiful blue water was calm on the surface, but the work will be done from below, from deep down.

48

Farah

TONIGHT, I'M GOING DOWN. I am sinking little by little. There's nothing in my head except for where I am now. My thoughts wend their way toward every beautiful thing. A sinking that feels like going up. I'm not sure if I'm sinking or rising. All I know with crystal clarity is that my eyes are open and my head is clear. As if I've finally found peace and there's nothing more that will keep me up at night. There's no longer any need to hurry. There's no longer anything that will drive me to despair. My heart is still beating—*thump thump thump thump.* Splendid memories accompany me. The heart always remains beating because that's where all that is beautiful is kept. I try to find the bad things that have happened, but I can't. Life is neither long nor short. I took my time and crossed bridges. I saw the cities I had to see, and I made my voice heard to whoever wanted to hear it. Whoever doesn't know anything about life will never know that it was a beautiful life, filled with whatever any life could be filled with. When night fell, I went down. At this hour my mother and two sisters will have gone to bed. Have they fallen asleep? My father doesn't sleep; hasn't slept since he came back from the Western Sahara with a missing leg. Is he looking for me? No one is looking for me. Father won't come. He has enough good reasons not to. His amputated leg being one of them. How could he go from Azemmour to Casablanca with this missing leg, his money stolen, while waiting for an extinct fish to appear?

At the start of this night, a desire I was unable to resist overcame me, as if it was preparing to become a final memory. My nipples gently hardened, even before he lay down next to me. I closed my eyes so he wouldn't get scared and back off. His agitation moved into me. His fingers were rough. I pictured fingers that had worked with wood for a long time, having mixed many colors. His thigh was cold as it touched my side. Would he move now? His hands were as rough as granite. The granite passed smoothly over my belly. I closed my eyes as if sleeping. I don't know his name. I didn't ask him his name. What would have been the use? His palms are the same size as my breasts. Big enough. The hand continues to rub and rub. Then I feel his lips getting closer, little by little. They lick my nipples greedily, the first, then the second. Gently, like two well-trained lips. Should I wake up or follow my dream to its end? The granite goes down between my thighs and I become wet. My muscles soften as his tense up and harden. I feel a delicious wave washing over me. I think he's going to lie on top of me. Then he gently lies down, as if afraid that I'll break. When he rises, he feels lighter rather than heavier. My eyes are too drowsy to see what the body perched over me is doing, where he's taking me. My bones pop with happiness as he enters me. A light sting that's closer to a tickle. My legs are spread open as if to receive the water of the ocean that resonates next to me. His penis slips in and moves slowly, warmly inside me, like a sweet, rare fruit. His penis slips confidently inside me, easily because I'm moist and ready. I hold tightly to his arms in order to keep him inside me. I pull him to me as if afraid he'll run away. My thighs open wider, grabbing onto his back to keep us from leaning to the side from the violence of the movements and convulsions and the rising and falling. Little by little his colors invade me. I don't want them to stop before my body has restored its form, and he doesn't stop. I've always needed something good to hold on to. His eyes are closed. The smell of the moon is in my mouth, as is the smell of wood and everything good. He moves up and down calmly, gently, lovingly, while I hold on to his sweaty shoulders. I'm sweating as much as he is. My thighs are open wide enough for me to embrace the waters of the ocean, and to let them drip their honey into my womb and veins and mouth and every part of my body. It's as if I'm falling into an abyss. My skin heals. Little by little I go back to how I was before, beautiful, with shining skin and no disfigurement. Yearningly, I scoop the water of his life, drinking one mouthful at a time before his well dries up. As if apricot-flavored ice has started to flow from between my thighs.

Life is what it is. Neither short nor long. Tears of joy come to my eyes. The smell of wood shares in my joy. I don't know how I was swept so suddenly into loving this smell. There's a light shining all around us. The red cats laugh. I wonder if God can see us right now, and I'm comforted by the thought that God sees all of this, and that He will know how to put our affairs in order. I cry out to keep the pleasure going, even though I don't know that it's my ship that will take me to the other shore, healthy, clean, calm, healed, satisfied. Life surges inside me. A rich life perfumed with the fragrance of other lives. This tumult fills the small, arid field inside me. I'm lying down, relaxed, on the water's surface. New smells surround me—the smell of nighttime seaweed—as well as some old smells. The smell of paint. The smell of wood. And between the cracks in the boards, the night's light enters. As I sink, I carry enough provisions with me for the road. Every traveler needs to carry provisions. A lot of cats, first of all. So that their moonlike faces can light up the night of my new home. The dark sky takes on a purple hue. Dawn. It's time to go. Slowly I rise up. A second soul takes the place of the first. A small, happy cricket's soul. That's right. Humans will turn into crickets when they die. Their lives dedicated to singing. The only pleasure that will remain. They'll sing all the time. With their legs and their wings and everything inside them. They will realize how much singing they have missed. Singing is life.

Who do you want to return with in the darkness
of the road?
You haven't lit a fire and you don't have a friend . . .

All of this brings much joy to my heart as I sink. I rise. Alone,
naked, accompanied by the moonlike cats, the young lover
without a name, and the eternal voice that is no longer sad—
the cricket's voice.

I wish we could have lit the old lamp in El Kantara
Maybe someone would have found their way.

SELECTED HOOPOE TITLES

A Rare Blue Bird Flies with Me
by Youssef Fadel, translated by Jonathan Smolin

A Beautiful White Cat Walks with Me
by Youssef Fadel, translated by Alexander E. Elinson

Velvet
by Huzama Habayeb, translated by Kay Heikkinen

＊

hoopoe is an imprint for engaged, open-minded readers hungry for outstanding fiction that challenges headlines, re-imagines histories, and celebrates original storytelling. Through elegant paperback and digital editions, **hoopoe** champions bold, contemporary writers from across the Middle East alongside some of the finest, groundbreaking authors of earlier generations.

At hoopoefiction.com, curious and adventurous readers from around the world will find new writing, interviews, and criticism from our authors, translators, and editors.